THE
PRIEST
HUNTER

For David,
I hope you enjoy it.

Jeff.

JEFF SPENCE

For those who may be wheat among the tares,
but wouldn't bet the farm on it.

ONE

A cardboard box. A bottle of single malt Glenlivet. A decent cigar. He took a long pull on the scotch and let it sit on his tongue. Linger. Sweet at first but then it bit, that leather-sucked aftertaste of old saddle in every brand of scotch he had ever tried. It was the cloud amid the silver lining.

So was the box.

He hadn't looked through it yet, hadn't even pulled back the interlocked flaps, but he knew what he would find. It would be the same as it had been so many times before, and each time more difficult for him to begin. This time, it seemed the standoff between the two sides of his will had come to something like an equilibrium. He willed his hand to pull back the cardboard flap, mustered up thoughts of duty, separation, and the need for someone to *step unto the breach* for the sake of the little ones.

But that someone had been him, for years now, and the parts of him that were tortured by it — the inner child part, the memories of fatherhood part, the simple decent human being part — were raw from the exposure. Those parts rose up against it, fought back, and the last few months had been exhibiting signs of damage. In the moment he acknowledged the damage though, and pondered alternatives to enduring more of it, the face of duty reared up and locked its gaze full upon him. On one side there were hundreds of thousands of files discovered in the Vatican, billions spent in compensation to victims that would still never heal from the wounds that had been inflicted. On the other, standing in the face of it like wooden posts crashed against by an incoming tide, were the few who would not stand for it, even at the cost of becoming pariahs among their peers. He had been one of these men for years now, but as his eyes drifted back to the closed box on the carpet, he questioned whether even his strength and dedication were enough.

The box contained magazines, pictures, and a stack of discs. He had seen as much when he had found it, enough to know that it was the evidence he had been looking for. The magazines would be disturbing, but tame in comparison to what he knew the discs were likely to contain. Videos, made by the man, or men, whom he had been tasked with identifying as the owners and producers of the illegal material. It would be the videos that would hit him the hardest, do the most damage, and plant the images in his mind that he could not scrub away. It was that cache of cancer in his mind that he struggled to carry, a cache already populated by images of war and destruction, of what he had thought was the worst that human beings could be. But he had learned of other, dark recesses of the depraved mind, hidden behind a veneer of peacetime and civilian life.

Part of those minds, despite every effort to prevent it, would stick in the memory of the men who fought against them. He didn't think he could bear much more. And yet duty called.

It would be sweet at first, like somebody's lost home movie: a little girl in a sun dress playing on a swing, or twin boys playing in soap suds on a nondescript kitchenette floor.

It wouldn't stay sweet.

The mood would change.

The television screen would seem to bleed out its colours, fade to sepia and then lose all hue entirely — like a black and white TV show. *Black and white*, they say, but it was all just grey. Everything.

From there it would bite. Get harder. Colder. The mouths would lose their smiles and the eyes, already too-big pools on little faces, would widen in fear. Instinct, that fear. They had it no matter how small they were. Teens, kids, toddlers… even infants could tell when things went there, to the dark grey, the black. They could tell when their play was over and someone else's had begun.

He held up the forty-dollar tumbler in his right hand, elbow on the plush armrest, and swirled the bronze liquid against the light of the floor lamp. The edge of a tattoo showed at the extremity of his unbuttoned cuff, the fletching of the arrows and handle of the sword that stood above the motto: *De oppresso liber* — "Free the oppressed." Mantra of the Green Berets. And of others.

He took another pull on the scotch and lifted the thick, smouldering cigar from a marble tray beside the chair. Swallowing a generous shot of the fragrant liquid, he drew in on the tobacco, rolled the smoke in his mouth, and pondered the rich blend of flavours — the intertwining of those two vices in his head. The whole of the experience was a ritual, a means to get through the work and out the other side, pleasure pushing him through the pain. But the blending of them had sunken into his skin, become part of him. There was pleasure there, the silver lining, but always there was the cloud. The edge to the scotch. The sting of smoke in the eyes.

The cardboard box.

He stared at nothing until the falling ash from the cigar tapped against the leg of his pants. He looked down to see tiny flakes on the front of his shirt and his thigh, showing white against the black material. He brushed them to the floor. The remote was sitting on the table. Near the box.

Soon, he thought to himself, *I'll have to. But not yet*.

He sat, and stared into memory and thought, letting his mind wander and drift, empty itself into the weariness of the night, and drift toward fitful sleep. The inner demons hovered nearby, watching and waiting.

The telephone rang, a small wireless hand-held with a digital beep, incongruous with the antique Georgian furniture and rich, blood-red carpets. The sound jarred him back from the edge of sleep.

4

"Hello?"

"Fa- *ah*, Danny?" The voice was familiar, but he couldn't place it.

"Yes, this is Daniel Wolfe."

"Yes, sorry. It's Billy Jackson, Kevin's friend from Thursday night? You told me to call you Danny."

Right. Kevin's pal from work.

"Yes, hi Billy. Yeah, call me Danny, that's fine." He rubbed a hand up over his face, "I didn't mean to sound too formal, I think it comes with my present lodgings." He said it with a smile, but there was no chuckle on the other end of the line, no polite hiss of air into the receiver to betray any type of levity, feigned or otherwise. "What's up?"

"Can you meet me… I need you to meet me. Near U of M."

"It's pretty late… I can meet you, but what's going on? Are you with Kevin?"

"I can't say much on the phone, and I just have a second. It's about Kevin. You'd better come down here. Will you come?"

"What's wrong? Is he okay?"

"It's a police matter. That's all I can say over the phone. I'm at a church. You know Saint Mary's, on forty-third?"

"Yes."

"I'm there. Just come, I'll meet you outside and tell you everything then."

"Okay, I'm on my way."

"And Danny…"

"Yeah?"

"I think you'd better wear your uniform. Can you do that?"

"Of course."

"Good. Good." The voice sank to a whisper. "Don't tell them who you are. I'll meet you out front."

"I'll be there in fifteen."

The line clicked.

He looked at the amber colours of the remaining scotch through the cut crystal, at the thin tendril of smoke wandering up from the end of the cigar, and then at the box, sitting still shut-up beside the heavy television cabinet. He crushed out the cigar and tipped the last of the liquid into his mouth. Grabbed the keys down from the hook by the door and opened it to step out. At the last moment he remembered Billy's request and jerked open a drawer in a narrow hall cabinet.

He pulled out the thin strip of stiff white linen and slid either end of it into his shirt collar, leaving only a small white square exposed beneath his chin, then reached into his shirtfront and pulled out a long, gold chain. A light tug and a crucifix pulled loose, the tiny likeness of the crucified Jesus dangling crazily, like a circus acrobat on a golden rope. He let it fall into place over his chest. He looked at the tiny bowed head, thought of his brother, and made something like a prayer to whatever unimaginable form the little symbol represented.

A single, brief look at the haggard face in the mirror by the door and Father Daniel Wolfe stepped out into the heavy heat of the Miami night.

He pulled the car up to the curb and turned the lights out. There were squad cars in a cluster in front of the church, headlights pointed in toward the main doors like a crowd of curious onlookers. It was possible that Kevin wanted his professional advice on something — an impartial opinion from a trusted source. Had a priest been killed? A member of the congregation?

But it wasn't Wolfe's church. Wolfe didn't have a church.

It had to be a murder, or there wouldn't be that many squad cars parked carelessly in the street. It had to be a murder. But his mind refused to take in the implications. Maybe it was a priest… Why else ask him to wear his uniform? Maybe that was it, he thought, maybe Kevin had found a priest murdered and hoped that his brother could help him weave through the intricacies of ecclesiastic life, of Catholic nuances and church politics. To be an insider, on *his* side.

Maybe.

But Kevin hadn't called.

He turned off the ignition and opened the door to the blanket of heat and humidity. The stones of the front wall of the churchyard were only a few feet high, but gave the place a feeling of security and longevity, like a vault… or a tomb. The scent of night-blooming jasmine wafted up from the ground somewhere near the stones, a

7

river of sweet fragrance in the dark air, a draft of insubstantial hope. The lights were sharp in his eyes, the police cars in disarray. He wished that they hadn't been there, that it was just a priest walking into a church to meet his brother's friend. *If wishes were dollars…*

Billy Jackson peeked out from beside the heavy wooden doors and, when he spotted Wolfe, moved down the stairs, two at a time. As a uniform cop stepped forward to ask for an ID, Jackson trotted up behind him.

"It's okay, Nick, I've got him, he's with me."

The cop nodded and waved Wolfe through. The hum of an engine behind the headlight glare, the murmur of the investigators and the background sounds of the night came together in his head like a deep throb, a base rhythm pulsing from the interior of a car, but the interior was in his head, in his veins, in the throbbing pain of his hands and the needling sense that he already knew what it was that Jackson was telling him. He could smell the musty odour of the night, the jasmine dissipated and lost. It was already getting difficult to focus on anything, to hear clearly above the unexplained rushing in his ears.

"It's Kevin, Danny. He's been killed."

A hand came up toward his face, a glass of cool water in it. He hadn't passed out or anything, of that he was certain, but wherever his mind had gone in the moments between hearing of his brother's death and the cool touch of the water on his lips, it had taken in no other facts or impressions. Two words echoed in his skull, like a clear but faraway voice, "Kevin… killed."

"There you are, Father, that's better, I can see it." The voice was that of a young man, Hispanic, with the kind of face one would imagine Saint Francis to have had: strength of will, but calm, contemplative. He wore a sweatshirt, but had the particular bearing of a priest — the way a cop looks like a cop.

"Where's Billy?"

"Billy?" He shook his head, eyebrows high.

"The detective I was talking to before. I don't know his last name. I don't remember. Uh... Jackson."

"I can check for you. Are you alright sitting for a moment? You are feeling better now, yes? It was quite a shock to lose a member of your congregation in such a violent manner. You must have been particularly close to him." The priest's brown eyes were concerned. Genuine.

"Yes, yes. It was a shock." He tried a meek smile. "I'm alright now." He sucked in a deep breath and blew it out.

He was alright, yes, but inwardly kicked himself for stupidity and weakness. He had been a soldier, a trained sniper, a specialist in battle and death. He had seen combat many times in Somalia and Iraq, Afghanistan — even a few places where American forces had officially never been. He had seen terrible atrocities, *done* terrible things. In a very real way he had started to become something terrible himself, to crumble away from the inside out.

So he had left the marines, trained for the priesthood, took his vows at the Vatican at the feet of the pope himself. He had been a counsellor at the deathbeds of those about to cross into the Undiscovered Country, a deliverer of the *Viaticum*, the Extreme Unction, the Last Rites. Death was nothing new to him; it had been his stock and trade for many years, in one way or another.

But Kevin was different. Yes, technically they were only half-brothers, but still, the man had been his own flesh and blood. It had been just Wolfe and his mother for a while after his father left, then she had died less than a year from the first signs of the cancer. A tumour in her brain. She had gone even before death took the rest of her body. After that, he had been with Aunt Ruby for a few years, off and on, and then the military. Signed up for the marines on his eighteenth birthday. Waited in the line alone. He hadn't even met his brother until the age of twenty-five. Still, Kevin had quickly become a part of his life. Started with a quiet drink, a word or two about their father, John. Condolences for the loss of Wolfe's mother. Then his studies ended and he was chosen to undergo his ordination at the Vatican. It had been a profound moment, during which Wolfe pledged his life to serve the church. Took an oath.

As he lay there, face down on the gold and red carpet, the supreme pontiff of the Catholic Church intoning words of ritual and encouragement to the eighteen prone forms, the thought uppermost in Wolfe's mind was that he wished Kevin were there, watching from one of the four massive galleries that fanned out from the centre.

They'd kept in touch. Spent more time together whenever Wolfe was in Florida and once even when Kevin vacationed in France and they met in Lille for two days. Nothing much happening in Lille... Best vacation either of them could remember. They had become family. And his brother was all the family he had left.

He had been.

Wolfe stood up, shaking off whatever weakness or shock that had gripped him, and walked toward the modern, steel doors with his knees only slightly fighting control. He missed the heavy wooden doors of the old style buildings. These modern ones didn't seem right, heavy steel barricades on the fronts of churches, tiny windows in them with the thin black wires of unwelcome running in the midst of the clear glass, side to side, top to bottom, like the bars of a cage. They should be open, warm. Like he had been when he had started his theological training. Not cold, unwelcoming — like so many things had become since then.

He passed through the doors into the empty lobby and from there on into the sanctuary, the 'nave' by the old nomenclature. There were muted spotlights aimed from the high ceiling, soft yellow cones of Rembrandt illumination. Spotlights on the space before the altar. Lower down were the tops of the lighting tripods brought in by CSI. They held the harsh, white lights, cutting through the soft glow with clinical efficiency. As he stepped down the long open space between the dark shining wood of the pews, he stared down the beams of yellow light, into the stark, white glow, to the tight cluster of men and women bent low over the floor.

Kevin would be at the centre of it — Kevin's body, that is — the centre of attention, the heart of the hive, just like he had been in life. Maybe, Wolfe thought, his brother would have wanted it that way.

The room smelled of faint must: the dry breath of aged, decaying books and humidified fabrics. He could smell, too, the under-odours of furniture polish, candle wax and the sweat of the detectives and crime scene technicians who walked here and there in the room, the former in rumpled suit jackets and ill-fitting trousers, the latter in the white paper coveralls of their trade, their tight, lilac gloves giving them the air of something alien.

There was another smell in the room though, familiar. Blood. The excretions of a body devoid of life and energy, passed into that state of ultimate relaxation and the settling of purposeless flesh. And it was his brother.

It used to be his brother.

Kevin was prone, his face against the granite floor and slightly to the side, away from Wolfe and the front doors. Toward the altar. Billy Jackson was there, speaking with a couple of detectives by the built-in organ. A crime tech crouched over Kevin's body, taking high definition flash-photos with a digital SLR. Wolfe wondered if he had any pictures of Kevin back at home. Pictures from before. A bit of the tech's shirt showed through his paper suit. Salmon-coloured Miami print.

Festive. Wolfe wondered what party he had left to come to this one.

Jackson noticed his approach and motioned for the two of them to meet in the narrow open space along the side wall.

"Hey, you doing okay?" Whispers.

"Yes, I'm better now, thank you. A shock, that's all."

"Look, maybe I should have told you on the phone…"

"I knew, Billy. I guessed before I got here. Don't worry about it, I knew what I was coming to."

Jackson nodded.

"How did you know to call me? And why did you ask me to wear the collar?"

"After you left last weekend, we kept on for a while, put away a bottle of decent Irish and… and we just hung out, really. He talked about you some, about the work you do. When I saw… when this happened, I thought he would want you to know. I lifted his cell and gave you a call."

Wolfe nodded. The movement was a "thank you" maybe, or a sign of understanding. He was still too numb to know which.

"And the collar? Because it's in a church?"

"No. It's a *cop*-killing, man. Every uniform and suit in the city is ready to kill the guy who did this. People are really amped up. They aren't going to go for anyone wandering around in here who hasn't got business. And they're as likely as not to think that someone who's here without good reason might be returning for a peek at his handiwork — or to mess with evidence."

"So you told them…?"

"I told them that you were his priest, and that he would have liked for you to give him the Last Rites, or whatever you do… normally."

"They believed you?"

"Most of these guys never met Kevin. The ones who did, well, you know how people get when somebody dies… suddenly everybody's a saint."

Yes, he knew. When he had first started with the Vatican, started investigating the misdeeds of the men who abused their power, he was sickened to learn of the white-washed reputations they gained in death. Even, in more than one case, *actual* sainthood.

A grim smile. Wolfe thought Kevin would have appreciated the irony of a disillusioned, agnostic priest praying for his atheist half-brother as an excuse to be present at the scene, at the altar, to see for himself what had happened… maybe to say goodbye. His brother would have liked that.

He was a bit of a contradiction himself, was Kevin. A policeman, but the life of the party. Self-disciplined, but with all the starched stiffness of a golden Labrador. Red-haired son of an Irish box salesman and a Cuban dancer. It had been a difficult time for Danny Wolfe, when his father had left for a new life in Miami, but for Kevin Ortez it would have been the good years. Childhood innocence.

One family chosen, the other left behind.

He brushed those thoughts aside and smiled, remembering for a moment his brother as he was when alive. But it faded quickly. The time had come. It was time to face the man as he was now, the remains of a life cut short in its brimming prime. The final remains of his last blood relative on earth, soon to become earth once again. Dust to dust. He stepped forward, assuming the slightly-bowed countenance of a priest in service, and looked down over the scene.

The murder.

Jackson may have seen it first — maybe that was why he had called — or maybe he hadn't. Maybe it took a man whose reverence for the temple had faded, to see the situation as any other data set, like he had been trained to do in the Special Forces and like he did now, too often, in the name of the Vatican.

The body was where it had fallen — at least there was no sign that it had been moved. The killer, it seemed, had clubbed the young policeman on the back of the skull with a heavy, gold-plated candlestick. He must have approached from the rear, or else Kevin had turned his back on him.

The problem was that Kevin, prior to falling, had been facing the altar, his back toward the exit, as if the cop had stood between his attacker and the altar. The candlestick was off toward the right side. Way off. Dropped, not thrown, judging by the circular dots of blood spatter, not elongated by the motion of a moving source. Whoever hit him would have had to then run past him to stop and drop the candlestick before doubling back and fleeing through the front or side door. Hardly the best plan for escape. Had the killer not known the layout of the building? He got in, he would know how to go back out. Or had it been panic?

But there were other things that tugged at his mind.

The attacker would have had to take the candlestick from the front, then get behind Kevin to hit him over the head, knocking him, face-forward, toward the altar, where the other candlestick still stood undisturbed. Otherwise the body would have been facing away from the altar, toward the door, or the wound placement on the front of his head, in the face.

Grab a candlestick, move back around the cop, hit him over the head… Run past him, deeper into the room, drop the candlestick, then turn and run back past him to the exits?

He looked down at the unnaturally still head, careful not to touch anything, and listened to the speech around him as his lips began to mutter prayers, the Latin words so engrained through study and repetition as to come almost on their own, his mouth a true proxy of another will.

"It's a fuckin' tragedy is what it is: killin' a cop in a church." The speaker was a heavy-set detective who looked as if he had cut his teeth in the days when a good back-alley beating took care of most of the neighbourhood trouble. A true veteran.

"Keep your voice down, or at least don't swear so much. We're in a church, for God's sake!" The next generation: treadmill, free-weights, shooting range twice a week.

"I ain't here for *God's* sake, that's for fuckin' sure, I'm here to nail the prick that thinks it's okay to kill cops."

Wolfe made a mental note of the veteran. A good cop? Maybe. But a bully too. He knew the type, met enough of them when he was on the lowest rung of the military ladder... and at school before that. Unsure. Afraid. Too ready to push himself up on the backs of the weak. Wolfe had hated that, being the weaker boy.

He raised his gaze, past the altar, to look through his eyebrows at the three priests who stood in the shadows below the crucifix, waiting to be interviewed by one of the cops he had overheard. Two of the priests were in uniform, the other in a Notre-Dame sweatshirt and seminary cross: the one who'd given him the water. He looked at the water-bearer again, now that his head had cleared. Late twenties, thirty at most, and in good shape. Hint of a belly, so he wasn't a gym rat, just an active, healthy young man. The youthful face was drawn with worry as he looked down at the fallen form. Then at Wolfe.

He continued a few phrases of his Latin with his eyes back on the floor beside Kevin's head, then looked up at the other two priests.

The eldest had a full head of white hair and a goatee, some threads of black still holding on under the bottom lip, amid the white. This man paid little heed to the body, but looked toward the veteran cop as if in pain. He carried himself with authority and the younger priest glanced toward him often. The senior man, then, an acute sense of the intrusion clear in his expression.

The third was maybe in his sixties, salt-and-pepper hair, black eyebrows and a good four inches taller than the other two. Maybe six-two, or three. Fit enough for his age. He was muttering to the senior man and, if Wolfe caught the words correctly, was upset by the sacrilege of a murder in the sanctuary, and of the body still left on the floor of the holy place.

Wolfe glanced up at the heavy wooden crucifix, the focus of the room the gory likeness of a dead Jewish preacher hanging from a tool of execution. He thought of the many hundreds, or thousands of funerals a church of this age had held, right on that spot. In older times, in churches yet more reverent than this one, they'd have buried the distinguished dead beneath their feet, and poured the remains of less notable members into the demon hole, to rest beneath the flagstones in an unruly pile.

He returned his attention to other voices.

He learned that a drawer had been forced open and an uncertain amount of money stolen, perhaps a few hundred dollars in cash. Maybe less. Donations… hard to know what was there. The drawer was to the left, Kevin in the centre, before the altar, and the candlestick to the right, away from the drawer. Away from the doors. *Colonel Mustard. Candlestick. Conservatory.* His mind began to wander, to lose its train of thought as he neared the end of the ritual prayer for the dying. But his brother was already dead.

Then a different voice cut through the others, not due to a higher volume, but to the quality of the sound itself, something in the timbre. It was a woman's voice, rich, but tremulous.

He followed her speech for some time, not detecting anything of interest in the words, except in the emotional content. Perhaps she was shaken up, or under stress. Someone uncomfortable near bodies, maybe? Someone uncomfortable near this body in particular? The voice was clearer now. He focused on the tones, trying to discern a cause: nervousness or fear… or guilt?

"Father?" A pause. "Father?"

Wolfe looked up and realised with a start that he had finished the unction and that the woman attached to the voice was now crouching beside him. She was a uniform cop. Her face was thin and smooth, the cheekbones high and protruding just enough to be unusual without detracting from her beauty. Her mouth was thick-lipped and strained in the corners, tiny lines, as if she were doing her best to stay calm, but the resulting tension was plain to read — for anyone who chose to look there. Her hair was black and pulled back into a low ponytail. Her eyes were large and dark. Moist. Stunning.

"I'm sorry, Father. Are you finished?"

"Yes, I'm finished. I was just offering a little extra prayer for him. Such a terrible way to die."

"But in a good place, maybe… here." He was not sure, but he thought he saw her hand move in a quick, miniature sign of the cross. She was a Latina, so there was a pretty good chance that she was Catholic as well, to one degree or another. Wolfe said nothing. "You know I never knew Kevin to go to church. He didn't seem too religious."

"No?"

"He has a brother who is a priest though."

Wolfe said nothing.

"I am to show you out when you're finished. Could you follow me please?" She turned and walked down the side aisle, slightly in front of him. When they reached the shadowed corner, near the sanctuary doors, she stopped and pulled him to the side, into the dimness behind the font, the ornate stone vessel which held the holy water, and there she grasped his hand.

"Father, before you go, will you bless me?"

"Bless you?"

"This thing, here, before the altar, it is *El Diablo*, I can feel him in this place. Kevin was a good man. He was a good policeman… I think you already know that?"

Wolfe nodded.

"Please, then, bless me before you go."

"You're Catholic?" Not that it mattered to him personally, but there were protocols. Rituals. Guidelines to keep things straight when nothing else seemed to make sense. Often.

She nodded.

He lifted his right hand and she bowed her head below it. He spoke: "*Veni, Sancte Spiritus, et in nobis absume quicquid impedit ne nos absumamur in te. Amen.*" — Come, Holy Spirit, and consume in us whatever impedes us from being consumed in thee. It was the prayer he used to say to himself when the new lightness of his heart had begun to fade, when his faith had first begun to waver in the face of the constant onslaught of human darkness. There, in that other kind of darkness at the back of the sanctuary, it seemed most to belong.

"Amen." She lifted his left hand and he felt her lips press against his skin as she kissed it, hesitated a moment, and then turned abruptly back down the aisle, calling on a fierce strength of will to master her emotions once again.

As the spot on the back of his hand cooled and the woman strode back to the front, where the body of his brother still lay, Father Daniel Wolfe pulled his eyes from the scene and stepped out, through to the lobby. He stood for a moment, his eyes staring out through the small wire-crossed windows in the steel doors. Blue and red lights played through the wires in the glass, like it was Christmas outside of the cage.

He had spent his adult life training to protect the weak, to bring down those who exploit their strength against them. Kevin hadn't been a weak man, but whatever had happened in the echoing room where his body now lay had been too much for the man. His little brother. And Wolfe hadn't been there.

21

He pushed against the metal bar and stepped out into the deepening night. The scent of the jasmine must have still been there, but he couldn't smell it anymore. Even the heat seemed no longer to matter. His skin was chilled.

As he pulled open the car door and slid in behind the wheel he heard the lone wail of a siren in the distance, but the only crime that he cared about that night was left behind him, laid out on the cold marble floor amid evidence that, to him, said anything but a theft gone wrong.

TWO

Wolfe passed into the wall of cool air like pushing through a curtain. He walked through the open lobby, the tiles cold and loud beneath the *clack, clack, clack* of his footfalls, then all sound fell to a muffled hush as he reached the gaudy carpeting of the hallway. The cheap prints of ocean fish seemed to stare at him as he passed by, watching him, knowing that who he had come to see would not be there. But they said nothing.

Everything he touched was hyper-real: the key, as it bumped its rough way into the hole, jostling tumblers before striking home against the back of the deadbolt mechanism, the grainy slide of the bolt from its metal stable, even the short pop of sticking paint as the door came free and swung inward, revealing the apartment. Kevin's apartment.

Wolfe walked in and closed the door behind him, placing his key back in his jacket pocket. He wasn't wearing his collar and his cross was tucked away inside his shirt. He had risen that morning with a feeling of detachment and had gone for a walk, hoping to clear his head. Instead he had stepped into the car, turned the engine on and driven to Kevin's. Maybe he had hoped to find his brother there, alive, to reveal the previous night as just a dream, a sick fantasy brought on by too many restless hours immersed in the bloodiness of war. And darker evils.

But the rooms were silent and still.

A plate on the counter with the remains of meal preparation: cut bits of tomato core and onion skins. A couple of egg-shells and fragments of chopped mushroom. They hadn't yet had time to spoil and the one who had eaten the rest of them lay dead, a coroner pulling a scalpel blade though his body, preparing to weigh the organs, to open the stomach, perhaps to place the remains of this meal in a stainless steel bowl to read its story, poking through it with a shiny rod. Wolfe's finger reached out and touched the skin-like surface of a mushroom, felt a peculiar connection.

He walked over to the living room area and smiled at the magazines on the table. *Dirt Biker* and *Guns and Ammo* issues piled three-deep, well-thumbed. Beside them a thin hardcover book on the logic of Kant. That was Kevin: simple man, complicated man. Wolfe wondered if he had been dating anyone, if there was anyone special. His mind flitted back to the woman at the crime scene, the Latina.

He stepped through to the bedroom and breathed in the heady smell. The sheets could have used a spin in the washer, but all in all the room wasn't that bad. Clean for a youngish bachelor. He sat on the edge of the bed and lifted the pillow up onto his lap. It smelled of Kevin. The whole place smelled of Kevin. How could a man be gone and his scent still linger like that? The one should have to go with the other, like the soul, leaving nothing but a sterile world behind where those who remained could get on with things unbothered and unburdened by the need to sift through belongings that were now no one's, treasures that were now junk, and stacks of nameless faces in photographs and cryptic notes.

But it wasn't that way. The soul might go as the body stills, but the fragrances of a life, good and bad, remain for those who are left to pick up the pieces, to sweep up detritus, and to move on. *Maybe better this way*, he thought, *a few more minutes with him.*

He reached over to the bedside table and pulled the drawer open. A gun, trigger-locked, sat beside a couple of prescription bottles, a jar of Vapo-Rub and a brass police badge on a necklace. The bottles were nothing special: Aspirin and some kind of antibiotic; Kevin had just beaten a throat infection a couple of weeks before. Didn't finish the prescription.

"Bad for you brother," Wolfe whispered, "not finishing the 'biotics."

He picked up the badge, the one Kevin wore around his neck when they stormed buildings and that kind of thing. His other would be in his wallet, or on his belt. Wolfe scooped the chain up and shoved the whole thing into his pocket. He would grab a picture, too, then he would have something, some memory of his family.

His eyes scanned the shelf by the dresser. Kevin was there, on his motocross bike at about age ten. Wild.

Full of bravado. There was one of Rosa, Kevin's mother, arm in arm with John, their dad.

Even in the flatness of the photograph, Rosa looked vibrant and full of playful mischief. John just looked worn. Handsome enough, Wolfe conceded, and he could be charming, Wolfe's mother had said. Life was heavy on him though, and it showed in his face. He had worked most of his life as a packaging salesman in Portland. Hadn't been great at it, but got a break at some point and moved the family out to Chicago for a job selling over his own, exclusive region. He had travelled — New York, Atlanta... Miami. It wasn't long after the move that he had begun to spend a lot of time away. Then he had simply stopped coming home.

New woman. New kid. New family.

There was another photo there: Kevin, back when he was a uniform cop. He had joined up after two years of criminology at the University of Miami, and by twenty-eight was a rising detective with a commendation for bravery in his file and a growing reputation for being a balanced, but driven, homicide investigator.

Wolfe set the pillow down and rose to his feet, but did not leave. He wasn't yet ready to move on. He stood a long time in the room, feeling as if he should be rifling through drawers for lost journals, seeking clues on notepads or discarded in the garbage, seeking some structure for what he knew was his brother's murder — not a theft gone wrong, but the deliberate actions of a person who had seen Kevin as some kind of a threat and taken him out. Killed him.

"Kevin is dead." The sound of his voice not much more than another shadow in the room. "Kevin is *dead*."

The scrape of the deadbolt alerted him. It rattled. Locked. The door thudded as someone tried to push their way in, then the deadbolt slid again, returning to the unlocked position. He could hear soft voices as the door popped open again and two more figures entered the room.

He could see them through the open bedroom doorway and recognised them both, one from the pictures on the cabinet by the dining table, the other from last night, from the sanctuary where Kevin's body had lain. The first, the one from the photographs, was Kevin's mother. She was slim and stood about five foot four inches tall. Her skin was fair, despite her Cuban descent, and it was plain to see that she had been a stunning woman in her youth — she was still handsome now, with streaks of grey in her hair and grief on her face.

The second person was a priest, salt-and-pepper-hair, tall, the one who had been shocked by the desecration of the sanctuary at Saint Mary of the Sea. Both figures froze as Wolfe stepped toward them and they caught the movement in the dim room.

"It's okay, Mrs. Ortez," he said, stepping out into the living room, "It's Daniel Wolfe, John's other son. Kevin would have mentioned me I think."

She was startled for a moment, but recovered herself admirably. "*Si*, Daniel. Kevin say about you to me. He was very proud he have his brother. He show me

27

a picture too." She paused. "You look like my Johnnie. A little like Kevin too."

Her strained face smiled as she came forward and put a hand on each of his shoulders, pulling him into an embrace. Her body tensed and then began to shake, without sound. She didn't take her face from his chest until the other priest came forward and moved her away, guiding her to an easy chair across from the television. Wolfe took in a deep breath and blew it out; he had never been good at that kind of thing. She sat down and pulled a kerchief from her handbag, dabbing at the corners of her eyes, her shoulders shuddering in silence with each intake of breath. He just felt like someone was standing on his shoulders, pressing him into the unrelenting floor.

"Why are you here?" the priest demanded, rising to his full, imposing height, his dark eyebrows pulling together over his nose.

"I'm Father Wolfe, Kevin's half-brother…"

"Yes, I know that, but why are you *here*? This is for a mother to take care of, not a brother who is barely related and didn't even know him until a few years ago."

Wolfe didn't understand the hostility, especially from a priest. Had the man no tact?

"Look, Father…?"

"Cisco, Antony Cisco."

"Look Father Cisco, he was my brother, and if his mother doesn't mind, I don't see why it should be any of your business why I'm here or what I'm doing."

"Oh I know what it is you do, Father Wolfe. I know what you do." A long finger jutted out toward him.

Wolfe looked at the man, long and hard.

"I think you'll need to explain that, Father."

"I think you know exactly what I'm talking about, and I think it's time you left. You have quite a record of sticking your nose in where it doesn't belong. We are meant to be caregivers, fonts of God's grace, and not to dig around and cause problems for Mother Church, or for those who serve her. A priest, even one without faith, should know better. Pull out the tares the way you do, and you root up good plants. You ruin fertile ground with your meddling."

Ah, so that was it. Cisco really did know who he was and, for whatever reason, it irked him. People, the clergy included, reacted in all manner of ways when confronted with Wolfe, and what he did for the church. There was no telling what reaction he would get when people found out.

One corner of his mouth pulled back in a half-smile and he nodded.

"Alright, Father, I don't mind going…"

"Good."

"…If Mrs. Ortez would prefer your services to mine."

Both men looked over to her as she looked up from the chair, such a tiny form in the presence of two big men. She had caught only the last part of the conversation and seemed a little confused at the tension.

"Father Wolfe wants to be assured that I am your priest, Rosa, before he leaves."

"*Si*, Daniel. Father Cisco — he is my priest."

Wolfe sighed and relaxed his hands. It wasn't worth the effort or the collateral damage. She had had a hard enough day. So had he. He walked over to the door.

"Since this is no longer Kevin's apartment, perhaps Mrs. Ortez should have your key returned to her — assuming you used a key to gain entrance."

Wolfe paused a moment, the soldier in him welling up, struggling with his priesthood. It was a battle he had often fought, in the beginning of his clerical training, and had thought mastered until his unusual assignment to a special team with Vatican Internal Investigations, the special duty he had been performing faithfully for the last three years. Now the soldier came up often, wanting to shoot, to stab, or to beat. And right then it wanted to beat. One good punch, a slap even, would release what he held inside. It would be quick, cathartic, perhaps even forgiven afterward, if he were penitent enough.

Wolfe dropped his key on the counter without turning around, picked up a photo of Kevin from the cabinet by the door, and walked out down the hall.

Father Gonzales hung up the phone and sat down in the stiff leather of his office chair behind the carved mahogany desk. He tugged on his goatee and blew out a long, heavy breath. Fathers Cisco and Pascal sat in chairs across from him. Gonzales had not even been aware that he had stood, sometime during the call, but the other two had seen his emotion and knew that the old man was coming close to losing his temper with the priest on the other line. He was disciplined though, and understood the chain of command.

"A secretary, and he brushes me off like that," he snapped his fingers, "a *secretary!*"

"Secretary to a Bishop," Cisco added softly. Gonzales looked sharply at him, but said nothing. "He is unwilling to discipline this man?"

"No. He is not willing."

"But he was not the policeman's priest," Father Pascal said, "He came in under false pretences and committed... a sacrilege! It must be!"

"Calm yourself, Father, the man is a genuine priest, after all."

"Genuine?" Cisco asked, looking down at Gonzales, "You call a priest without faith who hunts down other priests 'genuine'?"

Gonzales shook his head and leaned back in his chair. "He is employed by the Vatican, by His Holiness, the Pope." He looked over his glasses at the other man. "If such authority says he is genuine, who are we to say he's not?"

"Surely Scripture is a higher authority than even the Vatican-" Pascal stopped his thought short at the sharp stares of the other Fathers, "-great respect though we give to His Holiness."

"The Papal Throne is the See of Peter, the rock upon which Christ built his church and the Pope himself is God's voice on earth. And don't bring Pope Pius into this or any crusade-related arguments! I know it is in fashion for churches to see the pope as a figurehead, and to act as if authority were more localised now, than in the past, but there is nothing I have seen or heard to justify such actions. Nothing! Nothing has changed from the moment Christ commissioned Peter to lead his flock, and we shall continue to do so here, at least as long as I draw breath. We deal here and now with the pope God has placed above us, and with the officers of Mother Church who have been chosen to serve below him — ourselves included. Without this, all is anarchy and ego."

Cisco caught the glint of the gold-plated letter-opener on Gonzales's desk and began to fidget with it. It was a habit he had picked up in a long life of working with tools. Building. Digging. Tinkering with cars. "And are the Scriptures not also God's voice on earth, immutable and eternal?"

"Yes," Gonzales nodded, "And each supports the other. Papal decree to clarify interpretation, even when earthly eyes cannot see the accord. The position of pope was sanctified to prevent this kind of argument and the factions they might create. Of that I am assured in my soul. Such mysteries are our stock in trade, brothers, we had best get comfortable with them."

Pascal spoke again, "But if what Father Cisco tells me is true — and I do not doubt it — then how can we support such a man acting as we do, and wielding the same authority?"

Father Gonzales smiled at the young priest. "And what has the good father here told you about this man?"

Cisco cut in. "I told him who — what — Father Wolfe is. That he is a meddler in the affairs of true priests while wearing the frock as a mockery. His joy, it seems, is to ferret out weakness in others and drag it out to the shame and infamy of the church. You may call it his 'office,' Father Gonzales, and it may be, but it seems to me that this man is a menace, a creator of problems where no problems exist, and a seeker of trouble when he *should* be a maker of peace. He no more respects us than he does God himself, and should not be allowed to wear the collar — though the cross of execution becomes him."

"Father Cisco!" Gonzales half rose from his seat, "I will not have such innuendo here! Remember yourself or you shall be the one doing penance. The sin of one man does not permit the sin of another — and don't tell me that Father Wolfe should learn as much, for I already know your feelings on the man quite clearly. I would remind you that no man truly knows the heart of another, even when such things seem plain. Many do not even know their own hearts well, and it is best to begin and end there. All else is speculation. Hypocrisy, even. I suspect that, if each of us knew how often others had looked away from our shortcomings, or gave each of us the benefit of the doubt, we would be humbled indeed. Let us not react to sin, with sin. Even if his actions bring damage, they may be enacted from a place of good intention."

He settled himself down into his chair again and turned his attention back to Pascal. "It is true that he is a meddler, Father Cisco is correct in that, but he is such by the orders of the Vatican itself. His apparent lack of faith might best suit the unsavoury necessities of his work — or perhaps it is that particular work which brings on a crisis of faith, I don't know. Such things are common enough. But I do know something of the man myself, and I think you are wrong when you say that he is without respect. On the contrary, I suspect it is only respect, or loyalty, which keeps him in that frock you so begrudge him. Not respect for God, perhaps, but for his own vow to men, and the church."

"And that is *admirable*?" Cisco asked.

"To keep his word to men? More admirable than a man who claims faithfulness before God and yet shows none to his authorities in the church. How can such a person be trusted? Remember the rich man's sons, and which truly did the will of his father."

Cisco scowled.

"But this man, I have heard, cannot be trusted," Pascal said, more to Cisco this time than to Gonzales, "Are we to let him come and go as he pleases?"

"He cannot be trusted," Gonzales said, drawing the younger priest's attention back to himself, "not in some areas, but this is not to say he is not worthy of it. It is a tricky thing when one deals with the hearts of men, which scripture itself tells us cannot be trusted in full. He hunts priests for the Vatican and perhaps this is a kind of betrayal to some, but he does it in order to find the tares among the wheat and to carefully remove them. Is it then such a terrible thing?"

"And the wheat which he ruins in his hunt for the tares?" Cisco raised his eyebrows as he spoke, "Of mistakes made? Misunderstandings? False accusations? What of these?"

Gonzales leaned back in his chair and closed his eyes. A deep sigh escaped his lips and with it was revealed the strain and care that this situation brought down upon him. "That, Father Cisco, is indeed the sense in which he *cannot* be trusted. He may see degrees of evil in the actions of priests he finds, but he does not show it. He seeks and lays bare whatever he finds. He is an indiscriminate hunter, and it is in that lack of gradation that the danger lay."

Pascal eyed the trim along the bottom of the desk, lost in thought.

"So they will not remove him from this case?" Cisco asked.

"That is the interesting thing," Gonzales said, wrapping his hand around his goatee and frowning, "The secretary tells me that Father Wolfe is not on this case. He tells me that he is here on another matter entirely — he would say no more — but to his knowledge, the two are unrelated."

"Then we must ban him from the premises!" Cisco said, dropping the opener back on the desk and clapping his hands together.

"I agree with Father Cisco," Pascal said, "We cannot have him snooping around here, acting as if he is one thing while secreting another. If he is not here on official investigation, why is he here? Is the poor soul who-" emotion almost overcame him for a moment, anger, or sadness. Both. He cleared his throat and went on, before the others could take up the floor. "Has the poor soul who died before the altar been given his proper prayers or no? Is a soul already in peril due to this man? Is a priest in good standing with the church able to give unction despite his own spiritual unfitness? None of us can know. We stood by while this man uttered words that may hold no power at all. What are we to do? Is this irresponsibility ours as well? It must be!"

Gonzales raised his hands as if to ward off the questions. "I don't know, Father Pascal. I give no answers to either of you now... I have none."

"I have one answer. I can tell you why he came last night, though I cannot tell you how he knew of it."

Both Gonzales and Pascal turned to look at Cisco. Gonzales spoke. "What do you know?"

"Father Wolfe is the dead policeman's half-brother. They shared a father."

"Brothers?" Pascal whispered. He looked up at Gonzales with a new understanding. "When he was here then, he came to see the murdered body of his own brother. It is no wonder he was in such shock." He fingered the crucifix that hung over his chest.

"Yes," Cisco said, "Shock as if he did not know what he was coming to see. So why did he come? And who called him? Not one of us, surely. And it was no coincidence."

Gonzales shook his head. "There is sometimes no preparation for what one is about to see, regardless if there is foreknowledge of it, or not. This explanation is enough for me to understand his odd behaviour. What I do not understand, Father Cisco, is how you know this and why you have not said so before — before I called the bishopric, for example. I might have been made to look a fool! It is only chance that the bishop himself was not in."

"I did not tell you because I did not think it germane. Besides, you were already on the phone when I arrived."

Gonzales nodded, but the frown remained on his face.

"I found out myself only today. I knew who he was as a priest, at least by reputation if not his official office. That business in Sydney was his. I knew one of the exonerated men... no longer a priest." He shook his head and drew in a breath, "But I did not know his relation to Detective Ortez until I went to his apartment with the grieving mother, with the purpose of helping her put some things in order there. Father Wolfe was already on the premises, in the bedroom, fishing through the chattels I have no doubt."

"Come now, Father Cisco," Gonzales said, "Petty innuendo is beneath your station, bitter though you may feel about this man. If he was the brother, and had been given a key — which we can assume Kevin Ortez himself gave to him — then we can assume his reasonable right to be there. Had I lost my brother I would do the same."

"And would you pretend to be his priest and give him sacred prayers in which you did not believe?" Cisco asked.

"I might be moved to do the former, though the latter does not apply."

"I would not... I cannot abide it, Father Gonzales. It is not right."

"I understand your emotion, Father Cisco, but would remind you, both of you, of your own vows. Our responsibility is to God, to Mother Church, and to our own consciences — we have our own promises, that we must not break, especially out of indignation at others breaking theirs. To do so would be to always sit in judgement over half of the world and spiritual envy over the other half. None of us knows the heart of another man, not even you, Father Cisco, with all of your gifts and talents."

"And yet trees are known by their fruit."

"Let us wait for the harvest then, shall we? I will not let this rest, brothers, I assure you. This is my parish and what happens in it falls under my rightful office to oversee and to protect. I will make an appointment to speak with the bishop and see what can be done. At the very least I will seek censure for last night's deception — but I will do so with some new understanding of the motives behind it. With the compassion appropriate to our vocation. I do not think the actions were evil, merely... ill-considered. And who can blame a man for unclear thinking at such a time?"

There was little the other two could say, despite their feelings on the matter. Gonzales, for any faults he might have, was at least a fair man and a merciful one. Neither could argue with his judgment so far, once they had calmed down. Cisco left the room with a look of pained resignation on his face. Pascal remained to give a report regarding the running of the community centre, a responsibility he had only just begun to take over.

In a Vatican-owned mansion on the Miami coast, just outside the private office of Bishop David Grippe, Secretary Vittorio Sanchez was also issuing orders to a young priest under his care and authority. A message needed to be delivered to an agent of the Vatican Internal Investigations branch, to Father Wolfe: a request for information and clarification.

Daniel Wolfe was a special project of the bishop's, and Bishop Grippe would want to know if anything undesirable were going on. Sanchez sent the priest out on his errand and then settled back in his chair, looking out through the plate glass window. The yard below, the tree-lined pool, and then out over the cloud-laden Atlantic. Something was brewing in the air. Rough weather was on its way.

Grippe would be back that night and would receive, Sanchez had no doubt, a direct call from Father Gonzales, the senior priest of Saint Mary of the Sea. It would be best to have full knowledge of the situation prior to the bishop's return. Issues with Wolfe were seldom small ones and when one considered the case he was currently working on... well, they all knew the stakes. A thing like that could burst the seams of a church, of a community. The destruction and collateral damage could be devastating. Such a calling required great strength. But to leave it alone? To ignore such a responsibility?

Thoughts of the alternative pushed them all forward, and into the storm.

THREE

Wolfe's phone was off because of the box. He had found his way over to it earlier that evening, as if he had had some other errand in that corner of the room, and flipped open the interlocked cardboard flaps. He hadn't looked in the thing since he had taken it from the fifth-floor office four days ago.

It had been like a black op, getting in, but once he had the box, he had simply walked out the rear fire exit. Perhaps an alarm sounded somewhere in the bowels of the building, but by then it was too late.

The people for whom he had stolen the box owned the building. The man from whom he had stolen it was under their authority and, if it contained what both Wolfe and his employer thought it did, the last thing that man would want to do is draw attention to the fact that it had been stolen, or that it was his.

Some magazines were stacked on top: banal topics, nothing to draw suspicion. Beneath them were several others with various popular covers re-stapled onto less forgivable contents: underage teens mostly. Post-pubescent, at least. Didn't matter to him though, his mandate was clear, and underage was underage. He would let the higher pay grades sort out what needed to be done. Besides, Wolfe was pretty certain that the trail didn't stop there.

He flipped through the rest of the mags, ascertaining the genre without taking in too much of the content. Still, images latched onto his brain like snapshots. They were in there, unwelcome but vivid lodgers now. He would make notes of it all later, in an encrypted file at the bishopric. No damning conclusions would be given a chance for exposure — not unless his superiors decided it should be so. He set the magazines down and moved on to the DVD cases. Old technology, yes, but virtually untraceable. Downloads could be followed, detected electronically; a DVD though, might as well be a vinyl disk or a cassette tape. It could be in someone's hand, and nobody else would have a clue. It was here where the live action material would be housed, the material that his target was suspected of not only possessing, but having a part in the production of footage... and the supply of victims from the orphanage under his care.

Seven of them. Shiny-black cases with clear plastic over blank paper labels. Inside, the discs were merely numbered, four to ten. Handwritten. That meant he had missed three, at least. Maybe more. He wasn't concerned about it from a prosecution standpoint — there would be more than enough in what he had. The disguised magazines assured him of that. There was a chance that the missing discs would appear as part of the bargaining process, but it didn't always happen that way. Too often such things had already been passed on to some other person in some other place, just as the people in them had been passed around, one predator to another. Too often.

He popped number four from the brackets and let the DVD player pull it in, away from his fingers. He returned to his chair then, scotch at his side, cigar in his mouth, and remote in his hand. This was business. No, not 'business,' but he could sell himself on it being work. Duty, maybe. Whatever it was, it was unpleasant and it stirred in him memories of things long suppressed, images of rape and murder, children and adults alike stripped of all dignity and security in the mayhem and rot of war. These discs — all of them — did the same thing, held all of it, past crimes constantly renewed through time and repeated viewing, never ending because they had been captured on the silver discs. The aboriginals believed a photograph steals a soul. Wolfe had always thought it to be a quaint, primitive belief. Not so sure anymore.

He took a pull on the cigar, offsetting the unsavoury task with a pleasant compensation, and pressed the power button. The machine whirred into motion and a moment later the screen lit up.

It was a little girl, brown-haired and freckled. She was sitting on a small school desk on a plain white kitchen floor. Though the sound was off, Wolfe knew that someone was asking her questions. He turned the volume slowly up, trying to catch the voice on the other side of the camera.

Helium.

"Mother-*fucker*!" He couldn't help it. The words came to his mouth as automatically as the Latin had rolled out at Kevin's death, the 'old' man still present within the new, the soldier within the priest. He rolled the volume back down to almost nothing. They would need a sound tech to return the voice to something like its original timbre. The result would be low. Slow. And beastly. In any case, the use of helium meant that, even with a reconstructed voice, they wouldn't be able to prove whether his current suspect had been there for the recording or not. It made a big difference to the consequences, possessing child pornography compared to producing it. Wolfe wished it didn't — the one wouldn't exist without the other — but there it was: the legal difference.

Not everything hinged on the legal difference, however. Wolfe wasn't a cop and he wasn't a fed. Technically, he was a diplomat of the Papal State, an attaché. He worked directly for Vatican Internal Investigations — nicknamed 'Seven' for the Roman numeral VII — under the supervision of Bishop David Alexander Grippe. Grippe reported to a Cardinal Agresta, and above that Wolfe had no idea what information went to whom, if to anyone at all. He hadn't even known the organisation existed until the evening after his ordination at the Vatican itself. Bishop Grippe had approached him for a casual talk that had lasted long into the darkness. His eyes had been opened again that night. His already-waning satisfaction with a life of normal religious service had been snuffed out like a candle. Something else relit.

The blessing and curse of more, a vocation that could draw on the darker skills of his past as a stealthy dealer of death, but apply it to an institution of life. Renewal. His internal monstrosity might help someone, someone otherwise defenceless. It was a rope he had needed at the time, a life-line thrown out to him just as the last one had lost its ability to keep him above the dark waters. It had served him well enough.

Even so, the cases of late had become heavier, the offences more depraved. More organised. He had only been in Miami a couple of weeks, familiarising himself with the allegations against his latest target, when a feeling of weight had descended onto his shoulder, like some great beast had laid heavy hands upon him and pressed down. He had spent a full day walking a huge circuit — over one bridge, along the edge of the island, back over another — all in the blistering heat of the Florida sunshine. When the evening had fallen and the sea wind was pulled in by the low pressure of the preceding day, a coolness slipped in under the blanket of humidity and oppression. He passed a stressed vendor and bought a cheap jacket, covered up the black clothing he almost always wore, and stepped up to the side of the water, the line between the land and sea. There was so much space and mass and distance in the world, and he was just a speck on the edge of it.

Maybe it was time. Time to let it go. He had served his country, served the god he used to believe in, and served justice upon many who had previously stalked unchecked through the ranks of the innocent. Maybe he had done his time and it was okay to walk away, release himself from vows made in a more naive time. Somehow, though, he knew that the voices wouldn't stop merely because he had stopped responding. He needed a rest maybe, a break from it to clear his head, but some shred of self-awareness hummed below all of these thoughts and made it clear: he was not yet released from duty. Not yet. Accusations had been made, and powerful people still stifled the voices of the weak.

De oppresso liber. Free the oppressed. He could not leave such actions unanswered.

He couldn't leave them to the law alone, either. There were too many constraints on justice there. Proof was needed for both Vatican and secular courts, but the rules around gathering those proofs, and the strictures of police behaviour and protocols too often bound them up into inaction and impotence. The courts within VII had far fewer strictures of protocol, and proof was proof, regardless of how it was obtained, or from whom. If a crime was uncovered, it was prosecuted, in one way or another.

Most accusations never made it out of the Vatican courts, if they even made it that far. There were categories of inappropriate actions, such as having an affair with a youth between the ages of fifteen and eighteen, which were considered less serious. Vatican civil law, if it could be called by that name, was adopted centuries ago, from the existing local statutes, and had not been changed much in several significant ways. The legal age of consent, for example, was twelve. It was a medieval opinion, and not widely held anymore, but there it was: Legal distinction. Those who committed these so-called lesser crimes were handled in one of two ways. If they were old enough and the crimes far enough in the past, all might be forgiven and forgotten. If the situation were considered more serious, or was contemporary, they were sequestered, shifted into a life much more like a monk's existence than a typical priest's: a house arrest, as it were.

Child pornography was a growing problem, fuelled by the ease of private access granted by technology. Some offenders, those not involved directly with production or face to face abuse, were moved to offices where they were closely supervised and had no access to children. Even that policy was changing, increasing in severity. Those priests who were younger men used to be shifted to another parish in the hopes that efforts at rehabilitation would be successful.

They never were.

Now those who broke clerical law but not the laws of the country in which they resided, might be defrocked and quietly sent away. Those whose actions broke civil law as well were usually exposed to the police of the country in which the offence occurred and then denounced by the church and defrocked.

There was a third group, though, much lesser known. There were men and, though only twice on record, women, who went further than this. Some were involved in producing child pornography, others in the direct molestation of children far too young to be willing participants. These were difficult to deal with, difficult for the church to put away without drawing unwanted attention to the depths of the problem. Difficult to give over to the state without the same negative publicity and a rekindling of the public blaze ever the mistakes of past administrations and attitudes, a stirring up of mistrust.

Some, the darkest of offenders, abused others to the point of injury or death. Torture and mutilation were mingled with sexual intercourse and display. Permanent damage, in every sense, resulted from such acts and often a ritualistic aspect added to it a sense that true, demonic evil had permeated and overcome the offender. In some such cases professional exorcists were brought in, in other cases Vatican professionals of a more secret kind got involved. Their methods were quick. And permanent. He hadn't worked on such extreme cases yet, even after three years of successive investigations, but he knew such things existed. He had heard the rumours. The whispers. The stories in the dark.

Wolfe was a gateway between that dark world and that of the normal, working priests, a filter through which the suspects and offenders were sifted and categorised. He hated dealing with any of them, but there were some who stirred such thoughts of rage in his head that he was often tempted to take their punishment into his own hands. Maybe that's what they had in mind for him, eventually. But for now he was just the gatekeeper and that was as far as his conscience, self-constructed though it was, was willing to go. His focus returned to the video.

The girl was smiling until she was told to take off her sundress. She didn't like the idea. She was told not to be naughty, that the ice cream depended on being a good girl. Confusion remained, but compliance followed, an awkward, child's compliance, messing the hair and leaving the garment in a small pile on the floor.

"Now," said the barely-audible helium voice, "stand up and twirl like a dancer…"

Wolfe pushed the power button and threw the remote onto the other chair, staring at the reflection of his face in the dark screen, superimposed with yet another sordid image he would not be able to forget. He sat in the silent room, alone. Took another drink from the scotch and slid the unlit cigar into his breast pocket. He lifted himself from the seat and grabbed a jacket on his way out the door. He didn't want to be there, just then, not in a room with the little freckled girl and the high, distorted voice of the man, with the things he was about to do — had already done — present there on those discs, as if the action were playing over and over, constantly, in the corner of his room. He wished there were some way he could destroy it, nullify it, make it as if it had never happened.

There wasn't.

FOUR

The church was quiet outside. Wolfe didn't know why he had come, really, but for some reason he needed to see the place again, perhaps to convince himself that Kevin wasn't still lying there on the cold stone slabs of the floor, left alone and ignored. *No*, Wolfe thought, *He's on the cold metal slab of some morgue, with his organs weighed and neatly replaced in the cavity of his violated chest, Frankenstein stitches in a V from shoulders to sternum and in a long line from there to his pubis. Like zippers on a suitcase.*

As he approached the front, he could hear shouting off to his left, across the street from the church. He looked. A basketball game on a small, asphalt court. Maybe eight guys. Pretty good from the looks of it, and at the tail end of a solid mix-up under the basket. He was about to turn back to the front of the church when he recognised one of them from the other night. The young priest. The shouting intensified and the young man lunged forward at another player. Others intervened. There was some profanity, Wolfe couldn't tell from whom. Calming words were spoken. A shirt pulled off and thrown hard on the ground, but no violence ensued. He continued his course to the church and stepped into the lobby.

The *narthex*, it was called in ancient times. Wolfe wished it was still so. 'Lobby' seemed too hotelish. 'Reception area' too much like a perpetual wedding party. Neither one suited the solemnity of the older buildings, the stone ones, like Saint Mary's. He wandered over to the rack of brochures and pretended to browse through them, keeping an eye on the game breaking up across the street. The players went their various ways, in pairs or triplets, and Father Pascal said his goodbyes and walked across the street alone, back toward the quiet shade of the church, shaking his frown off to leave most of it on the court behind him.

When the young priest pushed open the door, pulling his tee-shirt back on as he did so, Wolfe looked up and their eyes met. A moment of confusion, he thought, tension between anger and something else. Then a warm enough smile and a hand extended in greeting.

"Hello Father Wolfe."

"Father Pascal."

"What brings you back here?" He glanced toward the sanctuary as he spoke the words, knowing the true answer without the other priest having to give it. Shrugging to acknowledge the banality of the question.

"Thought I might spend some time. Maybe have a word with a couple of you?"

Pascal shook his head. "Can't right now. I've got to get to the community centre, lock up for the night. Just came in to grab the keys and my gym bag."

"Maybe tomorrow?"

Pascal nodded. "Yeah, I'll be around."

They nodded goodbyes and the young priest walked up the side stairs which led to the ecclesiastical offices. He himself stood for a moment. Pondered the man. Then entered the sanctuary.

He could smell burning wax and knew that people had been coming in and out, lighting candles for the dead, the lost, the wandering. For Kevin too, probably. Two people sat in the pews, still and quiet: a young man in a hoody, a street kid maybe, more likely there for the relative coolness and safety than for religious reasons. On the other side of the central aisle and several pews farther up, sat a woman. Even from the back of her shoulders and head there was something about her that struck Wolfe as familiar. He walked quietly up the aisle until he was certain, then slipped in beside her.

"Hello," he said.

"Father," she whispered, "Hello. Are you serving here tonight?" The cop. The woman. Ana.

"No, I just came by."

"To pray for your brother?" She looked up at him with a kind of pleading in her eyes, as if knowing that she sat there in the presence of the Kevin's brother might help her gain access to the dead man somehow, to have a few more moments of mortal time before his life was over and his soul moved on to the other side. Forgotten, in time.

He wouldn't pray, but nodded. "How did you know? Last night?"

"Billy told me about you. I knew Kevin, socially," her eyes fluttered to the floor for an instant, "and guessed who the priest was who came here, but wasn't one of the regular fathers. I saw your face when they told you. I've seen the look before. Billy told me more today, about what he had done. He thought I ought to know. I'm glad. It would have seemed strange, otherwise, that you came all the way over here just to pray for a man already... gone. I know it's important, but Kevin wouldn't have thought so, and anyway one of the priests here could have done it." There was a long pause where neither spoke. "It was good that you came." She turned her eyes away from him, studied the confessionals.

"Are you here to pray for him?" he asked.

"I don't know. Maybe. I think I'm here just to be near the place where he was. Maybe God will tell me something, you know? Maybe I can find some reason. I felt so... powerless. I hate feeling that way." He believed her. She didn't look the type to feel that way very often.

"Do you know why he was here?"

"No. Walked in on a robbery, the official report says."

He pondered how to respond, how much of his own suspicions to reveal to this near stranger. She had been special to his brother though. She was here. That said something. "Unlikely though, that it was a robbery."

53

She nodded. "Yeah, me and Billy thought so too, but it's complicated. They don't want anything to get into the press that isn't substantiated. Church-related killing, volatile enough. At the altar… Ripe for crazies. Copycats even. And most of the detectives won't tell me much, anyway, not 'till I make my shield."

Wolfe nodded. They were always complicated, cop matters. Church matters. "Did Billy tell you anything else?"

"A little."

"Was anything stolen besides the money from the drawer?"

"No, nothing that they know of."

"Anything else broken, other drawers, maybe?"

"No."

"Did he have his wallet?"

"Yeah. In his pocket. Candlesticks were on the altar — except for the one on the floor. Whoever it was took nothing." She crossed herself and looked at the floor.

"Nothing but the cash from the one drawer that contained any."

"Yeah."

"Was it widely known that money was kept in that drawer?" It had begun to feel like an interrogation to Wolfe, but she didn't seem to notice.

She shrugged. "Any altar boy, even from years ago, would know where it was. Every priest, anyone who saw money placed in there after a service. There was a slot in the drawer for envelopes and cash, to keep it safe between collections. Anyone in the service who paid attention might see where he put it as well. It was not safe, I suppose, but the priests here trust the parishioners. There's been no reason not to. Well... not before."

"This is your church?"

She nodded. "It is a terrible thing, this death. I can't believe it was anyone I know — the killer, I mean."

Wolfe nodded. Still, it was strange. Whoever had killed him had been trusted enough for Kevin to let him, or her, stand behind him with a heavy candlestick. A friend maybe... or a priest. Priests wore their uniforms for a reason, it was a flag of truce, ostensibly, a symbol of safety and protection, of trust, as if anyone who wore the black suit and collar stood in the place of benevolent Jesus, Son of God and Saviour of Mankind. Wolfe knew better. Lots of people knew better.

She shifted in her seat, fidgeting with her rosary and averting her eyes. Signs of guilt. Wolfe remained where he was for a while, letting her nervous energy build. Guilt alone was nothing unusual; many people, most people in fact, had a sense of guilt when they sat next to a priest. Catholics were the worst, for obvious reasons. There was something nagging him about her guilt though, something he couldn't nail down.

He decided to leave her in peace, to regain her ease. She had been there first, after all, and if what she implied about her relationship with Kevin was at all serious, then she needed to grieve in this place just as much as Wolfe did, maybe more. A nod to her, and to his own surprise he grabbed her hand and squeezed it, then stood.

"I'll see you again, Miss Cruz."

She nodded. "Thank you Father."

He walked back down the aisle under the direct gaze of the street kid, and out into the deepening night.

The ghosts of the place followed him out, swirled around him in the night air.

Wolfe walked past the car. He followed the cracked sidewalk through the growing dark of the quiet neighbourhood until he heard the murmur of falling water off to his left. He turned down a narrow walking path in the direction of the sound. His shoes clicked and scuffed on the dark stones of the walkway and all other noise but that of the water faded away, blocked by a three story building on the left and a ten-foot wall on the right. A minute later the wall ended and a wider path opened up, with a concrete bridge over some kind of drainage canal, trees and bushes across the water, crouching in the dark. He stepped up onto the bridge and rested his hands on the rough-painted railings. Green, or blue; he couldn't tell in the dim light. He stared past them at the rippled surface of the canal.

Inky-black in the twilight, the water sparkled as it fell over each step, a foot-long drop into white foam and then a return to blackness and secrecy. The cool fragrance of disturbed liquid filled Wolfe's nostrils and he breathed it in deeply. Smelled like coming rain. He pulled the cigar from his pocket and fumbled for his lighter. He flared the tiny stream of fire across the front of the exposed tobacco. The full, rich scent wafted around him a moment, pulled quickly away in the air current, but comforting in fleeting moments.

His father had smoked cigars. The smell of the rich cloud, even the hazy quality it gave to the air in an enclosed space, made him feel closer to John Wolfe. It made him feel closer to Kevin now too, somehow. The two together gave him a sense of family, a false impression of being part of a home. He would often return to his Vatican-owned lodgings in whatever city they had him in and close his eyes as he passed through the door, letting the scent of stale tobacco bring him back, for a moment, to his early childhood, to the years before the loneliness, the wars and the pain, the penance and the service, neck-deep in depravity. Most of the rooms they gave him were technically non-smoking now. Nobody paid it any heed.

His dad had been like that in most aspects of his life: unencumbered by the expectations of others. After John Wolfe had stopped coming home, young Danny had become the man of the house. He had taken care of things: washed dishes, run the laundry, made childlike meals for his mother as she wasted quickly away, her beautiful skin turning to patches of unnatural yellow darkness and stretched, shiny white. The hollows of her face deepened as if her bones were trying to push their way out, until her son thought there was no further for them to go. But they had. Near the end it was as if someone had dropped worried eyeballs into a yellow skull. That was the face he remembered.

After her death, those last few days in the hushed, expectant palliative care ward, he had returned home to find the locks had been changed. The money had run out. He was on his own.

He took in a pull of smoke and blew it out over the water, lifting the cigar in a kind of toast to his fallen father, his fallen brother, the faded memory of his mother and aunt — to his own loneliness, in a way. Loneliness. He thought about the word. Perhaps that was the wrong term. 'Solitude' would be the better description, he told himself.

To his own solitude then, and to the last of his father's line.

It was really something to be the head of a great family, the first notable soul in a string of men and women spreading out over the globe, enacting dominion over the many forces that strive to eradicate human life. The great heritage of kings and queens, tycoons of industry, and the grand families of early America. It was another thing, no less great in its way, to be the end of such a line. In this case, for his father's particular branch of that line, Daniel Wolfe was the last one: a priest sworn to celibacy. A lifeless bud on the tip of the last twig of his father's family tree. He tasted the smoke.

Kevin had been with Ana. He had 'known her' as the conservative fathers would say. In Wolfe's more cacophonistic world he would call them lovers, or "sexual partners" when need for clarity was considered paramount.

Kevin probably trusted her. She might have reason to kill him, nonetheless; lovers were always the first suspects. She was Catholic, and had knowledge of that particular church. She felt guilty, too. One must not forget that. But guilty for what? Were their last words harsh? Did she forbid him sexual intercourse the night before, not knowing that it would be their last chance to be together? Did she cancel lunch, never to see him alive again? Had she been unfaithful? Had he? Any of these might evoke feelings of guilt, directly or indirectly, in a lover left behind.

Or did Ana Cruz kill his brother in front of the altar and leave him to cool in his own blood while she staged — and staged not very well — a scenario of robbery?

The killing had not been premeditated, not by more than a few seconds, at any rate. If it had been, a different weapon would have been used. The killer would have had to come up with some excuse to pick up the item, and then get behind Kevin in order to strike...

Wolfe pulled again on the cigar, suppressing the urge to allow the tears that blurred his vision to overflow his eyes. Catharsis could come, but later, not now while he was trying to keep his thoughts clear, clear of pain, clear of other distracting emotions and desires. Memories. And while he struggled against anything that distracted good investigation, he would push forward. Do what needed to be done.

One foot, then the other.

The breeze flowed by and helped to dry his eyes. He held the thick, chipped paint of the railing and let its roughness ground him. He scuffed a foot along the concrete pad of the bridge, reminded himself that some things were solid. Some things were reliable.

But not feelings.

He knew as much as anyone that it was impossible to clear them all, to be totally objective and detached. Still, what he needed were facts. Facts were the only things that didn't lie — if they were read correctly. No, Cruz could not be ruled out, not yet. He would have to spend a little more time there, gather a little more data.

Who else could it have been? One of the priests maybe. Pascal had seemed the epitome of the peaceful young priest the night of Kevin's death, but there had been that outburst on the basketball court. Might be nothing. Might not.

Cisco knew who Wolfe was, and obviously held his job in some contempt. That didn't mean anything though. Opinions on the efficacy and even the morality of what he did varied widely, and were seldom passionless. Collateral damage was far from unknown. Such sin dealt damage, even to those innocent of it. *Mostly* to those.

And the senior man? Hadn't met him yet. Didn't have much to go on there.

No, Wolfe was the last person to think that religious vows were any kind of assurance of morality. The things he had seen... Still, he hadn't had any immediate feelings of suspicion in the few dealings he had had with the Fathers at Saint Mary's. If it were a Vatican-sanctioned investigation he would be able to find out more, but as things were, his hands were mostly tied; he had little power there.

But Billy Jackson did.

Jackson: Kevin's friend and an obvious ally to Wolfe. He wasn't the chief investigator, nor even officially involved with the case at all, but Detective Delaney was, and Jackson knew Delaney well enough to remain in the loop if he wanted to do so. Maybe, Wolfe thought, he should be cultivating that relationship a bit, keeping communication open and doing a little mining for information on his brother's death. Why had he been there? Was he meeting someone? Investigating something officially? Unofficially?

If Jackson could give him something to go on — anything — he could at least have a look around, ask better questions. People opened up to priests, a spillover from the confessional, probably, and they told them things that they would never tell a cop, even if the conversation was outside of the confessional itself, and not technically bound under the ecclesiastical laws of confidentiality.

So it could be Cruz, it could be a priest, it could even be another cop — or none of these. Day one of an investigation usually meant that everyone could be a suspect. His lips turned down and he shook his head. No, he reminded himself, nothing was ever clear and simple. Especially early on.

He finished most of the cigar before the relative chill of the night air started to bother him, and then he let the stub of it fall. A tiny hiss, and it was gone. That tribute to his father and brother found a home in the tumbling dark waters of the drainage canal and floated away into the distance. He turned then and retraced his steps back down the path, toward the church.

The street out front was devoid of parked cars and only one pair of taillights drove off down the street as he pulled open his car door and climbed inside. The little covered area beside the church offices also appeared empty. Ana Cruz had gone, it seemed, as had the priests. Only a lone boy remained, this one long-haired and looking chilled in a thin tee-shirt, shuffling his feet around the edge of the basketball court, smoking a cigarette in the shadows of leaves growing up and over a leaning chain-link fence.

Wolfe turned the engine over and, with a reluctant sigh, returned home to his other duties and to the empty Vatican lodgings which had become his last, tenuous refuge in a world that was rotting away beneath his feet.

The struggle had been brief and was decided before it had begun. The boy in the hoodie was dead. His killer pulled the murder weapon from the boy's back and rolled him onto a raincoat before the blood could seep through the clothing and onto the thick carpet of the little office. Nine crisp, one-hundred-dollar bills stuck out from the pocket of the hoody; these too, were removed.

The killer wrapped the coat around the body and dragged it out toward the back of the building. A silent look to ensure that no one was around to see, and then out. One shadow pulled another over the landing at the rear of the church and into the back of a parked van. The vehicle's doors were closed on the motionless shadow, locked as if to keep the secret thing safe from escape or theft, and then the other crawled in behind the steering wheel.

The rumble of an engine in the night and the van pulled out into the street just as Wolfe stepped out of the dark walking path by the water and walked toward his waiting vehicle. As the priest drove his car off to the apartment and the unsavoury tasks the night yet held for him, stillness again descended on Saint Mary of the Sea and storm clouds rumbled quietly in the east.

FIVE

Wolfe, with some effort, lifted his heavy lids. He could feel the dull throb of a hangover through both temples. His tongue felt like it was covered in half-dried glue.

He closed his eyes again, feeling the softness of the pillow against his cheek and the night-warmth of the bed beneath the covers. He slid a foot over and felt the coolness of the sheets near the edge of the bed. It was his favourite time of day — minus the hangover. He could stay like that for hours, if nothing pressing stirred his thoughts up into a tempest that stole the pleasure from it. The tempest had been in his dreams through the night, in the waking moments between them, and lingered near with his waking thoughts. There would be no languishing that morning.

The bell rang. The door. That must have been what had stirred him from his sleep. He glanced at the clock. Eight nineteen. He rolled his legs out of bed and grabbed the robe from the footboard. Pulled it on, tying the belt as he made his way to the door of the suite. He paused at the peephole to see who was there. It wasn't a face he recognised. Wolfe knocked one sharp rap against the door from the inside. Rather than a startled jump, the man stood much as he had been doing, but his eyes darted up to look at the little peephole, as if he had heard the sound but didn't really know what it was yet.

Mild puzzlement. No fear. No threat.

That was good enough — the man was not there for any malevolent reasons at least, or he would have been more on edge. Wolfe opened the door.

"Good morning. Are you Daniel Wolfe?"

"Yes."

"Hello Father Wolfe, I'm Father Edwin Marsh, Father Sanchez sent me to you with a message from the bishopric."

"That's a lot of Fathers for one sentence. Would you like to come in?"

"I really shouldn't," the man said, smiling, "I have much more to do this morning."

"I understand, busy day or two here as well. The message?"

"He wants to know what the death at Saint Mary of the Sea has to do with your current work. He wishes for you to telephone and speak with him before the bishop returns."

"When is he due, the bishop?"

"Just before noon."

The man looked to the side then. They heard approaching footsteps. The footfalls slowed as they approached the door until Wolfe saw Rosa Ortez, Kevin's mother, standing timidly behind the messenger-priest. Wolfe smiled, to his own surprise, feeling a connection to his late brother through the presence of his mother, despite what it had meant to Wolfe's own childhood realities.

"Mrs. Ortez. It is good to see you, please, come in, Father Marsh was just leaving anyway and I could use the excuse for a break."

She did not move, but spoke to him as if the other priest were not there. Her words were breathless, the power taken from her by some inward pain at what she had heard.

"So it is true," she whispered, "Kevin was there because of me. *Ai*, I killed my son." In the final few syllables, her voice faded away to almost nothing.

"Mrs. Ortez?" she had begun to sway on her feet and Wolfe motioned for Marsh to assist him in getting her inside. They helped her to the deep couch beside the television, Wolfe hiding away the notes and lists he had been making as he inventoried and graded the severity of the offending items from the cardboard box.

He went to the kitchen area for water and a moist towel for Rosa. Before taking them in to her, he ducked into his room and put on a pair of jeans and a tee-shirt, throwing his bathrobe on the bed.

Father Marsh steadied her while they waited, saying nothing until Wolfe returned and sat beside her. He did not take her hand. Marsh opened his mouth as if to speak, but a subtle gesture from Wolfe stilled him. He watched.

"Are you alright?"

She nodded.

"Now please, tell me what you mean. How do you think you killed Kevin?"

Her voice was small, not the understated power of a confident woman, but the broken tones of a mourning mother. "It was me. I ask Kevin to go to the church. Terrible things… I think *terrible* things happen!"

"Okay. Let's start from the beginning. Tell me what you saw and then how Kevin got involved. If I can help, I will."

She took a drink of the water and steadied herself.

"It is my church, Saint Mary of the Sea, and I love it. Praise the Lord I *love* it." She crossed herself and kissed the crucifix that hung around her neck. "I work there sometimes, in the community centre and with clothing collection for homeless ones. In the soup kitchen too, when they need more hands."

"Bless you," Father Marsh said, but got a sharp look from Wolfe. First rule of investigation: don't kick a moving target. An object in motion tends to stay in motion unless acted upon by an outside force. If words are coming, let her talk. Don't risk breaking the flow without a damn good reason.

A brief pause, then she continued. "I was folding the clothing near the back when I hear some coins fall from a pocket and bend to pick them up. I am there, picking up quarters and dimes when a boy comes, he's name Douglas, and he talks to another boy, tells him things that I do not understand. I am not sure I understand him, Daniel — maybe not." She fell silent.

"What did he say? What do you think he said?"

"He say things about a priest."

"What kind of things?"

"*Your* kind of things."

Wolfe sat there silently in thought. He didn't push her further. Father Marsh, not fully understanding the communication that had just passed between the two others just sat and watched, unsure whether he should stay longer in hopes of having more to tell the bishop's secretary, or just go. He made no move.

"But you are not sure?"

"I am not sure now, but I think so then."

"And you asked Kevin to look into it?"

"I want no trouble, so I just tell him to tell you what I say to him. He says no, he will look first. He says if he finds something serious he will talk to you and help together, you and him. He liked that idea, I think, working with his big brother…"

"Kevin went to see if there were any-" he glanced at Marsh, "-problems at the church, the kind of problems I deal with?"

"Yes. Kevin tell me what you do. Like him."

Wolfe nodded. Yes, a little like him. "Rest a bit, I'll take you home in a few minutes."

He got up and motioned Marsh toward the door. The two priests stepped out into the hall for a moment and Wolfe shook his hand.

"Thank you Father, for helping with her. She's my half-brother's mother."

"Of course, you're welcome. Will she be okay?"

"Yes, I'll take care of her."

"And the telephone call?"

"I'll do my best to make it, but if you will tell Father Sanchez what you heard, I think he'll know what he needs to know."

"Still, if you can call him…"

"I'll do my best, really. Tell him that. And tell him there is progress on the other issue as well, but no conclusion yet."

Father Marsh nodded and walked off down the hallway. Wolfe waited a moment and then stepped back inside, locked the door, and returned to his conversation with Kevin's mother.

"Mrs. Ortez, these things are very serious, these things I deal with. Our goal is to protect innocent people. Any innocent people. Accusations, even false ones, can end a priest's career… or worse… and so we must be very certain before we take open action. There are things, though, that we can do, quietly, to find out if there is likely a problem. This boy you heard, for example, we can talk to him. He might tell me his story if he knows I'm on his side."

"That is why I come, Daniel," her tears began to flow again and she wiped them with a handkerchief, "That boy is gone!"

"Gone how? Where?"

"His friend say he went into the church last night, to talk to the priest. His friend wait a long time, but Douglas never come out again. This boy went to the church but it is locked, everybody gone home. Douglas did *not* go home last night. The boys look this morning:

No Douglas. I pray and pray but I think something is wrong, something terrible is wrong!"

"The church was Saint Mary's?"

Rosa nodded, fighting back another sob.

Wolfe ran his fingers through his hair. This was not good. Had Kevin not been killed in the church two nights ago — had Wolfe even had an alternative reason for his half-brother having been there — then this vague suspicion on the part of a grieving woman who'd just lost her son would not have been worth more than a head's-up call to the bishop. Had it not been for Kevin. But this was different.

And he had no intention of handing it off to someone else.

Now Wolfe knew why his brother had been there. He knew Kevin had been questioning priests, men the young detective suspected of being corrupt, perhaps, but he might not have known what such men were capable of when backed into a corner. Probably not, anyway. *If* that's what happened.

And then there was the boy. Wolfe remembered seeing the hoody, sitting silently in the pew several rows behind Ana Cruz. He even remembered the long-haired kid with the cigarette, outside in the cool darkness.

Ana.

He hadn't ruled her out before, as the killer, and now she might have been present at the boy's disappearance too? Very unlikely that she was an abuser, but not entirely unheard-of... and it was common for women to support and protect the men who perpetrated actual abuse. These women were predators too, in his mind, and enjoyed a similar degree of cover as most priests would. *A woman wouldn't do that… A priest wouldn't do that…* he had heard those phrases a thousand times. It may be very rare for a woman to be the primary actor, but he couldn't assume one wasn't involved.

Even if she weren't involved in the abuse, he wouldn't underestimate the passion of a devout believer to defend the institution's public reputation. Clergy had it. Laypersons had it. Sometimes it made no logical sense at all, and otherwise-rational people would do terrible things to cover up other terrible things on the part of officers of the church. His job, in many respects, existed because of this peculiar dynamic. If Cruz had learned something, if she and Kevin had been working together and had turned over the wrong rock in her own church… could she be such a person?

He wouldn't assume a priest was not a killer either — strange and powerful passions sometimes raged inside men of the cloth, and he had seen many things in the past few years, sliding through the bowels and poking through the refuse of the church. Pascal had been at Saint Mary's last night too, he remembered.

He took Rosa's hand. Squeezed it as much for himself as for her. "I'll look into it, Mrs. Ortez. I'll find out what happened to the boy. It may be nothing."

She smiled. "You will come to the service?"

"The funeral?"

"A service for now. They won't let him go until they investigate. But we will have some time together to remember him. You will come?"

"Of course. When is it?"

"Today, four o'clock. I thought maybe no one knew to tell you."

"No," he said, suddenly feeling very alone once again, "No one told me."

He drove her home, a half an hour each way in the light traffic of late morning, past Starbucks for a bite to eat and a coffee on his way back. All the while, thinking.

There were too few data points and too many loose ends among them. Things needed to be whittled down, threads followed and eliminated from consideration. But where to start? When investigating abuse, he had most often gone to the abused for initial leads, for answers. If he had no access to the victim, there might be other evidence. Pictures. Video. In this case, it was a murder he wanted to solve. Couldn't go to the victim. No pictures. No video. Didn't have access to forensic labs or even reports... but he did have one thing: Rosa had told him what Kevin had been doing at the church, why he was there and about whom. Maybe that was information he could trade with Jackson for a little inside information. First though, he had take a look around on his own.

An hour later he pulled into the parking area of the community outreach centre, fully-garbed in his priestly clothing — and ready for a fight.

The front doors were closed but there was a sign on them in faded green card-paper which read "Come in, all are welcome," in both English and Spanish. Wolfe pulled back the big door and stepped through into relative darkness and cool air. He scanned the room once and saw nothing menacing. Kids were playing ping-pong in the back, two girls on one side, giggling and obviously throwing the game as a big thug of a kid played the other end, swatting the ball in their general direction and grinning like a toddler.

Between the ping-pong match and Wolfe were several benches and tables, arranged in rows and presently undergoing a thorough cleaning at the hands of a round Latina who looked to be in her seventies and every bit as in control of the room as she had been in her thirties, if not more so. A few kids played cards at the far right end of one table and a small knot of others sat in a huddle to his far left, discussing in earnest whatever it was that interested teens these days; Wolfe had lost track long ago, if he had ever known.

As he stood and took in the scene, the round lady finished up the table she was working on and looked over at him with a smile.

"*Buenos Dias, Padre. ¿Cómo está usted?*"

Wolfe smiled at the formal greeting. He assured her that he was fine and asked if she knew all of the young people who frequented the place.

She nodded. "*La mayor parte de ellos,*" Yes, most of them.

"*¿Usted conoce el Douglas? ¿Está Douglas aquí?*" Do you know Douglas? Is he here?

"*El no, Douglas no está aquí.*" She knew him, but he wasn't there.

"*¿Está Albany aquí?*" Is Albany here?

"*Sí, él está allá. El sombrero verde.*" Yes, he's over there, the green hat.

Wolfe thanked her and walked over to the huddled group on his left. Albany wasn't hard to spot, his lime-green stocking cap pulled low over his forehead, long hair tumbling out the back.

"Hey, Albany, can I talk to you for a second."

"I don't know, *can* you?" Giggles from his friends.

"I need a private moment."

"I bet you do," he grinned to more giggles from the group.

It had been the wrong tack to take with Father Wolfe that day. He grabbed the kid by the shirt and jerked him up over the back of the chair. With a hand under an arm for direction and one under the chin for motivation, Wolfe led Albany out into the short hallway by the entrance doors and thrust him up against the wall at arm's length.

The kid was rattled, but as his friends followed close behind, Albany put on another front of bravado.

Wolfe spoke. "Are your comments finished? I need information on Douglas, kid, and I need it in a hurry."

Albany squirmed against the hold but it was obvious that this priest knew what he was doing when it came to physical force. He choked out a reply for the

74

benefit of his friends: "I don't think I can talk to a guy who doesn't believe in screwing."

A chuckle here and there, but most of them knew that this was no joke; they'd never seen a priest do this before. One of them called for the round woman. She was already on her way.

Wolfe thrust his hand up under the chin for a moment, then relaxed a bit, letting the tension ebb out of his grip. "I'm not sure I believe in anything, Albany, but I do know that my brother is dead, that the reason Douglas was at that church last night might have something to do with it, and that any little punk who keeps me from finding out, will find himself in a bad place."

Albany, reading the release to mean a loss of will, shrugged his tee-shirt back into place and turned to leave. Wolfe grabbed the boy's throat again and threw him up against the wall, hard. The round woman came in just as he did this and shouted out in alarm. Everyone else was silent and watching. Wolfe ignored the woman.

"Okay, okay!" Albany whined through clenched teeth, "I'll tell you!"

Wolfe relaxed a little, but kept his face close to the kid, his eyes steely, letting all of the rancid emotions of the last few days — Kevin's murder and the evil crimes he had been witnessing on the discs — wash out through his stare. The kid felt it. The kid talked.

"It was a priest, from Saint Mary's that started it."

"You other kids go back to the tables. *Now*."

They went.

75

"*Señora*, you too. I think Albany and I understand each other." Wolfe let his arms down to his sides.

A pause, then the woman backed up into the other room, but positioned herself cleaning a table with a clear line of sight to the priest and boy in the hallway. She watched as Wolfe spoke.

"Go on."

"It was a priest from there who started it, you know, with Doug."

"Started what?"

"Started fooling around with him, touching him and stuff."

"And how do you know this?"

"Because Doug told me."

"Just talk? Sometimes these things are just talk."

"Not with Doug, he was real pissed when it first happened, didn't talk much about it and avoided the place for a while."

"And then?"

"And then he came back. He told me that he had seen the priest and that they'd made a deal. He had money, too, hundred-dollar bills."

"What kind of deal do you think they made?"

"Well, you know, hookin` up. I thought Doug was getting paid to let the guy do stuff."

"You thought so... Do you think so still?"

"I don't know. We went there last night, Doug and me. He was going to get some money. He said it would only take a minute or two and I laughed, but he got real pissed. He said it wasn't like that, that he had kill somebody before he had let them use him like that."

"You believed him?"

"I did at first, but…"

"But what?"

"He never came back out. I thought maybe they'd hooked up and he was just going to take a while. We were gonna go eat later, and buy new jackets. I waited. But then when I noticed the last cars leaving and the lights out, I went to check. The doors were locked. Nobody was there. I went home."

"Do you live with Doug?"

"No.

"Do you know where he lives?"

"Yeah. Same building as me, but I live on the third floor. He's on ground."

"Where?"

"About six blocks from here in the *Mansiones Blancas*, but he wasn't there this morning."

"Is it a decent place, or a squat?"

"A squat, pretty much. Abandoned, except for us and some crack-heads."

"What number?"

"I don't know, but if you go in the bottom floor of the first building, Block A, and walk through right to the back you'll see a room with plastic nailed over the door, that's his."

"And there's nobody there?"

"Crack heads."

"But no Doug."

"Yeah. He was gone. But I've been here an hour. I don't know where he is now."

"One more thing."

"Yeah?"

"Who is the priest Doug was talking about?"

"I don't know."

Wolfe let his eyes go cold, pictured snapping the kid's neck... and let the thought show.

"Really, Father, I don't know, I swear. Doug never said who it was, only that it was one of the Saint Mary priests."

"And do you have a theory?"

The kid shrugged and shook his head.

He believed him, stepped back. Albany stood, stock-still, until the priest nodded for him to go, then it was like he was shot out into the neighbourhood.

Wolfe lifted a hand to the round woman, letting her know that all was well and that the crisis had passed, then he walked out into the parking lot. He got into his car, noticing a long silver scrape in the fender paint that hadn't been there before, and started the engine. It was a rental. Fully insured. The powerless were ever powerless, but maybe the kid felt better at least.

He typed in *Mansiones Blancas* to the GPS. There were two hits and he selected the closest. Four blocks south, one west.

He drove the car through the cluttered streets and soon pulled up in front of the place young Douglas called home. It was a six-story concrete structure with heavy roof damage and obvious signs of squatting. The upper floors were the more desirable, as the rats tended to prefer lower ones which had better proximity to water and to good foraging, and the waste of those above flowed ever downward, increasing in volume with each occupied floor. On the lowest of these would be the room Douglas slept in and hid his worldly belongings.

Wolfe found Block A and stepped through the opening, pausing while his eyes adjusted to the dim light. Boards and broken concrete cluttered the floor. There was the acrid smell of urine wafting up from the corners and the clear sense that mould had been flourishing there for some years.

The structure seemed sound enough, but there were rat faeces in clusters around any gap or opening in the walls, where pipes or wires once ran but had been scavenged out and sold for scrap. Raw sewage leaked out from one of the holes, obviously the result of some floor above using it as a latrine. He had seen worse, but not in a place that wasn't a war zone. Hell, maybe it was, in its way.

Wolfe walked the full length of the open room and down the only corridor until he reached the back of the building. Twice he passed rooms where he felt the stares of occupants upon him, sometimes eyes lit with the glow of a lighter or candle flame.

He spoke to no one yet, looking ahead at the doorway with the plastic curtain hanging over it, torn and translucent in the dim light. When he reached it, he passed through and looked upon Douglas's home.

It smelled of urine and mould. Expected. There was an old sleeping bag in the corner, stained and damp, with tufts of yellowed stuffing sticking out of it everywhere, pressed down by body weight at night, pulled out again by rats and birds in the daytime, each day seeing less of it there to insulate and to cushion. A metal box with a broken lid sat on the floor beside the bedding, nothing in it but some damaged plastic toys and a ragged Sports Illustrated magazine. The walls were covered in the scrawl of the streets, the melodrama of runaway poetry and expressions of inspired hate and hopelessness. Wolfe paid little attention to these. They would no-doubt have themes that would support the worst case scenario. But all teenaged poetry seemed to have such themes. It would do him no good without names or details, and a brief look revealed that these had none, except that someone named Julio was an asshole.

He scanned the room for hiding places but found very little. He turned over the sleeping bag with a stick he found on the floor, but nothing came out save a few fleeing insects that had holed up there for the day. Douglas could have had a hiding place somewhere else in the building, but it was futile to go looking for it; he had likely die of tetanus — or worse — before he ever uncovered anything of value. There was only one piece of information the priest was likely to get from this place, and that was that Douglas was not in it. Not a definite sign of anything foul — the homeless often disappeared for reasons of their own — but it was also not a good sign.

He walked back out down the hallway, calling softly into each room, asking for Douglas, telling him to come out if he was nearby, that he was there to help him.

It was a long shot at best. After all, if he had just been molested by a priest and was getting paid to continue the activities, or if he had tried blackmailing the older man, would he come out and show himself to another one, one who'd just invaded his only refuge in a world which had shown itself so much less than kind?

No, Wolfe knew he wouldn't.

Still, he felt sure enough that the boy was not in the building. He returned to the car and sped off toward home, hoping to squeeze in the phone call to the bishop, anxious that he put this situation together in his head before the clues got too cold.

His musings in the darkness intrigued him though: blackmail. Blackmail was a possibility. It would explain Douglas's return to the church last night, his new-found wealth, and even the reasons that a priest might stage a robbery and get rid of a police investigator. Or why a young man with a good financial deal going might want to get rid of an interfering police officer. Maybe both of them together.

It still wasn't wrapped in a tight bow, no, it wasn't all there yet, but Wolfe felt like he was nibbling at the edges of it, getting closer with each short step. He wondered how the police were doing with their own investigations. He thought of Jackson again.

And he thought of Ana Cruz.

SIX

"Good afternoon, office of Bishop Grippe," the voice was male: Vittorio Sanchez.

"Hello, it's Danny Wolfe for the bishop."

"Yes Father, he just got in. Please hold for a moment and I'll put you through."

There was a pause of about a minute. Wolfe propped his pillows into a pile against the headboard and reclined on the bed, kicking his shoes off onto the floor. A minute more and a somewhat breathless bishop said "Hello? Daniel?" at the other end of the line.

"Hi David."

"Hello, how are things going on the case? Have you seen the evidence?"

"We're looking at a dozen hours of it, at least… it will take me a few days." Twelve hours straight of child pornography would drive a sane man mad and imprint the images on his waking sight. Wolfe could only handle small doses at a time. Less as the years went on.

"Of course."

"We'll need the audio guys in, though."

"Find some interesting sound?"

"He used helium to disguise his voice."

"Can they do anything with that?"

"*I* can't, that's for sure. Maybe they can come up with something that we can use, even if it wouldn't stand up in a secular court. Maybe background noise for a location…"

"Of course, of course. And your lodgings, are they sufficient?"

"Very much so. The Vatican does have a penchant for providing elaborate rooms."

"Vatican nothing, I chose those for you — I can't have you in my home state and staying at the Motel 6."

"I wouldn't have minded."

"All the more reason."

"It doesn't make much difference, the hours I've been logging here — but I'm being ungracious, I do like the suite, really. I just haven't had much time to enjoy it."

"Of course, of course, we have been busy. Vittorio tells me you've expanded your investigation. Is Saint Mary's involved in the primary case then?"

Wolfe smiled. He knew, despite the words spoken, that nothing much got past the old bishop, and that David Grippe knew exactly the connection that Wolfe had with the little church. The official talk was finished then and the rhythm of the conversation shifted.

"There might be a connection."

"Yes, there might. What evidence do you have that there *is*?"

"There is a boy named Douglas, a street kid. He's missing."

"Yes."

"Kevin Ortez's mother attends there. She tells me that the boy reported being sexually abused by a priest."

"Reported to whom?"

"Just a friend. Nothing official."

"Worthy of a look of course. And the connection?"

"Kevin was killed there, while checking out the story about the boy. The boy is missing after an accusation against a priest. What more do we need?"

"We don't need anything else — for an investigation to be launched — but I'll repeat the question, Daniel. What connection does it have to your current investigation?"

"None… That I know of. It would be a coincidence if it weren't, though."

"Ah, my friend. I know this has a personal aspect for you and I promise I won't ignore it, but you know as well as I do the stakes we're dealing with on the other case — the impact could be world-wide."

"I know."

"Besides that, I got a call." Wolfe didn't comment. "A priest named Father Jésus Gonzales — senior priest of Saint Mary of the Sea, no less — gave me a call just this morning. Tracked down my mobile number, in fact. Assuming you didn't give it to him, I have to admit he's quite a resourceful old fellow."

Wolfe smiled, despite himself. Grippe was at least ten years older than Gonzales.

"Do you know what it was the man wanted, Daniel?"

"To have me out of his hair, I expect."

"That was an aspect of the call, but — and I have to give him credit here again — his call was primarily one of information. He let the reaction remain mine."

"What information?"

"Do you know a young man named Albany? A boy in the care of the Catholic Community Outreach Centre?"

Wolfe's gut knotted. "Yes."

"And for what reason did you think it appropriate to throw the boy against a wall, to 'rough him up' I believe the vernacular still is, and worse yet, to do so in the full sight of everyone there?"

"I needed information."

"Information? And for that information you, in priest's clothing and therefore as an official representative of the church, no less, abused a boy — yes, I said 'abused' — and frightened a dozen others? Do you understand the depth of that? The implications, especially considering your office with the church?"

"You and I both know that far more severe measures are taken in the course of these investigations, and their resolutions, and I was way back from the grey area on this one."

"No, that's where you went wrong. You and I both suspect, have an educated guess even, the extent to which our authorities in the church will go to ensure the safety of those under her care and the longevity of God's arm on earth — but we *know* nothing. Do you know why we are ignorant, why we are in the dark?"

Wolfe made no comment.

"It is because of the extreme discretion used when extreme measures are deemed necessary. Never, not since the dark times of the Inquisition, has the modern church been linked even tangentially to any of these extreme measures. Either they never occurred or those charged with the responsibility of carrying them out did so with extreme care, care which you did not show yesterday. You know the saying 'it is not enough to do good, one must be *seen* to do good'?" He didn't wait for a reply. "It goes just the same that one must not be seen to do evil, even if doing the evil was actually for the good. I take it you understand me."

"I'm sorry, David."

"Thank you, though I didn't expect you to say so. I expected more of a fight."

"On that you'll get no fight. I was wrong."

"So you'll back off then?"

"That's a different issue."

"You know you'll need to. I can't have you in there throwing teens against the wall and charging through the affairs of priests in good standing — even if it is to find the one who killed your brother."

"But there is something going on there, there is a reason Kevin was killed in Saint Mary's."

"I know. At least I believe it had some connection to something wicked. And believe me, you have my condolences — I began praying for you the moment I heard."

Wolfe grunted something like thanks.

"I'll look into it, I promise. But you need to let it go."

"I can't. How can I?"

. "You need to. Even if it weren't for the politics of it all, even if it weren't for the emotion interfering with a good investigation, aside from all of these things, you can't investigate your own brother's murder. It would damage you."

"And what do you propose I do then, forget about it?"

"Oh no, not forget. Grieve. Grieve for your lost loved one and follow the investigation as a bystander. Talk to the police. Talk to me. But stay back. Let it go, I beg you."

"You beg me?"

"And order you, if I must."

Silence.

"Aim these energies at your given task, pour yourself into your work for a time — as I say it, I realise that to do so would be no great change from the norm for you — and burn your energy in an area which will bring benefit and relief to others."

"And who will bring benefit and relief to me?"

"I will."

"How?"

"Put it in my care. Give it to me. On the authority of Holy Mother Church and your vows — let it go."

No reply.

"Promise me."

"I don't know that I can."

"In effect, my friend, you already have, when you vowed obedience to the church."

"Then why do you ask?"

"By way of reminder and by way of reinforcement. Willing obedience is always better than coercion. But I trust you. I trust you fully. I know what a vow means to you and trust it more than any other man's word — save our Lord himself — but I understand your pressure and emotional strain."

"Do you?" Some edge had crept into Wolfe's voice.

"Don't be a fool. I've been through two wars and buried three brothers, parents and a dear little sister. Your pain is real, but it is not unique. Remember your vows. And Daniel?"

"Yes?"

"I will be praying for you, my dear friend."

The phone call ended on that note and Wolfe checked the time on the clock by his bed. The little numbers glowed in red and switched from 1:17 to 1:18 as he watched.

The bishop was right: he had made vows of obedience and had not been released from them. As long as he didn't have a concrete reason to leave, some sense that the other side had broken their part of the deal, he wasn't going anywhere. He wore the collar as a constant reminder that he was not his own. The chain around his neck held him fast just as much as it held the little golden figure at the lower end of it. To walk away from his responsibilities and promises would have been too much like... like John, the father who had seemed so distant, then had gone altogether and left his mother to die alone, watched silently by her young and powerless son.

Wolfe had made promises to his country — and kept them. He had made vows to the Catholic church at the feet of the pope himself, despite the slow erosion of his religious fire throughout his seminary training. His faith had waned and withered and still Bishop Grippe had not let him go, had held him to his promise of service to Mother Church. The broken priest didn't understand why. He didn't see what use an agnostic clergyman was to the church or to whatever God might exist — at least no use in a spiritual sense. A thug. He often felt like nothing more.

Perhaps it was useful to have someone around to do the things that a believer wouldn't. But even that logic was flawed. The Vatican had fanatics ready to steal, kill, destroy or leap off cliffs in the name of the pope and the Catholic Church. It was nothing unique to Catholicism either; every religion had its share of crazies; they didn't need him to fill that quota. Then for what?

He blew out his air. He needed time to think.

It was an hour to the funeral parlour. They had decided against holding the service on the very ground where Kevin had been killed. Wolfe wanted to get there early, to spend some quiet time in a place devoted, for a brief hour or two, to the memory of his departed brother and, though he wouldn't admit it to himself, perhaps glean some comfort from the presence of Rosa Ortez, and even Ana Cruz, those others who were close to his brother. He had little sense of family, a thin thread only, now broken. It did not take much to increase his feeling of connection. Or loss.

He sat on the edge of the bed and laced his shoes up. A deep sigh and he rose to his feet. He grabbed his black suit jacket from the wooden hanger inside the closet door and put it on. Gold cross. Collar. Black suit. Work wear. Everyday wear. Funeral garb.

He pulled open the door and stepped out into the hallway. That was when the apartment behind him exploded with a burst of flame and threw him across the hall, through the opposing door with crushing impact, and onto the floor of the neighbouring suite.

His body did not move.

SEVEN

It was dark when Wolfe awoke, and he strained to breathe. His eyes couldn't focus on distance at first and the blurred sensation of motion gave him a feeling of nausea. He vomited, crying out as the strain of the stomach spasm sent sharp shocks of pain through his ribs, and hacking at the burn in his throat when he sucked his breath back in.

Smoke. The darkness was smoke.

Thick arms of black fumes reached out from the open door behind him and bent off down the hall or across into the room where he lay on the floor. It was hot and acrid, dark chemical-smoke and deadly gasses. He forced himself to his knees, groaning at the pain along his back and down his sides. Cracked ribs... maybe worse. Wind. Could he really feel the wind? He teetered.

He closed his eyes for a moment and called up the reserves he had been taught to tap into in his military training, in Special Ops. He remembered the forced drownings and being revived. The first time, he had thought that no fear could be so paralysing, that no urge could be so intense as the one to breathe when air was denied. By the third time he underwent the terrifying exercise, he was able to perform small tasks while drowning: thread a nut onto a bolt, fire a weapon. By the time he had finished his training he was aware of every second he had left before unconsciousness took him. Fear of unknown limits had been changed into an awareness of his true strength and ability, far beyond what he had thought a human being could endure.

That kind of awareness was what he needed now.

He closed his mouth, squinted, and rose to his feet in a deep crouch. Tears flowed from his eyes, both from the fumes and from the strain of ignored pain in his ribs and face as he moved out of the room and off down the hallway. He blinked them away.

His heart began to pound harder, the physical awareness of the throbbing beat radiated in widening pulses from his chest and head to his shoulders and down over his arms. His face began to tingle and he sensed numbness below his wrists and ankles.

He staggered against the wall once, but kept going. Dark drops of liquid seemed to strike his field of vision from somewhere off in front of him and remain, reducing his clear field of vision with each passing second until there was nothing but a narrow tunnel of fading light straight ahead of him. A stairwell, a flight of stairs, an open door at the head of them. It all waved from side to side. Looked too far away. Receding.

He staggered onward, passed through the door and kicked the stopper away from its base, letting the heavy swing of the metal knock him firmly to the side and against the cold concrete wall. As the sound of the latch registered in his ears as if from some distant room, he allowed his knees to buckle and he slid down the cold blocks, opened his mouth and let the first painful rush of semi-clean air wash into his lungs, like drinking a glass of sweet water tainted with gasoline.

He sat there, allowing his coughing breath to oxygenate his blood and the blood to reclaim control over his body. The feeling of vertigo returned and he could feel a tingling sensation moving up his spine from between his shoulder blades to the base of his skull, like a wide, flat hand reaching up from behind him, sliding up and over the surface of his skull. He knew what it meant. He tried to fight it — he had always tried to fight it — but as the phantom grip tightened, he knew that his efforts were futile. He moved his head to the side, balanced between the two walls and at rest in the cool corner, felt as if he slid backward, through the solid concrete slabs. And there his body slumped.

He awoke again in a hospital room — private — with the curtains pulled and a dimmed, artificial light illuminating the walls from recesses in the paneled ceiling. He heard the rustle of clothing beside him and turned his head enough to see Father Sanchez hunched over in a chair, a *Modern Catholic* magazine open on his lap.

Wolfe's ribs hurt when he breathed in, but not nearly to the degree they had before. He had been medicated then, probably morphine. From the look of the curtains it was night, but he had no way of knowing how much time had passed since he had been injured — one day or many. If the bishop had had Sanchez wait with him though, it could not have been too long.

Wolfe cleared his throat, wincing at the pain the action caused him around the ribs. The other man stirred and looked up.

"Ah, Father Wolfe, the bishop will be pleased to hear that you have awakened." His smile was genuine.

"He must have been worried, to have you sit with me personally. I'd have thought you would be busy on more important matters."

"In fact yes, for the most part I've been working on other matters in the bishop's absence. He's been sitting here with you himself, through the night and most of the day. Had he not been compelled to a certain meeting today, he would be with you still. There is a cot in the corner there where he slept through the night."

From the height of his bed Wolfe couldn't see the cot, but trusted that it was there. So the old bishop was truly worried about him. He tried to smile. His fingers went immediately to his face. Sanchez stood and reached for his hand.

"No, don't touch it. You have some burns."

"My face, when I smile… is it swollen?" It felt thick and immobile, like a layer of putty, or thick mud, had been pressed all over it.

"A little, but it is also gauzed and anaesthetised. It will feel numb around your cheek and ear for a while, and then not. They say the burns are not too bad, but you will have preferred it numb, though, I suspect."

It was the secretary's attempt at light-hearted humour. It was a trait of all of the men who worked Vatican Internal Investigations that their light-heartedness quickly fled them, leaving most with only cynical heaviness after a while. Wolfe felt it in his own heart and wondered if it ever went away when the job was done. He doubted it.

"A bomb?"

Sanchez nodded. "Yes, it seems so."

Wolfe's eyes widened as a sudden thought occurred to him. "The box in the living room, the papers and DVDs?"

"Gone."

"Everything?"

"If it was in the suite, especially if it was in the bedroom, it is gone. You're lucky to have survived at all, from what I hear. Firefighters found you in the stairwell, the back of your jacket peppered with bits of burning debris and your face covered in blood. You're lucky to be alive. Had you been even a little closer to your apartment door, who knows what might have happened? One might even say you were looked after there."

Wolfe thought a moment, disappointment at the loss of the evidence mingled with a deep relief that the need to view it, to analyse and take notes on the contents, had been removed by this act of violence. "You went over there?"

"Yes, the bishop sent me to survey the scene. Your door and the door across the hall blown open, scorch-marks running the length of the hall. I was only able to get into the apartment proper for a few moments, but what I saw was devastation. I could see out into the street through the hole blown in the wall by the charge."

"The bedroom, you said before?"

"Yes, the worst damage was in the bedroom — that is how I ruled out a kitchen accident."

"The stove is electric."

"I would not have known. The appliance was no longer where I suspect it should have been — nor was most the wall behind it. Removed by authorities, or by the blast, I don't know. The internal walls, it seems, were not as solid as the structure as a whole. Only the weight-bearing walls remain intact, the ones around the apartment itself. The others burned or were destroyed by the initial blast."

"Were others hurt?"

"No, it was mainly your own apartment that was damaged, and most were not home, or were home awake, so the smoke did no real harm."

"You said you could see outside… was there debris in the parking area?"

"Yes, and several damaged cars."

"Did you smell anything? Anything identifiable I mean."

"It smelled of fire… burnt rubber and something like Styrofoam. And gasoline, maybe."

"Maybe?"

"Some kind of fuel smell — I must admit I am more of an administrator than a hands-on type of person. The reconnaissance of a bomb site goes a bit beyond my skill set."

"Of course, yes... but you did well just the same. When is Bishop Grippe due to return?"

Sanchez glanced at his watch. "He was not certain, but I expect him within the hour or not much past."

Wolfe nodded.

"I should text him," Sanchez continued, "I was to leave a message when you awoke. I was asked not to use the mobile phone near the equipment. May I get you anything, while I am gone?"

"I think so, if you don't mind."

"Not at all."

"I am a little hungry."

When Sanchez opened the door, Wolfe was able to see out of the room. Instead of the normal bustle of a busy hospital ward, there was no sound from the hallway. The only other individual in sight was a man in a black suit who sat on a chair — no magazine or book, no coffee. Wolfe scanned his body as the door swung back into place and saw the tell-tale signs. His conclusions were immediate.

Armed. Shoulder-holstered handguns generally produce an obvious bulge in the suit jacket, just below the arm on the side the weapon is holstered, in this case the left. That kind of bulge told him a certain story. This particular suit, however, was of the two-thousand-dollar variety and tailored so as to make this bulge as subtle as possible. That told him another story. So did the expensive shoes. He would have expected guards of some kind, probably FBI; any victim of a bombing would be under protective custody until the investigators could determine whether he was a bomb-maker blown up in the process of device-construction, or if he had been the target and therefore still in danger. But these men were not FBI, not unless the feds had recently quadrupled agent incomes or issued expensive tailored suits.

So, Vatican personal security forces. Private hospital room. Vacant floor.

The bishop must think it was related to his most recent case, Wolfe decided. The case was a big one. They had evidence that a Vatican-run agency was being used as the backdrop for the production of child pornography. Due to the nature of this particular agency, it was thought that orphaned infants in the church's care might be their steady source of victims. Several properties were under the same overseer, as was a foundling orphanage supported by the local diocese — the church's answer to the cries of despair sent up by young mothers and troubled women who desired freedom from the burden of motherhood without having to contravene the contraception and abortion rulings of previous popes and thereby risk damnation.

The children were sometimes adopted from the institution, or eventually released on their own recognisance at the age of seventeen, if they hadn't run away first. But it seemed there might be some interference in the interim; interference which gave some church authorities grave concern. The suspected perpetrator was a high-level member of the clergy. The repercussions of such a thing finding public expression were potentially devastating.

It was Wolfe's job to determine who was involved and to hand that information over to the bishop. From there it would travel up lines of authority well above Wolfe's pay grade and far from his knowledge. Men might be moved around. Some would retire from the cloth and seek a life removed from the public eye. Occasionally such civil discipline was not necessary — accidents or situations sometimes occurred.

Wolfe didn't much mind the loss of those particular lives. All the same he made it a point to avoid any information about the subjects of his investigations once the cases had left his care. His business was information gathering and assessment. After that, he had nothing to do with those he investigated.

The bomb was something new, at least new to his life on this side of the military. Wolfe had few fans in the underbelly of the church, but he didn't like the idea of blatant assassination attempts. Besides, a bomb was too flashy, too obvious... too desperate. Whoever this person was, he — or they — was not coming in easily.

The details of the aftermath in the suite led him to believe that the bomb was constructed for the dual purpose of removing the evidence and the primary investigator in one go. Perhaps once the bomb squad people had taken a look he could find out for certain. Maybe Jackson could help him there, or Cruz. He made a mental note to check. Still, that could take weeks — months even.

He forced himself to a sitting position. Scanned the room. The cot was there, and beside it was the item Wolfe had hoped to see: a clear-plastic cover over a set of fresh clothes, and a smaller plastic bag with his personal effects — everything he had had in his pockets when he had been found. The badge was there, the photographs. His wallet. The bishop would not have thought him ready to get up and about yet, but came prepared nonetheless.

David Grippe was the closest thing Wolfe had to a friend. Hell, he was the closest thing to family, now. Almost forty years of age separated them, but the common experience of war and resulting self-loathing gave them a great deal of common ground. Both had moved into the priesthood in an attempt to find redemption — peace even — from the unbidden images that floated in front of eyes, open or closed.

Their immersion into the sordid world they investigated, however, had given them even more of these disturbing visions. Peace, at least for Wolfe, remained elusive. Maybe Grippe, with his faith intact, had a better time of it.

Wolfe often wondered if either of them would get to live in the normal world again, that of true priests and bright, sunny Sunday gatherings and melancholy midnight masses. He wondered if such a world existed after a person was exposed to the other extreme. Perhaps once dipped in the grime, the smell never quite came off, like fermented fish. He envied those who never had to know such things.

He stood to his feet, pausing for a moment, part way up. Then a long breath.

A few hesitant steps, then movement got easier. His rib cage was a grinding fury of stabs and bites, but if he concentrated on keeping it still and moving only his arms and legs, he did alright. Slow. Easy. No flowing rhythm, just minimal lean and motion to get the job done.

He was able to get the underwear on, the stretchy white undershirt and black socks. He dropped the pants on the floor and was able to shuffle into them with the use of the cot. The shirt was more difficult. It required him to stretch an arm backward and twist it, bringing the second sleeve up over his forearm until his other hand could grasp it and pull it up over the shoulder. Dislocated, maybe, from the impact of the shock wave. Put back in place of course, but that was one joint that held a grudge. Ah well, not the first time he had had a run-in with a bad shoulder. His fingers closed over the crisp fabric and he pulled.

The first effort failed. The second made him grunt in pain and forced a short break while he calmed himself and let his breathing return to normal. Pain brought adrenaline and he had no way of burning it off. Movement with damaged ribs was all about conservation of energy: one moves things only if absolutely necessary… because *everything* hurts.

The nurse came in with the tray of food as he was fastening the last of the buttons on his shirt. She was a young woman, perhaps twenty-two, and a nun.

"Father Edwards! You shouldn't be up."

Father Edwards. 'Daniel Edwards' was his alternate identity, that of an Italian national of Canadian birth. It had been issued to him by the Vatican for emergency use. Grippe must have had him admitted to the hospital under that name for safety's sake.

"But I *am* up, and I'm leaving." A light accent, Roman, taught and practiced while training for VII service at the Vatican.

"You can't leave, Father, you're injured."

"I'm better aware of my injuries than you are, Sister, but I'm afraid there is no question to the matter: I need to go. Call the doctor if you must, but have him bring the AMA form with him."

She left the room, muttering to herself, as he stepped over to the little table and began to eat the food she had left. From the first bite he became ravenous and wolfed the bulk of it down before settling to wait for the doctor and the fight to sign the *Against Medical Advice* discharge and get back to work. Twenty minutes and a bitter argument later, he was walking out the front of the building.

He met the bishop on his own way in.

EIGHT

"Whoever it was, tried to kill me, David."

"All the more reason to stay here."

"I can't just lie there and let whoever it is come for me again... I just can't."

"And what is your alternative? To wander around in the streets and make yourself a better target, an easier target? Look at you moving! That nun could take you down."

"No, not that either."

"Then what?"

"I need to find out what happened, what triggered the bombing. It could have been something to do with Kevin, or it could have been someone else, someone we've been investigating — who knows? But I need to do something. Sitting there just isn't right, somehow. It just isn't. I can't do it."

The bishop stood for a moment in the cool evening air. A breeze wandered in from the sea. Wolfe resisted the urge to say more, to continue to convince the old man that he needed to keep moving, to keep searching.

Instead he waited. The bishop's mind was in motion; let it move.

"You know I do not condone vengeance."

"I know. Vengeance isn't what I'm after. I'm after the truth, that's all. I'll let you decide what justice is from then on. I do trust you, you know."

The old man nodded. "I trust you too." He studied the brick wall for a moment. "I have new orders for you."

"New orders?"

"Yes. You are to continue to investigate the original molestation and child pornography case — and whatever peripheral leads you think might pertain to it."

"Does that include-"

"These are your only orders, Father Wolfe. I can give no others, nor do I wish to clarify, other than with one last thing."

"Yes?"

"Take care of yourself. This old man's grown fond of you."

"I will."

"I will be praying for you."

Wolfe made no comment, but nodded to his friend and limped to his car.

His first call was to Billy Jackson, to set up a meet with the munitions tech and find out what he could about what had happened in the suite. Jackson was on his way to a case, but promised to meet the next day, pending some information from the bomb squad.

His second call was to Cruz. He had asked her to meet him for coffee and she, just coming off the end of a twelve-hour shift, had agreed. A jostling, painful ride of twenty-five minutes and Wolfe stepped out in front of *Deluco's*, a quaint little coffee shop with light jazz piped onto the patio seating from the counter inside.

College-aged baristas brewed, poured and foamed behind the counter, their various piercings glittering in the night air. Young men bobbed and wove through the tightly-packed tables with trays of oversized cups and baked treats, tattoos like the Sistine Chapel. The rich aroma of the coffee mixed with the sweet taste of chocolate and fudge in the air. It was a mental break that Wolfe needed; he felt most at ease in places like this, solitary, but steeping in the motion and constant thrum of social interaction. The rumble and swoosh of passing traffic, the pockets of friendly laughter, and all through it the malty aroma of fresh bread and rich, dark coffee. Compared to the sterile environment of the hospital — sterile at best — this place was a little spot of paradise.

Cruz pulled up in her own car, a Civic coupe, but still wore the uniform. He watched her get out and walk up to the front door, waving as she came.

That uniform.

He had heard of women being beguiled by men in uniform, but had not really understood the attraction until he had seen Ana Cruz. Her body pressed out against the black material in all the right places, the folds shifting and changing as she walked, the utility belt with the flashlight, cuffs and radio alternately dipping or rising, accentuating the movement of her hips.

He saw what had attracted his brother, at least the physical part. She was a good-looking woman, no doubts there. And the gun. Why was a woman with a gun so enticing? Power? The juxtaposition of the feminine form with the killing power of the weapon? He had seen plenty of women toting firearms in Iraq. They'd been mainly for show, though, a PC concession by the boys in green to let the girls have some representation in the armed forces. It was changing fast now though, their combat roles were becoming more real. But when he had been in there, it was still just a token, a gesture without substance.

But Cruz had substance.

The Glock 22 on her hip was not for show. She knew how to use it and carried herself as if she were willing to do so. She seemed confident about the use of force where necessary, though Wolfe doubted she had had much call to it yet. Too young. But maybe he was just being naïve.

He returned her wave as she approached the table, a look of concern wiping away her smile.

"Hello Father Wolfe. I heard what happened. Is your face badly hurt?"

"My face will be fine. The bandages are just for show at this point... mostly." He grinned. "And please, call me Danny."

"Oh no, I can't call you just 'Danny' when you're like this, in your uniform." He considered pulling the dog collar from his shirt, transforming into a regular, hip, man in black, out with a pretty cop. He didn't.

"Father Danny, then, at the most." He reached out to take her hand in his, but stopped the compulsion, just in time, grabbing instead for his glass of icy water. Weakness, camouflaged by the heat.

"Okay… Father Danny."

They ordered coffee and a couple of slices of lemon-loaf, the sugary cake made on the premises each morning. It was so sweet it made his teeth hurt, but the coffee was excellent: strong. The two together were a good mix. They brought a little life back into his limbs and seemed to sharpen his senses.

"Is it painful?" she asked.

"A little. The ribs, mostly. Not too bad." A lie hardly worth the penance.

"Do you know who?"

"No, not really, and 'why' will also be a bit difficult… there is more than one possibility."

"Something to do with Kevin?"

"Might be. I'll know more when I know more about the bomb itself."

She nodded.

"Ana?"

"Yes?"

"Do you think you might tell me more about you and my brother?"

She blushed, there was no mistaking it. Full of more than a girl-like flirtation, this held grown-woman pain, complexity and discomfort. He had seen it before, broaching issues of sex with females and males alike. Was it discomfort for the subject though, or the audience?

"I'm not asking as a priest or as an investigator," he said, "I'm just asking as his brother. Knowing more about him, about his life as far as it got... it might help. Somehow."

She nodded again. Sipped her coffee. When she was ready, she spoke. "We met seven months ago, at a community policing seminar. He was talking about the importance of 'beat cops' in the neighbourhoods, officers who knew the people and were known by them. You know, minimise the adversarial tone. He was a good speaker. He was handsome, with his bright blue eyes and red hair. So tall.

"After the seminar we went for coffee in the lounge of the hotel, then stayed for a drink." Her flush renewed, but she gave no more detail of their first day. "We started seeing each other after that. It wasn't really serious, but it was regular, and nice — to have someone who understands the job, you know? He went through the same things before he made detective. Late nights, long shifts and stress. And the people sometimes, 'knuckle-heads,' he called them."

Wolfe smiled, "Yes, Kevin and his disdain for knuckle-heads."

"Well, I knew what he meant. People can be so good sometimes, if they want to be, so noble. But other times, so dark. Why must so many people be so dark?"

He shrugged; it needed no explanation, he felt just the same. "And you were still seeing each other when he was — when he died?"

She shook her head. "Not really. We had a little fight, not serious."

Wolfe nodded. "Anything to do with the reason he was at the church?"

"No." She shrugged. "I'm buying a little house. I'd mentioned trying the roommate thing... sharing the place as a trial run. It didn't go so well. Bad idea maybe. Anyway, we made up on the phone, mostly. But then it was a little different after that. Maybe we would have gotten there in the end, but we didn't. And now he's gone."

Wolfe did reach out and hold her hand then, as her thick lashed welled up with moisture, glistening in the patio lanterns and the shine from the counter. She didn't pull away. "You remind me so much of him, Danny."

No *Father*. Just Danny. Danny and Ana.

Priest and cop.

They sat like that for some time, occasionally sipping the coffees, but not talking again, letting the darkness and the bustle around them serve as a wall against the world beyond. It was Cruz who broke their silence.

"Billy told me what you do."

"Did he?"

"Yes."

"What did he tell you?"

"That you help the children. That you work directly for the pope himself and that you are a powerful man in the church — but a strange one."

There was more than one thing Wolfe felt he had like to correct in her sentence, or at least to comment on. He chose the last.

"Strange? Why am I strange?"

"Do you believe in God?"

"What do you mean when you say 'God'?"

"Your answer tells you why you're strange. You're a priest. You should say 'yes,' quickly, but you need to think."

"And is that so strange?"

"In a priest, yes."

"You haven't known too many priests then." An attempt at levity.

"I've known enough."

"And *you* believe in God."

"Yes, of course."

"You say 'of course,' but not many cops do believe."

"More than you think. More than like to show it. But you're right, it's difficult sometimes."

"Have you considered, maybe there are more priests who harbour doubts, and don't like to show it either?"

"Maybe. Why don't you believe?"

"I don't know if I do."

"But why don't you? Did you become a priest this way? Did no one notice?"

"I wasn't this way when I became a priest. Not really."

"What happened?"

Her fingers tightened a little on his and he felt the heat rise to his face. The touch of a woman, especially this woman, was so moving, so welcome in a way, but he also knew the spectacle they might make for anyone who chose to look: a priest and a lady cop, holding hands at a coffee shop in the middle of the night. He might be able to justify it as simple human comfort, if he could convince himself of that, but he wasn't sure he could. He remembered what Grippe had told him, the dressing down he had received for pushing Albany in the public eye. The church had enough trouble in the rumour mill. He wished she had at least tear up again, maybe let a drop trickle down her cheek so that it would look like he was consoling her. He was, wasn't he? Yes. Whatever else he might be feeling, he was certain of that.

"I don't know what happened. I was a soldier before. I fought in Afghanistan, Somalia, in Iraq — Desert Storm — and in other places. I saw terrible things. And I did terrible things. When I got out of the service I... I don't know... I was lost. I needed something to grab hold of. I tried this. I thought it would be enough. A solution."

"And you believed in God then?"

"I thought I did. Yes, I did. A good Irish son. I tried to be the best Catholic I could be, just like in the military I'd been the best soldier I could be. In the Army, that meant Special Forces, Green Berets. And in the church that meant the priesthood. The Vatican, as it turned out."

"But when you lost your faith, you didn't quit?"

"I can't."

"Why not?"

"I made a vow."

She thought for moment, in silence, mulling that over.

"If you made a vow to God, but you don't believe in God, why must you keep the vow? Isn't it meaningless now?"

It sounded almost like pleading, like an attempt to pull apart the façade — or perhaps this was just more of his yearning for human contact, the inner voice of his loneliness and isolation. It made his own judgments unreliable. But his creed was immutable. That's the point of creeds, he supposed, not a lot of room for interpretation.

"I made a vow to God which I guess I wouldn't have to keep, if I knew there wasn't a God, but I don't know — I just don't know if he's out there. More importantly though, to your question, I also made a vow to serve the Church, and the Church is made up of men — and women."

"A vow to men?"

"Yes. To my bishop, and the pope."

"And to women?"

"I suppose so."

"Like me."

He was silent.

"And of course these men are real."

"Yes." *And the women. The ones like you.*

"And so you cannot leave them."

"No, not yet. Maybe someday, but not yet."

She smiled and squeezed his hand again before slowly withdrawing it. That act of withdrawal, of a woman removing herself from a man who had designated himself as unavailable. He knew, then, without doubts, that she wanted him, that he could have her if he left his vows behind, even for a brief time, but he shoved that knowledge deep down inside, and locked it away. She was missing Kevin. His brother. A strange priest was a poor substitute, but it was a connection at least. Broken. Vulnerable. Even if he could... he wouldn't. Would he?

"Do you know what Kevin was investigating?" he asked.

"A little."

"Like what?"

"He heard there was a boy molested at the church. He went to ask some questions. That's all I know — but the boy's name was Douglas."

Wolfe nodded. Cruz, it seemed, had nothing new to offer him as far as information went, and yet he searched his mind for some reason to see her again. She was not the only one seeking tangential contact with Kevin, it seemed. He could call and he knew she would come, but he needed some justification for meeting with a beautiful woman. Something more than his own will.

"Danny?"

113

"Yes."

"Do you think it would be okay if I called you sometime. To talk, like this. It would be a comfort to me, to know Kevin's brother and to talk to him. You make me feel… still close to him."

"Yeah, that would be fine. I would like that." He shouldn't have added this last sentiment. The words sounded a bit too eager to his ears, the silence unnaturally long. But maybe it wasn't.

"I'm tired now though, a long day." She suppressed a yawn brought on by the confession.

"Of course."

"I hope you find what you're looking for, Danny."

He noted again the lack of 'Father' in her words, nodded and raised a hand as a parting gesture. She walked to the car and then turned around and returned to the little railing around the patio. He stood, slowly, and walked over to meet her.

"I almost forgot," she said, thrusting a hand down into her pockets, and then extending it to him. "Kevin's mobile phone. Billy gave it to me to give to Rosa at the service, but it didn't seem the right time. Here, you take it."

He did. "Was it a nice service?" he asked.

"Yes," she nodded, her eyes flooding again, "a nice service."

She turned back toward the car, got in and pulled out into the street, a short wave, unreturned, was her final goodbye.

The priest walked back to his table, sat down, and ordered another coffee. Grippe had arranged for a hotel room for him, for as long as he wanted it. He wasn't quite ready to go there. Not yet. He popped open the back of the phone and removed the battery, then sat with the little jumble of parts in his hand, the plastic against his palm the way it had been in Kevin's so often. He sat in the midst of the crowd and listened to the distant sounds of the night: sirens, dogs, traffic and the weather above it all, buffeting through the black shadows of palm leaves among the stars, the subtle thunder of tropical winds. And he thought of his brother. He thought of the little children who, perhaps at that very moment in time, were cowering in fear before men who wore the uniform of God's peace and protection.

Uniforms like his.

And sometime later, amid those thoughts, he rose up from his chair and went to the car, leaving his money unasked-for on the table. He had work to do and was smart enough to know that he couldn't do it without rest. He would sleep the remainder of the night away and then start in the morning. If he could find the bomber, he believed, he could find the one who had killed Kevin. If he could do it, that is, before they tried again to kill him, perhaps with more luck than the last time.

Behind it all, with the faint scent of flowers on the wind, he thought of his vows, his loneliness, and the empty night ahead of him.

NINE

Wolfe slept late. Perhaps it was the last of the morphine in his system, or the prolonged night with Cruz at the café. He awoke to that displaced feeling one often gets when sleeping in a strange place. He had thought himself immune to it, having spent so many nights in Vatican lodgings, suites, and hotels across the world, shifted here and there by the Church depending on which allegations they deemed worthy of internal investigation prior to involving secular authorities, if at all. He awoke with little expectation to know where he was, maybe that was it. In any case, the disorientation was unusual.

Likely it was the nature of the shift this time: it hadn't been time to move on — his accommodations were simply no longer available. Moved on, as it were, without him. Leaving him behind instead of the other way around.

Still, the pillows in his new room were soft and of the highest quality. The sheets cool where his foot wandered out, just beyond the heat of his body and the duvet heavy and soothing in the comfort of the air conditioned room. Familiar comforts.

And familiar pains.

His sides ached and he reached over for the water and one of the little tablet bottles with which he had been sent home. He took two of the big pills and washed them down, then settled back into his sheets.

Room service: that's what he needed. Here was a perk he hadn't had in the other suite and he decided that being nearly blown up on Vatican business was enough to warrant a little extra expense on their behalf. They never complained when he treated himself now and then, anyway. He was efficient and discreet... usually. Qualities his authorities appreciated.

Besides, he had need energy to move around and he was already hungry. Breakfast in bed would be just the ticket.

While he waited for his spicy omelet, fried plantains, sausage and orange juice to arrive, he gingerly rose out of bed and shuffled to the bathroom to void his bladder. His image loomed large in the mirror. His eyes were droopy, it seemed to him, with dark circles beneath them. The bandage had begun to lose its adhesiveness and he reached up and pulled at the taped edges. It came off fairly easily and without as much pain as he had expected. The swelling had gone down and the shape of his head on that side more or less back to normal. Red and angry skin, but devoid of the warbled waves of destroyed flesh that he had pictured in his mind. He had heard "second degree burns" from someone at the hospital, but had nonetheless had pictured something much worse. *Phantom of the Opera* worse. That or

Freddie Kruger. This was nothing more than painful redness: tissue damage, yes, but mild enough to heal without grafts or major scarring. He had be good as new before long. Nearly so.

"Good," he said to the face in the mirror, "You were ugly enough before," and returned to his bed.

As per instructions, room service brought the food right into the bedroom and set it up beside the bed. Wolfe, letting the bandaged ribs show and leaving the pill bottles in plain sight — a vanity of the normally self-reliant — apologised for the young man's extra trouble and tipped him well. The food was excellent, the kind of spicy Americana one could only find in Miami.

The day was starting well.

Preparation, though, was slow and arduous, dressing only slightly less difficult than the day before, and the cracks in his ribs even more painful. He had only taken the two pills first thing in the morning though, and it was now after noon. Nothing since, so the pain he felt was all his, nothing hidden by morphine or codeine or Percocet.

He had never trusted drugs; he saw their use as a form of self-delusion. If he was sick or injured, he didn't want to be out there thinking he wasn't, acting like he wasn't and maybe making things worse. No, he was more at ease when he could feel all of his pain and gauge for himself whether an activity was too much for him. Pain-killers were fine if he resigned himself to lie there in bed, or if the stress of pain was making things worse, impeding the healing. But if action was needed, then so was a true understanding of one's condition and abilities.

His Special Forces training hadn't taught him to think of himself as invincible, as some outsiders thought; it had taught him to know exactly how much trauma he could stand and how much would kill him. Anything less than that fatal line and it was his clear duty to keep going, to complete the mission. That day he was virtually drugless and still able to move around. That was a good thing.

Grippe had generalised the orders once again and freed him up to seek answers with the priests at Saint Mary's. Considering the loss of his evidence in the other case, the little church's possible connection to a local pedophilia ring within the Catholic clergy was about all he had to go on. The building where he had initially obtained the box of contraband would be cleaned out by now, no sign of impropriety left and everyone on their best behaviour, such as it might be. In truth, that investigation was effectively dead. He would pass on what he knew, and they would act on it — or not — based solely on what he had to tell them, and what they had gathered before assigning him to the case. It was compelling, despite being based on Wolfe's word alone. The Vatican courts didn't need the same proof that a secular court of law needed, but they still had a problem: what they had so far was evidence of repeated crimes without the identity of the criminals involved. One suspect, that was all, and it was possible his office was being used to store the box without his knowing what was inside it. Not likely, but possible. Then there was the problem of finding out which of those around him were in on it, and which were just innocent bystanders. Something in the box might have helped. It was a hard blow to the case, the loss of that box and whatever other clues it contained. Not for the first time, nor the last, Wolfe felt the stinging guilt of having put off his viewing, of having spread it out over time. If they could even have identified some of the victims, perhaps that might have led them to the name of a perpetrator, a description at least.

In the meantime, keeping it active in the field was little more than an excuse to keep him working on Kevin's murder. He had little doubt that Grippe knew this as well, and thanked the old man in his thoughts. Maybe he would remember to do so in person sometime.

Saint Mary's was where he most wanted to investigate. He told himself he would dull the frustration of the first case with the personal immediacy of the second.

If he were fully honest, Kevin's murder was pressing on his mind with even more urgency than the other case, and the realisation of it weighed on him. How could he set aside the search for abused children and their attackers in order to sort out something that had happened to a dead man, a man for whom there would no longer be any pain or suffering? Had his mind begun to slip? Had he really become that cold to such things? Or simply newly engaged with others?

Well, it was what it was, he decided, and held on to the tiny scrap of delusion that this present case might lead him to the centre of that other one, to the solution to the murder and the saving of the children all at once. The part of him that knew it wasn't so? He buried that.

He pulled in beside the church van in the staff parking lot, rather than park on the street as he had before, and hung the *VII* tag on his rearview mirror — parking access on any Catholic Church owned property and unquestioned entrance to any but the most exclusive Catholic enclaves. He walked up the little landing at the back and pulled on the door. The thumb-plunger didn't depress, but the door responded to his pull: locked, but not latched properly. Yet another single piece of data that opened up a dozen new possibilities.

He stepped in. To his left was a short ascending stairway with a door, closed, with the words "Father J. Gonzales" engraved on a plastic placard and mounted on it. To his right was a short hallway leading to the secretary's desk and to spaces for whatever other uses the short string of rooms were put to. Storage, mostly, if experience was any guide. There was a stairway there too, leading up into a dark hallway. Straight ahead was another door, and it was to this one that his steps carried him. The plastic placard said "Nave." It was the room in which Kevin had been killed.

He closed the door and looked around. It was not changed much from the other night he had been there, other than the present silence and a lack of visitors other than himself. The faint musty smell was still there, mixed with the perfumes of pine cleaner and bleach. He walked over to the place where Kevin had fallen, and bent to one knee to touch the floor with his open palm.

Cool.

Hard.

He tried to imagine what it would have felt like, smashing down onto the unforgiving stone. He wondered if Kevin had felt it. Or if he had already been dead.

"Father Wolfe?" It was Emilio Pascal, the man whom he would forever remember as the priest who gave him water at his brother's death. *I was thirsty, and you gave me drink.*

"Hello." The greeting ended in a grunt as Wolfe forced himself to his feet again.

"Are you in much pain? I heard what happened."

"Oh? How did you hear?"

"It was a Vatican building, bombed two days ago." He shrugged. "Besides that I am a Catholic from a family in which there are only two professions: the police, or..." he held his arms out to the sides in a gesture of self-display, "...and I am a terrible shot."

Wolfe doubted that.

Pascal smiled, "You are not badly hurt?"

"No, I'm fine. I do forget that it was already two days ago, mind you — the first one is a little hazy."

"May I help you? I must confess, I was under the impression that your presence was not welcome here. Not my own sentiments — not now — but those of others here."

"My directions have been altered," he said, making his way to the first pew and lowering himself to the thinly-cushioned seat, "So welcome, or not, doesn't really enter into it."

Pascal joined him. "It is a terrible thing, what happened here. More so because of where it happened, if you'll pardon my saying it."

"Terrible for me wherever it might have been."

"Of course. But this is meant to be a place of peace. Sanctuary. Yet too often it is not."

A long silence followed, a hallowed moment of looking upon empty stone in an empty room. The quieting of minds.

"Well?" Pascal asked at last, smiling, but without joy.

"Well what?"

"I know why you are here: to find out who did this thing. I am a priest in service here and have been for five years. I have known both of my colleagues that whole time. If you have questions, if you need information, perhaps even insight into anyone here, I am prepared to offer my service."

"It's unusual for a priest to do so. Most are circling the wagons before I close my car door."

Pascal smiled. "I am a priest, a true one, if you'll grant me pardon for saying so, and my loyalty is first to God, then to the Church, and then to my fellow man. I have a temper, I know that, but it does not stay hot long. This terrible crime, this desecration of God's image in God's house... It angers and saddens me. If I can help you, I will. I shall even let my colleagues know to be fully open when describing my own habits and character, should you wish to question them — though I fear they may be more inclined to the wagon-circling you mentioned. They are good men, please understand, but of a different generation. The mindset can be different."

Wolfe hoped it was so, that this new generation might be different. "So you have heard rumours about me then, that I am not a true priest." He didn't say it as a challenge, but as a statement of fact.

"Of that I cannot judge. I do not know your heart, just what I see. But I have heard that your faith is shaken and yet you continue to serve. Is that correct?"

"It's correct enough."

"Well some might think it courageous, to speak of weakness when in a position of authority."

Wolfe smiled. "Others think it's foolishness."

"'Insults from fools are compliments,' my uncle used to say."

"Sounds like a wise man, your uncle."

"He was."

"He a priest too?"

"A shift sergeant. Now what do you need to know?"

He thought for a minute. Men who offered assistance were often those who had an interest in deflecting the truth. Pascal didn't seem like such a person, but impressions couldn't always be trusted. They were great for surface evaluations. Near useless for the deeper things. Whatever questions were asked, Wolfe had to take care not to reveal too much about the focus of the investigation, the possible scope of it. He couldn't be specific. Still, a little background wouldn't hurt.

"Tell me about yourself first."

"Anything in particular?"

"Whatever you think might be worth knowing."

"I can tell you that I am familiar with explosives."

Wolfe stared hard at the young priest, who kept his own eyes aimed straight ahead toward the altar. This was a particularly interesting start to the interview. "How so?"

"Well, when I said before that everyone in my family was either a cop or a priest, I was exaggerating slightly. My father owns a company, *JP Demo*, and one of the things they do is multi-level building demolition. As a kid I used to sweep up his shop for extra cash. Later I worked summers as a demolition assistant to pay for school. It was a good job and he paid me well on the condition that I spent it well, or saved it. I left university and then seminary with no debt and little burden on my family."

"Why are you telling me this?"

"In light of the bomb attack, I assumed you'd be checking into these kinds of things. You might not have found out about it, but if you had, especially at a later time, it might have seemed incriminating. In any case, you'd have spent time looking into it and, since I know I didn't set any bomb, maybe the saved time will benefit elsewhere. I am a priest, after all, and the blowing up of a colleague is of special importance to me, whether I would normally admit it or not, much like it is among police when one of their own is killed."

If Pascal thought bringing that out in the beginning would mean it was looked at with less vigour, he was profoundly mistaken. "Anything else incriminating on your dossier?"

"No, I don't think so. I wasn't here when your brother was killed."

The priest's eyes turned to look again at the floor as he said this, to the spot where Kevin had fallen. His eyes stayed there while he continued.

"I am taking over the running of the community centres from Father Cisco. I was over there that night, assembling a ping-pong table with a woman named Maria and a few of the kids. They can verify it. I came back and forth a few times, but not into this room. Just grabbed a thing or two from my office upstairs."

"Do you oversee the workers there?"

"Yes. I heard what happened of course, with you and Albany, though I did not lodge the official complaint. They felt seniority and reputation would elicit greater response. Besides, I think they sensed my reticence to do so."

"You wouldn't have reported me?"

"I admit my first reaction to you was not a positive one. The giving of prayers for the dead and dying is a sacred and solemn duty. They are under profound circumstances, after all. I was angry that you, in your present spiritual condition, would undertake to deliver to someone so important a service."

"But?"

"But it was your brother. I didn't know that then. I cannot help but think you were sincere in your own heart. As for the office of the church, I found a way to satisfy myself on the matter which caused offence to no one."

"I'm curious what that was."

Pascal smiled and seemed a little embarrassed. "I used to tease my cousins for superstition," he said, "and yet I find myself more inclined to it than I care to admit."

"And so you did what?"

"And so, despite my thoughts that God would honour the prayers of a grieving brother, a priest in office if not belief, I still felt the nagging fear that it might not be so."

Wolfe nodded. Let him continue without interruption.

"And so I went down to the morgue," Pascal said, looking his fellow priest in the eye with either challenge or apology, Wolfe could not tell which, "And I performed the rites there, in the quiet of the night, with one respectfully skeptical orderly and a scoffing security guard looking on."

"And this satisfaction you found led you also to overlook my violence at the centre?"

"In a sense." He paused to gather his thoughts. "We tend today to paint all violence as evil, or to pass the responsibility for it off to the police and the military. Albany was being difficult and disrespectful. He often is. Not all violence is forbidden, sometimes it is the only communication broken individuals can understand. Jesus cast out the money-changers from the temple with a whip, for desecration and dishonesty, and he sent the apostles out with swords, the second time." Pascal looked Wolfe in the eye. "At least you didn't use a whip or a sword. In a way, you were more meek than the Saviour himself was at times."

Time to change tack.

"And Father Cisco, anything about him that you think I should know?"

"Well, he has been a priest most of his adult life. A missionary much of his time of service."

"Where?"

"South and Central America, somewhere. Amerindians were his passion. He has several pictures from that time in frames at his house. None here."

"What did he do, specifically? Do you know?"

"Not really. Likely setting up schools and facilitating clinics and medical visits — alongside spiritual development of course. Missionaries in remote places become Jacks of all trades, help out however they can to gain credibility and respect for what they've come to share. Make the village better off, then share the Gospel. That's the usual thing down there. Suits him well for the community centre work here… though the circumstances down there were more primitive. His heart is not here. Not that he does a substandard job. No. He's a very dedicated man, and a hard worker for a man even half his age. But, his heart is in the field. The jungle is beautiful, he says."

Yes, Wolfe had seen it in another life. Seen much of it burn under the thumb of less benevolent powers. "And since he's been here? How long has he been at Saint Mary's?"

"He's been here for ten years now, or something like it, building up the centre, developing youth programs for the disadvantaged."

"Kids then?"

"Yes, mostly," Pascal looked Wolfe in the eye, "Just like me. Same job."

"Anything else?"

"I don't think so, other than…"

"Other than what?"

"Well, it's nothing, just a detail. He was the one who insisted it would be okay to leave the money from the midnight and morning masses in the locked drawer until the afternoon, when we made the bank run or put it in the safe."

"Why would he insist on that?"

"It seemed strange to me, but he said it would allow him to maintain unbroken contact with those who came to mass, from their arrival until they left."

"Why is that strange?"

"Well, there are not normally many who come to morning masses for one thing, even fewer to midnight. For another, the safe is in Father Gonzales's office, which is right through that door," he pointed up across the dais to a door on the far side — a second door to the office Wolfe had passed on his way in, "and it has a cash deposit slot cut in the side. It would have only taken a few seconds to drop it in there, but it would have required him to leave the room. It was his preference, I guess. Father Gonzales felt much the same as I did, that leaving the room for a few moments wasn't a big deal, but it didn't seem an important issue. Father Cisco got his way, at least on days he was officiating. We took turns, of course. Had the drawer not been robbed when your brother was killed, I would not have thought it worth mentioning, but if the thief took only the contents of the one drawer, then it was almost certainly someone who had been at service with Father Cisco, and saw where the money was kept."

"But such a person would also have been present for masses with you and Father Gonzales."

"Yes, I suppose so. I thought at first it might have narrowed the list of suspects."

Wolfe nodded, seeming to brush it off as nothing. He would broach the subject when he interviewed Cisco.

"And Father Gonzales?"

"He is a good man, a good priest. He has taught me many things, theologically and practically. He did missionary work too, in Korea and China. He served in the military, I think, before that. Viet Nam era, but I don't know if he served over there or stateside. He's tight-lipped about it. It's never mentioned. Never. Father Cisco even warned me against it when I first arrived."

"How did you know then, that he served?"

"I've seen pictures, in his home, of himself and his brother in uniform. His brother was killed, or died, around that time, I think. Father Gonzales became a priest."

Wolfe was familiar with the progression from soldier to priest. "Has he been here very long then?"

"Thirty years and," he paused a moment, "seventeen days." Wolfe raised his eyebrows. "We had a small party for him, for his thirty-year anniversary of coming here. He was a junior then, like me now, but he turned down any offers to move to better positions in other parishes. He wanted to stay here, and he did so. His rise to the senior position might have been slowed by it, but he does not seem to mind, if it did. It's the place that is most important to him. Or maybe the people."

"So you respect him."

"Yes, I do. He is of another generation, to be sure. The church and God cannot be separated, in the minds of those men. They see them as one and the same. Papal authority, as well, is seen differently by many of us now. Respected, to be sure, but not necessarily…"

"Divine?"

"Infallible."

"But for you?"

"We both know that the church is made up of people. Many faults and weaknesses, from the pope to the altar boy. We can look to the church for our image of God. Many have done so. Or we can look to God and strive to fashion the church in his image. The one leads to bitterness and distrust. The other, perhaps, to something better."

Wolfe looked at the flagstones and said nothing. He had heard the speeches before. Many priests had tried to save him with such words. They were impotent sentiments, but he didn't wish his own disillusion on anyone else, certainly not on a young idealist who was making a positive difference in his community. He suspected that Pascal was such a man. Not likely a killer there. All men had it in them of course, but in some it was buried deep. It seemed that way with the young priest. But then again, buried things can come out in explosive ways.

"Nothing else you can think of? Nothing else seems important?"

"Nothing comes to mind. I will answer any questions you have though, if I can."

"Was Father Cisco here, or Father Gonzales, the night of the murder?" Wolfe watched Pascal carefully then, without appearing to do so, seeking any faint twitch or avoidance, any sign that he was attempting to incriminate either one without cause — or with it. He watched his eyes: up and to the left, accessing memory, rather than the creative portions of the brain. Not definitive on its own, but a good sign. No sudden itches around the face or neck. That was good too.

"They were both here, I think, at different times... Father Gonzales for sure. Again, I was at the centre most of the evening, but his car was in the lot, and so was the van. I took my own car over. They were back and forth a bit. Me too, really, but less so."

"Father Cisco drives the van?"

"We all do, but he doesn't have a car since the engine died on his old Mercury. He gave it to his mechanic, I think, a member of the congregation with whom he's close. He prefers to walk to the church, anyway. He only lives a few blocks from here, and since we all have access to the church vehicles, he decided to save himself the expense of a personal one. He's hoping to take on a similar centre in Panama. That will use church money of course, but he will set himself up with a home of his own choosing when he gets there. He's been working on the prep work for years. Once I start running the centres here on my own, I'll use the van more often, but in the meantime it works best this way."

"When will that be?"

"My takeover?"

"Yes."

"It's hard to say. It's kind of an undefined process so far, but we're moving steadily in that direction, so I'm not too worried about it. I have most of the control and do most of the work. He's not delaying any more than he feels is necessary, I know that. Like I said though, a good job is important to him. I just need to run things past him for a while longer, make sure I don't make any mistakes while he's still in charge on paper. He's very adamant about that. My dad was the same way."

Both men smiled.

"Most are," Wolfe said. "I've been over there, to the centre... I guess you know that. It looks almost new."

"Long-running ministry, new location. We had an old clinic building before. The new one has been donated on long-term lease by the estate of a local woman. Virtually rent-free for twenty years. It's saved us a great deal in potential renovation costs. We own the old building outright, but it's coming apart at the seams. Renovation would have been a great burden... half a million, maybe more. Flooding problems, old wiring, bad windows... We've been able to redo the whole set-up now, for next to nothing. Furniture, paint. New place, new face. Building, van, everything. Give the kids some pride in their community centre, and then maybe in themselves. That's the theory."

The thud of the door, followed by the sound of high heels clicking down the centre aisle approached them. Pascal turned his head, but Wolfe remained gazing at the floor near the altar, unable to turn his throbbing neck to look anyhow. The footfalls stopped when they reached them.

"Hello Father Pascal. Hello Father Wolfe."

It was Cruz.

No 'Danny,' once again.

TEN

"Hi Ana, what brings you here?" Wolfe knew it was an odd question to ask a member of the congregation when he, himself, was the intruder. And especially considering recent events.

"I've come to talk to Father Gonzales. He's expecting me, but not for a little while."

"Yes," Pascal said, "He mentioned that he had an appointment this evening, but he isn't in yet. I expect him any time."

She nodded and sat down into the awkward silence. It was obvious why she had come early: a moment or two with the shadows and ghosts of a lost lover.

"Well," Wolfe said, the universal signal of ended visits and imminent partings, "I need to have a word with Father Cisco, if he's in, then I should get going."

"He's not here either," Pascal shook his head. "Left for home a half hour ago, had some errands to do too, I think."

"But it's close?"

Pascal nodded.

"You have an address for him?"

The young priest pulled out a pen and wrote on the back of an offering envelope. "There you go. You might want to phone first. He doesn't have a lot of visitors."

Wolfe nodded, but had no intention of warning the man of his coming. He gave both Pascal and Cruz his new number at the hotel — in case she needed to get in touch with him after talking to Father Gonzales, he said — and then the two priests left her and went out on their own business, Pascal to the community centre and Wolfe to Cisco's place.

Cisco's home was the last one on a row of townhouses, each one sharing a wall with the neighbours on either side. Cisco's, despite being on the end and therefore only having one neighbour, still had a high, windowless wall on that side. Cookie-cutter. Too cheap to add in a couple of windows where they would have done great good to the light and mood of the interior. Still, the grounds weren't too bad. They had that slightly run-down, over-baked feel that all but the best communities had in South Florida, fighting a losing battle with the heat and the displaced sawgrass. But for all that, they were neat, devoid of litter, and the landscaping full and mature.

He placed an eye over the peephole and saw the light coming in from the windows at the far end of the room. Nothing moved within. No shadow passed over the bright opening at the far end.

He knocked on the door.

No answer. Nothing moved.

He backtracked the concrete walkway and then stepped over the border of vegetation that ran its length. Tiny lizards bolted off to either side. He walked along the blank face of the windowless wall and past the rear corner of the building. There was Cisco's patio.

To call it a patio is misleading. It was structurally little more than a tiled concrete pad with support poles at the outermost corners, but Cisco, or someone before him, had been hard at work. Two-by-fours had been run along the bottom edge of the tiled pad, attached to the posts by iron clamps. From them, similar boards rose up to support a running beam around the perimeter of the structure, flush with the overhanging plastic awning that ran out at a slight declination from the edge of the rear wall. It was a screened-in solarium now. A conservatory, open to the breezes and winds of the nearby Atlantic, and to those that came in from the other direction, from the gulf and over the swamplands of the Everglades. The plastic awning cast a strange, yellow light over the proliferation of plants within the room. Fruit trees, baskets of exotic flowers, wooden beds of dark earth built up and filled with growing things, edible and otherwise.

It was a jungle. There was no better word. Cisco had built himself a small patch of jungle. In the heart of it, in a tiny clearing in the foliage, Wolfe could see a small iron table, a couple of books lying beside an empty glass tea cup. And a single chair.

But Cisco was not home. Wolfe would have to wait for his interview.

A check-up with the doctor at Mercy Hospital would fill the time. He had promised Grippe that he had do at least that much to ensure that the damage wasn't permanent. His body was fine, healing well and gaining further mobility by the day. Lunch in a decent restaurant by way of private celebration, then he returned to his hotel room and spent some time brainstorming and analysing his present predicament with regard to his investigations.

Leads were few. He lay in his shorts on his bed, staring at the ceiling. He often practiced this exercise, drawing mental lines on a clean surface, filling the blank space with imaginary mind maps, Venn diagrams and flowcharts. He would draw connections between each piece of data and see which other relationships might come to mind as he did so. When one network had come to its end, no more intriguing paths to run between one point and another, he would start again, with a new connection, and build another one. He had found, over the years of doing this, that eventually his mind would identify connections that were common to all of the hypothetical networks. Those structures would be noted, kept in memory, and he would run the collection of possible extensions through his mind as he worked. As the trickle of new data continued to flow, the common connections would extend, some of the hypotheticals would no longer fit and, in time and if he were lucky and tenacious, a solution would form out of the whole mental process, like stalactites forming in the constant drip of lime-rich water, in a dark and unknown cave. But this took time. Data. Patience.

He sat up, grabbed a quick shower and dressed for his appointment with Billy Jackson at the police station. He was about to leave his suite when the telephone rang. He reached for the door handle, intending to ignore the call, then changed his mind and walked over to pick up the receiver.

"Father Wolfe," he said.

"Danny!" It was Cruz, she sounded agitated — more than agitated, she sounded terrified.

"What's happened?"

"Someone is shooting at me. *Was* shooting at me. They missed, but the bullets hit my house, my car... I don't even have my gun with me!"

"Okay, okay. Where are you?"

"I'm just driving, getting the hell out of there. The shots came out of nowhere, in broad daylight."

"Who was it?"

"I don't know, but... I can't go to work. Can I come to you?"

"Why can't you go to work?"

"He was dressed in black. A uniform. Like a cop. I don't know who else to call."

In black, like a cop, he thought, *or like a priest.* "Here is not the best place. I'm coming to you. The coffee shop, the one we met in. Can you meet me there?"

"Yes. I don't want to stay outside like that though. I feel exposed. I need a safe place to think."

"You wait there — inside. Maybe go into the restroom and wait fifteen minutes, then come to the front and I should be there. Just get straight into my car and we'll go. Yes?"

"Okay, I can do that."

"Did you call it in?"

"I called you first. They try to kill you, then me. Why?"

"Call Billy. Let him know you were shot at and that you're hiding. Then take the battery out of your phone and wait. Is there a tracker on your car?"

"No. But he'll want me to come in. He'll want to know where I am."

"That's all you need to tell him for now. Just that you're safe. We'll try to figure out what's going on here. You don't have your gun?"

"No. It's locked up in the house. I was shopping."

"Okay. That's okay. You won't need it anyway. If we need one, they're easy enough to get."

He hurried down to his car and pulled out into traffic, nearly running a delivery truck onto the sidewalk as he did so. He reminded himself to stay calm; having a car wreck wouldn't help anything. He pulled up in front of the café and waited for two minutes. They seemed like an hour each. He must have looked at his watch ten times.

Cruz poked her head out of the restroom door and saw him. She walked through the crowded tables and chairs and across the sidewalk with all the calm and poise of a person expecting a bullet from the alley at any moment. She fumbled with the door handle, yanked it open and tumbled into the car next to him in a wash of fear and floral perfume. She slid onto the seat and leaned sideways until her shoulder butted up against his. He winced in pain but said nothing, leaning back into her in an act of comfort, either for himself or for her — perhaps both — and then sped off down the street.

"Were you hit? Were you hurt?" He asked, knowing the answer before he had said the question, but feeling a need for her to talk, to assure him that she was okay. To assure herself.

"I'm okay, Danny… I needed a minute… I'm okay now…"

Danny.

He had decided before picking her up that his hotel room was, in fact, the safest place to keep her. He was registered under his Vatican alternate identity and was fairly certain that some kind of security force was watching the building for anything suspicious. Something like a priest bringing a flushed woman cop back to his room for the night, perhaps.

"Look Ana," he said, "It's very important that we keep your presence here a secret. My people might be watching the hotel, which has its own set of issues for me, but so might whoever it was that set that bomb or shot at you. They might not notice you coming in alone, because it's obviously not expected, but if you come in with me…"

"Is it the same people, you think, trying to kill us?"

"It would be a strong coincidence if it weren't. I think it's a safe assumption for now. Look though, we can't allow them to see you coming in with me, do you understand? You need to come in on your own and make your way up to my room. I'll let you in as you pass the door. Room 607."

He handed her the key card to his hotel room. He would grab another from the front desk when he got there.

"I can do that." She seemed to steel herself, but a faint tremor in her voice was still there. "I wish I had my gun."

"Just for a little, Ana, that's all. Just a quick walk and then you're safe inside. He won't have followed us here. I've been watching."

"Right."

He pulled up to the side of the road a block from his hotel and let her out. He watched her as she moved up the street and for the first time took real notice that she was not in uniform. She wore a stunning green and red dress, some kind of stylised flower print, form-fitting and very flattering to her already impressive figure. He shook his head in amusement, despite the danger: why couldn't it be a frumpy old man he needed to hide from assassins? Why a woman who might be mistaken for any kind of illegitimate visitor were she to be seen entering his room?

No, not any kind, he corrected himself, *the very expensive kind.*

He pulled out onto the street and drove past her just before she came alongside the edge of the hotel. He gave his keys to the valet and went straight to the front counter for an additional key card. A few seconds later he was at the elevator just as the doors opened up to let out an elderly couple with nasty sunburns. He nodded; they smiled. Canadians, no-doubt, down from Quebec to soak up some sun. He slid his card through the reader and pressed the button. The doors closed just as he saw Cruz enter the front of the lobby.

He rode up to the sixth floor, and stepped into his room. There he waited, ear to the door or eye to the peephole, waiting for the woman to arrive. Intent on the silent, empty corridor. At last the bell rang softly in the hall and she stepped out. She looked at the brass placard opposite the elevator doors: room numbers with arrows indicating their locations. A deep breath and she made her way down the hallway toward his room.

Just as she reached it, before she could even knock or use her key card, he opened the door and she stepped in, a wave of beautiful scent following in her wake. He closed the door and turned to face her as she threw her arms around him and held there, in a mix of unaccustomed human warmth and the intense pain of his injuries. He angled his head to the side and his lips brushed — not a kiss — against her neck at the corner of her jaw, beneath her ear. Not a kiss. Her face pressed into his neck for a moment, then she withdrew, blushing, but seemingly much relieved.

"It must seem silly," she said, "a cop so scared of being shot at. If Delaney heard about this…"

"Not at all. And he won't, not about this part. Anyway, you weren't on duty, not wearing your vest. It wasn't a crime you were investigating, it was a shot without warning, an assassination attempt. And bullets kill cops, too. You can bet Delaney would've been rattled in the same circumstance. At least you're healthy enough to take the shock. Now Delaney, on the other hand…"

His encouragement seemed to shake her more than calm her and he decided to get her a drink instead. They could both use a drink, he decided.

"It isn't the first time, you know."

"What isn't?"

"Me being shot at."

"Really?" He paused, mid pour. "What happened?"

"It was a while ago. Kind of how I met Kevin, actually." He nodded, let her continue as he brought them each a tumbler of Glenlivet. "I'd been hit by a thirty-eight round in the vest. Knocked me back and I thought it had killed me. The kid who shot me, twelve years old, thought I was there to arrest his brother."

"Were you?" Wolfe felt the presence of his brother step into the edge of his vision. A phantom not present, but seen just the same.

"No. Just doing the beat cop thing. Inspired again by Kevin's speeches on community policing."

"What did you do?"

"I didn't do anything. I fell down. My partner at the time shot the kid."

"Dead?"

"In hospital later that night."

"Sometimes things are unavoidable. The reaction the kid had, really that wasn't to do with you. He'd been seeing criminal acts performed by his neighbours, maybe his family, and — I think we both know — by other police officers. He sees you through the lens of what he's been taught, what he's seen... He wasn't really seeing you. He was seeing social and political history."

"That's what Kevin said too, but the thing is, I could have avoided being there. I didn't have to be in a uniform, knocking on doors and chatting up preteens with pistols in their jacket pockets... it shook me. I didn't think I'd come back from it."

"But you did come back from it. You kept going. The only way to change things, to keep what happened to you from happening to others, is by doing what you were doing."

"Yeah, I guess so. With Kevin's help. He said the same thing as you, that it would be tough at first, because the people didn't know us yet. The whole idea was to get them to know us, so they wouldn't be so afraid next time. He would know what to do now. He would know how to deal with it."

"Is that why you called me, instead of Billy?"

"Maybe." She received the drink from his hand. "Probably."

"I'm not my brother, you know."

She looked him in the eye, a glisten there, from fire or fear or something else he couldn't tell. "Yes," she said, "I know."

She sipped the scotch with a look of pain on her face, almost disgust — but sipped it all the same. She was still standing, her figure showing well in bright colour with the white walls of the suite behind her, her black hair and deep-toned skin exuding warmth, sexuality. And the shake seemed to be leaving her hands.

Wolfe tried to focus on other parts of the room, but it was difficult. It had been a long time since he had been alone with a woman and an even longer time since one had hit him in the gut like this, made him feel awkward and... fumbly.

His vows, those he still held sacred, were to the Church, not to God. He wondered if they included abstinence, or mere celibacy. The first denied him sex, the second only marriage. It was a semantic point, perhaps, but semantics were sometimes all he had to hold him to some kind of reliable ideology. He remembered having the debates in seminary, covering the idea that social conventions of the past made celibacy and abstinence synonymous, and the opposing concept that the social changes that made sex outside of marriage publicly acceptable, also made the distinction valid. If one based moral choice on those grounds, a priest perhaps had opportunity to exercise sexual expression. Celibacy might imply a life without sex, but it wasn't explicitly so. Such arguments, so seemingly complex in academia, and the conclusions so easy to accept; so much more simple in real life... and the burdensome conclusions so difficult to bear. He looked over at her again as she worked her way through the strong alcohol. The phantom Kevin stood, still just beyond his sight. Wolfe's stomach growled.

With an act of will he moved his mind away from sexual musings and onto more important matters: they were, both of them, targets of assassination, it seemed. It could be the abuse investigation in his case — it went deep into the aristocracy of the church after all; it was high stakes — but it made no sense that the same people would go after Cruz. The only connection between them was Kevin, or Saint Mary of the Sea itself.

Would a priest of a small Catholic parish have the motive and means to bomb a Vatican investigator? To destroy church-owned property? To shoot an off-duty police officer, a woman, in cold blood? The church building in his mind's eye, so placid and quaint before, took on a sinister quality, a squatting, dark beast with shining, stained-glass eyes and rottenness within.

The image fled as Cruz sat down beside him, too close.

"What are you thinking about, Danny?" No 'Father' again. It was fear before. What was it now?

"I was thinking of the church where Kevin died. About who might want to kill us."

"The one who killed Kevin."

"Yes, probably, but who is that?"

She made no answer. "I miss him." She looked into a corner by the little bar. Perhaps she too felt a third presence in the room. "Do you?"

Wolfe nodded.

She shifted her weight, moving a little closer to him. Resting her shoulder against his arm. Her hair near his face, touching his shoulder, filling his nostrils with deep scents of perfume and pheromones. Some scientists think pheromones don't exist. *Bullshit*, he thought.

"Will we find who did it, Danny?" She had used his name again. Too often. He didn't like it, because of how much he liked it. He leaned into her a little, telling himself it was to relieve the strain and sharpness in his ribs. The comfort of human contact. Of a friend. Nothing more. It did take his mind off of the pain... He turned, as if to look at her as he spoke, and drew in a deep breath, his nose just an inch from touching the softness of her hair.

"Yes," he whispered, "We will."

There was a long silence then, neither one wanting to move away nor daring to move closer, priest to woman, woman to priest. Wolfe must have drifted a little, and in adjusting his posture he felt the sharp stab of pain in his side and woke fully, unable to hide his discomfort for a moment.

"Are you okay?"

"My ribs, that's all. Bruised from the explosion."

"Oh my God, that must be so painful."

"A little, but not too bad, I just fell asleep the wrong way."

148

"Yes, I've kept you out here looking after me all evening and forgotten that your escape was closer than mine. You need your rest. I can sleep out here on the couch."

"No, no, you can use the bedroom, I only ask a bit of help opening the pullout. There are extra pillows in the closet. I'll grab them."

She didn't argue, perhaps preferring the increased safety of the inner reaches of the suite. Each look at the door evoked a flash of intensity on her face, an involuntary shiver up her arms and spine. The shock of the shooting was still raw. He could sense her stress. Guessed at her feelings of shame. He said nothing about it.

She piled the cushions on the surrounding chairs and was opening the pullout bed as Wolfe came back into the room. She left it half-open and stepped quickly over to him in the doorway to the bedroom.

"Are you sure you won't use the bed? Or share it? Just to sleep? I feel so guilty, taking it all and leaving you out here."

"We're Catholic, aren't we supposed to feel guilty?"

Her face became quite serious. "I heard different about you... that you weren't really Catholic. God might have expectations on a priest, if you believed in God. Those men you vowed to, do they have the same expectations?" As she spoke she moved closer, until she stood directly in front of him, a hand near his waist, somewhere between touching and not.

149

He said nothing.

"Well," she said softly in the silent room, "I'll be in here I guess. If you are uncomfortable, let me know. We could trade or something."

Still he said nothing and she gave him the smallest of hugs, the breath of "Thank you" from lips brushing his cheek and the sparkle of — something — in her eyes as she passed through into the bedroom.

He paused a moment and then silently closed the French doors between the two rooms. A thin glass wall between one reality and another.

He grabbed a bag of pretzels and the tube of Pringles from the minibar to feed the growl of his empty stomach, opened the pullout the rest of the way, and lay down, still dressed, on the soft pillows.

A little while later he shrugged out of his clothing and pulled a blanket up over his naked form, grasped a pillow in front of him, remembering the feel of the woman in his arms, sensing still her scent lingering in the room, there on the couch, and re-living the moments spent so closely there, in the silence. The French doors stood silently at the corner of his vision, his stomach twisted in knots, and he watched the possibilities parade by in his mind's eye like the ghostly kings in Macbeth. He felt just as doomed. Just as much at the mercy of profound flaws and human weakness. Maybe fate, as well. The door to his own kind of doom, just a few welcome steps away.

ELEVEN

Wolfe awoke while the sky was still a dull, predawn grey. He left a brief note for Cruz to stay in the suite, to telephone no one, and to order whatever food she liked. He was then off, safely, into the day. He had missed his appointment with Jackson the day before and seeing him was important. He needed information on the bomb and on yesterday's shooting. Jackson would want information on Cruz as well. He had not been happy that she had gone into hiding without so much as a statement. Wolfe would have to make that right for her, if he could. He also wanted to know what Jackson could tell him about his brother's case... had Detective Delaney found anything yet?

He pressed the button for the elevator and waited. He looked up at the numbers and saw them moving slowly downward; 5, 4, 3, 2, L.

A long pause at L.

He gave up. He turned to the side and opened the door to the stairwell. Five flights wasn't bad, going downward, and he could probably use the exercise. His ribs had started to tighten up again after the sleep on the pullout and he needed all of the mobility he could get. He grabbed the railing and started down.

As he passed the fourth floor landing, the numbered elevator lights in the hallway outside of his suite turned from 4 to 5 to 6. The soft bell. The door opened and a man stepped out. He was dressed in decent suit jacket, white shirt and dark slacks. Nothing noteworthy. He had a small burgundy athletics bag in his hand. He glanced at the brass sign with the room numbers and arrows to direct new guests. He then turned left from the elevator and walked down the hallway to room 607. There he stopped, looked both ways down the hallway to ensure that he was alone, and reached into the bag.

Wolfe arrived at the police station only to meet Jackson heading for the car park.

"C'mon, Danny, let's go. We can talk in the car."

Wolfe followed.

"Where are we going?"

"Saint Mary of the Sea."

"Why?"

"It seems Father Pascal is missing."

"I just saw him yesterday, how can he be missing?" It was a silly thing to say, but Jackson let it pass. Stress messes with clear thinking, and he knew Wolfe was not immune, however resilient he may be.

"He didn't show up for an appointment last night at the community centre, then didn't show up for mass this morning. When Gonzales found out, he sent Cisco to his apartment."

"And?"

"Door open, signs of theft, according to Gonzales — and no Pascal."

"You know about Ana."

"Of course."

"It doesn't bother you that she didn't come in?"

"It would, if it was my case, but they put Delaney on it, so technically she's hiding out from him, not from me, which is good."

"Why is that good?"

"Because I have a pretty good idea where she might be. He doesn't." Jackson looked straight ahead, as if the road were all the world.

"Did they find anything at her home?"

"Bullet holes in her building and in the door of her car. They look like nines, which narrows it down to about sixteen thousand registered firearms in Miami alone, let alone the illegal ones. She was lucky, the guy was sporadic, six shots into the apartment's outer wall, the rest into the car. Makes things open up a bit though."

"What do you mean?"

Jackson shrugged. "We all thought the thing with Kevin, then the explosion that nearly took you…"

"Yeah?"

"They both seemed related to something at Saint Mary's."

"That would make sense, wouldn't it?"

"Sure."

"Then what?"

"This attack on Ana…" he paused, "She goes to Saint Mary's, true — at least sometimes — and she was seeing Kevin. Those are both connections to the church, since Kevin was killed, but they might also be connections between her and Kevin that have nothing to do with the church. It might be that she and Kevin are one issue, and the explosion another. Or, it could be that Kevin's death and the attempt on you were connected. Maybe all three. But all three… that seems a bit of a stretch."

Wolfe thought back to his mental diagrams, the webworks of connections and possibilities. "More of a stretch than all three violent acts being connected? Pretty random if they aren't."

Jackson waved a hand at the word outside the car window, at the people and buildings swishing by, and the hundreds of cars rolling along around them. "This is the land of random violence, Danny. We found a head in a bucket last week. Just sitting on the sidewalk in a bucket. A fuckin' jogger found it. Coulda been a kid walking by, seeing something like that. Sure, probably gang related. Mexicans maybe, they're into that kind of thing. But there were also two more killings on the same block, same weekend. Connected? No. Two of them solved, the bucket filed under *nobody gives a fuck*. We can't assume any of this is connected. And we can't assume not. It's fucked up, but that's Miami."

Wolfe thought about that a while. It hadn't occurred to him, the statistical probability that the crimes were related had seemed sure to him. Maybe not. After all,

Jackson would know; it was his business even more than it was Wolfe's. He shook his head. He needed to get back on the ball, to get his head clear before his slowness did some real damage. He couldn't afford to miss anything.

"How many bullets hit the car?"

"Three I think — Delaney knows for sure."

"Grouped?"

"Reasonably, yes."

"But no leads on the shooter."

"None so far, but together with Kevin getting killed, you can bet things are pretty squirrely back at the station."

"Did Delaney tell you anything about Kevin's case?"

"Not much yet, but we're on it, you can bet. A cop-killing doesn't go by without a lot of digging. This Ana thing just pours fuel on the fire. It was Kevin, but could have been any of us, so everybody wants it done."

"And?"

"We're running out of places to dig. We know that he was there to ask a few questions, but we don't know what he was asking about. Maybe he walked into the middle of a theft, but the set-up is off."

"Yes, I noticed that too."

"Still, if nothing else comes up, it's the most likely scenario. Maybe there was more than one thief. Maybe they didn't *look* dangerous to Kevin. Could even be that somebody followed him in. A revenge thing. It happens now. Somebody wanting a cop dead, seeing him go in alone… maybe."

"Chances, then, of catching whoever did it?"

"Realistically? Not much. The cash was taken, the checks left. The bills had just been handed in from whoever came to morning mass, so there isn't any way to know serial numbers or to track it. There aren't any fingerprints that shouldn't be there, we checked the priests for blood on clothing…"

"And no luck."

"Nope. All three had some blood on their shoes, Gonzales and Cisco had it on their hands as well, but none had spatter… the rest could be explained by finding the body and checking for vitals. With the wound as it was, there might not even have been any spatter. It cracked his skull, but not a lot of blood until after he fell, so the paper suits tell us." He glanced at Wolfe, not sure if he should continue. "Even what we do have to go on wouldn't be conclusive. Can't nail anybody, or exclude them for sure."

"When was he killed?"

"Anywhere from two to five hours before I called you that night."

"The attack with the candlestick was cause of death?"

"Yeah, blunt force trauma delivered by an altar furnishing. *Fuck.*"

"Did you confirm the whereabouts of the priests?"

"There was an event happening at the community centre, a grand opening for the new building or something. All three priests were involved, moving back and forth from the church to the centre, but none of them report having seen anything strange until the body was found when they returned from the event."

"All three?"

"Sort of. Pascal was here, but came in afterward."

"How did that happen?"

"Pascal drove. He was unloading a few things from the van. Gonzales and Cisco came in together after closing down the centre. They had donations from the event, and when they entered the sanctuary to get the cash from earlier in the day, to count it and add it to the safe as well…"

"They saw him there."

"Yes."

"And nobody else?"

"Nope. Pascal came in just after the other two."

"Then how did he get in? Kevin I mean."

"That we don't know for sure, but he had choices. One of the main doors was left unlocked, and apparently the rear exit door sticks a little, can be opened if it's not pulled tight. He could have entered that way too."

"And so could the killer."

"Right. Delaney's pissed. The priests would be prime suspects — the *only* ones really, if the place had been locked up — but their story seems to check out."

"Well locked up, and Kevin wouldn't have been in there in the first place."

Jackson grunted. "Father Gonzales claimed that, since one or other of them is almost always there and with the front doors open most days, he didn't place too high a priority on fixing the single back door. It worked, if pulled-to each time. He figured it would be enough to tell everyone to pull them closed behind them. Apparently not."

"And the bomb?"

"I got you a number for a tech on the bomb squad. Rob's his name. He's a good guy and he owes me a favour, so if you want to buy him a beer he'll get candid about whatever he knows. He's a veteran as well, did demolitions for Uncle Sam before he joined the force. I told him you'd served too. Quite a while."

"You called in a favour? That sounds big, Billy, thanks."

"Did Kevin ever tell you how we met?"

Wolfe shook his head.

"We came up together, joined the force the same day, met right there at the job fair recruitment booth. We signed up for a prep thing too, to get ready for the tests. I did okay on the written stuff, but the P.T. was fuckin' *killing* me. I was never an athlete in school, not used to the discipline."

"You look in pretty good shape to me."

"I am now. That's Kevin. He pushed me to do more. To be more. After I thought I'd given everything I had on the courses, on the runs… he would tell me to do one more lap, one more pushup. Just one. I did. He'd do it alongside me. He'd tell me I could do another if I wanted. Optional. But I did. So did he. Every time."

Wolfe smiled. Sounded a lot like his military training: push the body as far as a man thinks it can go, then show him that it can go a hell of a lot further than that. Show that others had done it, and bring the next guy along. He wondered where Kevin had picked up the idea. He had never served in the military.

"If it wasn't for him, I'd have never become a cop. I believe that to be true." He paused a moment. Screened a memory or two across his mind's eye. "The favour's not all that big, anyway. It's my sister. Rob saw her at some weekend thing and he wanted to meet her. What he didn't know was that she wanted to meet him too. So, being the stand-up guy I am, I agreed to talk her into it — if he owed me one for the gesture."

"And you'll spend it on me?"

"Sure. You're Kevin's brother and Kevin was a good cop, a good friend. Besides, that was almost a year ago and him and my sister are an item now — it's only a matter of time before he gets the full story and I'm outed. Surprised I haven't taken heat on it already. Better to use the favour while I can. So how's Ana doing, anyway, is she hurt?"

"No, she's-" Wolfe stopped himself and turned to look at Jackson. It wasn't often that a man could catch the Priest Hunter in a trap.

Jackson smiled. "Good. That's all I need to know."

They drove in silence for a little while, Wolfe ruminating on this sparse new information, Jackson navigating the awakening streets and humming along with vintage Ozzy on the radio: Wolfe, too, felt like he was *going off the rails on a crazy train…*

They were then only twenty minutes from the church.

Father Gonzales met them as they walked in through the sanctuary. He had had his office door open and was listening for any visitors, anxious, in light of the recent violence, that Father Pascal be found and his safety ensured.

"When was he last seen, Father?" Jackson began.

"Last night, or rather, yesterday afternoon I suppose. Around two o'clock, at the centre."

"And his absence was noticed?"

"By myself, actually. He had a scheduled meeting with me at four. He didn't arrive. Such an oversight is very unlike him. He is generally very punctual and will call or text if there is some kind of delay."

"No calls?"

"None."

"Does he always carry a mobile phone?"

"Yes, he does, I have the number here, on his card."

Jackson phoned in the number to have its usage checked. Pascal hadn't been gone long enough for a formal missing person's report and the warrants such a report would enable. The recent murder might pull it into the realm of possibility, if they claimed Pascal as a person of interest, but the young detective knew a better workaround. Because the phone was technically owned by Saint Mary's, Father Gonzales could authorise the release of the records via the Web and they had them in half an hour. No calls after 1:45pm, the day before. His last call was to a second-hand store downtown. A quick check from Jackson revealed that it had concerned the purchase of a box of discount curtains of a size usable in the centre — nothing relevant. The battery must have been removed shortly after that. Nothing to trace.

"You've been to his apartment, Father Gonzales?"

"Not me personally. Not lately. Father Cisco went to check on him. He is over there now."

Jackson nodded. "Now as I said, adults can't normally be declared missing until they've been gone for twenty-four hours or more. Circumstances here are a little different, so I'm going to get the ball rolling, but it's still unofficial, okay? Let's see if we can track him down. Often these things turn out to be something small, misunderstandings, unforeseen delays, that kind of thing. Okay?"

"I understand, Detective, thank you for looking into it."

"We'll take a quick look in his office first." It hadn't escaped the thoughts of either Jackson or Wolfe that the young priest might have fled, might have taken an opportunity to get away from the pressure of those hunting a cop killer. Were they, in fact, hunting him? Impressions said no. But impressions could be wrong, despite what movies and TV might depict. If there weren't hard facts networking behind the gut feeling, then it was as likely a bad burrito as a good idea.

The old man seemed a little uncomfortable with Wolfe's presence, but was obviously more concerned with his missing priest. He said nothing more, but led them to the front of the church and upstairs to a little row of offices. The one at the far end was Pascal's. It was small, but obviously full of activity when in use. Papers were stacked in precarious piles under the desk hutch. There was an *ad hoc* collage of pictures on the wall above it: local youth at the centre, playing dodge-ball or ping pong, sometimes just posing in rowdy groups, trying to look tough, but obviously having a good time.

Wolfe leaned in close to these, searched the young faces. Everybody seemed to be having a good time, at least at that moment. No obvious signs of fear. None of loathing. Albany was there, and Douglas.

Behind the desk was a chair worn bare with use, a Notre-Dame sweatshirt hanging off of the back of it to match the pennant on the wall behind. A basketball was stuffed in the corner, kept from falling off the end table by a pair of rolled-up athletic shorts. Several pairs of shoes, athletic and formal, lined the back baseboard in a ragged line, mostly paired but obviously dropped there by a busy man. There was a paper calendar on the desk, but it was more of a heavily-doodled schedule for centre events than a personal diary. He must have had a PDA or daily planner on his phone, or at the apartment. That, or a phenomenal memory.

"Okay," Jackson said, "I'll need his address and we'll head over right now."

In fifteen minutes, they were there.

Cisco wasn't waiting to buzz them up, as they'd been told he would be. Apparently he had gotten tired of waiting and decided that someone had gotten the directions mixed up. He had gone from there to the centre where he was held up with some counselling issue. They were on their own.

Jackson showed his badge to the super and the elderly man let them into Pascal's apartment. The old eyes flicked from one to the other of them, as if taking in a different single detail each time. Once the lock snapped open and the key pulled free, he turned and walked back the way he had come, without a discernible word. Wolfe got the distinct impression that the ready cooperation was because it was another priest who wanted in, not because of the cop. That said something about the kind of neighbourhood it was: not bad, *per se*, but not eye-to-eye with the law. Just the kind of place for a young, idealist priest to live.

Or for a criminal.

The building was an average apartment block, nothing too flash or run-down, but it had clean halls and wide balconies. The entry door was next to the kitchen and, once inside, Jackson closed the door for privacy.

Silence, then the air conditioner thudded and hummed to life. Both men jumped, then smiled.

The kitchen was empty, no dishes on the counter or in the sink, no sign of breakfast. A few pieces of paper stuck to the fridge under magnets, neatly arranged. The entry closet was open and full of jackets and sweatshirts lined up on hangers. A row of cardboard boxes, tipped on their sides along the rear wall of the closet, kept the shoes organised.

The living room was small, but stuffed with furniture. A couch and love-seat butted up against each other at the corner, a deep chair sat opposite, comfortable-looking, but mismatched from each other and from the carefully vacuumed carpet. A coffee table took up the space in the middle, a crystal dish of candy in the centre of it on a white doily, like an old woman lived there and not a young, athletic man.

The balcony was wide and ran the width of the living room. Pascal made use of the extra space with two bicycles — one of the road variety, one mountain — a covered solo-flex machine and a small, metal table with a mini-grill on it.

The bedroom was furnished with bed, dresser and chair. A Notre Dame poster decorated the wall beside the bed, a crucifix adorned the wall at its head. The bed was made, an extra blanket folded neatly at its foot. Wolfe opened the top drawer: clothes neatly folded in half of it, the other half empty. He opened the remaining two and found much the same.

There was no sign of a struggle, no sign of theft. For the life of him, he couldn't think what it might be that had made Cisco think there had been a robbery. He would have to ask him — or better yet ask Jackson to do it. Wolfe guessed, and did so accurately, that he was not high on Cisco's welcome list. Agents of VII had that same effect on the priesthood as Internal Affairs did on cops, good *and* bad. It was a dynamic he had never really understood, but, with rare exceptions, exceptions like Father Pascal himself, the name 'Father Wolfe' seemed to close far more doors, and mouths, than it opened — at least willingly. Curse of the job.

Jackson was in the bathroom, checking for clues, out of sight. Wolfe walked back into the kitchen and scanned the papers on the fridge door. Two kinds of handwriting. He read them all quickly, pulled a certain slip of paper out from under its magnet and tucked it into his pocket. He moved back around the counter and into the living room.

He slid the glass doors wide and stepped out onto the balcony. Below him was a low row of abused bushes, and the fringe of grass beside the car park, which was nearly deserted, but for Jackson's car and a few others, two of which looked like they didn't run at all. Instinctively, he held his hand over the grill lid, then set it flat against the metal. Cold, of course, save for the heat of the Miami sun.

Father Pascal was gone.

TWELVE

They let in the lone CSI tech with his uniform escort, and then returned to the police station. They hadn't spoken to Father Gonzales yet; Jackson thought it was better to contact Cisco first, since he had been the one to enter the apartment and claimed to detect signs of burglary. Wolfe wished that Cisco had some kind of mobile phone. It was unusual that he didn't. Tough to be too critical though, considering Wolfe didn't carry one either.

Wolfe didn't carry one because he could, in theory, be tracked by it, and his line of work required a degree of privacy and stealth not usually desired by regular priests. He suspected that Father Cisco was simply 'old school' as so many of the older clergy were. He wondered if Jackson had a way to determine where Pascal's mobile might be at that moment. He was about to ask, when the cop's own mobile burst into a static-laden version of *The Shape of You*.

"Jackson here… yeah. Uh huh. Okay, can we say…" he looked at his watch, "Twenty minutes? Good. See you there." He hung it up.

"What is it?"

"Cisco is heading over to the church. I'm going to head back there and have a chat."

"We're what, five minutes from the station?" Wolfe asked.

"Yeah, why?"

"Would you mind my bringing my own car? I have a few things I'd like to check on."

"No problem here. I'd like to be in on it, though."

"Maybe we can help each other more by dividing our time — two places at once."

"Did you see something at the apartment?"

"I'll know more later."

"C'mon, what is it?"

"I'll let you know if I get something from it. In the meantime, a little bit of plausible deniability can't hurt you. I won't keep anything big from you. That I can promise."

"All right, I can live with that for now, but remember, that knife cuts both ways."

"No knife, Billy, just keeping my unofficial status from muddying up your official reports or constraints. I'll pass on what I get."

Jackson remained quiet.

They pulled up to the police station and Wolfe got out. The air was still a little tense, but there was no time to clear it just then. The cruiser pulled away and u-turned back toward the church. Wolfe went inside the building and pulled the paper from his pocket. A quick call and he had an appointment for five that afternoon. He returned to his car and struck out for the church, only a few minutes behind the young policeman.

Father Gonzales was in the lobby, speaking with one of the parishioners.

"I sent them into my office," he said to Wolfe, "They'll have more privacy in there. You are welcome to wait here." The old man motioned to a seat by the door to the sanctuary.

Wolfe didn't break stride on his way into the nave.

He didn't know why he flaunted his independence in front of the local, senior priest, but for some reason he couldn't put his finger on, Gonzales rubbed him the wrong way. His gut was just a little tighter in the presence of the old man. He trusted his gut. Usually. More than he trusted Gonzales, anyway.

The office was quiet when he entered, Cisco sitting in one of the visitor's chairs, Jackson in the other, listening to his mobile telephone. Focused. Wolfe closed the door behind him and, mindful of his recent disrespect to Gonzales, sat on a bench by the bookcase, rather than in the thick leather chair behind the desk.

"I see," Jackson said at last, "Thanks for letting me know." He tapped the phone and stood. "I'm sorry to hold you up. We're done here for now."

The priest seemed surprised. "What is it?"

"Police business, Father, I'm sorry. I'm sure you'll hear soon enough."

Jackson ushered Cisco out of the office and motioned for Wolfe to stay.

"What is it?"

"It's Father Pascal," he said, his brow furrowed, "It seems they found a gun in his apartment, a Luger P08... nine millimetre."

"A Luger?" Antique German pistol. WWII. "Was it a match for the one that shot at Ana?"

"Maybe, we'll know later today. Likely though, I should think. Don't you?"

"Maybe." Taking in the thought was like jamming a broom handle through a keyhole. "Where was it?"

"Behind the radiator, in a card-stock box."

"Extra ammunition with it?"

Jackson thought for a moment. "I don't know. Maybe. She didn't say."

"Doesn't sit right."

"The guys have been looking for somebody to blame for Kevin's death and the shots at Ana. Pascal had better hope we find him before any of them do, priest or not."

"What had Cisco seen?"

"What?"

"Father Cisco, he said that there were signs of burglary..."

"Yes, there's that too. Apparently Father Pascal kept a suitcase in his room — wouldn't fit in the closet. It was gone, the drawers of the desk were open, and the can of cash that he kept in the refrigerator is also missing."

"So he thought robbery?"

"Yeah."

"Not a quick getaway?"

"That's what I thought too, even before the gun was found, but Father Cisco swears it wasn't possible, that Father Pascal was a good man, a true priest, he said, and that he wouldn't just leave like that, despite what it looked like."

"Unless he had been backed into a corner, killed a cop and tried to kill another?"

"Unless that, maybe, but I didn't bring it up to Cisco. He was pretty adamant, and seemed concerned for Pascal's safety. Genuinely worried, even. Better not to stir him up, I figured. In any case, I have to go file a bulletin on Pascal, see if we can track him down."

"His car still out there?"

"Yeah."

Both men one that it was, either way, not a good sign.

Wolfe left Jackson at the church, talking with a determined Father Gonzales, not wanting to share information with the old man, but finding it hard to detach himself from the conversation without either giving the priest some kind of information or else appearing disrespectful. Wolfe was sure the cop would figure it out on his own. In the meantime, he had an errand.

Then he saw Cisco heading off toward home. A couple of blocks from the church already.

Wolfe pondered a moment. He pulled out the piece of paper from his pocket and set it on the seat beside him. The address was printed there in his own, pinched handwriting. His appointment wasn't for another two hours, but this new information was too much for him to wait on. He would drop in early, hoping to find out what he needed, then head back to the hotel to talk to Cruz. The drive was not a long one. But first, he had take a little time for another visit. No appointment.

He gave Cisco a good ten minutes on his own before walking up to the heavy steel door of the townhouse. He took the little knocker between two fingertips and rapped it against the anvil. Nothing for a while. He knocked again. Louder.

The door cracked open and Antony Cisco stood in the gap. "What do you want?"

"To talk to you for a moment."

"You can't use a telephone?"

"Needs to be in person."

"In my home?"

"Good a place as any, isn't it?"

"Better than most... but not for you. Make an appointment at the church."

The face disappeared and the door swung toward its frame, halted by Wolfe's outstretched foot.

The face reappeared, hints of rage now fleeting between mouth and eyes.

"I have the authority to question you as I will. If you prove to be a pain in the ass, I'll have you censured. Not only will future posting requests be in jeopardy, but believe me when I tell you, you don't want a censure request from my department on your record, retiring or not."

The eyes narrowed. The crack in the doorway widened. "Your methods are as evil as your intentions, Wolfe. Yet you bear your shame like a crown."

The priest-hunter said nothing to that, and stepped inside.

Cisco's home was sparsely furnished, to say the least. It had a cheap dining table and two chairs in the main room, a single easy chair with a pile of books around it and a small, older television on a travel trunk near the wall. The kitchen was neat, the counters devoid of any modern gadgets, but a small woven basket of spoons, whisks and a can opener sat prominently next to the electric stove. The room smelled of chilies and burnt dust.

Cisco himself was not in his regular clothing either. Or rather, he probably was. His black uniform was gone. He wore a linen shirt with an Asian collar. It was long-sleeved and looked to have been once a brilliant white, though now it was worn and the colour dimmed. His black trousers were replaced by a pair of knee-length khaki cargo shorts. He had a kerchief tied around his neck and needed only a broad straw hat to have looked quite at home in an Indochinese period piece.

"My tea will get cold. You can come and ask me your questions out here."

Cisco gave the protesting glass doors a heave to the side, opening them a little wider than they had been, and stepped through to the little patch of Jungle Wolfe had seen on his earlier visit. Cisco sat down and leaned into the back of his chair, taking up his steaming cup with

172

one hand as dismissively as a plantation owner addressing a slave. No offer was made to get Wolfe a chair. No chair was asked for. Wolfe stood just inside the plant-filled structure, feeling the gentle rub of air-conditioned draft rolling down over his back from the open sliders.

"The night Kevin Ortez was killed," Wolfe began, "What were you doing?"

"When your brother died? I was helping at the centre. I already made a statement."

"Not to me. And I want to know what you were doing at the centre. Specifically. In detail."

Cisco mastered his resentment, swallowed his outburst and answered in an even tone. "I was seeing that the cleanup for the food and beverages was properly arranged. It does not do to leave food out overnight in the centre. It will attract vermin. We are right now happily devoid of cockroaches, rats and the like."

"So you were on kitchen duty?"

"I was delegating tasks. That is my job."

"And you returned to find... the body, together with Fathers Gonzales and Pascal." The catch in his throat was not ignored by either man. It even seemed to soothe Cisco's anger a little. For a moment.

"Yes. The three of us."

"Convenient."

"None of this is particularly convenient, Father Wolfe. None of it."

"Why did it take three of you to retrieve the money from the drawer? Surely one could have done it while the other two began the counting and recording from the fundraiser…"

"We were in conversation. It is good manners to stay with one's conversation partners, is it not? But I forget myself. Manners are not your strong suit." He had hoped to anger his inquisitor. Wolfe showed no sign of offence. Cisco was probably right.

"What were you talking about?"

"Propitiation."

"Propitiation?"

"Do I need to define the term for you, or do you yet recall a fraction of your seminary training?"

"It seems a rare topic, that's all. And very specific."

"It is the latter, yes, as you requested, but it is hardly rare for the sanctified to speak of the sanctifier, or the freed man the liberator. It has its complexities, as you may know, and we were simply speaking of the theological details. We three are priests, after all." Another insult missed its mark.

"Where did you serve?"

"Pardon me?"

"Your missionary service, where was it?"

"Columbia. Paraguay. Costa Rica for a time. Why?"

"Background. Any military service?"

"Not a violent man. It is incompatible with a life of peace."

Wolfe chose not to point out the number of clerics who once thought more of stripes on their arms than on their backs. Cisco knew of Gonzales's service, but he may not have known that Wolfe was aware of it. Another feeble attempt at attack. Perhaps Cisco was right, the man really was no good at the offensive game. Maybe Wolfe was just immune to the assaults used in normal society, like a bull being shouted at by a city kid.

"Any training in explosives? Jobs using dynamite, that kind of thing?"

Cisco's face turned sour. "I have been a priest. Always. Since I was a young man and long before you were born. I have no training in anything of the sort. It should shame you to ask me such things."

"I do my job, Father Cisco. That's all."

A snort from the older priest. A sip from the cup. A mutual pause in the process.

Wolfe basked in the fragrances of the plants around him. It was almost heady, but still maintained a kind of differentiated set of scents. A chimera of flavours on drifting air, rather than a muddy mass of perfumes.

"This place is beautiful." Wolfe hadn't even meant to say it. Just a thought out loud; a feeling made real through the voicing of it.

"What?"

"This patio. It's beautiful. All of the plants."

Cisco looked around in suspicion as if there were something in the greenery that Wolfe might use to trick him. Then he looked back at the man. No. He had meant it.

"I did serve in the military," Wolfe said, "Spent a lot of time in the jungle. This reminds me of the best parts of it."

"Though there are less idyllic aspects, to be sure."

"Yes. Those too. But not here. You've done a good job here."

A simple compliment. Simply given.

"Thank you." Mumbled. "Will that be all? I had intended to read." He nodded toward the books on the table.

"Only one more thing."

"What's that?"

"Did you ever see Father Pascal's gun?"

His answer had been incredulous at first. Then a moment of thought. Then an admission that the young priest had mentioned an interest in history — military police weapons. "Just a fleeting interest though, surely," Cisco had said, as if trying to convince both Wolfe and himself, "His grandfather, I believe, served as a military policeman in Korea. Or maybe it was Europe... In any case, he didn't *have* one. That I know for certain." When questioned as to just how he would know, the priest simply insisted that he would, and insisted that there could not have been a gun. "Very unlikely, at best," he had said, "At *best*."

So now Wolfe drove through the traffic-choked arteries of south Miami. Thinking. Working his way down Highway One to the cross street labeled on the little piece of paper. There it was. He signalled and turned to the west. Away from the sea, from the expense of the coastal real estate, and toward the sprawling grid of little, box-like, affordable homes. The drive took him less than an hour, the traffic easing up as he left the main arteries and made his way through the residential streets toward the address.

The patch of lawn was rimmed with low palm trees and cluttered with toys and bicycles ranging from little tricycle-types to a small mountain bike with a basket on the handlebars, log pink tassels trailing from the handles. The house behind it was modest, but well-kept; the yard full, but clean and mowed; the windows clear in shade cast down by the awnings in the stinging, early-afternoon sun. The place smelt of flowers.

He knocked on the door. A surprised-looking woman in her fifties answered, apron-clad and shooing three small children off into the house behind her. They ducked behind the nearest furniture and eyed the priest from just out of their grandmother's reach.

"Mrs. Barbosa?" he said, "I'm Father Wolfe, I spoke to you earlier."

"Yes, yes, so sorry, I expect you at five!"

"You were right, that's my fault. Some things have happened and I wonder if I might take just a moment of your time now."

"Of course Father, come in, sit down."

The place was as he had expected it to be: clean and tidy, the mess of toys relegated to the out-of-doors, the living room set up for peaceful visiting and, as he also expected, a candy dish upon a doily in the centre of the coffee table.

Mrs. Barbosa brought in some glasses, a bowl of ice, and two cans of juice-flavoured soda. She opened one and filled each of their glasses with two ice cubes, and the unnaturally bright red liquid. All the while, the children watched with curious smiles from behind the furniture. Wolfe waved at them and was answered with screeching giggles and a general stampede down the hallway, into the rooms beyond. Despite what was going on, he couldn't help but smile.

He turned his attention back to the woman, his expression more grave.

"How long did you work for Father Pascal?"

"I clean for the Father for…" she thought for a moment, "Five years now."

"You do a very good job."

"I clean for him like I clean for His Holiness himself. It is God's work to serve his priests."

"Thank you, I know he appreciates it." She blushed with pride. He had meant that Pascal appreciates it, but suspected the woman though he referred to God himself. Didn't matter to Wolfe. "I have to ask you something now. I don't want it to upset you. I think I know already what your answer will be, but it is a difficult question. Are you ready?"

Her face turned wary and serious. She grasped her hands together in her lap and nodded.

"Did Father Pascal have a gun?"

"*Oi* NO!" she said, nearly jumping up from her chair. "Father Pascal would never hurt anyone!"

Wolfe smiled and motioned for her to sit, "That's what I thought," he said, "That's just what I thought." More than his words, his smile seemed to calm her. She sat back down. "Just to be clear now, there is no way that he kept a gun in a box behind the radiator."

"No, nothing was behind radiator. I clean it, I know."

"I saw the apartment, Mrs. Barbosa, and I believe you. It was very well looked after. I saw his office, I know the difference you made to his home."

"He can be so messy, God forgive me," she crossed herself and looked to the ceiling with mock frustration, "So busy all the time! But it is a pleasure to clean for him, Father, a blessing to serve. He is so good with the children. A good man. A truly gentle soul."

"And you saw nothing in all your time there that gave you pause? Nothing that made you think something wrong was going on? I am a priest, too, and Father Pascal's friend," this was not quite true, "You can tell me."

She got very solemn and leaned forward in her chair. "No, Father Wolfe, nothing wrong. He is a saint among us. Will he be promoted, Father, will he go to the Vatican? Is that why you are here?"

Wolfe smiled, but felt little joy in it. "I hope he will stay right here to serve this community," he said, "His gifts would be of more use here than in Rome. Here is my number. I'm staying at a hotel here in the city. Keep it secret, secret from anyone. If you hear from Father Pascal, he may need my help. Call me. I will come."

She nodded, knowing now that this was no test for a job at the Vatican, that her adored priest was in trouble of some kind. He could see he had unsettled her.

"Don't be afraid. I don't know anything yet."

"I will pray, Father, I will do my rosaries." She pulled the chain of beads from the table beside her chair.

"He would like that, Mrs. Barbosa, I think he would like that."

He got up then and left the room. The small faces reappeared at the end of the hall and made their stealthy way toward the red cans on the table. The stunned woman remained seated, muttering in the cool shade of the house, fingering the small beads in faith and hope.

Wolfe left with little of either.

He left his car with the valet again. Moved through the lobby to the elevator. He went from there to the front door of the room and dipped the key card into the slot, pushing the door open and stepping inside. "Ana, I'm back."

He froze.

THIRTEEN

Something wasn't right. He could feel it — smell it — in the air. A few steps more and he saw a lamp overturned in the hallway. His Special Forces training kicked in and his body lowered, moving his centre of gravity closer to the floor for quicker movements and more powerful reactions. He stepped to the kitchenette and silently slid open a drawer. A knife into his left hand, heavy and long, a smaller one into his right for throwing or to follow up on a distraction from the bigger one. He stepped back toward the hallway.

He breathed out hard through his nose, silently but with enough force to pop his ears, sharpening his hearing to its maximum. He breathed in slowly then, taking in the air carefully. Her perfume. His unsmoked cigars. Coffee. But something else. Something that wasn't in the room the night before. Something that didn't belong.

It wasn't blood or visceral fluid — he had smelled enough of both to know them immediately. It was something else, not sinister in itself, but definitely foreign to the suite. He crept down the short hallway into the living-room area. The lamp was down but there was little other sign of struggle. The plush carpet showed footprints. Work boots maybe? A heavy-soled shoe like Doc Martin's? Either way, they were too deep and large to belong to Cruz. He stepped to where he could see through the French doors. No movement. No one there. The bed was unmade and a glass of water had been knocked from the bedside table to the floor. The bathroom door was closed.

He crept forward and dragged an outstretched finger through the patch of carpet where the water had fallen. Nearly dry. It had been there a long time. Hours.

He reversed his stance, right hand forward, ready for a quick jab, and stepped toward the bathroom. The fan was on inside, humming softly through the solid wood, obscuring any other sounds which might come from within. He turned the handle and kicked at the door, entering blade-first, wide-eyed, ready to strike.

He stood alone in the empty room, in the steady hum of the plastic fan.

Ana Cruz was gone.

He called the police station immediately. Jackson was in. "Hey Billy, we have a problem here."

"What is it?"

"Ana is gone. Taken."

"Are you sure? I mean are you sure she didn't just leave on her own. She can be a strong-willed woman… and she's a cop after all. She won't want to sit around doing nothing."

"I know. There are signs."

"Blood?" The voice on the other end was suddenly flat, quiet, serious.

"No, but signs of a struggle and of someone being here who shouldn't have been."

"You've called it in?"

"That's what I'm doing now."

"Any signs of forced entry?"

"None that I can see. I haven't checked windows, but I'm on the sixth floor."

"You've got to wait there. I'll come now with a few of the CSI guys and we'll see what we can find out, but you've got to stay there."

"I can't, there's no time."

"No time for what?"

"If they've got her, there's no telling what they'll do. Her life might be in danger, you know that."

"But you have to stay put. You can't do this on your own. You tell me what you know, we'll do this thing together."

"Look, somebody killed Kevin, then the kid went missing, then Pascal — now Ana. They shot at her before, but now they *have* her. What do you think her chances are if we don't get to her immediately?"

"Whoa, take it easy, who is the kid? What kid went missing?"

"From the community centre. Douglas. Ana thought he might be mixed up in something at the church."

"*Shit*, they just found a Douglas Kane buried in the upper Keys. I got a call from a social worker this morning. He was reported missing from Tampa a year ago, ran away here. I don't know much more about it, probably wouldn't have been my case, anyway. That'll change now. He was buried down there not more than a few days ago, wrapped in a sheet with his hands folded over his belly. That's all I know. The file's here somewhere though."

"So whoever buried him cared about him."

"So the shrinks tell us. It's a strange place for him to be dumped. Not a place runaways usually end up, dead *or* alive. A lot of trouble to take him all the way down there."

"Any other forensics?"

"Just that he had been dropped there in a truck or van, pretty generic tire treads, we had need a specific vehicle to tie it to the site."

"Have you checked the church van?"

"I can arrange that."

"Look, I don't need to tell you that anything you can get from that site might lead us to Ana — I think it might lead us to Pascal as well."

"You don't think he's already the major suspect?"

"He might be your major suspect, but he might also be another victim. I talked to his cleaning lady and he never had a gun there. Whatever happened to him, somebody's trying to make it look like he shot at Ana."

"Or else he did shoot at her and then fled."

"Leaving the gun behind?"

"Panic?"

"Didn't look like panic, half of a drawer empty, the other neatly folded... Besides, six shots into the side of the building and only three in the car. And grouped? Whoever shot at her wasn't trying to hit her."

"Or else he's a consistently lousy shot. But you were right about one thing, the gun was found fully reloaded, but without any spare ammo. I can agree that that's weird."

"Something else is going on... but my gut tells me we're in escalation, Billy. Whoever this is, is losing control. Whoever is the victim here, is in real danger. Pascal and Ana are in danger."

"I can't sell Pascal as a victim over here, they're dead set that he's not only our shooter, but Kevin's killer as well — it fits, he had access to everybody and every crime scene."

"Except mine." He didn't mention the explosives training.

"Maybe, we haven't checked an alibi for him for that. But she would have let him into your room at the hotel, wouldn't she?"

"Maybe. Yes. But the signs I see are of an intruder, not company. It doesn't fit. There's something I'm missing and I need time — time I'll not spend answering questions and going through processing as a suspect."

"It won't look good, you leaving the scene."

"Looking bad will be tolerable if I can find Ana and Pascal."

"And what about the resources spent looking for you instead of chasing down whoever did this? Have you thought of that? You have no resources for this, Danny, and by running, you'll drain ours. The best chance for any of the victims is for you to stay there and to tell us whatever you can. We'll work together on it."

"I have more resources than you know of. I also have more freedom. You need to operate within your regulations — I don't."

"Talk like that could lead to things that might get you arrested."

"If it gets Ana back, and Pascal? I'm okay with that."

There was a long pause on the other end. Heart pounding, Wolfe waited. Despite his talk of resources and freedom from regulations, he needed backup on this and Jackson was his best chance.

"Okay, what do you need from me?"

"Mainly time. That and any information you can give me."

"Okay. I can't give you much time, but I've got that number for the bomb squad guy... it's here somewhere... there." He read the number out. "He's got something to tell you, he said, though not much. You can call him any time."

"Will he know if there's an APB out on me, or a BOLO?"

"Not if you call him now. Right now you're just a citizen calling in a crime. When units get there and you're gone, that's when things will heat up. I would guess you have all of about forty minutes before they're there and pissed off, another ten before something gets done about it."

"Right. I'll call from somewhere else. Thanks Billy."

"Thanks? All I know is that you called to report a break-in. What's to thank me for?"

"I'll be in touch if I can."

"Public phones."

"Public phones."

Wolfe hung up and went to the closet. He typed in the combination to the room safe and pulled out a small black booklet, like a day planner. In it were both of his brand new passports, two sets of ID, including credit cards, and two short stacks of hundred-dollar bills held together with rubber bands — nine thousand nine hundred dollars in total, just under the maximum unreportable amount with which one could board an international commercial flight. There was an encoded list of passwords for various Vatican associations in several countries, two pair of plastic hand restraints and a lock-pick set. It was his arrest and escape kit, provided by the Vatican for times of emergency. He might need to work under the radar for a while and that was exactly what the kit was designed to facilitate.

He left the hotel by the side fire exit, leaving his car and the buzzing door alarm behind him. He pulled the white collar from the front of his shirt and thrust it down into his pocket. Rolled up his sleeves. A few open buttons at the neck and he would look normal enough, civilian enough to blend in. He crossed the street and hopped a bus two blocks down. He rode it for ten minutes exactly and then depressed the button for next stop. Should be far enough to evade any dragnet the police put out for him, and he needed to make a stop; he had a phone call to make.

The line rang twice before a woman's voice picked it up and he was transferred to the appropriate desk at the Miami Dade Bomb squad.

"Rob Connelly."

"Hi Rob, I'm a friend of Billy Jackson, Daniel Wolfe?"

"Ah yeah, the priest. Billy told me you'd be calling. You had a close one there."

"Yes, close."

"Doing okay though?"

"Rattled ribs and a little sunburn, but not bad."

"You're lucky, that thing was meant to take you out."

"Can you tell me anything in detail?"

"Yeah. Whoever built the thing was an amateur as far as bombs go, but educated I'd guess, and a smart son-of-a-bitch. Capable."

"How so?"

"First of all he used two types of explosive, one to blow the shit out of the bed it was under and another to flame the place. My guess is that the first was meant to kill you instantly, the second to remove any evidence of him being there."

"Effective."

"Not really, not from our end at least. People think bombs blow themselves up, disintegrating anything useful, but that's not true. Everything we need to reconstruct this thing is there — is always there somewhere — it's just sometimes in very small pieces, or spread out. We gather them up, we put them together. At least at your place the weight-bearing walls held most of the blast in — and the pieces with it."

"And what have you learned?"

"Not everything, not yet, but we have a little. The detonation rig was attached to the alarm clock. Do you know when you last used it?"

"I've never touched it. I normally wake up early so I don't need one."

"I think that saved your life, Padre. We found two batteries... this thing was set up on a collapsible circuit."

"So? What does that mean in practical terms?"

"A bomb needs a power source to detonate. That's normal. A collapsible circuit is a kind of bomb-maker's backup. It needs power to *keep* the bomb from detonating. A collapsible circuit is made so that a loss of power to the system closes the switch and sets the device off, using a battery to do it. Makes it harder to disarm it. In this case, it had a motion circuit, and then the other one. I think it was set up so that any movement of the alarm clock — setting it, turning it off, even turning it to face another direction — and the second battery is cut off from the system: *boom*. Touch it, boom. Don't touch it for long enough, and boom. Construction wouldn't have required a pro... just somebody with the smarts to do it and some steely nerves. Somebody's looking out for you. Your prayers may have pulled you through, Padre. The thing went off without you. The bomber unplugged the clock, let it run on its backup battery power, which was attached to the collapsable circuit. When that died, the trigger engaged. You set your alarm at night, or turn it off that morning, and *boom*. You don't use it and the system just sits there, the circuit draining power little by little until the main battery can't hold the switch open anymore and it collapses. Either way…"

"*Boom*."

"Yeah. And if it didn't get you, it would go off anyway and blast any fingerprints to hell, maybe get lucky and take you with it."

"Risky. Could have taken anyone out. A maid, the next guest."

"Yeah."

"So no information on the maker so far?"

"Not without something to compare it to. You're looking for someone with some technical know-how and the desire to take out everything in your apartment without dropping the whole building. Everything a guy like that needs is easy enough to find on the Internet, I'm sad to say."

"He could have? Taken out the whole building I mean."

"He could have, yes. He had the knowledge to do it, I'd guess. It's harder to limit an explosion than to let a big one loose. I'd say he held back… or you and your neighbours got really lucky."

"Good to know. Look, thanks for the info, if there's ever anything I can do, let me know."

"My pleasure... Billy thinks I owed him a major anyway, and this was a good way to let him keep his delusion and not have any family strife."

Wolfe laughed, "Yes, I heard about that."

"Hey, don't mention this to Billy yet, but if you manage to keep yourself alive for six or seven more months, maybe you could help us. I'm Catholic, Sonya's not. My mother's heart is set on a church wedding. Helps getting a church with a priest in our corner..."

"I'm not much of a priest, Rob."

"I'm not much of a Catholic — match made in Heaven."

"I'll see what I can do."

"I appreciate that, I'll be in touch."

Wolfe wasn't sure if the information helped or not. At least he knew that it probably wasn't a professional out to get him, but it was little comfort; amateur bombs blow real holes in people too. He picked up the taxi company's courtesy phone and waited for the click. Ten minutes later he was seated in the back seat of the car and on his way to the airport.

He had had to wait almost all night for the authorities to finish at Cruz's home and tape up the door. They'd cut short the usual twenty-four hours to start an investigation of her disappearance, for her, a cop who'd been shot at the night before and now was missing. He had no doubt that they'd already issued something on him as well. Person of interest... at best.

At the airport he had booked an eleven o'clock flight in his own name. He had no intention of being on it, but it would sap their resources, give them a place to look for him that was far from where he needed to be. He had then rented a car under his Daniel Edwards identity and camped out a block from Cruz's home, in front of a taco joint that had a busy takeout business: lots of traffic to serve as cover. A good place to hide.

As the first breath of darkness slipped silently over the area, and he worked his way through a greasy burrito, lights came on and went out again at various points along the building. He carefully noted each change and, as residents came and went, tried to ascertain who had left which unit, removing them from the mental list of possibles. At last he saw the techs leave the building. A single officer remained behind, slipping into a shadowy stoop just to the side of her building's entry.

He calculated back in his mind, to the bank of lights that had most recently been extinguished. A front unit. At the corner. That was the most likely place then. He had her address from Jackson. Once inside, he could tell if it was a corner unit on the front of the building, then he could be sure enough of its emptiness. If not... well, he couldn't wait around all night. Sometimes chances had to be taken. At least he knew most of the techs had gone. If the unit was somewhere else in the building, with lights still on and somebody still inside, he would deal with that when he saw them.

He had been scanning the structure all evening, looking for the best points of egress. Laundry hung on lines strung between the lightning pole at the front corner of the building and some structure or anchor point further over on the roof. That would mean an open door to the roof. If he could get up there unseen, it would be a covert point of access to the rest of the place. He rounded the block on foot, avoiding the sentry, and entered the apartment building next door, attached and only one story higher. He took the stairs to the sixth floor. Above him was a long stack of furniture and boxes piled inside a chain link barrier; access to that building's roof was blocked.

He went instead into the hall. It was narrow and smelled of stale cigarettes and the faint waft of urine. At the far end, facing onto the back alley, was a window.

He prised it open, stepped through onto the fire escape, and climbed up onto the rusted railing, six stories above the pavement below. This part would be hardest. Not bad, normally, but with his injuries... He sucked in as much air as he could and pulled himself upward.

The injured ribs screamed at him, but he stifled any outward sound. His arms continued to pull, lifting him up until he could swing his body to the right and let the answering momentum lift his left arm high enough to thrust an elbow up and over the tin lip of the roof. He caught a glimpse of the pavement, now almost seven floors below him. There was a dumpster with half of the lid open and a broken toaster oven sitting atop a pile of white plastic grocery bags full of cans. His imagination scrolled through probable contents. Glass. Tin cans. Animal bones. Even the solid edge of it made any fantasy of landing safely amid cushioned refuse a silly fantasy. No. If he fell, it would be the end of him… and probably an agonising, terrible end.

As his torso swung back to the right he thrust that arm up and hooked his hands on the inner side of the low ledge that ran the perimeter of the rooftop. He pushed his feet against the brick below and hunched his body forward, this time grunting in pain, and managed a point of equilibrium for a moment, before one last toe-nudge pushed him up and over.

He allowed himself a moan while he caught his breath, looked up at the darkening sky, the passing clouds, and remembered other climbs, other pain. Much worse than this. He was getting soft. Or old.

He willed himself to his feet and made his way toward Cruz's tenement. Across the roof he found the drop down to her building a little easier. There was a built-up area of the roof which housed air ducts for the heat and air conditioning system. The drop was less than six feet, nothing, under normal circumstances, but he knew his ribs would take another beating from it.

No choice.

He swung his legs over the edge and pushed himself forward into a short free-fall. The impact was sharp and excruciating. His vision blurred for a moment and he fought against faintness. Blood-red fog rubbed hard across his sight and he lowered himself down until his cheek rested on the warn, unforgiving metal. A painful breath or two and the sharpness dulled a little. With each inhalation he took in a little more air, stretched out the protesting muscles and bones just a little bit more. His fingers probed his ribs and, despite the throbbing, they seemed none the worse for wear. He had made it, that was the main thing. The pain had sent its message of alarm, but all was well enough. It could now be dismissed.

As he had suspected when he saw the rooftop laundry line from down below, the door to the roof wasn't locked. It opened easily at his pull. Down the stairs to the third floor, and then down the empty hallway. Room thirty-four... thirty-five... thirty-six. That was hers. Corner unit. On the front. The door was locked, as he had expected, and there was no missing it. It had the four usual strips of yellow police tape fastened across it: one top, one bottom and a big, forbidding X down the middle. Subtle.

He pulled out the lock-picks and went to work on the deadbolt. It was a pretty good one. The irony of low-end neighbourhoods was often high-end deadbolts. He had been in mansions which housed million-dollar works of art and were protected by hardware less challenging than this lock on a third-story walk-up just outside of the slums. Still, he was well-trained and in good practice; in fifteen seconds he felt the slide of metal on metal and the bolt slid back.

He didn't want to spend any more time than he had to, exposed in the open hallway. A hunched step into the room without displacing the yellow tape and he closed and locked the door. If the sentry came to check the place, everything would be secure as expected.

The curtains were pulled. He didn't dare open them, in case there was a second sentry who spotted the change from the street below. Likewise, he couldn't turn on any lights to help him see and he hadn't brought a flashlight. At least it wasn't completely dark, and the lack of light assured him that he was alone. At least for the moment.

He didn't know what he expected to find there. For the right or wrong reasons, he had all but excluded her from his list of suspicious persons. Her abduction, if it were real, only bolstered that position.

If it were real.

He had no reason to think it wasn't. Shots had been fired after all and, even if she could have faked those, how could she have gotten the gun into Pascal's apartment? She couldn't have. Not if she came to Wolfe immediately after the shooting. It would be too risky to shoot up her own place and then wait an hour to report it while she raced over to Pascal's, who may or may not have been at home, to hide the gun in his apartment. It was also unlikely that she was working as part of a duo or a team. He was no profiler, but the M.O. didn't fit for multiple perpetrators.

Besides, all of this somehow had connections to Kevin's murder — and she wasn't mixed up in that. His gut told him that she wasn't the one. At least he thought it was his gut. Sometimes other parts spoke up that had no right to be in the deliberations. It could be that too. She was attractive, after all. She was also close to his

196

brother. They had cared for each other, in some way. Unfortunately, if statistics could be trusted, that was far from a reason not to kill somebody.

While he stood thinking, his eyes adjusted and the room took shape around him.

He looked in the kitchen, briefly, then moved through to the combination living and dining room area. There were pictures in the bookcase by the opening to the hallway: Hispanic children playing at a wading pool, an elderly couple smiling so broadly that their eyes disappeared in the wrinkled fastness of their faces. There was a photo, faded with age, of a black dog, mostly Labrador, with a little girl standing beside him. Wolfe leaned in close. Yes, it was Ana Cruz, he guessed, or a lookalike sister. As he straightened up again another photo caught his eye.

Kevin.

He was alone in the picture, but Wolfe recognised the expression on his face, the look in his eyes. Whoever held the camera for that shot wasn't some pal from work. He had seen the same look in the old pictures they'd shared not long after meeting. Kevin's first love. The girl from the theatre with the big hair and the daggers for earrings — too old for him, but that never mattered back then. Fantasies don't care for such things. And this one, he knew, was a look aimed at the woman in whose apartment he now stood.

He moved from the living area, down the hall and into the first bedroom. It was full of boxes and bags of fabric, a sewing machine, a bicycle and several cases of canned goods. A spare room for company, turned into a workshop, a shed and a larder. The other was her bedroom.

Wolfe smelled her scent more poignantly there — the perfume, the soap, the hair products. It was a messy room. Clothing thrown over chair backs and an over-filled laundry basket. Myriad bottles tumbled over each other on a vanity that was lightly dusted in powder, drifted down from weeks' worth of makeup sessions. Blushes, skin tones, and darker hues of violet and amber. Wilted flowers sat atop stiff stems in a vase on the bedside table beside a neat row of inhalers. Three of them. One label read *Flunisolide*, the other two: *Salmeterol*. Meaningless to Wolfe. He pocketed one of each type and left the duplicate untouched.

He moved to the dresser and began with the top drawer, pulling it open, pushing the clothing around inside to look for anything hard, foreign, hidden — even the soft crinkle of paper. Nothing. The second one down was likewise devoid of anything more interesting that tee-shirts and socks. The third was her underwear drawer and he paused.

He had been investigating pedophiles for years. Before that he was in seminary, devoutly studious and celibate in spirit as well as well as law. The years before were years of violence, blood and inner coldness. The items in that drawer were as far from all such things as his mind could imagine.

He lifted up a pair of her purple lace underwear and pressed them to his cheek, breathing in the flowery scent of laundry detergent and feeling the dainty softness even before any sexual thoughts rose to the surface of his mind. He laid them back down and lifted another pair. Tiny. A patch of lace, smaller than the palm of his hand, and strings with miniature bows in white ribbon. He couldn't imagine that these had much of a practical use as underwear; they were not for everyday wear, he suspected. They were for show. Attraction. Seduction.

Had his brother taken these from her body? The thoughts came unbidden to his mind, visions of the woman and the man interlocked in passion played across the screen in his head. He wondered if they'd been lovers, or just played with the thought, thinking they had time to explore, to tease, to let the new thrill of first-passions linger just a little while.

Lovers, he thought, *of course they were.*

In the outside world, such things happen quickly and easily. Unlike his world. In his world no real pleasure was quick, and nothing at all was easy. In that moment a swell pressed outward and upward from the base of his neck, his face fought back a scowl, and a brittle bitterness settled onto his thoughts. He pushed the feelings back in. Back down. Settled and relaxed the muscles in his cheeks and mouth. He laid the little lace thing back in its place and closed it. He left the fourth and final drawer unsearched.

As he passed through the living room he reached out to pick up the picture of Kevin and shoved it into his belt at the small of his back. He intended to give it back to her if he found her, if she was still alive. If not, he wanted it, as a memory of who his brother was with this woman… and as a reminder of who she had been to Kevin.

He opened the door and stepped out, tearing the tape from the frame as he passed, not heeding where it fell or if it still clung in futility to its humble duty. He pulled the latch shut behind him, unlocked, and walked down the stairwell, out the front door, to the right, and across the street. The sentry didn't see him, or didn't recognise him from the back, or had no orders to stop him if he did. To Wolfe it was all the same. He had lost his brother, and all of the finality that that statement represented was finally starting to sink in. The world stretched out away from him, wider and more empty than he ever remembered it being before, and growing more expansive with each step he took.

He got into his rental car, revved the engine, and squealed out into traffic. To the church. To the priests hiding in its stone walls. To the one place where he felt he could get some answers.

Part of him wished he had a gun, for the effect it would have on them, the fear of death it would instil. The greater part of him knew that he didn't need a weapon to kill, and that those black-clad men, used as they were to reading human hearts, would know it.

FOURTEEN

Wolfe's rage had cooled to a grim determination by the time he reached Saint Mary of the Sea. He pulled on the side door. It was locked and latched. He pounded on it and it was almost immediately opened by a young Hispanic man, muscled and tattooed, wearing all of the local gang paraphernalia but looking less than deadly there, in that setting. Behind him was the reason why. His mother had, apparently, brought him in to speak to Father Gonzales. They had just arrived and were waiting for the clergyman to greet them.

Wolfe didn't wait.

He opened the door to Gonzales's office and stepped in, startling the old man as he tore open bills and letters on his big desk.

"Father Wolfe. It is customary to knock before entering another's office, or does your appointment to the Vatican exempt you from common courtesy as well as vowed obedience?" The older priest stopped tearing at the envelope and slowly set the papers down on his desk, mustering all of the solemn authority he felt his office afforded. His impetuous visitor did not seem to notice. Wolfe stepped straight over to the desk and stood in front of the old man, staring him down with his own sense of authority and watching the colour drain from the older man's face.

"What is it you could want, Father Wolfe, 'Priest-Hunter'?"

"I want to know what it is you're hiding."

"Why would I have anything to hide?"

"I've had enough, Gonzales."

"*Father* Gonzales... You forget yourself."

"I don't care what title you cling to, I know there's something going on that insults that collar you wear more than the omission of your honorific. What is it?"

Wolfe couldn't be sure, but it seemed some colour drained from the old man's face. Then he reddened.

"You honestly come in here thinking that this kind of badgering will get you somewhere? How dare you? How naïve you are to believe such a thing! If I did have something to hide, do you think I'd reveal it to you, a man who is known throughout the priesthood as a betrayer of confidences, a defiler of the confessional and a persecutor of his brethren? Come now, you insult me with your simple thinking."

"I insult you with much more and feel less guilt than I suspect you live with every day. Isn't it time to show loyalty to something more worthy of it? You're a priest. If your duty meant as much to you as your title does then you'd know that."

"Out with it then! What do you imply?!" His voice was raised now, his anger stirred.

Wolfe raised his own voice, appeared to lose his composure. If he could amp up the emotion in the room, Gonzales might slip, a momentary loss of control and a brief revelation of whatever it was the old man was hiding. And Wolfe knew, knew it in his bones, that there was something in there.

"My brother is dead, killed not twenty feet from here by someone trying to cover something up. What was it? He was here to investigate a sex crime, Father Gonzales, though I suspect you already know that. Why do you think he was killed? Do you honestly think he stumbled upon a simple robbery, turned his back on the thief so he could be clubbed to death? I suspect you're immoral, but I do not think you're stupid."

Gonzales's face reddened. He rose from his chair.

"Get out! Get out of my office and my church! You are not welcome here with your disrespect and your accusations! Your superiors will hear of this, I assure you, and I will not let it rest as I have your other interferences, believe me!"

"Involved in kiddy porn, Gonzales? Do you know more than you're telling about my brother's death?"

"GET OUT!"

Wolfe heard a click behind him and the door to the office opened. The young Hispanic and his mother came in, the former with a look of menace on his face. His mother wide-eyed with worry.

"A problem here, Father Gonzales?" the young man asked, "Who is this?"

"There is no problem, Rico, he was just leaving."

Wolfe didn't move. Gonzales held his hand out, motioning to the door and staring steadily back at the other priest. Now that his anger had been stirred and there was backup in the room, however unlikely it might seem, the old cleric seemed confident that he was protected.

"Go."

Rico stepped forward, chin out and head cocked, ready to fight. Wolfe didn't fear that, but he knew his limits. He could get away with charging in and insulting a priest suspected of wrongdoing, but fighting with a young parishioner, and in the church itself, would not be easy to explain.

"Do what the father says, *punta,* or I fuck you up."

The youth's mother crossed herself, deep distress on her face.

Wolfe stood his ground, looked steadily into Father Gonzales's eyes. "It's not over."

"You bet your ass it's over, *homes.*" The boy stepped forward, jaw still thrust forward and hands back. An elbow to his chin, in that posture, and he would go down like a dropped sack of potatoes. Even with his ribs the way they were, Wolfe could finish it in less than a second.

"Rico," Gonzales said in a softened voice, motioning for the youth to be still, "Thank you, but that's enough. It is over now."

Wolfe turned then, without another word, and left the building.

He got into his car and drove north, quickly but aimlessly, up Highway One until he saw a Cuban diner with a public phone. He pulled in and dialed.

"Billy Jackson," he sounded tired.

Wolfe cleared his throat. "Hey, it's me. Is it a good time?"

"Yeah, yeah, it's fine. You're calling about the Kane autopsy, right?"

"Okay." Jackson must have something to tell him about Douglas, and there must be other ears around.

"We were right about him being stabbed. Three punctures, all with the same weapon, probably a screwdriver or something like that — it was pointy enough, but not a sharp blade. We're waiting to hear if there are any metal fragments in the wound, but it seems the lucky bastard missed the bones all three hits."

"Lucky?"

"Well, they'd be lucky to miss bone on all three strikes, especially if it was in the midst of a struggle."

"Right," Wolfe lied, "Anything else?"

"Yes, he was wrapped in a raincoat — nothing special about it, very common, you can buy it in any gas station or home goods store — and transported in a vehicle with green paint."

"You're certain about it being green?"

"Yup. The buttons of the coat scraped the surface of whatever he was lying on, probably while being driven down there. Green paint."

"The church vans are blue."

"Yup."

Damn. "What's up with regard to me… are they looking?"

"Yes, but not as much as we had thought. It seems, for now, the situation has the benefit of the doubt. Still, I think it would be a good idea to deal with it."

"And lose the time?"

"Maybe, but what's happening in the meantime? Gain any ground?"

"No, I can't honestly say I have." He paused a moment, the two of them silent in thought. "Any word of Ana?"

"No, not yet."

"No ransom call, or demands? Nothing?"

"Nothing."

"You know that's not good, right Billy?"

"Yes, I know."

"I don't think I can come in yet. I need to keep pushing, to find something. Anything. There has to be a thread dangling behind this guy, if I can get a hint of it I can follow it… that's all I need."

"Sometimes we don't get that."

"I know."

"It'll get worse with more time, you know that too."

"For me?"

"Yeah."

"I know. For Ana too." Another pause. Wolfe could hear the bustle of the police station on the other end of the line. Jackson remained silent. "I'll call again later tonight. Sooner if I find something."

"Sure. I'll be here."

"Thanks Billy, really."

"Yeah. Later. Take care."

They hung up the phones and Wolfe stepped into the diner. He was frustrated, spinning his wheels. Everything was there, somewhere, he was sure of it. Some nagging feeling told him that he could pull it all together with the right thought, the right focus.

He ordered the *pan con lechon* and a cup of coffee. He needed nourishment, and he needed rest — he hated to take it — but he needed to let his mind unclench, to wander, and to find its own way to the conclusion that he knew hovered just beyond his conscious thought. Over the sound system, the rapid concussion of hands on bongo drums blended with the acrobatic fingers of the guitarist, the rhythmic mantra of the whole backing up the lead singer, making his case for perfect love and the perfect woman he sang it to. Wolfe closed his eyes and took it in, let his mind rest on it.

Somewhere, likely not too many miles from where he sat, Ana Cruz, and maybe Emilio Pascal too, were either captive or already dead. The clock was ticking. Time was running out. And Father Wolfe sat and ate his meal.

Somalia, 1994. Wolfe and his partner had been assigned a target and set out for the event two days before it was scheduled to happen. They waited two days. Nothing. They waited still longer, watching the small cluster of stone buildings twenty-four hours a day. They'd gone easy on the food, but after the fourth day they were out… and still had a return journey once the shot was made. Still they waited.

In the afternoon, Wolfe awoke from dreams of night-visioned images to the glare of bright sunshine. His eyes adjusted to find his partner sighting the rifle. He rolled over, grabbed the distance-finders and focused in on the shacks.

A woman was there. Not the target.

But they were raping her.

His partner's finger was on the trigger, hand trembling.

Wolfe reached over and removed it with a light touch, pulling the hand to the side first, then back. He reached out again and eased the weapon toward him until he bore the full weight of it. Snugged it up under his right shoulder and slid his hand down the composite-moulded stock beneath the barrel. The scope to his eye. A few soft clicks as he adjusted for the wind, then he drew the lead man between the crosshairs.

And waited.

His partner lay his face down in his hands and appeared to sleep. Wolfe didn't pull the trigger. This man wasn't his primary target. He watched as they raped the woman, barely more than a girl. He saw her, too- clearly through the powerful scope.

Her fear.

Her helplessness.

Pain.

He watched while her body was broken, her mind shattered. It went on, man after man, from mid-afternoon to nearly sunset.

Still he waited.

Just before nineteen hundred hours, local time, a cloud of dust on the horizon revealed a vehicle coming. It was a large truck, Russian manufacture, military-issue and made for rough roads and combat zones. It rumbled up the lane, dropping several armed men from the back of the vehicle to take up perimeter positions.

He heard a whisper from beside him, the voice cracked and worn from a day of silent weeping. "Eighteen-hundred to near doorway. Wind, east at eight." Wolfe took in several breaths and let them out in long, silent sighs. Centering his thoughts. Calming his body. Slowing the beat of his heart.

A click to the scope. Another.

He waited until the vehicle stopped and a man got out, wearing the uniform of a high-ranking officer. He was bearded. Tall. Wolfe studied the dossier photo in his mind. Compared the two in a mental frame-by-frame.

"Target acquired," he said.

"Confirmed," hoarse, from beside him.

Wolfe leaned slightly forward, into the solid stillness of the stony bank. His breaths came deep and slow, drawn out as he relaxed his body and mind further until the minute, shaking thud of his heartbeat could be felt. Seen in the tremor of the crosshairs. Almost heard beneath the low hum of the wind through the eroded wadi. The tremulous thump of his heart, then a moment of stillness. Then another thump.

Thump. Rest. *Thump.* Rest. *Thump.* Rest.

The officer walked up to the young woman. Paused. Reached to the front of his pants and began, Wolfe could only guess, to unbuckle them.

Thump. Rest. *Thump.* Rest. *Thump. CRACK!*

He had squeezed the trigger between beats and paused a moment until the tiny figure in the distance shook once, then twisted down to the ground, a cloud of red, atomised blood drifting off over his fallen form. A direct hit. Centre mass. A clear kill. The other men stood for a moment, reading what they saw until the sound of the shot rolled over the gap between barrel and victim and assured them of what they had witnessed.

Wolfe's partner slid back, "Target neutralised — verified," falling into the background as Wolfe panned the weapon's sights to his right, carefully, breathing as slowly as he could and hearing the heartbeat remind him of his own, tenuous life.

Thump. Rest. *Thump. CRACK!*

The round seemed to take forever to reach the little cluster of buildings.

In truth, he shouldn't have fired. Unless one of the guards had been looking directly at him, scanning the featureless stones and desert at the exact place and time, it was virtually impossible for anyone on the ground to ascertain their position from a single shot. Not right away. The time it took them to figure it out would have given Wolfe a decent head start. The cluster of men might have set out in the wrong direction, thinking the sniper to be in the closer, more accessible ridges on the far side of the valley. They might even have holed up, hiding from other shots that might come from anywhere, thereby letting the two tired American snipers slip back over the far side of the hill and head for the safety of their pick-up zone.

But he did. He did fire again.

As the bullet struck the smooth skin of the young woman's chest, flashing in a small cloud of arterial blood and sternum fragments, a burst of gore flew out behind her, instantly changing the dull brown stones to bright red. Her eyes went wide. She fell back from the man who held her by the arm, offering her already-broken body to his leader for further humiliation and pain.

Now faces turned to the hill. Men pointed. Flashes of muzzle fire sparkled here and there on the field, too far away for any real hope of effect. Wolfe opened the chamber and slid in a tracer bullet. He lined up the crosshairs and fired again. Just once more. This third shot streaked in a long yellow line from the gun muzzle to the armoured fuel tank at the mid-point of the heavy truck. He had aimed at the top few inches of it, knowing that it had traveled some distance to read the outpost, and so there would be sufficient air in the tank, along with the volatile fumes. A full fuel tank seldom exploded. The metal panel flickered for a moment then erupted into a cloud of smoke and flame, hurling shrapnel in a wide arc, downing some men with injury and others with fear.

He had shot fifty-nine men in the course of his military career, including five women — including the one in Somalia. He remembered all of them as necessary evils.

Except her.

He didn't know, afterward, why he had shot her. He told himself at first that it was to end her misery. In part that was true, but it wasn't all there was to tell. He knew that if he didn't do something to end her pain, then he would feel it with her. He would go his entire life not knowing how long her ordeal had lasted. What had happened to her once it was over. What tortured memories she would carry.

He would wake up each day knowing that he could have stopped it.

His tour lasted another four months. He never fired his weapon again in that time. The young Somali woman, wide-eyed and shattered, was his last victim in that terrible string of killings, his last act in a difficult conflict in which he was never an official participant. And he couldn't shake the feeling that he had done it for himself.

She had been a symbol of the end of his own pain, a sick-minded act of closure that made sense enough over there, but didn't translate back to civilian life, to the exaggerated problems of the everyday. Nothing of that time did — except, perhaps, for the constant feeling that the children he was supposed to be protecting had already been broken. Damage done long before anyone knew to look for it. Futility. Like the girl in the desert, the cardboard boxes he had gathered in his Vatican duties bore testament to ongoing pain. Pain he somehow shared.

But there was no bullet for the cardboard boxes. Not yet a bullet for him, either.

He wished he could say it was the last life he had taken in the name of duty, but it hadn't been. Special Ops in *Desert Storm* and a brief Black Op in the Philippine Islands, all demanded their own tolls in blood and fear — the taking of human life in the name of God and freedom. The scratching up of his own sense of peace.

When he had returned from active duty he completed his education, and became a priest, sidestepping civilian life once again. Perhaps it was a kind of penance for his part in the conflicts. He didn't know any of that for certain.

One thing he did know though: War had taught him how to wait.

FIFTEEN

Red and green lights passed by, the bright gold of the glowing high-rises behind them. The night was heavy with heat, but Wolfe had the windows down, the AC blowing, inviting in the sounds and smells of the South Beach night. Something was near the surface, in the air of the place. Something was close to poking its ugly little head up and proclaiming the murderer as clearly as church-bells on a Sunday morning.

But not yet. Not just yet.

The afternoon was long gone, evening ageing, and the thrum of night in restless waking.

He pulled the car up into a space just as the previous occupant pulled away. He stepped out and walked toward a pair of phone booths a little ahead. To his left, a meandering cliff-face of concrete and glass rose, its base ringed with hot lights, blaring music, cow bells, bongos, guitars, and throbbing dance music. Women in painted-on shorts and bikini tops thrust their hips to the music — and to the tourists — beckoning any and all into the packed bars behind them, calling, along with the rhythm, to the primal urges of the human instinct. And to the wish to belong. To be wanted. Part of the Tribe.

Wolfe passed them by.

To his right, the cool breeze of the Pacific brushed across his face, soothed his passions and called him to its darkness, to its cool refreshment and the vast permanence that is the sea. Shadows walked there, hand in hand in the trackless sands. Beach and city. City and beach. Each an alien existence to the other. Wolfe walked the thin, concrete line between those two worlds. Alone.

The police would have discovered his flight reservation by then and begun converging on the airport. They wouldn't know yet that he wasn't going to be there. He wouldn't be very popular once they had. But he wasn't now.

He dropped a quarter into the slot. Dialled. Jackson answered from his car.

"Hello?" the voice was cool, guarded.

"Hi. Any news?"

There was a brief pause. "Yes, there's news."

"Well?"

"I think it's time you came in."

"Yeah?"

"It's not a warrant yet, but they want you as a person of interest in the disappearance of Ana. You were the last one to see her."

"Not the last."

"Will you come in?"

"To you?"

"Delaney, technically, but I can be there."

"Any chance of a look at the police file first?"

"The kid?"

"Ana too... all of it."

"That a condition?"

"If it helps."

"Alright then. You come in, to see *me*. Don't give a name, just come right to the front desk and tell whoever's there you're my ten o'clock. I'll let them know you have some information but won't be giving your name. I'll tell Delaney ten-thirty."

"Make Delaney eleven. We might need to talk."

"Ten forty-five. I don't want to push things. I have a lot at stake here too."

"Fine."

"So you're coming in?"

"You'll know at ten."

"Good. Good. I'll hope to see you in an hour then."

Jackson was in his office, looking relieved. He led the priest into one of the interrogation rooms. When they entered, Jackson made sure that none of the recording equipment was on and slapped a thick file down on the little table, on top of a thin one that already rested there.

"Here they are," he said, "Douglas Kane's autopsy report. Ana's file."

'Kane,' Wolfe read the boy's family name as he flipped open the blue manila folder. The pages inside were tightly secured with aluminium tie-down plates. He left the papers secured and flipped through to the external examination and evidence of injury. He scanned for the bits he wanted, muttering them aloud to himself.

"Three puncture wounds on the back. No other signs of premortem injuries. Peri- or postmortem abrasions evident on the back, buttocks, and heels... consistent with dragging. Trace amounts of gypsum dust and flakes of green paint retrieved from clothing and sent for analysis."

He scanned the internal description and toxicology — cannabis and methamphetamine in his system — and the other lab tests, most of which he didn't understand. On the last page were a few brief paragraphs containing the M.E.'s summary. One section caught Wolfe's eye.

"The weapon is a ten to fifteen centimetre metal object, pointed at the end, such as a blunt knife or screwdriver. The assailant was likely behind the victim at the time of the first two strikes, the third being consistent with the body falling with a twisting motion. Any of the three could have been fatal. Death by stabbing."

"Anything ring a bell?" Jackson asked.

Wolfe shook his head. "Poor kid."

"Yeah."

He then took a look at Ana's report. Nothing much of interest there. Wolfe himself was named as a person of interest, which he already knew, and Pascal was listed as primary suspect, believed fled. There was a question mark in red ink in the margin beside Wolfe's name, crossed out then written in again.

The two men sat there, stared at the walls. Jackson at last grabbed the report, flipped it closed and tucked both of them under his arm.

"Delaney will be in in less than fifteen minutes. You need to watch out for him."

"I do?"

"He's a good cop, don't get me wrong, but that's the point. He likes you for Ana's disappearance and doesn't mind that you also have a connection to Kevin and to the church."

"I'm his pet suspect."

"You're his *only* suspect. He doesn't buy that Pascal shot at Ana, and your only alibi is that you were with her. Now that she's gone…"

"So is my alibi. Right." At some point, he had been a suspect, then not. That's why the first question mark had been crossed out. Then he had been placed back on the list. Could have been anything that brought him back under suspicion, but it may well have been because of Cruz being taken. He wondered if the hotel lobby had him on camera at the time.

"All I'm saying is be open with him, but careful."

"Open *and* careful…"

"Yeah, so much as it can be done."

"Well, there's no need for you to get in trouble too. Go get him, or call him… whatever. Let him know I came in early."

Jackson nodded, stood up and walked out of the room with the folder under his arm. Wolfe calmed his breathing, consciously relaxed his shoulders and neck, down his back, his legs.

He had need to focus here. He had need to be sharp. He had little doubt that he could keep the probing thoughts of Detective Delaney from getting anything concrete that could be used against him, but there was more potential to this interview: Delaney didn't think Pascal was guilty. That meant that he had more information than he was telling Jackson. It might be the same details that Wolfe had, or it might be more. This was a chance to find out.

Five minutes later, it began.

Delaney stepped into the room, smelling of sweat and coffee. Each puff of air brought the fragrance to Wolfe's nostrils, along with the slightly sickening thought that the air he now held in his lungs had shortly before been in the body of this leather-skinned, cynical homicide detective... and who-knows-where before that.

Delaney turned the chair backwards, dropped himself down into it, and leaned forward with his forearms on the backrest, legs spread wide on either side of it. Wolfe glanced down at the crotch, stretched tight by the fat legs, looking like the seams might split at any moment and the man's sweat-soaked genitalia burst out onto the chair.

Wolfe smiled a little at the morose thought of where his day had taken him.

"You like that, Father?"

"What's that?"

"My package. Made you smile. I'm asking if you like that kind of thing. Perverts and cock-sucking? Little boys?"

Wolfe's eyes narrowed. One didn't need to walk long in the midst of the abuse he had seen to develop a short fuse for that line of questioning.

"You know what I do for a living?"

"I know what they say you do. Watch kiddy porn, chase around the other Fathers in their black skirts. That your thing? Bet you have a list somewhere of the real sickos."

"You're a cop, Delaney, so I'll let that go this time, but if you expect to get anything in the way of information from me, anything at all, you'll change tack or I walk right out of here. I am here willingly, as you know, and nothing says I can't get up and walk away."

"You know, for now that's true, but I've got a gut, see" he leaned back and patted his bulbous pot-belly, "And my gut says there's something I don't like about you, Father Wolfe, that you and I might not get along. You know why that might be?"

"I should think it happens a lot, Detective, why should I be a special case."

Delaney's smile faded from his face. He leaned in again, taking a deep breath as if to control himself.

"Now you'll notice, *Father*, that I haven't arrested you. I haven't turned on the camera, or the tape. You know why that is?"

Wolfe didn't reply.

"How about you and I cut the bullshit, huh? I know you aren't a real priest anymore. I know you spend a lot of your time lookin' at sick shit and chasing faggots. What I want to know is: you go over to the other side once in a while? Just for a poke?" He thrust his finger forward in the air, "It's a serious question."

Wolfe shook his head. "You say I'm not a real priest," he said, "And you may be right, but you should know that I'm a real man, a former soldier, and was once a father — a real one, not a priest — and what you say offends me. I made a vow of peace to men and obedience to the church when I took on my orders... but I have limits to what I will tolerate, just like any man."

Delaney smiled, evidently pleased that he had broken through the skin a bit.

"So you're saying no... no poking little boys."

Wolfe shook his head.

"Priests?"

Shook his head again.

"You fuck Ana Cruz?"

The urge to stand up and knock Detective Alfred Delaney to the ground welled up in Wolfe's chest and it was all he could do to stay in his chair. All the same, his body leaned forward and his fingers twitched, betraying the urge to clench his fists. Delaney didn't miss any of it. He nodded, a little smile playing around the corners of his mouth and eyes.

"I see," he said, "But you wanted to. Obviously. Hey, I don't blame you," he said, holding his hands up in a gesture of peace, "The whole detachment wanted a piece of that, and lots of those are women! A fine piece of ass, Father... titty to write home about."

"Are you finished?"

The smile faded. A sharp blow of air through the nostrils: coffee fumes. A hint of tooth decay. "Why do you think your brother got killed?"

Wolfe thought a moment, adjusted his posture and stared back at Delaney.

"I have an idea for this little interrogation," he said.

Delaney's eyes went wide with mock surprise. "Really?! Well son-of-a-bitch, man, share, share."

"I answer your questions, truthfully, and you answer mine."

Now how is that fair when I'm the cop and you're the priest? Aren't you supposed to be listening, not asking questions?"

"If you're right, and that fat gut of yours knows something about my involvement that you don't, then I have something important to give. If I *have* done something wrong, if I'm guilty of what you think I am, what could you tell me that I don't already know? Where would be the harm in the trade? An honest trade?"

He pondered the proposal. "Alright, I go first..."

"You already went first," Wolfe cut him off, "With your stupidity about me buggering young boys. It's my turn. What do you know about the priests at Saint Mary's? Are any of them capable of making the bomb that hit my rooms?"

"Now that's two questions, which one would you like to know?"

"The second."

"Then the answer is yes. My turn. Where did you spend the hours between six yesterday morning and now?"

"You didn't answer my question."

"You're a smart man, I think you'll find I did. It's your turn now, or we're done this little game. Where were you?"

"Airport, rental car agency, Ana's apartment, diner, driving around, and here. Which priest?"

"Any of them, they're all educated men and any precocious fourteen-year-old with an internet connection could have made that thing — with the right materials. Do you know where Ana Cruz is now?"

"No..." Wolfe was about to ask which priest might have access to the materials, when a different, more pressing compulsion welled up. "Do you?"

Delaney paused. He looked at Wolfe a little sideways, his eyebrows drawing together and his mind working hard at what he heard and saw. "You really don't." It wasn't a question.

"No, I don't."

"And Pascal?"

Wolfe shook his head.

"Well I'll be god-damned if I don't believe you. I guess we're done here — for now."

"Wait, I'm not finished."

"And yet that's not your call to make. You're free to go, like you said."

"About my brother, just tell me one thing."

Delaney paused and raised his eyebrows.

"Do you have any leads, any information at all on who killed him… or why?"

The detective shook his head, pulled his belt up tight under his belly, and left the room. Wolfe sat down again, not yet ready to leave. A few moments later, Jackson knocked on the door and entered.

"I thought you might be waiting for me before you left," he said.

"No. Just taking a minute."

"It went well I gather. He's not keeping you."

"I suppose it went well. I found out what I needed to know."

"Well," Jackson grinned, "That's more than most get when they're the ones being interrogated." Wolfe didn't react and the smile faded from the young cop's face. "Look, at least they aren't holding you on suspicion of murder or kidnapping, that's good."

"It's not good enough."

"What would be? You just lost your brother, you should expect a tough time."

"It's not that," Wolfe said, "it's not being able to do anything about it. He's lying there, in my head, skull smashed in on the floor in front of an altar. When I daydream about it he turns his head to me and kind of smiles. 'Find him, Danny-boy,' he says, 'Find the son-of-a-bitch.' But I haven't, Billy, and I won't — not the way I've been doing it."

"What do you mean, 'the way you're doing it?' You're not a cop, you can't do anything more than you have been."

"Yes, I can. I can do a lot more."

"Don't get involved that way. Don't do it. You're a priest, not a cop, I don't care what kind of investigating you do within the church, you'll get arrested for it out here. Or worse. Stay back. It's probably at least as much my fault as yours, feeding you information and keeping you in the loop, but I did it for Kevin. I won't anymore though, no more. Kevin wouldn't want you mixed up in it like this."

"Yes, he would."

"With all due respect, I've known Kevin — I *knew* Kevin — for a lot longer than you did, brothers or not, and I can guarantee you that he wouldn't want to see you in a cage, or worse, for doing something that the police will do anyway. He wouldn't. You know it."

"And what else would he expect me to do?"

"Do what you're supposed to do. You're a priest: pray."

"Now we both know better than to think that's what he had want."

"I'm asking you — and I'm telling you. Please, stay out of it from now on."

Wolfe got up from the table, shook Jackson's reluctant hand, and walked from the station without answering.

Wolfe picked up a new key card at the front desk and went up to his room. There was no police tape up on door, and there was no guard. Delaney probably pulled them the moment he decided Wolfe didn't have Cruz. He stepped through the doorway and straight to the bed. The pain in his ribs was less sharp than it had been, so maybe they were already starting to heal. Or maybe it was the drink or two he had had at lunch. He lowered his head onto the soft pillow and closed his eyes. Kevin was there, pale against the red-black pool of blood congealing on the floor in front of the altar, the saints staring down, mute and bound from speech as if by the sanctity of confession. All of them staring, staring at the priest in his black shirt and white collar, a sniper rifle strapped across his back. He imagined blood on his hands, his wrists, his face. Some terrifying kind of stigmata.

In the darkness of his room, Daniel Wolfe pulled a pillow up over his face and howled his jagged rage into the softness of it, muffling the sound from any physical listener.

Again.

Again.

And once more his soul cried out with words his mind could not express: a shuddering, primeval prayer for Emilio Pascal. For Ana Cruz. Most of all for his dead brother. Then he let the pillow fall to the side, wet with saliva and tears, his face worn and blank, staring at the ceiling in the darkness, pleading for some answer he could hear, some inner voice not his own.

But there was nothing.

And then another figure entered the imagined space. A woman. In pain. Suffering, like the Somalian girl, in the hands of the wicked... the deranged. Waiting — waiting in a deep, cold darkness of her own.

SIXTEEN

Shiny black shoes stepped one after the other down the thick wooden stairs. The wearer was below ground, in the thick darkness of a concrete basement, high-ceilinged and capped with tin ducts and heavy cast-iron pipes running the length and width of the structure, secured to the ceiling with dust-caked steel brackets. The only sound, aside from his own footfalls, was the steady, echoing drip in the darkness.

He reached the bottom of the stairs and pulled a black balaclava over his face. To this he added sunglasses, a light tint, just enough to see in the electric lantern light without revealing his eyes.

With one of his gloved hands, he pulled a pistol, an antique Walther P-38, from his trouser pocket. He tucked it into his belt at the back. In his other hand was a white paper bag with grease-spots working their way through the bottom.

He was ready.

He stepped across a jack-hammered sump hole in the floor and through a rough, wooden doorway into the main room. Boxes lined one side of the lower level and, above him, running like balconies around the perimeter, catwalks of aluminium mesh could be partially seen in the faint light. Bits of discarded construction material littered the floor. In the farthest corner sat Ana Cruz.

Her area had been hastily swept clear of debris, the wall brushed clean of cobwebs and any loose bits of brick or pipework. A blanket was spread on the floor like a rug, with a single, military-style cot laid out against the wall, amply covered in an assortment of blankets and with a thick pillow at one end. It had been all set up when the man had dragged her down the stairs into the dark basement, as if someone had been there before her. But whoever that was, they were not there anymore. It was only Cruz, and the man with the greasy paper bags.

Beside her was another white bag, this one empty except for the Styrofoam shells of the take-out dishes and a few others, from previous meals, crumpled on the ground at the edge of the rug.

As he neared the woman, a motor kicked in somewhere in a distant room, a sump pump that ran like the air conditioner in her apartment, running in unnoticed cycles throughout the twenty-four hours of the day, pulling the dark puddle of water from the hole by the door and depositing it in the sewer system beside the building, a never-ending fight against the seeping waters of the ocean and the Everglades. A common, mundane thing. Here though, in the black and silence, she jumped at each sudden *thrum* of sound. Each interruption a shock in the otherwise unpunctuated stillness and captivity. It covered the silence, covered the approach of whatever unseen terror might creep its way through the darkness as she slept. And so she seldom did. She held on to every shred of consciousness, fighting the sensory deprivation, until exertion took hold and she lay a long time, only nightmares and foraging visitors startling her from the unwilling rest.

"You should take them with you," she said to the man as he entered and she pointed to the bag on the floor, "The rats — I think it's rats — are attracted by the smell."

"There are no rats in here," the man said, his voice gruff and severe.

"Tell that to the rats." She was bold, acting as if she were unafraid, though in truth her legs shook whenever the man was there. She could smell the fear in her own sweat. Could he? Over the damp air? The stench of the urine and faeces in the plastic bucket?

She had been surprised by the man in the hotel suite. She had heard the door opening and closing, and thought it might be Wolfe coming back. She had walked out of the bedroom, running a towel over her hair to dry it a bit before pulling it back into a ponytail. She had seen a hint of him below the towel as she ruffled it through her hair, and in the moment it took to register something amiss and lift up her eyes, he was ready for her. She was not ready for him. In retrospect, she decided that he had seemed as surprised by her presence as she had been at his.

She had reacted in an instant, but the man had a head start on her, a moment of early realisation. She tried a trick to knock an attacker's arms to the sides and clap the ears: a stun-blow.

It hadn't worked.

Her hands had clapped together just as a heavy blow landed on her sternum, stunning her before another one landed alongside her head. It had hurt a lot. It still hurt. The side of her face was swollen, and she was sure she had a nasty bruise on her chest... wasn't about to check it when this bastard was in the room. It was dark the rest of the time.

She had bent forward after the impact, winded and surprised, and there her memory ended. She woke up in the dark basement of some large, empty building, a headache like there was a tiny horse trying to kick its way out of her skull, and a throbbing pain each time she breathed too deeply.

He had surprised her, outfought her even, a trained police officer with two older brothers and a boyfriend or two in her past who'd gotten rude awakenings when they had tried to put hands on her in anger.

This one though, he had won. Everybody gets lucky now and then. Maybe that was his time. If he ever let himself get close enough, she decided, she would make sure he would never get that lucky again.

But in the meantime she felt useless. Defeated and small. Female in all of the ways used against her as a kid, when her dad had wanted a son, when teams were picked on the playing field at lunchtime, and when coed obstacle runs were staged at the academy. She loved being a woman, most of the time, but hated those attributes that made her weaker in a fight. She hated herself for hating them.

He had done her no other harm, except to cuff her ankle to a pipe set into the concrete wall and leave her there, alone, with whatever rodents wandered the floors in the darkness. She had no weapons. She had no phone. She had no watch. Time did not exist and yet she was aware of each disembodied second as if it were her last. Counting, silently in the darkness, waiting for the unknown.

The man came in, occasionally — she had no reliable way of knowing how often — and brought her food, greasy take-out and soda. He had brought a second bag in, the first time, taken it off to where a thick metal door stood, built into the concrete wall about halfway between her area and the opening with the hole in the floor. Whatever was on the other side of it, haunted him. The last couple of times he had gone in, but had taken no white bag. He seemed troubled by the room, often glancing over to it and then back to her. It made the skin draw tight across her face and her heart feel like it was skipping.

Survival depended on keeping her wits and looking for opportunities. It probably also depended on somebody from the outside being able to find her. She determined to spend her time gathering as much intelligence as she could, as much identifying information on the man and the place as she could discern or draw out from him. She also needed to test his intentions, to find out what kind of danger she was really in.

She began with one of the few interactions they had: the greasy food bags. They had been from McDonald's at first, but she had asked him instead for something else. The next meal was from Sonic. Still greasy, but compliant with her request. The man had not refused. He had not threatened her. He had not hurt her.

And so she was bold.

"You need to let me go."

The man looked at her through his tinted glasses. She memorised the way he moved, his height, the length of his strides, every minute detail she could discern of his clothing in the dim light.

He seemed to study her, as well.

"Be quiet."

He had altered his voice. Whispered, though no one was around to overhear them.

She knew him then. Somehow.

And "be quiet," he had said, not 'shut up' or 'shut up bitch,' but "be quiet." She didn't know if this second thing was a good sign: a gentle man, a soft heart, taking her out of necessity, when she had surprised him in the midst of a burglary… or if it was a bad sign: *a quiet man, seemed normal, not an enemy in the world, shocking that he could be capable of such a thing, such a sick thing…*

"I need my inhaler. If I don't have it, I will get sick. It's not a maybe, it's just time. It will happen."

He didn't answer.

"I'm not lying to you. I take one puff almost every day, then another when it gets bad. If I don't take the everyday one, it is only time. It *is* coming — I could die."

The man looked at her a moment, thoughtful, glanced again at the metal door and then dropped the food at her feet, without coming close enough for her to kick, or grab, or take a swing at him. Then he turned around.

"I'm not joking, you sick bastard! I will *die* without my inhaler! You want a cop-killing on your hands? You won't live out the month." It then occurred to her that he may already have a cop-killing on his hands. The realisation stilled her rage, and a chill dropped like a damp blanket, cool on her back and shoulders.

He paid her no heed, but instead walked across the room, toward the metal door and paused there to peer into the little window. He reached into his pocket and pulled out a small flashlight — her service flashlight, she realised, or one just like it — and clicked it on, aiming the beam through the small square of glass. He clicked it off, opened the door and entered. She heard nothing for a while, then thought she could pick up stifled weeping. Before she was certain, all was quiet again.

They were following him. He couldn't be quite sure who 'they' were, but there was no mistake. No easy task, as a general rule, following Danny Wolfe; the priest had a heavy foot, and a growing sheaf of speeding fines to prove it.

234

He had slept in, holed up in a little motel near Homestead, just south of Miami, paranoid that every passing set of footfalls, every slam of a car door, was another unseen attack. Worse were the unfamiliar hums and tics, the creaks and whirs of the ageing AC unit perched precariously on the window sill, the light scuttle of a palmetto cockroach across the bathroom tiles. The distant bark of a dog.

Unsettled sleep had come reluctantly, and just before the rising of the sun. He had awakened feeling weary, and washed away the fruitless night with a lukewarm shower. How, in a place where the sun burnt down with relentless fury, could the water remain so tepid, despite ostensive efforts at heating it? He missed the places Grippe arranged for him: quiet and well-equipped — even if they did sometimes explode.

He returned to the car, grabbed breakfast at a fruit and yogurt kiosk, and made his way back northward, into the bustling city itself. That's when he had seen them, sometimes just a little too close and, after a while, there just a little too long.

Wolfe couldn't say with any confidence if it was the police, or some minion of the pedophilia producers he had been hunting, or someone having something to do with Kevin's death. Maybe the latter two in one. He didn't like the idea though, regardless of who it was. Someone had already tried to kill him once, likely a second time when Cruz was taken, and he had no intention of letting them continue as his tail. But first he needed to find out just how good they were. With any luck, they'd been up half the night too, keeping an eye on his room and motionless car.

There is a figure, in literature and film, a figure that every priest is familiar with, as it is as much a part of their history as slavery is to the American psyche: that of the Jesuit spy. There are still Jesuit priests, the current pope even, was of a Jesuit order, and most are good and honest men, so it seems, but the medieval image of the backroom, black-cloaked strategist persists. He is a master manipulator, a stealthy hearer of secrets and a mysterious tool of the faceless authorities above him, a walker of empty hallways and a seer of covered-over things. Though not a Jesuit himself, Daniel Wolfe was just such a man, and his skills in the world of intelligence and counter-intelligence were sharp.

He had noticed the car two turns back: a blue Chevy Malibu with a man driving and a woman in the passenger seat. He hadn't made any peculiar turns yet, just picked a destination at random — the Bayside shopping area — and drove in that direction. The car remained in the lane it was in, one left of his, thirty yards back from Wolfe's car.

If their lane was a forced turn, or traffic slowed in one stream or the other, then they signalled and pulled in behind him, with two or three cars between. When he slowed his speed slightly, they hung back. When he sped up or overtook another vehicle, they waited a few moments. Maybe forty yards back. Then a creep forward, returning to a comfortable thirty yards: too far to be obvious, too close to lose the target, even in heavy traffic.

He was certain: he was being followed.

He stepped on the gas a little, deciding to have some fun with his new companions without being too obvious, and pulled out into the centre lane... the turning lane. The car behind him signalled to do the same. He then turned back into the former lane, skipping the turnout and acting as though he had started too early. The Malibu maintained its line, despite its flashing signal, and skipped the turn as well. It earned them a wailing horn from behind and a gesture Wolfe wanted all-too-much to give them himself. He then drifted over into the next turnout, last-moment, and pulled onto Highway One. A small-but-busy corridor. Lots of lights.

The Malibu did the same.

He had seen better tails, but the people behind him were not amateurs. Had he not known they were there, nothing they had done would have stuck out as particularly strange — not in Miami's frantic, unpredictable traffic. Had his manoeuvres been more obvious, he had no doubt, they would have taken measures to hang back further, take a few more chances, or maybe hand him off to another observer.

This last was tricky: it was hard enough to spot one tail in busy traffic. If there were a team on him, they could make it next to impossible to figure out which of the thousands of people walking the sidewalks and driving the roads were the ones tracking his progress. It would take a major team though, and a good one. These two didn't peel off when he had started his play, so maybe they were alone. Or maybe they were optimists.

Kevin's death was a cop-killing, so they'd take that seriously, and Ana's disappearance wouldn't help him to look less guilty in their eyes. But Delaney didn't think it was Wolfe. Delaney had let him go. If the cop thought him innocent, then he wouldn't have put a whole team on him, that was for sure... Unless he had let him go on purpose, in the hopes that the priest would lead police forces to where he had hidden the girl. False confidence... then a trap.

Wolfe had some investigation of his own to do. He had an idea that might led him to Cruz, but he needed to confirm a couple of things first. If he was right, he would need to get in there, quick and without any kind of warning, and put himself between Kevin's killer and Ana Cruz. He was pretty confident that she was still alive, and didn't want a clumsy police presence messing that up. He could do it himself, but not with a tail.

He couldn't do much about it if they were police following him, except for losing them, which he was fairly certain he could do if he found the right conditions. The problem lay in the possibility that they were not police, that they were instead in the employ of the person or persons who wanted him dead, perhaps the same ones who had killed Kevin and killed or held Cruz and Pascal.

If the latter were the case, he couldn't just lose them, he needed to get his hands on them, to hammer his way through to their employer if he could. Something in this said "cops," but he had to make sure. He breathed out something like a curse, or a prayer — it was getting difficult to tell which.

As he neared the stadium, he saw what he was looking for: Bayside Marina and Shopping Plaza.

He pulled into the lane which led to the paid parking area and glanced in his side-view mirror to see the Malibu do the same. For his twenty bucks, the attendant handed him a ticket from the dispenser and Wolfe pulled through the parking garage, to the far end. The tail entered and drove the other way, across the lot closest to the mall entrance. They cruised to a stop and idled there, set apart from the main traffic, but still with a clear view of the main entrances. Wolfe backed into a parking space near the vehicle exit. The parking area was about half full. People walked back and forth from the mail entrance. A small group of young men lounged around near the mall, pulling tricks on skateboards and taking videos with their phones. All tattoos, piercings, and youth. Wolfe wondered what he had been doing at that age. Probably boot camp. It seemed an eternity ago.

He pulled a short stack of twenties from his emergency kit and tucked them into his wallet. He then walked casually into the shopping concourse area as if he had the whole afternoon to waste.

It was busy, but not as crowded as he had hoped it would be. Wolfe was sure that at least one of the people in the car would follow him in, and hoped the other would hang back, ready to go, ensuring that their quarry didn't get back to his car and leave the parking area if they should lose sight of him for a while inside. As much as he would have preferred more crowd, the lack of people had its advantages too: once on foot his tail had to fall back a long way to stay inconspicuous.

He maintained the casual stroll at first, but made a couple of abrupt stops, as if something in a store window or booth had caught his eye. He even picked up a pair of shorts with hot pink flamingos on them, as if he were interested, just to toy with the tail a little and try to catch a glimpse of which one followed him. He dared a quick glance.

The guy. Good, he had hoped so. The woman was in her forties, he guessed, probably had teen-aged sons, or daughters who brought young men around the house. Wolfe hoped her maternal instinct was good and strong. He hoped the young men were a handful. They usually were.

He walked again, a little faster this time. His tail hanging back, keeping a good distance between them, maybe getting a little suspicious. Wolfe found what he was looking for then, a small group of tourists, a couple of them big, tall men, heading for one of the narrow cross-hallways of the complex. He upped his pace a little and slipped in ahead of them.

The moment he rounded the corner into the narrow connector hall, he burst into a run and almost dove around the corner at the other end, not daring to look behind him, and hoped that his follower had reached the hallway too late to see him double back toward the parking area. If all went as planned, the line of sight would be blocked by the tourists, at least for a few moments, and the delay might be enough to make the guy hesitate, avoid a scene, to maintain his cover and look around for a minute or two — just long enough.

Down the mall on the far side of the connector, Wolfe walked with all the inconspicuous speed he could muster. He ducked through the food fair and down a short stairway to a sidewalk running the length of the building between a freshly-painted cement block wall and the parking area. He saw the small knot of young men, hanging around the entrance to the shopping area.

"Hey," he said, "Wanna make a hundred bucks?"

Detective Eloise Mason sat in the car, gazing off toward the plaza entrance and feeling the cool draft of the air conditioner against her face. "Hot as Hades," she said to herself, "Glad I'm not the one running around the marina today." The radio was on, and she was muttering along with the lyrics as best she could, enjoying the playful rhythm of the song.

She was, as Wolfe had hoped, a mother with teen-aged children: two boys and a girl. Peter was almost twenty and more than a handful. It had been all she could do to keep him from getting caught up in all the crap that goes on in the schools these days.

Then there was William, thirteen going on thirty, and involved in a fight last week at a soccer game of all places. He was only in soccer because she didn't like the violence of football. She still didn't know if he would be kicked off of the team — it seemed to her that the other boy had started it.

Then she saw them. Three young men, not much older than Peter, she guessed, walking out of the plaza entrance with wide grins on their faces. Cats with canaries; she knew the look. A moment later, another ran out, leaping onto the back of the biggest guy there, shouting obscenities and seemingly beating him about the head with his one fist and elbow while the other arm hung on for dear life. The big kid had a tattoo on his neck — maybe gang-related. It was so hard to tell these days, with the hip-hop and the tattoos on every second kid on the street. As he toppled to the ground behind a car, the attacker still on his shoulders, the two other kids jumped in as if they were kicking at one or the other youth on the ground. It was too much, surveillance or no surveillance.

She pushed the car door open and jumped out, ran across the lot, palming her badge as she did so and drawing her sidearm.

"Police! Show me your hands! Show me your hands!"

Both of the youths who were still standing shot their arms up in the air, followed soon after by the two on the ground. All she saw were fingers and wide eyes. No one was smiling anymore, nor were there any signs of blood or injury on any of them.

"What the hell's going on here?"

"Hey no problem, no problem lady, we're just fooling around!" The speaker was the big one with the tattoo.

"Fooling around?"

"Yeah," a second said. The apparent attacker.

"Why the fuck are you jumping around here like gang-bangers? You know that can get you killed?"

"It was just a joke, I swear, your partner said to act like we were fighting, that's all!"

"My partner?"

"Yeah, the other cop."

"Where?" Her eyes shot over to the empty space where the little blue rental car had been. She felt her gut tighten.

The one with the tattoo on his neck pointed to a vehicle that paused by the exit booth. "That one," he said. Wolfe looked back at her from the car, pressed down the pedal, and sped off into the congestion of downtown Miami. The only way they'd find him now is if they knew where he was going already.

She holstered her gun and walked back to the car. The priest was in the wind, and what made it worse was she was sure she had seen the smug bastard shrug as he looked at her. Delaney was going to eat her alive.

Wolfe parked down a side street a few blocks from the church. He didn't want a repeat of his last visit, when the local boy had taken it upon himself to defend Father Gonzales. Nor did he want to pick up his police tail again. This trip would be all about stealth. Besides, his intention wasn't with the interior of the church this time, nor with anyone in it. What he was interested in for the moment was what might be parked outside of it. The freshly painted wall by the mall parking lot had tweaked something in his mind. Given him an idea.

He crept around the corner of the building, near the back, and stepped through the thick grass to the rear of the churchyard. The stiff, green blades were too long, someone within had been remiss. But then who could really blame them for letting the grass grow a bit, considering the circumstances? Busy week.

He paused before moving out onto the gravel. He had not spent much time, lately, with his feet in the grass and it felt good, soothing somehow, to be standing on a wide carpet of living thing. It felt connected. He could smell the earthiness of the grass and, under different conditions, would have taken his shoes off and lingered a while. The flower bed to his left, overgrowing with fragrant weeds, sent up a sickly-sweet smell. The heat was starting to waver. The sun getting low in the sky. As it began to cool, there was a hopeful current in the air. Not yet comfortable, but it held some promise. The relief of evening and the breaking of the Miami heat.

The mosquitoes would be out soon.

He heard a door slam and crouched low against the building. No one would have reason to come back there, unless someone finally decided to care for the lawn, but Wolfe doubted they would. Sure enough, a few moments later he heard the slight scrape of the steel door sliding on its hinges and clunking against its metal frame. He moved.

He crept out toward the parking area, the gravel crunching beneath his feet as he went. No degree of stealth hid that sound. The best he could do was to stay low, stay behind something, and finish what he had come to do as soon as possible.

The first thing he did was creep around to the front of the van and feel for heat on the small hood. There was no need, he could see the radiating warmth in the air before his hand ever touched the metal. Good. That meant that whoever had closed the door had just returned from somewhere. It meant that they were less likely to come right back out again.

He peeked through the front of the van, leaning up over the hood and trying to get a good look at the cargo bed. No good, it was too dark already to penetrate the shadowy interior. He moved around to the back to see if he could make it out from the rear windows, but that was no good either. The tinting was too strong to make out colours. Dimness over dark hues, nothing more precise than that. He tried the doors. Locked.

He thought he heard a noise behind him, toward the door. A quick look.

Nothing.

Nothing? Had he seen it, a shape in the little pane of wired glass, ducking out of sight?

Something else, maybe. One of the phantoms at the edge of one's sight that tricks the mind and harasses the heart, the kind that comes more at night and with fuller shapes than in the daylight. More with guilt and feelings of powerlessness. He shrugged it off as imagination, but moved to the far side of the van nonetheless, out of sight of the tiny window in the door.

He dug into his pocket for the key to his car and scraped it slowly and firmly along the bottom edge of the van's rear panel. The dark blue paint came off in flakes that curled back on themselves before breaking off. Beneath the blue was a thick layer of green. New community centre. New name. New look.

New paint for the van.

He pocketed the flakes and stood up again. There was one other thing he needed to check, and he wanted privacy to do it. Not trusting the steel door by the parking area, he instead decided to risk something a little bolder.

He rounded the wall, back the way he had come, until he reached the front corner of the building, where the wheelchair ramp doubled-back in its rise to the top of the front steps. He sat on the low wall and swung his legs over it, feeling the gritty texture of the bricks beneath his hands. He rubbed his palms together to free the little particles of rock and mortar and walked straight up to the front doors of the church.

He stepped through the door, all calm industry, just like any other priest at any other church on any other errand.

He had been in a thousand of these buildings, each one striving in its own way for architectural identity within the confines of ecclesiastical purpose and community expectation. Each one leapt at the styles of an era: field stone or red brick walls, some covered in dark, rich woods, other times in light, Nordic slats cut in with open squares for art, or banners. Seventies contemporary, just a little behind the hippie movement, catching onto the fading, respectable end of it, with a partial grip already on the pendulum swing back to conservatism and a tighter gaze on tradition.

Some tended to collect artefacts of ages past: icons and coat racks, heavy cabinets for the new, thin pamphlets that let everyone know the times and places of picnics and bake-sales and clothing drive drop-off points. Soon these would be gone and it would all be apps and links.

But despite the myriad faces, beneath it all were the same solid bones of centuries past, the anatomy of a faith laid over the necessity of a congregation. South Florida was no exception, except that the skeleton would most often be on its head, or reclining across the lot, the high water table often demanding upper stories or side expansions in the place of basements.

He stepped off to the side and down the hallway that he knew would be there. The passage ran alongside the sanctuary, opposite the bank of offices. He knew that the priests would likely be at their desks and telephones upstairs, if they were there at all, and that the classrooms, the lair of Sunday Schools and floor-hockey and first kisses in shadowy corners, would be empty but for the resting flannel-graphs, old TVs and the stored flotsam and jetsam of the See of Peter.

At the end of the hall, the kitchen had the same things all such kitchens had, two stoves, two fridges, a deep-freeze with a tablecloth laid neatly over it, and plenty of counter space. Behind it was what he had hoped to find: a narrow wooden door. He opened it and stepped into the vestry.

The little room was windowless and accessed by three doors. One would lead to a staircase, to the offices of the priests on the second floor. The second was the one through which Wolfe had entered, and the third gave access to the nave. The walls were otherwise lined with tall cabinets, each holding the tools of the priesthood: candles, wine cups and boxes of the thin wafers for Eucharist, and the draping ceremonial robes for more formal services. The vestments hung on wire hangers in plastic dry-cleaning bags, another symbol of spiritual sanctity stripped bare before the eyes of the priests. On a low cabinet near the door sat the other item he needed... the telephone.

Wolfe went straight to it and smiled to see the numbers for each of the five church telephone lines neatly printed in the white tabs beside the buttons. It was the diligent service of the humble: everything just so. He picked up the receiver, pressed line three, and dialled the number listed for line one.

A woman answered. "Hello, Saint Mary of the Sea, how may I help you today?"

"Hello," he said in a voice just above that of a whisper, "May I speak to Father Gonzales, please?"

"I'll see if he's in. May I ask who's calling?"

"It's Father Wolfe," he said, "on behalf of the Vatican." This last was for her benefit. That word, "Vatican," in all its ancient glory and terror, was like a magic spell in places like this. He would be viewed as an emissary from the pope himself, a kind of angel or saint, and if Father Gonzales did not answer his phone she would go and find him until she knew he had. Faith demanded it.

But Father Gonzales would not take it the same way. If she passed that detail on to him, and Wolfe knew she would, in hushed tones even, the old priest would take it as a sign of pride, condescension. Even a territorial challenge. Wolfe would have some reparations to make, perhaps, before the old man did what he wanted him to do. But in the end he would do it. Vocational conscience demanded it.

"Hello? What is it Father Wolfe? I have a busy day."

"I'm sorry Father Gonzales. It is important that I speak to you. *With* you."

"What about?"

"About many things, things I don't want to get into on the phone."

"I can make an appointment, perhaps tomorrow around lunchtime?"

"No — I mean — It's very important... Father..."

"Yes?" Wolfe could hear the old man's voice gaining interest, skepticism and suspicion waning.

"You're a priest, Father Gonzales? A true priest?"

"Of course! Have you called just to insult me again?"

"No, no, I-" he let his voice falter there, crack a little. It was surprisingly easy to be convincing. "I need to talk to a *real* priest... about Kevin," this turn of topic surprised even Wolfe as he let the words come out on their own. He wouldn't have used his brother's death as a tool to manipulate the old priest. And yet the words had left his mouth, and yet more followed them. "I have some concerns about that night."

"You needn't, though I'm glad you've come forward in some penitence. Father Pascal performed a second rite on your brother's behalf, in the morgue, I believe. Your brother's soul is at rest, if his conscience was clear."

"If his conscience was clear," Wolfe repeated. "And my conscience, Father? Are you willing to hear mine?"

"To hear your confession?"

"Such as it is."

"You know that confession has its power only for the penitent man, the man with an intention to turn from his previous folly and walk the proper path."

"Can you meet me in front of the church?"

"In front? Why? Come into my office, we can talk alone here. It is far from the other offices for that reason, among others. I like my silence and my privacy when I work."

"Please, just meet me in front and maybe I'll come in, or we could go somewhere to talk, a café maybe, or a park."

"I am a busy man, Father, as I said. My day cannot be completely rearranged."

Wolfe made no answer. The wait became long.

"Okay," Gonzales said at last and with a long sigh, "I'll meet you out front and we can discuss location then.

I still think my office best, but perhaps there you can tell me your reasons against it. The young man who was here before is not here today, if that is your concern. His visits are sporadic at best, whenever his mother can drag him here to see me. A good boy, maybe, deep down, but he is in a bad place. A not uncommon problem."

"I'll be out front in five minutes, Father, thank you so much."

"Very well then, I'll be there."

The old priest hung up the phone and Wolfe waited a short while after, allowing the third line to remain lit a little longer. Habitual caution. He then set the phone at rest and moved over to the dark wooden door that opened off to the side and behind the altar, behind the granite stone slabs on which his brother had died. Like hiding behind a grave marker.

And also just behind the offices of Father Jésus Gonzales.

A few minutes later, when he heard the faint slap of footsteps across the nave floor, from there fading to the front of the church, he peeked out of the door used by each serving priest, waiting to admonish, to baptise, to confirm... Or waiting for the senior priest to leave his office unattended, for just one quick look around.

As he slipped through and into the nave, Wolfe had one fleeting doubt: that the old man might have left the nave door to his office locked. He wouldn't be able to use the other one without increasing his chance of being seen by the secretary — and even then, it would likely be locked as well, if Gonzales had taken the time to lock this one. No time to pick it either. Not without a high risk of being caught in the act.

His hand reached for the brass knob. It turned. The door opened.

He stepped straight over to the desk and began shifting papers this way and that, seeking anything that might be lost beneath them. He checked the oak board at the head of the desk, the one with the holes for two gold pens, both filled, the tiny metal basket for paper clips and eraser nubs, and a small, oblong hole... with nothing in it. The nameplate shone out in gold plate against the dark-stained wood, hiding behind it almost everything that belonged.

But the item he sought was not there.

Stepping over to the padded chair, he dropped to his belly on the thick carpet and looked beneath the desk. Nothing but an old Bic ballpoint, dropped, no-doubt, since the last time the cleaning had been done. Nowhere, despite the expensive desk set, was the gold-plated letter-opener that went with it. In the trash can were envelopes on top, torn open by hand, but others, lower down, slit neatly at the end, as if with the perfect tool for the job.

It had been there in the office, and not so very long ago.

Footsteps. A doorknob turning.

He pulled his feet up close and lay there, his head in the foot-well of the desk and his hips and feet, hopefully, covered by the bulk of the chair. The door opened and he watched the flat-heeled shoes of the secretary step through and over to the desk. A shuffle of papers. A muttered word or two in whispers to herself, and the woman turned back toward the door and out once again, humming an unidentifiable hymn as she walked.

Wolfe let out his breath.

He rose to his feet and reached for the phone on the desk, pressed the button for line two and dialled again. He made his apologies to the woman on the other end and cancelled his meeting with Father Gonzales. A moment's pause to let her leave her desk... He then left the room, turned through the metal door, out onto the landing in the deepening dusk, down the street toward his car. Other walkers were coming, gathering at the church that night. He was quickly lost in the scattered movements of people on their way to seek the Pearl of Great Price — but Wolfe felt he had already found his. Without a doubt in his mind he was convinced that one of the priests had killed his brother. Without a doubt, too, he knew that one of them had killed Douglas, possibly right there in Gonzales's office, and the same person or persons likely had Cruz and Pascal, too. He pictured the pair in his head, and they were alive, always alive.

He needed to get what he knew to Jackson, to have them seize the van and let the CSI techs at it. Then Delaney would unleash his own authority to get schedules, alibis, statements. It would be a great, deep stir of this place, and maybe among the resulting heap, the key piece of the puzzle would be found.

He had parked on a side street, tree-lined and away from too much church-related foot traffic. He reached his car and pulled out his keys, looking down at his pocket as he did so, careful to keep the paint flakes secure inside.

It was the look down that did it. Just a moment too slow, a fraction of an inch behind in his reaction. Something hard and unforgiving whacked against the crown of his head. He slumped against the side of the car, arresting his fall part-way down, mental fingernails clawing at consciousness, at sight, trying from the depth of his guts to see the figure that loomed up beside him.

He saw the black shape, silhouetted by the streetlamp above and behind it, and dark in the cloak of its own shadow and the swirling red clouds of his coming faint. Wolfe thought, just for a moment, that he saw a grim smile.

His knees buckled and he slid into darkness.

SEVENTEEN

His grandfather was there, the odour of pipe tobacco clinging to his undershirt, that strong, man-smell of an earlier generation, so assaulting to a child, and yet full of comfort. Strangeness.

The man wrapped the boy's soft fingers around the handle of the gun, a 38 Special, Police Revolver. "Like this, Danny. Here. Yup, that's right. Cup the other hand under here. Hold hard. Good. Set your feet apart, shoulder-width."

The boy glanced down at his feet, shuffled them to the sides of the orange-crate on which he stood and set them, firm.

"There you go boy, a *natural*. Okay, now pay attention, this is serious. Stretch your arms out. Solid? Good. Look down the barrel now, line up the sights, same as we did at home. See it?"

"Yes, Grandad."

"Okay then, slow your breathing. Nice and deep. Steady. Breath it in, then relax. When it's about half-way out, hold your breath, just for a moment, and squeeeeze…"

The boy breathed in, calmed himself in the scent of his grandfather's guarding presence, and let the air slowly flow out of his lungs.

A stop.

A moment.

Squeeze.

It was like being awakened by a mud-caked shoe to the head. One moment his world was small again, secure and familiar, the next it was stabbing pain, piercing lights, blurry vision. The ground bumped once beneath him, hard, then it seemed as if the world tilted sideways and, had it not been for the broad straps across his chest and thighs, he was sure he had have rolled to the floor. Everything spun, like the whole planet did a barrel roll.

"Father Wolfe?" a voice said, "Daniel?"

He looked up, struggling to focus his eyes in the bright light. A tiny globe of light swept across his vision and his eyes darted after it, right then left.

"He's awake and tracking," the voice said, off to the side. Both pupils reactive and even. Then, back down at Wolfe, quieter, "You're going to be alright, Daniel. My name is Chris, I'm an EMT. You're in an ambulance, but you're doing fine."

"What happened?" His voice caught, dry in his throat, nearly choking him. He coughed it out.

"You don't need to talk now, unless it's to tell me how you feel, okay? Don't nod. Just be still."

"But what happened?"

"You got a bump on the head, that's all. Can you tell me if you feel pain anywhere else? I saw your ribs are taped. Have you recently injured yourself?"

"New fashion statement. All the rage in priestly circles…"

"He's coming around," the voice said to the side again, a smile from half of the mouth, "Getting some sense of humour back." Then back to Wolfe, "That's a good sign, Daniel, a very good sign."

"I'm in an ambulance?"

"Yes. You got bumped on the head. Does it hurt anywhere else? Anywhere new, or any of the older injuries feel worse? Are you breathing okay? Do you need an inhaler?"

"An inhal- No, no... just the head."

"That's a blessing, Father."

"If you say so. Where are you taking me? Where is the car?"

"We're taking you to the hospital at the University of Miami. We'll be there in a few minutes. I don't know anything about a car."

"Stolen?"

"There were cars around where you were found, it might have been there. Did you see what happened to you? Did someone try to steal your car?"

Wolfe slid one of his hands from beneath the strap and placed it on his forehead, stroking down over his face to clear his vision a little more, to get a break from the lights. "I'm getting pretty sick of this," he mumbled.

"You just rest a bit then, Father, let me know if anything feels worse or changes, but keep your eyes open for me, okay?"

He nodded, scrunching up his face in pain as he did so, remembering the EMT's direction too late. Then he just rested, and collected his thoughts. In a few more minutes, they arrived at the hospital and the EMTs wheeled him in on the gurney. X-rays followed a visual examination, then a few more tests and an hour of 'observed rest.'

He was fine, the doctor said: a slight concussion and a little scalp lac. A few quick sutures. Nothing permanent or life threatening. He shouldn't go to sleep for a while, to give his injury some time to stabilise and to make sure nothing more serious was going on, like a stroke or some other haemorrhage. His ribs were checked, pronounced well on the mend, and he was given permission to leave, so long as he had someone who could stay with him through the night. He would call Grippe. Grippe would come.

"Doctor?"

"Yes?"

"Would you mind answering a quick question for me?"

"No, of course not. What is it?"

"I had a couple of inhalers with me, I think the ambulance attendant, uh, Chris, had them."

"Yes, they're right here. What about them? You breathing okay? They're not yours, I assumed from the name on the label."

"No, they're not mine. One of my parishioners. Can you tell me a little about them? How they work, or if they're for a serious problem? The woman who owns them left without them, by accident."

"Sure, I suppose so. I can tell you what the drugs are used for in general, anyway." The doctor picked up the two little tubes from the side counter and had a look at the labels again. "Well, first of all, any asthma is serious. This one is a regular-use inhaler, the other is for flare-ups. Emergencies."

"How dangerous can it be to miss taking them for a few days?"

"It depends mainly on the patient... and the conditions. The most serious issue is that not taking the regular one will increase the chances of an emergency. If the attack is severe, death can occur. If these are the only ones she has, I'd say get them back to her as soon as possible, before anything serious happens. Her doctor could arrange for her to pick up new ones at a pharmacy near her, as well."

"Oh, good. Can you tell me what conditions might make it worse?"

"Stress. Cold and damp... exertion. The best bet is to have the person stay restful and in a well-ventilated house until you get these back. Away from pets, probably, flowers, mould. Prevention is a lot easier — and a lot more successful — than treatment of an actual attack. Anything else?"

"No, that's what I needed to know. Thanks. I'll make that call for my ride."

"Alright. You have your prescription?"

"Yes, thank you."

"You're welcome, Father. Feel better."

Wolfe nodded and waited until the man walked away before dialling the bishop's mansion.

"David Grippe here."

"Hey David… it's me."

Wolfe puffed out a thick cloud of smoke and took a sip of wine, examining the flickering colour, like an art critic, the way the light played through the crimson liquid.

The bishop did the same and then turned to look at him, "Probably shouldn't be giving you either of those — especially the drink."

"I won't tell. And don't worry, I've no intention of dying on you tonight."

"It's not your intentions that worry me. It's other people's. This hasn't been a great week for you."

"I'll give you that. I'm close though. Close to something big."

"Yes, no doubt, but if you get much closer this way, you'll wind up on a slab. Try to stay in one piece for a week — you'll like it, I promise."

"What would I do to fill my empty Wednesday nights?"

"You don't like this?" The old man gestured to his rooms in the mansion, luxuriously furnished and provided for his use by the church. The man himself owned nearly nothing — there was no need to. He had the usual investments for a retirement he had no intention of taking, but nothing else to burden his spiritual walk. Or his physical one for that matter.

"I suppose it'll do now and then." Wolfe regarded the cigar and the wine for a moment, deep in thought. "I think it's one of the priests at Saint Mary's, David. One of them killed Kevin, and probably the Kane boy too."

"Yes, I was afraid of that. Any idea which one?"

Wolfe shook his head. "Not just yet," he said, "Small pool to choose from though."

"Pascal?"

A shrug. A subtle shake of his head.

"That's what's bothering you? You've seen this before. You've seen worse than murder perpetrated by the hands of priests. Why is this one weighing so heavily? Is it your brother? Is it too much?"

Wolfe shook his head and took a drink. "Kevin's part of it. More of it is that I'm just sick of the job, sick of seeing the shattered lives of the children — the babies — their whole childhood and all of its good… stolen and ruined. They'll never heal. You know that. They'll always be broken."

"Maybe not always."

"Please don't preach at me, not tonight."

"Preach 'at' you? Come on now, we're better than all that. Can't a friend try to give another hope without getting into religious conflict and theological debate?"

"You're telling me you weren't thinking about heaven, then? About a land at the end of all this with no tears or crying, no conflict? Golden streets and harps on clouds? We wouldn't know what to do with ourselves. Conflict is all we do well."

"Yes, we're masters at making messes of things, but in the mess we also see the depth of goodness in people."

"If you say so. I just see the mess."

"Occupational hazard, perhaps. But there's something else bothering you, I think, something you haven't told me yet."

"There's Father Pascal, and Ana."

"Ana?"

"Cruz."

"Oh I know her surname. It was your failure to use it that interests me."

"Maybe I'm just feeling casual."

"Maybe your 'Father Pascal' says you're not. You know her well?"

"No, not well. She was dating Kevin. They were close — lovers — and now she's gone, taken from my own hotel room, and likely dying of asthma as we speak. And there's nothing I can do about it. Nothing at all. Everything I could think of is already a dead end. If we can't nail down the right priest, we'll never find her, and we can't do much more with the priests because the police are involved already. So what then? She could be hidden anywhere in the city. I might as well go door to door asking if she's in. I sat in a diner most of the day because there really is very little left that I can do."

"Do you desire her?"

"What?"

"I must warn you, I take evasion and delay as signs of guilt."

"I'm not guilty of anything."

"I don't think you are, but that has little to do with feeling guilt, does it? You're Catholic, or at least you were... we're born and bred to wallow in guilt, regardless of whether we did anything or not. That's the nuns' doing. Blame the Holy Sisters. Perhaps it is intended to keep us ready for shrift."

Wolfe smiled. He was glad he couldn't get much past his old friend; the world felt less lonely and hostile that way.

"Is she beautiful?"

"Yes, she is."

"Catholic?"

"Yes."

"Oh dear."

"Why? What's wrong with her being Catholic, isn't that a good thing?"

"In general yes, but many women are drawn to uniforms, to power and symbols of social control. These symbols of larger powers act upon such women, drawing them sometimes, and exciting the emotions. A Catholic woman is much more likely to feel the effects of a Catholic priest."

"The dog collar and black slacks is a turn-on?"

"It is more common than you might believe. How do you think men such as Koresh, Jeffries, Rasputin and other so-called prophets fill their beds with the wives of their parishioners and followers? Each was a man with power, a perceived link to God. Followers see a superhuman security right there in human form." The bishop took a pull on his cigar, puffed a cloud of smoke out into the dim room. "A man like you. Add to it your background, your strength... you're quite a catch. A forbidden one, but that just adds to the allure."

"I can't have those things in my life. Women, I mean."

"No," the bishop's watery eyes turned to Wolfe, narrowed for effect, "No, you can't. Part of your oath was to set women aside from your life — to set sex itself aside — and focus on the things of God. The spiritual."

"And if those things are harder to see these past few years?"

"Then open your eyes wider, my pupil, and stop the foolishness of your mind before you, as well, are caught up in something you shouldn't be. Don't let frustration with the case drive you to sin."

"But I am frustrated. I'm at a standstill. Two people missing, at least two dead and nothing I can do about it."

"Nothing?"

"Why do you ask that? Do you know something I don't?"

"No, no, I'm just a humble bishop," he replied, smiling a little at the thought.

"But..."

"But I do hear things, now and then."

"And?"

"I heard that the Kane boy — Douglas was it? — Was covered up, that his face was covered up to protect it from the soil."

"And?"

"And you tell me that you think it was one of the priests."

"Yes, I think it likely."

"Then which priest could have done these things, physically, and still cared enough for the boy to show him respect in death? If you can figure that out, you would have him."

Oh, is that all? Wolfe thought, but said nothing. Based on that criteria, it could be any of them. The bishop was no longer an investigator himself, and showed little evidence that he had ever been one. Sometimes those revelations made Wolfe glance away, find something else in the room to look at. He did so in that moment too, but then something started tugging at the fringes of his thoughts again. A priest who can kill someone and care for them at the same time. His mind began to run ahead, grasping at something, something just beyond his reach.

To kill and care.

The bishop might have shot into the dark, but in this respect he was near enough the mark to reveal it to Wolfe. The killer was a priest, he was now sure of that in his own mind: if he could set Pascal aside, then either Father Gonzales or Father Cisco was guilty of bludgeoning Kevin to death, stabbing a homeless boy, kidnapping and maybe killing another priest and a good,

265

Catholic cop. Maybe — probably — a whole lot more besides. Each of them had the right connections to be the killer, neither one had a decent alibi, but that didn't help Wolfe to find a solution. That wasn't the key...

The telephone rang. Grippe reached over and picked up the handset. "Yes?" A pause. "Good. I'll let him know. Thank you Vittorio." He hung up and smiled. "Father Gonzales called. Your car is at the church. They found it a couple of blocks away, with the keys still in it."

"No one took it?"

"No, it seems not. Good amongst the mess, Daniel, 'sheep amongst the wolves.' Not everyone is a criminal."

"Come now, My Lord Bishop," Wolfe took a pull on his cigar and watched the smoke roll out as he blew, "you know your theology better than that."

She could feel the light tickle, high up in her chest. It was as if some tiny spider had slipped down her throat in the night and begun weaving a web. Thin strands of silk, back and forth, back and forth across her windpipe. Her lungs were heavy. Her forehead had begun to sweat. Cold against the heady air.

She knew she needed to remain calm, but of all places to grasp at peace, the dark, rat-infested lair of a kidnapper was perhaps among the worst. She knew that he didn't plan to kill her — or at least that he didn't *want* to kill her — but, green as she was, she had still seen enough of these scenarios to know that things didn't often go according to a criminal's plan, and that wants were sometimes sacrificed in times of perceived need.

She wished she had a gun. A baton. Anything she could use as a weapon. There was nothing.

She could feel the strain build in her muscles. Effort had so far kept the worst of the fear shoved down beneath the surface. It was rising though, prodding up against the skin and seeking a way out. With every rattle of its movement she could feel a little more resistance to the air that flowed, with intentional calm, in and out of her lungs. Imperceptibly heavier with each breath.

She was fighting it. But she was losing.

She crossed herself and began grasping the fingertips of her left hand in those of her right, counting imaginary rosaries over and over again, and whispering her mantra of hope, learned at the knee of her *abuela*, the aged, rasping voice the most comforting sound in her little-girl's world...

Hail Mary, full of grace, the Lord is with thee. Blessed art thou among women, and blessed is the fruit of thy womb, Jesus. O Lord, open my lips and my mouth will proclaim your praise. Incline your aid to me, O God. O Lord, make haste to help me. Glory be to the Father, and to the Son, and to the Holy Spirit, as it was in the beginning, is now, and ever shall be, world without end. Amen.

Hail Mary, full of grace...

She didn't know how long she lay there, praying and muttering in the darkness, before she saw the flickering light of the man coming again, moving down the stairs, quietly and slowly, electric lantern in hand. When he had approached close enough for her to see him in detail, something different gripped the back of her mind. He was not wearing the dark glasses. He still wore the mask, but the gloves were gone. Caucasian. Pale, bony hands with blue veins and knotted, elderly knuckles.

Less careful about secrecy was not good. It meant less worry about her identifying him — less chance that she would ever be free to do so. But the gun was not in his hand. Perhaps that was good. She fastened her mind to that one fact. Perhaps he was being worn down by the investigation on the outside. Perhaps he was getting ready to give up. Or to run away. She steeled herself and spoke.

"Please, I am not well. I need my medicine. I need my inhaler."

Even the act of asking for that life-line heightened the degree of stress on her body and her breathing began to labor, to grow more audible. The man reached into his pocket and her eyes followed his hand in the unlikely hope that the small aluminium tube would be there, ready to burst into her lungs with the gift of free-flowing life once again.

The smooth black metal of the pistol brought tears to her eyes and she began to sob and to wheeze. The fingers of panic were piercing the skin at last. She began again to count the absent rosaries on her fingertips, mumbling her prayers over and over again with rapid fervour.

Hail-Mary, full-of-grace...

The man set the lantern down in front of him, on the edge of the damp blanket. He raised his arm and looked down the barrel of the gun. Lined up the bead with the woman's head, gently rocking forward and back as she muttered her prayers and gasped for air.

But his aim would not hold. His hand shook against his will. He lowered the sights to her chest. A bigger target, less motion, but the knotted hand trembled and the old knees were restless. A struggle raged back and forth between two inner intentions, and the battle shook any hope of a clean kill from the mind of the shooter. Even the thought of a "clean" kill churned his stomach. It was this woman... not much more than a girl really, despite her occupation. A Catholic. Devout, it seemed... He had seen her at services more than once and could discern the prayer, spoken softly but with the fluidity and confidence of frequent practice — and she was preparing herself to die at his hands. His priest's hands.

His mind played back images of the falling policeman who had come by the church, asking thinly-veiled questions about Father Pascal and Douglas. The act had been one of instinct. Protection. Desperation even. But he could still feel the shudder of the candlestick in his hand as it hit the hard surface of the man's skull... felt the brittle break in resistance as it shattered the bone.

That same hand had snatched up the letter opener in reaction to the threats and insults hurled at him by Douglas. The boy had been talking to someone, had betrayed his elder friend to someone who had alerted the police. And then Wolfe had appeared, like some dark opposite of the Damascus Road, to make it plain that this was an ending of the way things had been. The boy had asked for money, then more money. That would have been acceptable, like a father or elder brother helping out a younger one, but it had not come with respect, or gratitude. His heart had felt the deep sting of it, but it had been his hand that acted. It had felt the soft press into the young flesh, the blade meeting no resistance at it thrust in, once, twice, and a third frantic time as the wide-eyed Judas slowly slid to the floor.

He had been saddened by that. Despite the need for it, it was a burden to him still. And now he faced another young soul, too new to the world to understand its complexities. Too innocent to deserve her fate. An accident of circumstance. Born into it… into the curse.

Weren't they all.

His arm lowered, giving the hand a brief reprieve from further violence. She would never know of the battle that had taken place there, never even see the man turn and walk back through the darkness, fighting back his own tears, leaving the lantern behind, glowing at the edge of the blanket in the cold room…

…and the young woman curled over on its farther edge, wheezing desperate prayers, clinging to the last few breaths of life and hope.

EIGHTEEN

Wolfe arrived at the church and received his keys from the secretary in the front office. He had no desire that day to face either of his primary suspects. Not knowing the fate of Cruz or Pascal was wearing heavily on him and sleep would not come, even in the comfortable guest room at the bishopric. Despite the pain killers and booze, a good rest was elusive. Even a bad one wouldn't come easily.

"It's in the parking lot at the side," she said, handing him the keys. "It's terrible what happened Father, that someone could do such a thing — and to a priest! But with what happened in the sanctuary… I just don't know anymore. I just don't know where people are at these days. Makes me want to stay at home and watch TV."

Wolfe nodded to her in that way priests learn early: non-committal, friendly, neither happy nor sad. Stoic, like he was in on some great secret that would be revealed to her one day, but in the meantime it was best if she just listened to what she was told, said her prayers, and maintained her faith. The men in black would steer the ship.

"Well, there is one good thing to come of this," she said, crossing herself.

"What's that?"

"Church attendance is up. Even at the morning masses we have close to the whole congregation — all of those who can make it before work, that is. Tragedy brings faith."

Or morbid fascination, Wolfe thought. He nodded his goodbye and left the office. There it was, parked with its trunk end toward the building on the gravel pad where the van used to be.

Used to be.

He changed his course and walked up the low platform to the side door. Locked and latched — for once. He headed back around to the front and asked the woman if she knew where the van was. She didn't. Who had taken it? No. Who it was that brought his car back to the church for him? One of the priests. No, no idea which one. There was a new one there, temporarily, a Father Macédone. No, she didn't know where anyone else was — it was Thursday night, they could be anywhere.

A dead end. He wondered what the woman did for them at Saint Mary's, besides lurk in the offices at all hours of the day, a less dramatic incarnation of Quasi Modo. He walked down the length of the nave and paused in front of the altar, standing back a little from the place where his brother had lain. He genuflected from habit and glanced up at the massive wooden crucifix hanging above the altar. He crossed himself.

It was getting dark, there was no bright sunlight outside to illuminate the stained glass and throw multi-hued beams of rich light down onto the polished, grained surface.

The saviour's body hung on a wooden cross, arms stretched gracefully to the sides, and his rib gaping open with a bloodless, wooden gash, painted gaudy red below. His genitalia were tastefully hidden by a strip of loin cloth carved as if to be blowing in a spiritual breeze — the *Ruach* of God, the Spirit-Wind, rushing past his crucified form. Below this, the shiny wooden skin of hanging legs, pinned down at the feet with iron nails.

He wondered if the woman who tended the place also dusted and polished the crucifix. Perhaps she fancied herself another of the faithful women, there with the Mother and Magdalene, wiping clean the slain body of her Lord and awaiting his special attention when once again he returned to reward the steadfast.

But the wooden form seemed only a bleak and lifeless idol to him, when held up in comparison to the form that had stained the floor just a few short days earlier. Even in death his brother's flesh was more quickened than the aged wood above the cloth-draped altar. The wooden effigy had never cradled a spark of human life, and Kevin had been a jinn of vitality.

Wolfe turned from this and walked toward the side door. He stepped down out of the church and into his rental car. Every action was deliberate, an intentional battle against the other thoughts and fears that crowded and distracted his mind, made each minuscule action a separate task.

He stuck the key in the ignition slot and turned.

The engine fired to life.

He clicked the transmission into drive and pressed the pedal.

Pulled out onto the street.

Clicked the headlights on as the wheels bumped down out of the semi-lit parking lot.

His thoughts wandered to Cruz as he drove and he wondered if, somehow, concentrating on her hard enough might help him to find her, to drive toward the spot where she was being held, coming near through some kind of cosmic thread or psychic connection, an extrasensory link... Two souls drawn to each other.

It was a foolish fantasy, but his nerves were raw, his injuries throbbing, and his frustration building hour by hour as his imagination painted ever-more grotesque possibilities of torture and agony which she might, even now, be suffering at the hands of a merciless killer.

He accelerated hard, followed the gentle curve of the road and approached the traffic lights for I-95 north. The light turned to yellow and he accelerated again, pushing the car through the intersection as the bank of lights turned to bright red. He drove up the incline and onto the high concrete overpass, the glitter of downtown Miami twinkling overhead. The speed felt good. The rushing air cleared his head a little, allowing him to run over the data again, to strain it for clues and direction.

Traffic slowed a little up ahead. The back of the car in front of his lit up red.

Wolfe's foot pressed down on the brake and with the action he heard a sharp, grating sound from somewhere under the hood in front of him. The frame of the car dropped and popped back up, jarring his ribs and knocking his head against the window beside him. He yanked the wheel to the right as the chassis dropped again and bare steel met the road, the car lurching to the left, across three lanes of traffic, and veering down the exit ramp.

The main brake was useless. He slammed his left foot down on the emergency brake, but again, to no effect. Sparks flew up in a great, orange cloud outside his door. The scenery blurred past behind them. Any fleeting thought that this was an accidental malfunction fell away onto the road behind him.

As he skidded to the lower end of the off-ramp, the steering gave way altogether and the front end slammed into the pavement. The airbag exploded, knocking his face backward and blocking his view of all in front of him save the sky. The wheel pulled right, then left, and he felt the sharp slam as the car hit something low, then lifted into a moment of flight.

Wolfe prayed and swore and heaved uselessly on the wheel as the thing landed and bounced again, this time drifting sideways in the air and dropping — leaving his stomach behind — down over the edge of the road.

A sickening, four-foot drop of sloping lawn and then he slammed into the edge of a drainage canal. The impact of the grille threw up a wall of water and the vehicle stopped dead, the driver's side lifting high, almost to the point of rollover, before settling back down, slowly with the sinking of the car into dark, cold water.

"Dismiss the pain," an echo in his head demanded, "Ignore it. There is *no* pain." There would be time for pain… later.

He was still for just a moment, allowing the sensation of rocking motion to abate a little. He felt his face, his ribs, his arms and legs. All seemed to be intact, or reasonably so. The car sat in water to the door-handles already, and slowly sank, passenger side first. The door would not budge.

He rolled down the window instead. It halted halfway, the spit and spark of electrics somewhere under the hood signalling the final demise of the car. He broke the exposed slab of glass with a sharp shove and began to pull himself from the vehicle when a man ran up, then down into the edge of the water, closely followed by a heavy woman in an evening gown, who stayed on the bank.

"Is he alright?" she called, "Is he dead?"

The man ignored her, pulled Wolfe from the car and helped him up onto the bank. As they crawled up toward the guardrail, the woman gasped.

"Are you a minister or something?"

"I don't care who he is," the man said, "He's got to be drunk out of his mind to pull something like that. Or high."

"Don't talk to a minister like that. It had to be an accident. Look at his car!"

"Why, 'cause he waves a Bible around on Sundays?" He scoffed.

The two of them argued briefly while Wolfe caught his breath and his bearings. He glanced at the car. The whole of the front wheel was missing. The grill and fenders smashed.

He was unhurt, at least, but it was obvious that whoever was trying to kill him wasn't going to give up until the job was done, and the battered priest didn't trust to luck enough to expect many more near-misses like this one. One of these times the bastard would succeed. As the wail of sirens erupted in the distant night and his rescuers exchanged fiery words, he stumbled his way around to the front of the woman's little Audi TT and slipped in behind the wheel. The man caught a glimpse of him out of the corner of his eye and pointed.

Wolfe hit the accelerator and shot out through the intersection, hearing "Mother *fucker!*" in a hysterical, female voice fade into the distance behind him.

Cruz huddled up to the lantern in the darkness, as if the little disc of light it cast on the floor was an island in the midst of dark waters, with the fins of hungry sharks circling around and around it. She had pulled the blanket toward her, across the rough floor until the glowing thing was within reach of her free foot. She tipped it toward her and pulled it up into her arms like a lost infant.

And there she sat, infant in arms on the tiny island, waiting for the return of one who might be death, the shark who moved on land. She threw the corner of the blanket back out over the floor, staking her territory, feeble though the assertion might be.

Any little bit helped.

Her breathing was laboured and the deficiency of oxygen was starting to show symptoms. She was pale, her lips bluish, and her thoughts at the edge delusion. All of her focus was on staying calm, on letting the air flow in and out... in and out, snaking past the spider webs through her bronchial tubes, the putty of her lungs... Keeping her thoughts strait, her mental sight clear.

But the lamp was growing dim.

She thought of Daniel Wolfe, out there looking for her or wondering if she had run off. She thought of Billy Jackson and his awkward consolations: a hand on her shoulder, a quick hug, all the while trying to keep his sexual tension and pleasure from showing through, perhaps even trying to stifle it altogether.

But she knew. She always knew.

She had developed early, her breasts forming while the others in her class still bore the frames of little boys. Her hips rounded, her throat even took on that subtle sub-tone, not the rough bass of a man, but the whole, full timbre of a sexually mature woman. She had learned early how to read the feelings and attractions of men. The boys at school would tease her, pull her hair or call her "Princess Titty-Ana." The boys in the older grades, in the building across the playground, would look at her through the chain links. Watch her run and play with her friends. Whisper comments to one-another. Smiles and laughter. Appraising glances.

And then there were the men. These were awkward, stifled reactions to her nubile womanhood. She caught occasional glances from a teacher, a bus-driver, the fathers of her friends. For a brief period in her teens she had even exploited it, experimented with how much she could get with this mysterious power, how far she could go.

Her *abuela* had put a stop to that.

Her grandmother, dear to her, but feared in her wrath, had taken her up to the bedroom on the top-floor of the narrow little slice of a house she had had back then and sat her on the knitted blanket at the foot of the bed.

From a drawer, the woman pulled out a picture album and set it on her lap. She then bade Ana to look into the face of her *abuela* — not just a glance, but to really see the wrinkles, the tiny scars, the sagging skin and dark spots of an old woman. Ana looked. Took it in. Studied the flaws and the marks of the passage of years and uncounted woes and untold worries.

She had never really noticed before. That was just how *abuelas* looked. Hers had always looked that way.

Then the old woman opened the album. There were pictures there of a young beauty, full-bosomed and proud, pouting lips so shiny that the red almost showed through the old black and white photo. There were more pictures: wedding pictures, special occasions, a portrait when her cousins came to America and opened the short-lived bakery business.

And in all of the pictures, there were the looks of the men. They looked on with a kind of hunger.

Then her grandmother had made Ana stand before the mirror and look into her own young, beautiful face. In Spanish, she had asked her grand-daughter a simple question: "Are you a thing to be devoured? A thing to be used up? Are you food, ready to be chewed and swallowed on a plate until the hunger is satisfied? And then whatever is left over, thrown into the bin, or handed over to another?"

She hadn't fully understood then, the life her grandmother had led, the abuse and pain and neglect she had suffered at the hands of her husband in the years before he died and she took the children from New York to Miami with the last few dollars he had left behind and a two-hundred-dollar policy from his work at the factory.

But young Ana had understood enough to stop the games, to make something of herself.

And yet there was another face that walked the dark basement, that of a handsome priest, an unattainable man who'd likely already had more tests to his faith and control than most men have in a lifetime. And yet she wanted to test him more. She was a fighter, a cop, a strong person who could take care of herself.

But she was also a woman.

She prized her sensuality and her beauty. She would never have admitted it, but a part of her wanted him to burst into the room, to save her, to hold her in the darkness and free her ankle from the scabbing pain of the steel cuff. She wanted to feel his kisses on the skin of her face and neck, and beyond, the power of his hands crushing her against him, pressing her breasts between their two bodies until the need overcame them both and he made love to her, in some safe, clean and shining place far from there. She longed for his rescue from the darkness.

But the footsteps she heard were not his. Not even the hopeful mind of a despairing captive, faint with illness and stress, could mistake the sound she had come to expect and to fear so intensely.

He had the flashlight again, and a small duffle bag. She watched each step in the near-darkness, gauged each inch between them, yearning for a brief lapse of judgment on the man's part. A step too close. An arm, just within reach. She may not win the fight in her weakened state, but she had give the bastard a run for his money. This time, the surprise would be to her benefit, and they'd see how things went then.

But he didn't come near. He didn't cross the invisible barrier that marked the full range of her reach. She cursed herself for not thinking more clearly, for inching the blanket closer to her after each visit, a little each time. He might not notice the change. He might walk, as he had before, right up to the edge of the frayed thing. He might then be within her reach.

But she hadn't. And so he wasn't.

He walked within a dozen feet of where she sat holding the lantern. He opened the duffle, reached in and pulled out a small white item and tossed it over to her. Her mind took a moment to register and then she snatched it up to her mouth and depressed the tube into the holder, breathing in hard as she did so, pulling the life-giving steroid as deep into her lungs as her condition allowed. She did it a second time. A third. Spider webs in the depths of her chest snapping, dissolving. The inner passages softening, expanding. The sweet flow of life.

She closed her eyes then, sucking in the gritty damp of the air, once again tasting the stale grease of the fast food and the rough film of uncleaned teeth. It was relief. All she cared to do was breathe. Just breathe. Dizzy and tired, she leaned forward, elbows on her knees, and placed the precious little canister onto the blanket between her feet. There she stayed, staring at the little thing. The gift of life given to her by the dark man. The shadow. The killer.

She did not notice as he tossed a newspaper on the floor near her, then another white bag of food and a plastic gallon-jug of water. He set his pistol down on the floor, well out of her reach, and turned on a digital camera. A brief flash in the dim light. He checked the photo. Seemed satisfied. Picked up the gun again and left her, walking instead into the room with the steel door. He didn't check the window this time.

The soft closing of the heavy door didn't pull her from her relieved weeping, each breath passing like beads on her rosary. Later, the retreating taps of his footsteps were little more than a whisper in the background of her thoughts. And again she was alone.

In time she wiped the tears from her eyes and picked up the bag of food. She was ashamed of herself. The feeling had been growing the whole time of her captivity. She was a strong woman, not some hunk of meat kept in money and diamonds in trade for sex and status, and she was better than this. On top of it all she was a police officer, a person trained in taking down criminals and keeping the peace. Not some whimpering victim.

And yet she could not deny that she *was* a victim, whimpering or not. In that darkness, alone. In her own bitter estimation, she was nothing more. The tiny, hard links of steel between her and the solid wall made it so. The thought galled her and she threw stares of hate toward the dark end of the room. She cursed the absent man in the most biting Spanish her lips could mouth.

Thoughts of escape had occurred to her. She had tried to squeeze her foot through the cuff until her ankle had become swollen and raw. Had he cuffed her hand, she might have gotten out of it, broken her thumb or something, like in the movies. But he hadn't. She had never heard of being able to get free from a shackle in the same way. No thumb there. Short of gnawing off her own foot, she saw no way of slipping the shiny ring from her body. She had even pondered the practicality of that — briefly.

She had tried the other end of the cuffs as well, but the bracelet was snug and secure around an old, cast-iron pipe which ran straight out from the poured concrete ceiling and then down, almost to the floor before there was a joint and another bend where it ran off along into the darkness. The joint was thick and prevented the bracelet from passing any further. It was corroded and rusty on the surface, naturally welded, over time, to the pipe to which it was linked. Both were solid and unyielding. There was no hope of that, either.

She had tapped on the pipes, long into the hours of her captivity, and still, sometimes, in the deep of her constant night she hammered an SOS call onto the cold steel. But it spooked her. Often the thought of anything, good or bad, materialising out of the darkness without warning terrified her. She seldom tapped anymore.

She had looked around the room when the man was there with his light, searching the extent of the cold beam for any means of escape or communication with the outside world. She had seen doorways at the far end, darkness beyond. Now that she had the lantern, she could make out a few more things in her spacious cell: crates and boxes piled up along one of the other walls and some kind of mezzanine or catwalk twenty or so feet to her left, above the room with the steel door. Nowhere in all of it could she see anything that gave her hope of escape. It was like she was in a disused prison.

She took another deep pull on the inhaler, thankful for the hope it gave her. The time. This was not the act of someone who intended to kill her. That was more than she had had a few short hours ago, as he had aimed the gun at her with trembling hands. It helped her to stay calm.

She chewed her cold, limp chicken strips slowly, drawing out the activity as long as possible in an effort to pass the featureless time.

Perhaps she drifted in and out of sleep. Perhaps not, but eventually the lamplight flickered and faded. She tapped the plastic casing, then knocked it hard with the heel of her hand, but it was no use. The light grew dim enough for her to see the tiny filaments glowing yellow, then orange, then fading away to a hint of red which threw no usable light or warmth, but rather reminded her of the eye of some monster, feared in her childhood years. She set the thing down beside the cot.

She drew her knees up to her chest and hugged them, pulling the bag of food between her thighs and bosom, overpowering the light stink of the basement air and the acrid bite of her own body odour, with that of breaded chicken strips and limp fries.

Comfort food.

There was a little cup of Coke tucked in beside the fries and she sipped it quickly, willing the caffeine to wash away the pain and hopelessness. But both remained.

She thought of those she knew were digging, asking, probing — trying against hope to find her before it was too late, or before they were too overwhelmed with new cases to worry about her anymore. *Missing, presumed dead*, it would read then. A cold case. A boxed file in yet another dark room. *Like this one.* Already filed away.

She closed her eyes in the stillness and swore that, were she ever to get the chance, she would make the bastard pay for this, for this nightmare come to life. She swore it, fantasised about it, planned out a hundred scenarios in her head and steeled her nerves.

Then she tucked the inhaler into her waistband, rolled up the top of the paper bag and tucked it in close to her belly, where she could protect it from any marauding rodents, and closed her eyes to sleep.

It was a priest who came to her dreams.

Wolfe didn't take the stolen car very far, just enough distance between himself and the crash site to avoid being picked up by police. Even if he were let go in the end, it would take time for them to do so, and that was time Cruz and Pascal might not have. He pulled into a residential area and stepped out into the heat, leaving the keys under the floor mat. The police would find it. Probably.

As for Wolfe himself, he had to lie low and figure out what his next move should be. He felt impotent, two steps behind whoever was trying to kill him, but he was, at least, enough of a threat for them to try to take him out. It meant he was getting close, somehow. But he was aimless. Relying too much on luck for both success and survival. He needed control.

The car sabotage had almost done him in and, as he walked down the street with no clear destination in mind, his hands started to shake and his knees felt wobbly. Against reason, his mind detected staring eyes from too many windows, shadowy figures crouched in any dark shadow. Waiting death with any tick of the clock. Distant reports from imagined weapons popped in his ears. Shrubs looked like jungle. Driveways like desert wadis. The present was slipping away in the midst of his shock. He needed to draw it back. Stay with the needs at hand.

He leaned on a concrete barrier.

They would arrest him if they found him. He could not ask Jackson for more help. Not without forcing an awkward choice between duty to the force and duty to a dead friend's brother.

And a missing woman.

Perhaps that was enough. Perhaps the desire to save her might be enough to call in one last favour from the detective, if need be. Wolfe could explain what happened, why he couldn't yet come in, and maybe Jackson would stall for a while.

But what to do while he stalled? He saw a Caribbean bar across the street with darkly-tinted windows and only two cars in the lot. It would be best to get off the street for a while. He stepped into the reggae-soaked dimness and ordered a shot of dark rum — brand didn't matter — and chicken wings. He had forgotten how hungry he was. Besides, the alcohol would need a little something to cling to in the stomach. He needed to get a grip, not to get stupid and make a simple mistake. He added a bottle of water to his order and drank it down in a few long gulps. The wet shins of his pants dripped on the floor, the sound distant to his thoughts.

He considered his two main suspects: Gonzales and Cisco. Each one relied for his alibi on the casual observances of the other two priests from Saint Mary's, and the alibis were shaky at best. Either one of them could have been alone in the church for the time it would have taken for Kevin to confront him and the murder to take place. If Kevin had been there to ask around about abuse, either one of them could have reacted out of guilt or self-preservation. Or even both of them...

But then again, neither of them had a history of prior accusations or charges. At their ages, to keep a long-running history of abuse quiet would be a cunning feat indeed. The chances of this being a first offence? Pretty much impossible. The lack of a record was an anomaly, but not unheard-of; some of these guys were pretty cunning about their habits, at least at first. Wolfe still didn't like it. Didn't like anomalies at all.

The bartender clinked the glass down in front of him. He took an appreciative sip of the rum. Then drained it. Not bad. A few deep breaths. That was it; things were settling down now, the spectres in the shadows fading away. He lifted a finger to indicate a second round.

His thoughts turned back to the case.

Both men were technologically savvy enough to use the internet and devise the bomb. What was it Delaney had said? "Either could have made the thing, if they could get the materials."

Maybe that was it. Maybe determining who could get the materials was the key to figuring out who the killer was. But the police would know that. That would be their first action once they got the details from the bomb squad. If it had led anywhere then surely they would have someone in custody by now and not be chasing around after Danny.

His booze arrived and he tilted it back. The pungent fumes flowed up into his sinuses, making his eyes water and clearing out his head, pushing out the jungles and deserts and sounds of warfare and death. Clearing out cobwebs of thought like a busy, benevolent spirit.

He would sip the third one.

He had a call to make first. He stepped over to the bar and asked to use the phone. Yes, local. He dialed the bishopric.

"Bishop Grippe's office, Father Vittorio speaking." The voice was rough, sleepy. Wolfe had not considered the time.

"It's Daniel Wolfe."

"Father Wolfe?"

"I'm sorry to call so late. Are you able to look something up for me in Vatican records?"

"Yes, I suppose so. It cannot wait until morning?"

"I'm sorry, no."

Wolfe could hear the light rustlings and sleep-heavy grunts and groans as the man pulled on a robe and walked through to his office.

"I'm ready, go ahead."

"I need the files on Fathers Jésus Gonzales and Antony Cisco." He waited.

"Okay, I have them."

"Did either of them serve in the military?"

"Just a moment." The secretary read through the files in silence. "Yes. Jésus Gonzales was a chaplain in Viet Nam, involved in Cedar Falls operations in '67, Tet Offensive. Left in '72, honourably discharged with a purple heart."

"And Cisco?"

"No record of military service."

Wolfe was silent, his mind working quickly.

"Anything else?"

"No, no thank you, that's what I needed. I'll let you get back to bed. Thank you."

"Go with God." The phone clicked on the other end, but Wolfe remained where he was, holding the receiver in a hand shaking with emotion.

He dialled Jackson's cell. It rang for a long time.

"Hello?" The voice echoed.

"Hi, Billy?"

"Who is this?"

"It's Danny."

"Just a second." There was some rustling again, a few dull bangs, like cupboard doors being swung shut. "There's a BOLO out for you... You stole a car?"

"Someone tried to kill me. I had to get away."

"So you stole a car?"

"Borrowed it. I just needed to get out of there prior to any complications. Look, I think I know who is holding Ana, but if I get caught up in red tape and-"

"Yeah, okay, I get it, but stealing a car is not going to help you. Wait a minute... who do you think has Ana?"

"I just needed to get out of there, that's all. They'll find the car, no damage done."

"So why are you calling me? Who has Ana?"

"Are you in a safe place to talk?"

"Yeah, I'm in the can. Go ahead."

"It's got to be Gonzales."

"Why him? He's got the best alibi of the three of them for Kevin's murder — his arthritis is so bad he can barely pick up those old candlesticks."

"No, it's got to be him. The one who set the bomb off in my suite knew what he was doing, limited the blast. Gonzales has a military background from Nam. The boy, Douglas, was stabbed with something like a letter opener, and the opener is missing from Gonzales's desk set. I knew there was something off about him from the beginning, I could feel it. The evidence fits. It's got to be him."

"I can't go on a hunch and a military record. What do you expect me to do?"

"There's got to be some way to put the pressure on him... find out where he's got Ana, or where he hid her body."

"She's not dead, Danny."

"I know, sorry. Of course she's not."

"No, I mean we know for sure that she's not dead."

"How?"

"Things have happened. We got a package with a picture. She's in a concrete room, cuffed to a pipe, but she doesn't appear injured and she's got food and water."

"Thank God! But with her asthma…"

"That's alright as well. She had her inhaler on the floor beside her bed."

"Her inhaler?"

"Yeah. The things they breathe in, you know."

Something about that seemed disjointed. She hadn't used one openly at his apartment, and she had left her place in a great hurry after the shooting, leaving her purse behind. Even if she had it, would she have grabbed for it during a kidnapping? In the heat of that moment would she have realised what was coming and had the presence of mind?

"So you talked to Rob about the bomb?"

"Yeah. Nothing much useful there yet."

"Maybe you should think more about the car then."

"The car?"

"Well, anyone can make a bomb these days, Rob tells me that ninety percent of their cases are kids playing with explosives they make from internet plans — pipe bombs and that shit. But to sabotage a car? Maybe we're looking for a mechanic, not a soldier."

Might be worth a thought. "There's another thing."

"What's that?"

"The van at the church."

"Yeah?"

"It was painted. Recently. The bed inside will still be green. I think that's the vehicle that Douglas was transported in."

"I'll check into it. The tread width of the model is right. That's a good indicator that it's a priest. Good. Doesn't help you much though. What are you going to do?"

"I don't know. I don't know." He pondered a moment. "Hey, why did the kidnapper send the photo? How much did he ask for?"

"He doesn't want anything."

"What? What do you mean?"

"He doesn't want any money, anyway. The note is for 'those looking for Ana Cruz' — not to the police specifically, you'll notice — to back off. He wants us to back off or he'll kill her. If we do what he says, or so he tells us, then the girl will be released in a short time, unharmed."

"Like the bishop said," Wolfe thought aloud.

"What's that?"

"The killer of the boy didn't want to kill him — or at least he cared about him in some way. It's got to be the same guy who has Ana, and I think this is the same thing. He doesn't want to hurt her."

"He may not want to, but he's capable."

"Will you back off then?"

"The police? No. We can appear to, a little, but it's not in our directive to listen to threats like that, hostage or not. What about you?"

"I don't know yet."

"Don't do anything stupid. You may think it's Gonzales, but without any proof of it you'll be landing yourself in prison and, in the words of your brother, you boys are too good-looking to last a night in there."

Wolfe smiled, despite himself. That was an echo of his brother alive, cocky and full of jokes. He needed that. Kevin was fading already, images and memories dropping away with each day that passed. Each hour even. He knew the loss hadn't truly hit him yet. But it would. When this was all over, he had no doubt, it would.

"Besides," Jackson continued, "if we bring him in without anything solid, she'll be rotting in a cell somewhere. The longer we keep him, the more risk to her. I know I'm not supposed to say this, but having you out there looking could help us out. At least you will if you can keep out of jail."

"I promise I'll do my very best to prevent becoming an inmate."

"Stealing cars is not a great start."

"Well, I'll deal with that when this is over. It'll be fine."

"Let's hope so."

"Bye for now then, thanks for the intel."

"Yeah, yeah. You just stay safe. Keep your head down."

Wolfe hung up the phone and returned to his table. The wings had come and he sat down and ate them mechanically, fulfilling a physical need without great pleasure or satisfaction. The third shot of rum was different. With each sip of the liquor his nerves calmed down a little bit more, and his thinking became easier, more relaxed. Whoever it was that had Cruz didn't want to kill her yet, and had just handed over a picture to the police. That meant that there was time, however little, to find out where she was and to verify who had her, before it was too late.

It also meant — something that Jackson had failed to mention, though surely it had been noticed — that Father Pascal was not a part of the deal. The priest had been a suspect at first, and might still be one in the eyes of some, but the weak attempt to frame him wouldn't fool a professional worth his pay grade.

Delaney may be an ass, but he was no fool. Nor was Jackson.

Pascal might have shot at Cruz if he were involved. He might even have fled afterward. But what he wouldn't have done was shoot at her, flee, reload his gun and then leave it behind a radiator in his abandoned apartment, taking the spare ammo with him.

Besides, if Wolfe could find the housekeeper and ascertain that the gun hadn't been there before, then surely the police could do the same. In all likelihood then, there was only one reasonable conclusion.

Father Emilio Pascal was dead.

NINETEEN

Wolfe looked on as Ana Cruz stared toward him. Her body moved, but the eyes held no remnant of life in the dry surface; they were fixed and vacant. She looked up at him from the depths of a well, with smooth green walls telescoping downward at a weird angle, carrying her farther away from him as he watched, off to some deeper horizon. He was alone.

He stood there, not waiting, but not having anywhere to go, or anyone to see. The world was still, except for a growing sensation that something was approaching him from a low place beyond his sight. He looked to the ground and a long, black snake was coiling about his ankles, its body silently undulating and growing in girth as it moved.

He looked beside him and the land sloped off like a field, jungle bubbling like emerald water in the distance, flashes of fire erupting here and there and, sharp and clear in his dream-sight, dark faces staring back at him through the deep of the foliage. Hate and fear shining in them, like flames.

His mind saw the form of an old priest then, black and scaled like the serpent at Wolfe's feet. The priest's face was obscure. It seemed translucent, as if the man had begun to fade away already. He held a military-style duffle bag and wore a broad-rimmed sun-hat, but black, like a Jesuit's.

He awoke.

He was in a new car, rented under his alias. The windows were covered with condensation and the interior was beginning to grow hot, humid like the jungle. He was missing something and he suspected that his subconscious mind was working hard to tell him. It had happened enough in the past that he did not panic at waking. It was close. He didn't need to look for the solution now; it was looking for him.

He relaxed and turned the key in the ignition, feeling the relief of the air conditioning flow over his skin. He felt the primal coiling at the back of his neck as he imagined the black snake slithering its way through the darkness under his seat, approaching his feet, his calves, already fixated on a target, ready to strike if he moved.

Ready to strike if he didn't.

He resisted the urge to shake off the feeling, to slough off the tangled remnant of the dream like an ill-fitting skin. Instead he let his mind hover there, loose, between the waking and sleeping worlds where the human mind loses its inhibition, where it reconstructs restricted thoughts and censored memory. He let mental images come easily and go easily, refusing to attach greater importance to any single one of them.

The photograph was an interesting development. It had meaning, if he could find a way to read it. The kidnapper hadn't wanted ransom. Wolfe even doubted if the guy wanted to be a kidnapper at all. More likely was the scenario that he had entered Wolfe's rooms with the intent to set another explosive charge, and Cruz had been there. Secret. Hiding. Perhaps the man felt he had had no choice. Why hadn't he run? Why hadn't she defended herself? Surely she could have fought off a man as old as Gonzales or even Cisco. Unless he had had a gun...

And now he had sent 'proof of life' and made a demand, albeit a strange one. The investigation had to be close, breathing right down the guy's neck, for him to take a chance like this. It felt desperate. If Wolfe could just sort the important from the unimportant and fabricate a picture of what was going on. The near-slumber continued, but he could feel himself losing it.

The snake moved around his ankles, the rough scales rasping on his skin.

His pool of suspects was small: without some new, earth-shattering bit of information, it *had* to be either Gonzales or Cisco. At their first meeting, his instinct had told him that Gonzales was hiding something, and that had not changed. Of Cisco, Wolfe was unsure. Open hatred was there... could that expression of hatred be hiding something darker? The were too damn similar, the two men.

So what was the key?

The priest cared for the people he had killed. The picture proved that. Blankets, food, a light and the very fact that Cruz had not yet been killed. The guy didn't *want* to kill her. But Wolfe knew that he would, if push came to shove. If time ran out. They all knew it. He had killed Douglas Kane. Probably Pascal too.

At least she had her inhaler.

He closed his eyes again, drifted in semi-wakefulness and placed himself in Cruz's position. She had been taken, chained up in a cellar somewhere by the man who likely had killed her lover and then shot at her the night before. She must fear for her life. And yet she had left the inhaler — a tiny device that meant the difference between life and death to her — lying on the floor beside her? What if he took it to ensure her good behaviour? What if he stepped on it in anger and destroyed it? What if he simply took it and allowed her to die? Wolfe had been a captive before and he knew the thousands of scenarios his own mind had scrolled through, each one more paranoid than the one it followed. Something like that, a device that meant his life to him, he would have hidden it.

But she had't hidden it, so she must have known that her captor wouldn't take it. How could she have known that?

Wolfe was fully awake, the snake dissipated in the light of day. It had found him.

She hadn't had her inhaler with her. How could she have grabbed it when trying to defend herself against an intruder? No, she was taken without it and, if left that way, she would certainly have died. The conditions of her cell proved that. But the kidnapper didn't want her to die, at least not yet. He *cared* about her. About life. There was one simple answer that explained it. She didn't fear the man taking the inhaler away, because it was the kidnapper who had brought it to her in the first place.

Wolfe glanced at the car clock. It was five a.m. The sun lighting the eastern sky, and would soon be up in full. There would be a mass at seven. If what the woman at the church had said was correct, a good portion of the congregation would attend. He hoped so. He turned on the little car and drove toward the church. He would need to park several blocks away; he couldn't risk an arrest if the police were watching the place.

He stopped on the way there at a twenty-four hour Walmart and went inside. He bought a change of clothes and some deodorant. A couple of bottles of water and a sandwich, in case his nerves calmed and his stomach woke up hungry. He also picked up a clipboard and a thin pad of writing paper. An hour later he was locking the car and setting out down the street in a light blue, short-sleeved button-up, and khaki walking shorts... with sandals. He even had the beginnings of a trendy brush of stubble. The day was warming, but not yet oppressive; under different circumstances, the walk would have been pleasant.

He came from the west end of the building, keeping to back streets and alleyways. With his clipboard in plain sight and his clean, casual clothing, he took the risk to

300

cut through the yard of the house behind the church, crossing the alley afterward and having only seven or eight yards of open ground to cover before reaching the side door of the church.

Locked.

He walked around the back and tried the other.

Locked.

Perhaps the woman had been right, perhaps some good things had come from this tragedy. At the very least, there was an obvious increase in vigilance with regard to the faulty exit doors.

It was ten to seven. Parishioners had started to arrive. There was nothing else for it. Wolfe would have to try the front door.

Had he seen the two men sitting in their unmarked van a block down from the church, listening to *Cold Play* and hammering out the one good solution to the national economic situation, he might have noticed that they gave him hardly a glance as he walked around the corner, his back to their surveillance, and entered the front door of the church. They were looking for a priest, a man who had only ever been seen clean shaven and in his ecclesiastical uniform. A man last seen in that uniform and driving a stolen Audi TT.

Wolfe walked through to the nave and ducked immediately to the side, into the shadows by the font. Father Gonzales would be officiating. The old priest was up at the front making a few last-minute preparations and directing the sleepy-eyed altar boys to tend to their duties with haste. "Earlier is better than later," he whispered, "and 'finished already,' is better yet."

Wolfe made his way to the front of the church, keeping himself obscured from Gonzales's view by the pillars which ran down either side. When Gonzales stepped through the side door and into his office, Wolfe strode into the central aisle and raised his hands to the congregation.

"Excuse me, good people," he said, "I need your attention for a moment."

The room grew quiet. He knew he had to be quick. If Father Gonzales came back out before he finished, there was no telling what the man's reaction might be.

"I'm Father Daniel Wolfe, from the Vatican, and I have an important question to ask you." He held up his I.D. for anyone close enough to see it. Most took him at his word; a few had seen him there in uniform and informed their neighbours. Murmurs from the pews, raised eyebrows and excited looks. "I need to know if any of you have recently been asked for an asthma inhaler. Has anyone here given their medication to one of the priests? A life hangs in the balance. In the name of His Holiness the Pope, I authorise you to answer, even if an agreement of secrecy was made." He couldn't technically give such authority, but he counted on no one there knowing the finer points of ecclesiastical law.

The room was quiet and still for a moment, and then the silence was broken.

"What is the meaning of this? Father Wolfe! What are you doing?! This is unacceptable! Cease this at once, this is a holy service of Mother Church!"

"The mass does not begin for another five minutes. I am here on the authority of the Vatican and you cannot stop me. I command you by that authority to be silent."

"You command? I will not have this! You might be a priest, but I do not recognise your authority over me in my own congregation with nothing more than the word of a renegade with no more reverence for this mass than to show up dressed for a day on the beach!"

"Please," Wolfe repeated, turning to address the congregation again in a loud voice, "All I need is for you to tell me if any of you have given an asthma inhaler to a priest."

"None of them has!" Father Gonzales shouted, "Now it is time for you to go. Leave this place and leave this service before you do any more damage."

"How can you possibly know that no one here gave an asthma inhaler to a priest, Father Gonzales?" Wolfe turned on the old man now, his own anger and impatience growing, "Unless for some reason of your own you do not wish them to say so?"

"Impudence!" Gonzales shouted. "Is this the quality of priests we have in Rome?"

Wolfe sucked in his air to speak again, but the old man thrust a hand up in a practiced motion of authority and gained the moment he needed to continue.

"I did not say that no one here gave an inhaler, I said that none of the congregants had. I know this because it was *I* who gave the inhaler to Father Cisco. The stress of this situation has weighed heavily on him. He is a much more sensitive soul than his gruff appearance would lead one to believe. These past days have aggravated minor health concerns and he needed a temporary relief. There! You have your answer, though I cannot see how this was worth the disruption. I will be lucky to recover even a hint of the peace this service is meant to impart on the morning worshipers! Go. You've done enough here."

The old man could be lying, of course, covering his own tracks, but Wolfe didn't think so. He got the sense from Gonzales that, even were it to save his own skin, outright lying would be one sin that he would not commit. Still, there was perhaps one way by which Wolfe could check.

"Thank you, Father Gonzales," he said, "I apologise for the disruption. I assure you it was necessary." He left the dais then, and walked quickly to the lobby. Once there, he turned and closed the doors as if to assist in the recovery of a peaceful service. He then bounded to the side and up the stairs. Down the short hallway, glancing at the plastic plate on each of the doors until he saw one which read "Father Cisco."

Locked.

A step back and he kicked hard at the door. He heard a deep crack in the wood and felt the fire of his injured ribs awaken. Another kick and it swung open, a long splinter broken from the jamb near the lock. He sank to his knee for a moment, breathing in deeply and thrusting the pain back down inside.

Later. Time for the hurt later.

He hauled himself up. Two steps into the room and he learned what he had wanted to know: The smell from his suite the morning he had returned to find Ana gone. A childhood memory, faded almost to disappearance: Pipe smoke. Cisco's office was filled with the rich, sharp smell of pipe tobacco.

On his way back down the stairs, Wolfe met Gonzales coming out from the nave, fury on his face. "Father Wolfe! What is the noise? What is the meaning of this? You are to leave at once!"

Wolfe said nothing. He stepped out onto the front steps with Father Gonzales close behind, shouting chastisement in the triune names of God, good form, and holiness. It was enough to draw attention to the man in the blue shirt and shorts. It was enough for the two men in the van to notice. In the quiet of the morning, at the edge of Father Gonzales's shouts, recognition at last bloomed and an ignition turned on. An unmarked police van pulled out into the street.

They'd found Daniel Wolfe.

The rev of the van's engine was unnatural on the quiet, early-morning street. His training kicked in and he bolted, leaving Father Gonzales open-mouthed on the front steps. Wolfe rounded the corner of the church at a full run, only then glancing backward to see what it was that had triggered his flight. The two faces staring out through the windshield of the van snapped into his head like a photograph and his mind continued to look at them even as he passed by the side of the building and turned his attention to the ground at his feet and a possible path to escape.

They were cops, of that he was sure. And they wanted him.

Every instinct in him pushed his feet to run faster, to get away from the two faces and the roar of the engine which now rounded the side of the building and fishtailed into the gravelled parking area in a cloud of dust. Wolfe leapt the low barrier and was across the alley in three long steps, slamming back through the gate by which he had entered that morning, hearing the van slide to a crunching stop behind him.

As he passed through the empty yard he heard the passenger-side door slam and the whine of the engine as the van backed out of the churchyard. He knew that there were footfalls behind him, even if his heart pounded too loudly for his ears to hear them.

He raced past the house and burst out onto the street on the other side, paying little heed to any traffic on the roadway, knowing that his only hope of evasion lay in full committal to his flight, utter determination to avoid capture. He forced air into his lungs and threw his legs forward with each step, thrusting backward in an effort to gain just a little more speed, a little more advantage. He relaxed his arms. Conserved energy where he could. Pressed on.

But his ribs ached.

His mind, however willing it was, could not completely overcome the sharp stabs of pain which shot through his core with each impact of shoe on pavement, each twist of his body as he ran. Pain sucked energy. It drained resources. Pain was exhausting.

Behind him he could hear his pursuer, clearly now, puffing air out in sharp heaves, drawing it in once with every two steps he took, each one just a little closer to Wolfe, a little less freedom between the two of them with each passing second. There was no hope of outrunning the pursuing cop. Wolfe knew it as surely as anything. Sweat poured down over his face in the ageing Miami morning. But his feet kept moving.

He could stop and fight. The cop would have a gun, a Taser, pepper spray. Still, if he could time it just right, turn at just the right moment to take him by surprise. He listened through the pounding of his heart and the slapping of his sandalled feet for the change in the pursuer's breathing. In the distance he heard the roar of the van's engine as it turned the corner and joined them on the street behind the church building, lined with sleepy houses just stirring for a Friday morning, people waking to wonder at the noise and shouting.

Then he dropped.

It wasn't even a conscious choice. It was a compulsion born of years in combat, skills and instincts heightened to a degree beyond anything needed in regular life. Something in him felt a change in the rhythm of the man behind him, a change in the quality of his foot-falls, perhaps something yet more subtle — Wolfe never knew what it was — but it kicked in, and he allowed his leading leg to buckle, rolling his body to the side as he fell and slammed painfully into the base of a rotting, wooden planter box in an innocent resident's front yard.

The cop went over him. Worse than that, for the officer involved, his body flew over the place the priest lay while his foot caught the edge of the planter wall, turning the final lunge into a headlong miss. The man's body came down with a heavy *thud* upon the far side of the planter. Even Wolfe could hear the moaning rush of air as the man was winded, incapacitated, removed from the equation of escape.

The cop rolled over a moment, stunned. Scrabbled for his weapon. Wolfe forced himself up, despite renewed pain in his ribs and a new throbbing in his left forearm from where it had hit the board and taken the lion's share of the impact.

He pushed himself toward the west, away from the church, past the side of the next house and through the yard, hearing the van screech to a halt behind him and the other officer begin shouting into his radio. The man's words were lost in distance as his prey kicked open the rear fence and turned southward down the alley, running, fighting the pain in his ribs and a growing stitch in his side.

Wolfe needed rest. He needed to think.

He needed a place to hide and he wouldn't find that as long as he had either one of these men on his tail. He heard the crunching of his second pursuer's footfalls in the loose gravel behind him, neatly alternating with his own rhythmic run. Would the stop-and-drop work a second time? Would he be able to disable one more man and find a way to get out of there, find his car and speed off into a place of safety where he could form a plan to get Cisco? To save the girl?

His own slowing, failing feet had allowed his second pursuer, fresh on the chase, to gain on him, to reach a position just a few yards back. This second man had seen what had happened to the first and was not about to fall prey to the same tactic or to underestimate the fleeing priest. Just as Wolfe pondered the wisdom of incapacitating the cop, nothing too bad, just something to keep him from pursuing any further, the steps behind him slid to a stop in a rattle of loose gravel and the next moment, Wolfe felt as if a vehicle had struck him from behind.

His body stiffened, his back arched and he fell to the ground in the alley, the sharp stones rolling under his skidding face, cutting through flesh already burned and bruised and worn. His head rang like an anvil under a steel hammer.

After a moment he rallied his will and attempted to move. Another blast. Another spasm.

"Stay the fuck down I said! Stay DOWN!"

He squeezed out a cry of pain through clenched teeth as the man jolted him a third time with the Taser and followed it with a harsh kick to his torso. Had his hands not been paralysed and by his sides, a weak protection at least, Wolfe was sure the kick would have broken the cracked ribs, perhaps pierced something internally. It was time to give up, for now, to stop the fight.

"Okay," he groaned, "okay, I'm finished. I'm finished!"

"Stay down!"

"I will, I'm down."

A rough hand pinned his neck against the gravel and a knee fell, without gentleness, between his shoulder-blades as the officer pulled handcuffs from belt and clicked them onto Wolfe's wrists.

"I should be beating the living shit out of you right now. What are you running for? You think running ever did anybody any good? All it shows is we're right, you *sonnovabitch!*" a downward thrust from the knee, a grunt from Wolfe, "All it shows is we're right."

The man knelt there for a minute or two to catch his breath. A quick call on the radio was answered by his panting partner. It was not long until the van pulled slowly around the corner and the first officer, in pain but not seriously injured, leaned his head out of the driver's side window.

"You call it in?"

"Not yet. You do it. Tell Delaney we're on our way right now. We've got the priest in custody."

TWENTY

Father Antony Cisco placed the last item into the suitcase and closed the lid, clipping the old-style clasps firmly into place. He didn't trust those plastic zippers. How could plastic zippers hold anything really securely? He didn't trust all of these new things. That's what had attracted him to church service in the first place: a respect for the tried and true. Tradition. Loyalty.

But even there, things had begun to change too quickly for his tastes.

His flight for Panama left in less than seven hours and he was nearly ready to go. He was packed, his business at the church wrapped up. Just a few things to do before leaving and he had no need to worry about the place anymore. His duty there would be done.

His flight would take him to San Jose first, then to Panama City. From there he could melt into the jungles and move southward into his old mission grounds. He would live there again. Serve there. Die there, in his own hammock. The trip had been planned for nearly two years, the flight booked eight months ago. His responsibilities at the community centre had been gradually passed on to Father Pascal, and any regulatory problems solved with the willing help of Father Gonzales. It was as if Gonzales had wanted him to go.

It was a shame about Father Pascal. Allegations put forth by a young man, a young man who knew nothing but rumours. He should have been turned away at once, but Pascal was ever the soft heart for those young men and women at the centre. He seldom saw the truth, that they were street-hardened. Mature beyond their years. Even crafty. Crafty like serpents. The young priest would not let it go. Pressed him. Cisco fought back the images from his mind: the confrontation, the hard words, the scuffle. He hadn't meant to hurt poor Emilio, but once he had, there was little he could do about it. He had tried to stop the bleeding. Didn't know there was other bleeding. Inside.

He shook himself from these thoughts. They would not help poor Emilio now. They would not help anyone now. His one hope lay in getting out of there alive and unsuspected. He had wanted to let the police woman go, but he had slipped up there too. In a moment of distraction he had let her see his skin. She had know his race, his age, his eyes — possibly even be able to identify him. He had seen her before, after all, at services now and then. The night he had killed Kevin Ortez. She had grown bold and almost mocking the last few visits and she seemed to know about the little room. He supposed she guessed what lay in there, carefully wrapped in plastic sheeting to keep the smell from overpowering the basement too soon.

He was ashamed of his tears and regret after doing such actions as he thought necessary to protect the reputation of the Church. He had done nothing wrong. He had never forced anyone to do anything they hadn't wanted to do. Yet still threats were made, demands.

The first cop, nosing around in the church and making innuendoes, accusations without a shred of evidence or understanding, as if he spoke to a common person rather than to a holy emissary of the church, however fallible. Pascal had demanded public confession and reparations. Douglas had demanded money. Easy enough. Then more money.

And the young woman: At first she had demanded very little, relieved to be alive, respectful… but she had changed. His kindness and care were repaid with harsh words and venom. His efforts to feed her had been held in contempt. He had wanted to do right by her. He had wanted to let her go. Once free, and him gone, any speculation of his involvement would be only that: unsubstantiated possibilities. Any blemish on the church would be avoided.

He had wanted to let her go.

From a drawer near his bed he drew out the small black duffle and lifted a Walther P-38 from the bottom of it. One of his father's weapons from Germany, one of the collection. A second Luger 9mm was also there, a twin to the one left in Pascal's apartment after their fight. He reached down and pulled the P-38's chamber open half an inch. The shiny brass casing of a round sat snugly in the confines of the chamber. In a little less than an hour he would be forced to pull the trigger, to let the little shell do what it was made to do.

In a way, he would have very little to do with the actual killing. His finger would pull the trigger, true, but it would be the release of the firing pin that would allow steel to strike the shell. It was the mechanism of the shell that would strike a spark within the chamber. It was the gunpowder that would ignite and expand and force the slug — spinning and warping with the urgency of its path — down through the barrel and out into the world, untouched and no longer guided by the hand of the man who held the gun.

Separation.

Almost innocence.

He would be distant from it as it struck her. Its shape would fragment and spread in reaction to the impact against her skin and each fragment would choose its own twisting path through her body, according to a thousand minute variations and influences. The priest himself: separate. Absent from it, in a way. The enactor of a necessary measure. What happened after his finger depressed the trigger was up to the providence of God.

There was a greater good at stake.

He placed the gun back in the duffle and picked up his newly-packed suitcase. He then double-checked that his travel documents were all in order and that he had left the key on the kitchen table as requested by the landlord.

He had left the plants.

Everything else was gone. A moment at the door to look over his little apartment for the last time. A deep breath. A few hours and it would all be over.

Just one more thing to do.

Wolfe was in a holding room, sitting at a little table on a plastic-moulded chair with metal legs. He looked into the one-way glass, mirrored on his side, and assessed the damage. His new shirt and shorts were stained with drops and smears of blood from his face where the gravel had scraped it and where the blood had congealed around the particles of dirt and pebbles from the alley.

It was already beginning to throb. Cleaning it later would be agony.

His knees were scraped up and one of his cheap sandal straps had torn, so each step now displayed an undignified *flapping* sound from his right foot. After the night in the car — the night after the booze in the little bar — he had no doubt that he smelled and looked like some addict brought in after being found asleep by a fountain somewhere, or on somebody's stoop. Even his hair was sticking up like a rooster's.

He was still cuffed, but they'd moved the metal restraints to the front, through a heavy pin in the table, so he could at least lean back in the chair normally. He sat and waited for Delaney. When the door opened and a figure walked in, Wolfe was relieved to find that it was not Delaney at all who stood there, but Jackson, holding a yellow plastic bag in his hands.

"Thank God it's you!"

"You might not want to thank him just yet, Father Wolfe."

Father Wolfe? Damn.

"Look, you've got to know I didn't do any of this. *You* phoned *me* to come to Kevin's killing. I have no reason to hurt Ana, no reason to hurt the boy, or Father Pascal."

"Just because I don't see any reasons, doesn't mean that there aren't any."

Wolfe shook his head. He had hoped that Jackson, at least, would be backing him. He had a difficult story to tell Delaney, one that he himself would have a hard time believing if it hadn't been for the last three years, years spent rummaging through the worst that the priesthood had to offer.

He had come to *expect* depravity in every dark corner — it was why he was brought into each situation, after all — but he knew that most people dealt primarily with the cleaner side, the true priests, the ones who could keep their pants zipped and their hearts in the right place. Even if they were cynical about those who did take advantage of their positions in the church, the true depth of their crimes was not in the public psyche.

Wolfe wondered if the virtuous ones could ever do more good than the damage done by their less numerous counterparts. Could they ever tip the scale in their favour? Delaney would think not. Wolfe might be able to win them over once the evidence from the car tampering was in, but that could take weeks. Pascal and

316

Cruz didn't have weeks. Delaney knew that too, and would come at Wolfe hard. The embittered cop already had it in for him, there was no way the detective would believe a story like this with no proof and only a vague guess at motive.

"If you don't believe me, why are you here?"

"Here," Billy said, tossing the bag onto the table, "A Father Sanchez dropped it off. It seems that someone from Saint Mary's made a call to inform the bishop of what was going on."

"That's it?"

"That's it. I don't know what you expected."

"I'm Kevin's brother."

"You're his half-brother and I've known you all of, what? A week? Two days before this shit all started with you in the middle of it? My best friend is gone, his girlfriend missing. Where's the common thread, Father? If not you, then what is the one thing that ties it all together?"

His voice was loud. Wolfe couldn't be sure, but it seemed to him that, as Jackson said these last words, something crept into his expression, some kind of frantic sincerity that made all of his former speech seem a put-on.

"Here," he said, tossing his handcuff key onto the table, "change your clothes." As he stepped out through the door into the hallway, Wolfe heard him say to someone in the observation room, "He's all yours." He grasped the key in his hand, feeling better knowing it was there.

A moment later, the door popped open and Delaney stepped in, engrossed, it seemed, in the contents of a thick manila file. He sat, without a word, as if this were a casual visit with a long-term inmate rather than a suspect interview with a man who'd just been brought in, resisting the arrest, on suspicion of car theft, up to three murders, and a kidnapping or two... a potential cop-killer who had another officer in a makeshift prison. At last the man looked up and smiled at Wolfe.

"And how are we?"

"We?"

The detective chuckled. "Well yes, I see what you mean... I'm doing quite well of course, though I'd be doing better if you'd help me clear up a few things."

"Such as?"

"Such as what motive you might have had for killing the boy."

"Which boy?"

"Douglas. There's more than one?"

Wolfe's eyes widened. This was new. "What do you mean?"

"*Douglas*. You remember, the kid with the letter opener stuck in his back... last time you saw him." Delaney knew about the letter opener? Jackson must have talked to him then.

"I didn't kill Douglas, but I do know who did."

"Oh yes? Interesting. Who did it then?"

"Father Cisco. And he's got Ana."

"Where?"

"I don't know yet, but we haven't much time."

"We don't?"

"No, we don't. I think Cisco's leaving the country — I don't know where to yet. Central America probably."

"Wow. Cisco. I wouldn't have thought it. Alright then," the big man rose as if to leave, stopping as his hand touched the doorknob. "Oh, one last thing though."

"What's that?" Wolfe didn't like the way this was going.

"How did the letter opener wind up in your rooms?"

"What? How did *what*?"

"See that's answering a question with a question, and where my wife's rabbi might get away with that, we're a little more picky down here at the precinct." The detective's eyes narrowed and grew cold. His little game was over. Now the hurt would begin.

"You need to listen to me, Detective, Ana's life is at stake."

"Is that a threat?"

"No, no, it's not a threat, but I know it was Cisco and I know that he's planning on leaving soon. If he gets away, we may never find Ana. Or worse, he might take care of loose ends before he goes, loose ends like a woman who can identify him."

"Fascinating!"

"Look, he was into something that Kevin either found out about, or was asking around about. Molesting the kid, I would guess, and he killed him."

"Killed Kevin, or the kid?"

"Both of them."

"Ah, yes, of *course*."

"I was getting close to him too, asking around the church. There was no opportunity to take care of me the way he had the other two, so he tried to blow me up — twice."

"Twice?"

"The second time he met, unexpectedly, I presume, Ana in my hotel room."

"Ah yes, the woman in the priest's hotel room... Do go on."

"He took her, and he's got her now. He tried to frame Father Pascal, then killed him, sabotaged my car and now he's obviously trying to frame me."

"Or you tried to frame Pascal."

"And myself? Only an idiot would leave a murder weapon in his own home!"

"Unless he had already seen how quickly we saw through it the other time. You ever see *The Princess Bride*? I know, that you know, that I know..." he was grinning, but there was no question that he was going in for a kill.

"Look, we're both priests, no stranger for me to have done it than for him — but think about it: what is my motive? Why would *I* do it?"

"And he did all this because...?"

"Because he didn't want to be outed for the molestation."

"Hmm. Interesting story. So what you're telling me is that, to prevent what might have been a short sentence, if convicted, for fondling a teenager, this guy — a priest

320

— kills a cop in front of an altar, in his own church, stabs a kid, sets off bombs, rigs cars, kidnaps an officer and plans an escape, all while going about his daily routine, praying prayers and doing whatever the *fuck* it is you guys do all day?"

"I think the escape was already planned. Before a crime ever happened — the violent ones at least."

"Do you." Voice as flat as his eyes.

"Yes."

"He planned the escape before the opportunistic crime? Before your brother came sniffing around for perverts in robes? I see. That's some good priest. He must really hear the voice of prophesy, eh Father? You know. I almost believed you before. Hell, let's tell it like it is: I did believe you. I won't make that mistake again."

Wolfe lowered his forehead to his empty hand. His explanation, wild as it seemed, all fit. It was plausible, even if it did sound outlandish all in one breath. These things didn't start complicated. They grew. Step by step. Small crime, avoidance, coverup... Bigger crime.

It was worth checking out.

But he knew that Delaney wouldn't do it. He knew that, in the cop's mind, the killer was already in custody. The detective felt like a fool for having let him go before, and he would do all he could to keep this fox from getting away before the judicial hounds got their teeth into it. Tick the boxes. Collect the credit. Move on.

Delaney chuckled to himself, "People think cops are rough. They have no friggin` idea where the real sadism is. A rogue-priest cop-killer won't last a week at trial. And a priest who killed a kid? Not a day in the general pop˙ of a prison. At best, you make a deal. Tell us where everybody is, alive or dead, and hope for protective incarceration. Might keep the shivs at bay... *Might*."

Wolfe was history, to Delaney's mind, and good riddance.

The big man grunted as he stretched and rose to his feet. "Well Father, I don't think you're quite ready to confess — maybe the irony is too much for you yet — so I'm gonna give you a few more minutes to think things over. Maybe an hour or two. I can't make you any deals, that's a given, unless we get some answers as to where Ana Cruz might be located." Delaney's gaze became sharp and he stared right into Wolfe's eyes. "You give me that, and I swear I'll get you every lenience I can dig up or improvise. You got me? Everything." He paused. "You *don't* do it, and I'll see you burn in hell — even if I'm the one to send you there. There's everything good on this side," he held his open hand out to his left, "and everything fucking horrible on this one," he held his right hand wide to the other side, in a fist. "Your choice."

He turned then, and stepped out of the room. Wolfe heard him tell someone to keep an eye on room three, let him stew for a few hours.

No one came in immediately, or even looked in on him, unless it was through the mirrored window. Using the key Billy had left, Wolfe uncuffed himself and rubbed his raw wrists. He pulled off the damaged clothing and wiped his face gently with the shirt to get the worst of the pebbles from the still-soft blood, where he could. He let the shorts fall to the ground and pulled on the neatly-creased black pants and shirt. In the bottom of the bag he found the white collar insert and slid it into place. The black socks and shoes felt like heaven.

His uniform, such as it was. His armour.

He saw himself in the one-way glass. Neat enough, now that the clothes held no sign of the struggle. His face was clearly injured, and freshly so, but he didn't look like he was in the midst of turmoil any longer. Fingers through the hair and it was passable. Stylish even.

He felt physically better — at least he felt cleaner — but his mind kept going back to Cruz, back to that room she was being kept in… back to how little time she might have left if no one did anything more than interrogate the wrong guy. He shoved the cuffs into his pocket.

His stomach couldn't take the strain of sitting down again. He began pacing the room. Outside, in the open area of the station, Delaney chatted up one of the young female officers for a few minutes, then strode off to the restrooms. Jackson was in the captain's office, briefing him on the progress of a case of his own. In the little room, shut off from it all and without pausing to hinder the compulsion, Wolfe turned, reached for the knob, and pulled the door open. There had been no need to lock a room in which the occupant is cuffed to the table.

He took in a wide glance of the open area office as he stepped out, but kept it casual. No familiar faces glanced back. The breeze of the air conditioning blew against the scrapes on his face as he walked, and he was conscious of how he must look to others. He did get a few stares from those he passed in the hall and open office area, but he was no more disturbing than the myriad prostitutes, beat-up homeless, incarcerated bullies or gang-bangers that often crowded the place. Much less so in fact.

He was a priest, and though he had come in wearing dirty shorts and a torn shirt, with blood and gravel ground into face and fabric, he now walked tall, unrestrained, and in fresh, ironed clothing.

He was a different man, obviously the victim of some kind of attack or accident, and had he known it, the stares he received were those of sympathy and regret that such a thing should happen to a person dedicated to peace and service. He walked out just like any other voluntary visitor. Anyone who might know different was absent from the room, or distracted by other work.

He passed through the intake area and down the front stairs. His pace quickened as he turned down the sidewalk and he fought the urge to run, to burst into flight and get as many miles between himself and the station as he could. He had made it almost a block when it hit him that he had just broken out of police custody. They'd read him his rights… hadn't they? His recall of those moments was blurred. Had they said he was under arrest? They did cuff him… but he had also been given a key. Was he allowed to just leave? No one had told him he couldn't. Not technically. Wasn't he allowed to go unless they charged him?

He tucked away the thoughts for later. They didn't matter now. The worst they had to threaten him with was not enough to keep him from going after Cruz anyway.

A block and a half from the station was a Cuban coffee shop, a hole-in-the-wall café with bills posted all over the windows, obscuring the inside from the view of road traffic while affording those inside a decent view of what was going on around the place.

Perfect.

He could hunker down, even for a few minutes, and formulate a plan. He was ten steps from the door when he heard the screech of tires and turned to see Jackson jumping out of the driver's side of his car. Wolfe kept walking, past the shop, and turned into an alley just as the cop caught up with him and grabbed his shoulder from behind.

Wolfe's fingers curled into a fist, and he struck.

TWENTY-ONE

"What the fuck do you think you're-"

Jackson's sentence was cut short as Wolfe dropped below the outstretched arm and spun, crouched low, rising up with the power of his toes, his foot, then the chain of muscles and bone up through his core to his fist, driving a blow into the young cop's solar plexus that knocked him back a pace and took the solidity from his knees. The strike forced the air from his lungs and stunned him long enough for the priest to swing Jackson's arm around behind him, to drop him to the ground with a shoulder lock and to place a demobilising foot on his friend's back.

Pulling the cuffs from his pocket, Wolfe snapped the outstretched wrist into one bracelet, leaned the other over to the wall and clipped it around a protruding gas line pipe. He then stepped back.

Jackson sucked in a deep breath, finally feeling the muscles of his chest relax. He spun around, pulling his sidearm from its holster and pointing it at the priest's chest. Wolfe, just out of reach, stood his ground.

"What the hell man," Jackson said through panting breaths, "Do you have any idea, *any* idea what you're doing?"

"I know what I have to do. Ana's life depends on it."

"You can't do this. I can't let you do this. My goddam key, man."

"You can't stop me. It's her only hope. By the time Delaney finishes with me… it could be too late."

"I can stop you," Jackson said, the gun growing steadier as his body reclaimed air and recovered from the shock of the attack.

"Yeah," Wolfe answered, "But you won't. Not that way."

Then he turned and left the alley, ignoring the shouts and threats from behind him.

He looked to the side, off down the street toward the heart of the city, and then to the other, back the way he had come. There sat, door slightly open and engine running, an unmarked silver sedan. Jackson's police cruiser.

He didn't want to get the young cop into any more trouble than he already had. But then again, extreme need justifies extreme action — wasn't that what they'd taught him in Special Forces? Isn't that more or less what his granddad had meant when he said 'Sometimes, son, a guy's got to man-up, do what he's gotta do'?

As he pulled away from the alley, he wound the window down and threw the handcuff key. It bounced and spun and settled nowhere near Jackson, as it happened, but at least the first person on scene could let him out, perhaps saving him a bit of embarrassment for having been out-manoeuvred in a fight by a priest.

The car sped toward Saint Mary's. Wolfe didn't know why, but he was certain that the answer to his final question must lay there. He knew the whole story, he felt sure, except for one thing: the location of Ana Cruz. He had little hope of finding Cisco out in the open, but if he could figure out where the priest could hide a kidnapping victim, then he could meet the predator in his lair. At the very least, he could give her a chance at survival. The crime hadn't been planned; there had to be an opportunistic place to put her. The picture gave him a sense of the kind of place it might be, but no real clues. The man had been careful.

He smiled grimly; the way his luck was going lately, he was more likely to be caught just as he found the place and further implicate himself. Ah well, no point wasting his head space on things he couldn't change. And even if that happened, Cruz would be safe.

The car sped on.

He was a fugitive at large, driving a stolen police car which probably had some kind of GPS tracker on it. Nothing to lose... he hit the sirens and the accelerator. Once they saw his general direction, they would assume he was on his way to the church. Maybe it was far-fetched, but he couldn't afford to take chances. He doubted he could pull off another jail-break, even if he resorted to violence and brought all of his skills to bear. No, there had been enough of that. But where else could he go for information? Someplace they might not look right away?

He redirected the car toward the community centre and it was then that the solution hit him: The community centre. Cisco had been looking after that particular ministry for some years, but things had changed recently. New guy coming in, new paint-jobs on the vans… new building. A new building meant there had to be an old building too.

He killed the siren as he pulled the car into the parking lot and screeched to a halt in front of the main doors. He ran inside and spotted Albany, the boy he had held against the wall on his last visit to the building, to loosen his tongue. Well, hopefully the boy was still primed, because Wolfe had even less patience this time, and was in a hurry.

As he approached he saw the blood drain from the boy's face and the little group of street-kids went silent.

"One thing," Wolfe said, "I want one thing and then I walk out of here. Got it?"

The boy nodded.

"Where was the community centre before it was here?"

"Over there," he said, pointing, "on Evans."

"What does it look like?"

"White. It has the old sign still."

"Thanks. Keep yourself out of shit." Then he turned and left.

The old centre was set on a raised field of maybe an acre and a half. The structure itself took up a good portion of that. It was a long, wide construction of concrete blocks, the floor of the main level raised up, so that a basement could be included and kept dry, despite the high water table. The windows were vandalised. Boarded up. Pascal had mentioned damage. Flooding. Bad windows.

It was quiet. There were a couple of cars nearby, but nothing parked right in front of the building or in the front lot. He watched the place for a few moments, seeking anything out of the ordinary before going in. From the outside, everything seemed fine: a nondescript, semi-abandoned building waiting for its next duty, or for destruction.

A little destruction was on the way.

There were two sets of doors visible on the front side of the place, the main set, where the public came and went, back in the days of its use, and the second set, smaller but still very prominent and with a porch-like structure of their own. Wolfe stepped out of the car and walked over to the main doors. They were locked securely with deadbolts in place and chains looped through the handles. Padlocks. Strolling along the front of the building, knowing that no one — except Cisco himself — would find the presence of a priest anything suspicious, he made his way to the second set of doors.

No chains, but the deadbolts were in place.

He followed the wall around the side and into the gravelled patch of make-shift parking stalls at the back.

There he saw an old camper-van. It seemed as if it had been abandoned some time though, as it was caked in dust and had that sun-baked look. Grass was growing up over one of the tires. If she were being held in there, she would have been dead from heat long ago. Besides, the picture had her in a concrete room.

He ignored the thing and walked instead over to the little loading dock, stepping up the cracked steps and over to the doors. No chains. The first door stayed fast as he pressed down the thumb-latch and pulled the handle. The second latch depressed and the door gave.

It was in times like these that Wolfe wished he carried a gun. He had no desire to shoot anyone else, but there were times when he was stepping into unknown situations that he would have liked one. Liked to wield at least the threat of a firearm, the deterrent of a 'big stick' of his own. He braced himself and stepped through into the darkness.

A moment or two gave his eyes time to adjust to the dim light. A flashlight would be useful. Maybe one in the car? No time to go back out. He was in. Time to find Cruz — if she was there. He pulled in air through his nose, trying to catch the scent of pipe-smoke, but there was none detectable, only the musty, slightly rotten smell of a disused building, almost a taste in the air. It was hot.

And still.

The room he was in was some kind of loading area, lined with metal shelving, empty, for the most part, and devoid of feature except for a pair of double-doors on two-way hinges opposite him. He stepped quietly toward them. He pressed an ear against the dusty wood of the door and listened.

Nothing.

He pushed through, ready for a sudden flurry of activity, an attack, a grisly scene of some kind — anything, really, except for what he saw: a large, empty room, dimly lit by the gaps in the boarded windows which dominated the long wall. Thin slivers of light shone through in places, casting furtive light deeper into the building.

Off to the right was a stage with a couple of microphone stands still sticking up from it. To the left the room went off into semi-darkness. Emptiness. Moving to his right, Wolfe hugged the wall until he came to a door.

Again he listened. Nothing.

He tried the knob. A long, narrow closet. The smell of rancid filth blew out from a forgotten mop bucket and he quickly closed the door again, thrusting down the urge to wretch.

The next door opened into a dark office, obviously disused, as did the third. On the wall of the third room, partially lit by a break in the plywood window covering, was a framed photograph of the building. Black and white, and taken long before it became a community centre. He walked over to it and leaned in close. "Henken House, Residential Asylum, 1949-1997." It looked posh. High end. But the windows were barred.

He turned around then, having cleared that end of the room, and moved quietly toward the dim expanse. It had obviously been used as some kind of meeting hall, though there were lines in the floor made of holes from old concrete nails. These signs of removed walls made him wonder what it had been like back when it was a mental hospital. Elite. For only the most privileged of the mentally ill. Part of this room might have been a reception or activity hall, large enough for intimate luxury, airy and well-lit from the tall windows behind the modern plywood.

The wealthy relatives of the unmanageable insane would have come here, signed the papers, left their loved ones behind. It wasn't that long ago that anyone with a mental illness or awkward condition — schizophrenia, depression, dementia, autism, even Down Syndrome — would have been sent to a place like this, strapped down or kept in a padded room, electro-shocked toward an appearance of normalcy.

Padded rooms, he thought, *a great place to hold a captive.*

It was the perfect place, the more he thought about it, the perfect place to hide someone, to keep them from interfering with a plan. A perfect place, even, to kill. Cruz's room didn't look padded in the photograph, but he had been careful not to show too much in the photograph. He might even have been deliberately deceptive. He would move her out of a padded room, if that' what he was using — too easy to find them otherwise. It was a good spot though. How long would it be, he wondered, until somebody hidden in this place would be found?

The Catholic Church is one of the largest landowners in the world and has hundreds, maybe thousands, of disused buildings waiting for new purposes, often gaining in resale value even as they rot and fall to pieces.

He returned to the main room. All of the doors had been checked, except for the three sets of double-doors which he knew led out into the front, to the parking lot across from which Jackson's stolen police car sat under the shade and cover of a large Banyan tree. Despite the situation, he smiled to himself; he had promised the man he wouldn't steal any more cars...

He stood to full height and stretched out his back, tired from crouching and creeping around. The material pulled free of his sweat-soaked skin, then settled onto it again, cooler. Almost refreshing.

He didn't see any other doors and he hadn't seen stairs in any of the rooms. It was dim, true, but they had been too small to hide something like a stairwell. Unless the entrance to the basement was like some Kansas-inspired tornado shelter, external and flush to the ground, then there must be a stairwell somewhere, and there was only one place left where it could reasonably be.

For the first time since realisation of his theory, doubts had begun to grow. All of this for nothing? If she wasn't there, then he had lost his chance. They wouldn't let him go again, and there were a good many charges they could lay against him now, charges that were true and verifiable... He didn't like to dwell on it.

He turned his gaze to the large, empty room with the stage in it and tried to make shapes out in the dimness. He walked closer to the far wall, under the boarded windows. They faced eastward and, as the sun sank further down in the west, the light they afforded continued to fade and withdraw from the room. By the time he found the gaping rectangular hole in the floor he had almost stepped out over the edge, almost fallen down through the deep end of the opening, to land on the sharp corners of the concrete steps below.

He walked around the outside of the hole and began to work his way down the long flight of stairs. As he did so, he thought he could hear, faintly down below, the cry of a woman. Relief and tension washed over him at once. She was there. She was alive. Were there also the deep tones of a male voice, or was that his imagination playing tricks on him?

He stepped down and followed the sound through the deepening darkness, to a doorless opening in the wall to his left. He saw Cruz in the circle of flashlight glow at the far end of the room and, his body in a crouch and ready for combat, he moved forward. His foot stepped out into nothing and he sprawled downward, grinding his shin against the rim of the chipped-out drainage hole. He heard the crack of gunfire and felt the sprinkling bits of shattered concrete as a bullet smashed into the wall somewhere above his head.

He grasped the edges of the ragged hole and threw himself backward, back through the way he had come, another bullet cracking through the darkness and shattering with its impact against the wall.

Wolfe ran toward the stairwell, but passed beside it rather than up. He had detected the faint outline of a door on the wall behind the diagonal slab of steps. He ran up against it and fumbled with the knob in the darkness. Light shone through the opening behind him, wavered and bounced wildly as a flashlight was picked up. The light in the doorway grew as the gunman began his pursuit of the unwelcome visitor. Wolfe heard the choking anger of a woman's voice in the darkness, shouting in relief or warning. Probably both.

Turning the knob and yanking the door open, he ran out into the pitch-dark of the unknown, a hand stretched out in front, wracking his brain for some estimation of how far it might go before its abrupt end, probably in a solid wall.

His headlong flight ceased before that. Just as the beam of light was thrust through the doorway, he met a knee-high box filled with something heavy and his momentum threw him forward, over a pile of junk and damaged sporting equipment.

Three more bullets cracked out of the muzzle-flash in the darkness, none of them finding their mark, as Wolfe hit the floor on the far side of the obstacle and grasped across the dusty floor for something to use as a weapon. He found a ping-pong paddle with a cracked handle.

A poor tool is often worse than no tool at all, but in that instance all he needed was a missile, and anything that would fly would do. He grasped the disk-like paddle face between his finger and thumb and rose up just high enough to get an accurate location for the flashlight. Then he hurled the little wooden paddle like a throwing star, spinning, cracked handle and all, through the air toward the shooter.

He never knew if he hit his target or not, but before the missile even made it to the man, Wolfe was off again. The flashes of light around the room had revealed a door in the wall which stood slightly ajar in the darkness. He took five frantic steps and then he was through, not sure whether the sound he had heard was a gunshot or his own heartbeat pounding against his eardrums.

The room was in complete darkness and Wolfe knew that running head-long through that inky air was as sure as death when his pursuer had a gun and a light, so when he made it through the opening he turned back again and hid behind the door, letting it creak slowly into place in the few seconds it would take for the gunman to reach it, to burst through it, and to put an end to the chase, one way or the other.

And then an end to Ana Cruz.

TWENTY-TWO

Jackson would have preferred Delaney tease him, but the big man was far too angry to take anything as a joke. The curses that flowed from his mouth were almost visible in the air around him as he threw the key against the brick wall beside Jackson's chest and let him unlock his own damn cuffs. It would have been better for the young cop if Wolfe had hit him in the face, though if he had needed to do so, Jackson could have lifted his shirt to reveal the beginnings of a dark bruise forming around the top of his belly.

"Where was he going?" Delaney demanded as his junior slid into the car beside him, two marked cruisers with lights on waiting patiently behind them, unable to suppress smiles at the thought of the future razzing this episode was sure to bring into the precinct locker room.

"Where do *you* think he's going, super-cop." Jackson said, forgetting his customary reverence for the older detective. Rather than bringing the explosion he would have expected though, his comment calmed the mood in the car and Delaney took a deep breath. He had been bested by the priest too.

"The church?"

"Unless he knows where Ana is."

"You think he does?" The big man looked sharply at Jackson.

"No, I don't, but I thought you did."

"I didn't discount it," Delaney said with a short shake of his head, "but I don't know. At first it didn't seem to stick quite right. Then I thought he duped me. Now? More has come in about his car. I had it rushed. Seems he wasn't lying about that. Somebody is trying to kill him. He's a pain in the ass, there's no doubt there, but I don't think he killed his brother."

"Why did you have him followed? Arrested?"

"Well he's obviously in this thing somehow, or he wouldn't have apartments exploding in his wake and somebody fucking with his car."

"If it wasn't him, he would be out looking for whoever it was killed Kevin and still has Ana, and probably Pascal," Jackson said.

"And that would probably mean the church."

"Unless he knows something else we don't know."

"Let's hope not," Delaney shook his head, "we're likely in enough shit for this fiasco as it is."

The radio popped to life and their suspicions were confirmed — the stolen cruiser was heading for Saint Mary's. They had a bead on their target. They pulled out into the street, speeding toward the church with sirens wailing, the grill lights on and the two marked cars following behind.

Father Jésus Gonzales picked up his phone on the fifth ring, panting from the effort of getting from the nave to his office in time to answer it. It was Rosa, from the community centre.

"Yes Rosa, what is it?"

"Hello Father," her accent was thick, but she always insisted on speaking to him in English, probably to demonstrate her determination to be the best helper she could be. Ironic, considering Gonzales was a native Spanish speaker, but the little oddity was nothing too taxing under normal circumstances. In truth, if she just continued spending as many hours as she did looking after the youth at the centre and didn't cause any trouble herself, Father Gonzales was as happy as could be.

"Hello Rosa, what can I do for you?"

"I don't know, but I think I should call you…"

She sounded upset.

"That's fine, is there a problem?"

"Oh I don' know, Father, maybe yes but maybe no. Maybe is nothing…"

Gonzales took a deep breath and mastered his impatience. "All the same, Rosa, perhaps it's best if you tell me what the problem might be, hmm? I would like to hear it."

"Oh, well, if you would like, I tell you. Is just the other priest, the one who fight with Albany…"

"Yes?" his interest was high again.

"He come back. He come in a car and ask where the other centre is, the old one. He race away. Jacob say he in a police car too. Is he police, Father? I tell him no, but he say is a police car. Other kids say yes too, police car, but no police."

"Thank you," he said, keeping his voice calm to hide the furious working of his brain, "I'm sure it's nothing, but all the same why don't we close up for the night, shut things down a little early."

"You sure, Father? The children…"

"It's okay, they'll be fine for one night without ping-pong and Kool-Aid. Shut it down for now. We'll resume as normal tomorrow night."

"Okay, if you sure."

"Yes," he said, not finding it amusing that he was forced to justify himself to the community centre cleaning woman, "I am sure. Close the doors and lock them. You go home as well."

"Okay, Father. Good-night and God bless you."

"God bless you as well. Good-night."

"I pray for you today."

"You too, Rosa, take care."

He hung up the phone and remained standing for a little while, pondering what this might mean. He couldn't think why the priest would want to know where the old centre was — at least no reason he was willing to entertain — but he was very certain that he didn't like Wolfe poking his nose around things, stirring up problems and rumours that Gonzales himself had already taken care of. He picked up the phone, pressed the button for an outside line, and dialled the number from the little card he had been given on the night of the murder.

"I'm sorry, Detective Delaney is out of the station right now, may I take a message?"

"Is it possible to be patched through to him?"

"If it is an emergency, yes."

Gonzales thought for a moment. "Yes, it is."

"Okay, please hold a moment."

The line crackled and beeped. A sound like the ticking of a fishing rod reel continued for a few seconds, then the line opened and Delaney was on the other end, patched through to his radio.

"Delaney here."

"Yes, Detective, so sorry to bother you, but I think I might have a problem here."

"Who is this?"

"Oh, I'm sorry, this is Father Gonzales from Saint Mary of the Sea."

"Really," he said, hoping the action hadn't started without him, "And what's the problem?"

"Well, it may be nothing of course, but Father Wolfe was seen at the community centre. The children believe he was driving an unmarked police car and, I don't need to tell you, those children would know. Were you aware of this?"

Delaney ignored the question. "Is he still there?" He had already altered the direction of the car. New destination. More speed.

"Well, he asked about the old centre, the old building. I'm not comfortable with his interest. It is difficult to explain."

"No need. Where is the old centre?"

"On Evans, just a few blocks north from the new one."

"Right. I'll check it out."

"Thank you, I hope I'm not being any trouble."

"No, none at all. And Father?"

"Yes?"

"Do you have keys to the building?"

"Yes, I have some around here somewhere. Father Cisco dropped them off with his relocation papers."

"Relocation papers?"

"Yes, he's leaving for the mission field again — perhaps already has."

"He's quit his job? You didn't think to inform us?"

"No, no, he just changes location and duties. It is nothing new."

Delaney cursed under his breath, just audible enough for Gonzales to guess at the content.

"Father Gonzales..."

"Yes?"

"I'm going to need you to meet me over there with the keys."

"I suppose I can do that. How long until you arrive?"

"I'm guessing about two minutes."

"Two minutes?!"

"Yes. And don't be late."

Delaney cut off the call. Cursed everything in sight. He pushed the pedal yet further to the floor as the car squealed out of a residential corner and onto the last straightaway toward Evans Drive. Jackson hung on and said nothing. Whatever was happening, both men knew that the culmination of the case, for good or for bad, was just a few blocks ahead of them.

Father Cisco came through the doorway into the dark office, flashlight leading the way. One sharp heave against the door as the older priest came through it and Wolfe pinned him against the wall. The flashlight fell to the ground with a metallic *ping-ping* and the light went out. One more shove against the door and the gun fell as well.

Still, if Wolfe had hoped for an easy fight, he was sorely disappointed. Cisco may not have been a soldier, but he had been a missionary in some of the harshest conditions South and Central America had to offer, and he was a tougher soul than he looked. He was older, but bigger, with no cracked ribs or burns to deal with. He also possessed the strength of desperation, that power loaned to any sentient thing when it knows that its life hangs in the balance. The door slammed open again and the older man threw himself forward, deeper into the office.

Wolfe dropped to his knees, feeling around for the pistol that he knew lay there, somewhere on the dark floor. As his fingers touched the flat, cold metal of the barrel. He smiled. Then he heard a familiar sound in the darkness of the office, the three sharp clicks of a round being chambered in an automatic pistol. Not his.

Cisco had another weapon.

Two bright shots filled the room with freeze-framed images of the two men and a cloud of acrid gunpowder fumes. Wolfe half-rolled into the doorway and kicked his feet out, launching himself back into the junk-filled room he had just fled, letting a scream of pain go as his ribs seemed to grind, bone-on-bone with the effort of his escape. One more shot rang out and he was on his feet, out through the door and past the stairs, turning the gun in his hand into a firing position and getting as much distance between himself and his enemy as he could, gaining time to recover, to set his weapon. To wait. Cover Cruz if he could.

He turned to his left, this time avoiding the chipped-out hole in the concrete floor, and staggered into the big room where she stood, tears of frustration streaming down her face, by the narrow military cot in the corner, the steel cuff holding her ankle fast to the pipe at the wall.

The room was dim and Wolfe's eyes were still seeing large, purple blotches from the muzzle-flash of the gunshots, but he could see enough to know that there was a large pile of boxes off to his left, and another to the right. He chose the right and shuffled across the floor to crouch behind the dim shapes.

He froze. There had been a sharp sound, like a hand slapping water, and then the feel of the room changed. A hum, like an army of insects all woke up at once. He waited a moment and became aware of illumination from the ceiling. Round lights, like bulbs hanging out from trashcan lids, began to glow in the heights of the ceiling beams, amid the A/C vents and pipes. It was enough to show him the layout of the space around him... It was also enough to make him an easy mark, hiding behind a stack of cardboard boxes in the growing light.

Scanning the room, he caught sight of one more thing he hadn't noticed before: catwalks running along two sides of the room, opposite each other, up near the ceiling. Evidently this place was once a common room for inmates — patients — and the high walkways served as observation decks for the doctors, or guards.

On Wolfe's side, near the wall with the entrance door in it, a long aluminium ladder leaned up against the near end of the catwalk. That was it: elevated position, some protection from gunfire provided by the steel mesh, possibly the element of surprise. He stepped over to it and scrambled quickly up to the top, sliding in under the aluminium railing and crouching there a moment before standing, gun aimed down toward the entrance doorway, waiting for the shape to enter.

It didn't.

He scanned the lower wall, but saw no door in the direction he had left his opponent. Behind him he could see that the wall did not reach right to the ceiling, but had a gap. Darkness below. Whoever manned this catwalk could observe other rooms too, it seemed. But it was good dark below to make anything out. Could Cisco get down there? Take a shot at him from the cover of darkness? Maybe. He crouched a little lower, letting the partial wall block him from the view of anyone lurking below.

He waited, in the layer of shadow just above the level of the hanging lights. He would be obscured, but not hidden. As he waited there, he felt the trickle of blood down his shin from where he had stumbled into the hole. The adrenaline ebbed and the pain of his injuries began to make its signal known to his brain once again. He heard the choked, almost sobbing breaths of the woman chained up below.

But there was no sign of Cisco.

He moved down the mezzanine, closer to the place where Cruz stood, staring wildly around the room from him to the doorway, to the dim glow of the lights, a glow which made her cover her face as if a bright glare were suddenly unleashed upon the room. To Wolfe, there was just about enough light to get a good shot in — if Cisco dared to step through.

He was halfway down the platform when some motion caught the peripheral of his vision and Cruz cried out to warn him. He turned, gun following his eyes, but not fast enough, as a shape emerged opposite him, level with him, on the far side of the other mezzanine. There was a door there, no-doubt connected to one of the offices they'd been through, fought in: the access door for the guards and doctors who watched their own captives all those years before, before the church turned the property into a community centre. Before Cisco had come. Before the old place had once again been abandoned in favour of newer, more appropriate facilities.

He saw the flash. He never heard the shot.

He remembered throwing himself backward, as if he could somehow dodge away from the unseen cone of lead and copper that sped across the room toward him. He hoped for a moment that the shot had been inaccurate, but he had had too much experience for that delusion. He could tell from the angle of the pistol in the darkness, even those several yards away, that the aim was true enough.

His lower back felt the pressure of a hand railing and then it was as if the world dropped in front of him, rotating the ceiling down to his eye level, the far wall to his feet and the floor behind him. The rotation continued as he fell until his vision saw the rear wall, the floor again, the fore wall, and then nothing.

Delaney swerved the car into the parking lot and came to a sliding halt on the crumbling asphalt. He and Jackson, followed by four uniformed officers from the other two cars, three men and a woman, ran through the settling dust to the front of the building and tested the doors. All secure.

"The car's here," Jackson said, "He's got to be in there somewhere. Maybe a back door."

"You two stay here," Delaney motioned to two of the uniforms as he spoke, "And call for a bus, or a few of them. We don't know what kind of shape she'll be in if we find her in there, and from the body count so far, this guy isn't going down without a fight."

"Are we waiting for Gonzales?" Jackson knew the answer before he had heard it.

Delaney shook his head once with a scowl. "Wolfe got in there, so can we. Cruz might be there, and following him gives us probable cause. Gonzales won't fight it. Let's go."

With that he moved past the chained-up front doors and around the side wall, closely followed by Jackson and the two remaining officers. The four of them checked the rear of the building and found the open door by the loading dock. Taking the flashlights from the uniformed officers, Delaney and Jackson prepared to enter the place.

"You stay here and watch the door," Delaney barked at the woman.

Jackson checked Delaney's motion with an outstretched hand, "Maybe it would be better to have a female officer inside. We don't know what shape Ana might be in."

Delaney sneered at the younger cop, his distaste evident on his face, but he nodded. "Don't get yourself killed." He said to the female officer, "Or me," he muttered, and then he opened the door. She rolled her eyes at Jackson and took her place behind the pair.

All of them drew their weapons.

When just inside the loading room, the three investigators heard the distinct report of a pistol shot somewhere else in the building, echoing from wall to wall. Impossible to tell a direction to its source.

They moved quickly into the main room and checked the doors in the same order Wolfe had, moving as a cooperative unit through each space, each officer moving in turn, covered by the other two. As they neared the far, dark end of the main room they heard echoes of voices from the hole where the stairwell descended, now emitting a dim light from below. They moved toward it and down, flashlights out and weapons ready.

Then came the second shot.

Wolfe woke up staring at a bright ceiling light. He felt sharp pains in his sides and back, but nothing felt broken... nothing that hadn't been broken already, anyway. He felt his side. There was blood still seeping slowly from under his left arm. The bullet had grazed the edge of his left pectoral, just outside of the nipple, and passed through and out. It was painful and inhibited the movement of his left arm, but was not, it seemed to him, fatal.

He had been lucky. Lucky on more than one count.

His hand felt around him. Softness. Firm, but with a good six inches of give, like a stiff couch. He turned his head to the side.

It seemed he had fallen from the mezzanine, but had landed in a padded room, a cell for detaining patients who were a danger to themselves, perhaps to others as well. They would have been strapped into straightjackets and thrown in through the door, left to burn out their rage or fear or frustration until their physical needs overcame their mental agony and they calmed, through necessity or exhaustion, into pliability, or until they succumbed to their medications.

Wolfe turned his face the other way and saw something he immediately recognised. For a brief moment his chest tightened as he thought the plastic-wrapped object might be the body of Ana Cruz, but the shape was wrong. Too big. Too tall. Pascal? He blew out his air and steadied himself.

Yes: Pascal. The young man who had given him water on the night his brother had been killed. Wrapped in plastic sheeting in the dark. Silenced. Dead men tell no tales, after all — at least it had been so before the advent of forensics and the scientific method brought to bear upon the dead. Even so, the tales they told were hard to read. The presence of the body was enough for him though. Anything else he needed to know would be in the next room.

He needed to get up. He needed to find out what was happening, how long he had been out. And there was something else he needed... He felt around him and there, in one of the shallow depressions in the plush floor, its hammer punctured through the rotten leather covering, was the gun. He wrapped his fingers around the grip and levered himself to his feet with his good arm.

The weapon felt natural in his hand. Familiar, like an extended finger. He held it up to the dim light that filtered in through the open ceiling. It was a Walther P-

38. Small. Automatic. Loaded, though he didn't know how many rounds were in it, and didn't have time to check.

No matter. It only took one.

He couldn't have been unconscious long, perhaps not much more than a moment or two, for what he saw through the little window in the steel door was Father Cisco, still breathing hard and with a trickle of blood down the side of his face from the struggle in the dark office, walking across the room toward Ana. His gun raised, and eyes wide, the old priest chanted prayers of the *Viaticum* in rhythmic Latin in preparation for her death. He stopped with his toes on the edge of the blanket, his prayer drawing to a whispered close. She stood erect, tears on her cheeks but her expression solemn, defiant even, staring death in the face as it came.

Wolfe didn't know if the padded cell was locked or even if he could get the door open fast enough to get a shot off at Cisco before the man killed Ana, or Wolfe himself, or both. But there was no more time. No other choices. It was this one thing or nothing at all.

He shoved.

The door swung open on near-silent hinges and he broke the serene stillness with a shout.

"Drop the gun! It's over!"

Cisco looked to the door in shock and surprise, his face blanched as if a ghost had materialised from the other side. A moment of pause, a break in the chant, and he swung his gun around.

TWENTY-THREE

Krack! The P-38 reported once and Father Cisco's body quivered. The gun fell from his hand to the blanket on the floor as he staggered backward a step, then regained his balance and turned toward the door where Wolfe stood. The shot had entered his shoulder, through the joint. His right arm hung useless at his side.

"Stop!" Wolfe shouted, "In the name of the Vatican, you sorry *son-of-a-bitch*, take one more step and I finish you!"

Cisco obeyed. He watched as Wolfe stepped out of the padded cell, Pascal's tomb, and shuffled out toward the centre of the room like a gun-toting Lazarus.

"You don't know what it is you do, Father Wolfe, you don't know."

"I don't know? I know I stop men like you from corrupting everything you touch."

"Corrupting? No... I am *purifying*." His chin lifted in pride as he spoke.

"Purifying? You call killing my brother in cold blood, 'purifying?'"

"That was an unfortunate sacrifice, but your brother would have brought shame on the church, with his questions and his poking around. I did not want to kill him, but I had no choice. What he would have caused... I've seen it before."

"I bet you have. I bet wherever you went you saw somebody poking around for perverts and predators."

"I am no predator. Nor a pervert for that matter. Do not be so medieval."

"What do you call killing Douglas? What do you call whatever you did prior to that? Was molesting the boy part of your purification?"

"What Douglas and I had was not molestation. It was love."

"Love? Such a pure love that you had to pay him to keep him quiet?"

"If you could ask the young man, and get the truth, he would say the same, though he was troubled by it. The money? Well, he was at a low place in life. His desire to better himself was common enough, though his methods were not what they could have been. We all have our thorn, Father Wolfe, even you. Mine is as Saint Paul's was: a thorn of the flesh, a desire not for a wife but for the comfort and companionship of my fellow men."

"Of boys."

"Oh, you can call him what you will, but he saw himself as a man and so did I. In most cultures of the world the gap in age would have been perfectly acceptable, as would his youth. Were it an old man with a young woman, many might have applauded my virility."

"You are a priest."

"And a man. You are one to lecture me on the priesthood, Daniel Wolfe, professed agnostic, believer in nothing at all. Do not forget that it was I who found the woman in your hotel room. Your brother's woman."

"There was never anything going on between us."

"Who is the deceiver now? Are you so skilled in lying that you yourself have fallen victim to your own wiles? Perhaps you too, are in need of purification."

"And Father Pascal? Was he another purification?"

At this Cisco's eyes sparkled with moisture and he smiled.

"No, no. Father Pascal — Emilio — had little need of purification. He was, if any of us is, a true priest. An idealist. His death was very sad to me, and an accident. I did what I could, but I am no doctor."

Wolfe began to speak but could never afterward remember what it was he had meant to say. Over the hushed tones of their conversation, a sharp report rang out, echoing across the room like a vibration.

He turned to see Cruz, standing by the edge of her cot, the blanket bunched up at her feet and a Luger in her hand. He turned back to look at Father Cisco only in time to see him look down once at the hole in the side of his chest, under his left arm, already starting to pump little bubbles of blood out onto his black shirt. He lifted his head once to Wolfe, turned to face the woman, and then fell, knees collapsing as he sank to his back on the floor. Crumpled. Dead.

Wolfe turned again to look at Ana, but her eyes had closed, squeezing out her tears above a relieved smile.

She let the gun drop to her feet.

It was all over by the time the three police officers reached the bottom of the stairs and moved into the big basement room. Delaney kept his gun trained on Wolfe and the uniform scanned the room for others as she approached Cruz. Jackson crouched down to check Cisco for life signs. There were none, except perhaps the warmth that remained. But that, too, would soon cool and the body be little more than dust waiting to crumble.

Jackson found a key in Cisco's pocket, moved over to assist the uniform with Cruz's release. She had sunk to her knees and then collapsed in exhaustion into the other woman's arms when the ring had been unlocked and pulled from her scabby, bleeding ankle. The officer half-carried her toward the stairs and up, into the darkening night where the sirens of the ambulance could now be heard howling and chirping into the parking area above.

Back down below, Delaney snapped the cuffs onto Wolfe's wrists and gave him a harsh knee to the soft belly, doubling him over.

"There you go, Father, a little hello from the guy you left behind in the alley. Find your way out of the station all right?"

Wolfe groaned as he fought for air.

"Good. Good to hear it. Finally got you to shut the fuck up."

Ten minutes later, Cruz was taken away in the ambulance, the CSIs were on scene to deal with Cisco and Pascal's remains and whatever evidence they might want to gather, and Jackson and Delaney were striding down the hospital hallway. Wolfe, a fresh bandage wrapped around his chest to stop the bleeding from his wound, was cuffed and led along between them.

"Honestly with the cuffs?" Jackson asked, his familiarity with Delaney growing to the point of a willingness to challenge his authority in front of others, "You're honestly going to do it this way?"

"You bet your hairy ass," he answered, jerking Wolfe along, despite the priest's injuries and near-exhaustion, "You should thank me, he made a bloody fool of you!"

"All the more reason why you should see it my way," Jackson held the door open and the three men walked through into the waiting area, cleared by security to give them some privacy. "We know it wasn't him. Cisco did all three."

"Yes, and yet this cock-sucker broke out of custody on my watch... No, not even that, this piece of shit *walked* out of custody on my watch. You might not mind being beaten and cuffed by this bastard — with your own bracelets, for Christ's sake — but I'm certainly not going to let him get away with resisting arrest, interfering in an ongoing police investigation, stealing two cars, including a police car, and withholding evidence in a capital crime. No fuckin' way! He goes down for that shit."

"No," a voice said from the doorway behind them, "I'm afraid he doesn't."

Delaney looked over to see an elderly man in a black cassock and wearing a purple skull-cap — the uniform of a bishop, had he known it. The man sat with a watch sergeant who had a look on his face like he had just been asked to tell his Rottweiler that there would be no more meals this week.

"And just what do you mean by that?" Delaney asked, "We're not in church, here, Father."

"It's not 'Father,' detective, it is customarily 'Your Excellency,' but I don't need to stand on ceremony with regard to my honorific. I will, however, have to insist on this." He held out a legal-sized sheet of paper filled with tiny type.

"And what is that?"

"It's Father Wolfe's verification of official Vatican agency. In terms germane to this situation, it's his diplomatic immunity."

"His what?"

"Diplomatic immunity. That's when-"

"I know what fuckin' diplomatic immunity means, but he's an American citizen for Christ's sake. He can't have immunity from his own government!"

"I'm afraid that Father Wolfe is also — for Christ's sake indeed — a citizen of the Vatican city-state, a diplomatic representative in its foreign office, and is therefore not detainable for the offences with which you have charged him — whether he did them or not. Anything short of murder, and he goes free. Right now."

Delaney grabbed the paper and scanned it, looking more for signs that it wasn't the real thing than making any attempt to read it.

"It's legit, Detective," the sergeant said, "It went up to the chief himself, and back down like a goddam hammer. We're to let Wolfe go."

Jackson, without a word, took the handcuff key from his pocket and released the priest from the tight metal bonds. Wolfe smiled his thanks to him and stood, rubbing his raw wrists until he began to sway with fatigue.

"Are you ready to go, Daniel?" the bishop asked, forgetting formality for a moment through concern for his friend. Wolfe simply nodded and the two men stepped through the door and to the room in which Grippe had arranged for a private doctor to meet them. Wolfe was checked over. Instructions for his care were given. Then both men left the building and walked the short path to a waiting car. Sanchez sat behind the wheel.

The big sedan pulled out from the busy hospital and headed for the bishop's mansion. Wolfe was asleep before the car had reached the first intersection.

TWENTY-FOUR

Rain spackled the windshield as Wolfe steered his rental car onto the treed lane on which Saint Mary of the Sea sat nestled in seeming peace. The trees had lost a little of their menace, but to him the place still felt cavelike and unwelcoming. Perhaps it wouldn't have seemed so, had his experience there been other than it had been, but to his eyes it was still a tomb more than a sanctuary.

Nevertheless, he had something he needed to do there. Unfinished business. He pulled up on the street in front and turned off the ignition.

Inside he passed one late-morning attendee, an elderly woman just finished with her prayers. Wolfe smiled at her, putting at ease her initial shock at the bandages taped over the gravel rash on almost half of his face, and his awkward, injured gait. She smiled back and passed peacefully out into the street. He continued on into the dimness.

From the inner side of the narthex he could see the altar area clearly. In the long, partially-lit nave it showed beneath the subdued spotlights in a soft glow, like the gaze of heaven rested on it in the midst of some Miltonian darkness and chaos.

Just a little to the near side of the altar itself, on the bare, flat space of granite floor, was the last place his brother had drawn breath.

Wolfe approached slowly and as near to a state of true prayer as he had reached in more than three years. When he neared the place, he stopped and knelt, signing the cross as a reflex, but feeling all the same as if he should do something, something which held more meaning than a habitual wave of his hand.

Nothing came to mind.

He didn't know how long he had knelt there, but when the pain on his knees finally forced him to stand, his joints cracked and popped with the effort. He groaned to his feet.

"It gets yet more difficult the older you get, Father Wolfe, despite practice."

He turned to his left. It was Gonzales.

"Good morning, Father."

"Are your wounds serious?"

"A few scrapes."

"I heard you'd been shot."

He shrugged, right shoulder only. "I don't even feel it... if I don't move."

The older priest smiled at the joke for a moment, then it faded from his face.

"I did not know that Father Cisco had killed anyone. He was flawed, as we all are, but I didn't think he was capable of that. I would have been more helpful."

"Would you have?"

"Yes," he raised his eyes to meet Wolfe's, "Of course."

"And yet you'd leave the other crime? You'd help to cover it up?"

"Cover it up? No. Not cover it up. But Father Cisco was leaving. I found out only after everything was prepared and set in motion... not before. In a short time he would be far away, unable to do more harm to the congregation. An elegant solution to a messy problem."

"Harm to this congregation, you mean."

"No, to *any* congregation. I have been to the jungles as well, when I was a soldier. There is little opportunity there to..."

"Rape little boys?"

Gonzales shot a brief but sharp glance at Wolfe.

"To engage in unsanctioned relationships."

"Is that what we're calling it these days."

"I know what you do, and it is a deep shame that there is need for it, but I do see the need." He frowned, his thoughts obviously troubled. "But Father Cisco was not molesting infants and children. He was a homosexual man and chose to express it, despite the restrictions of the church and his vows. The boy was no child. Maybe he shouldn't have been a priest, but were it not for the violence, I would struggle to name him a criminal."

"The boy was what, fifteen? Were it a sixty-year-old man with a fifteen-year-old girl, would it be seen as a meeting of adults?"

"Ah, but there you display your cultural bias. In the jungles with which Father Cisco was most familiar, fifteen is well into adulthood, and the value of a match more to do with security, than similar age. Were he not a priest, such a relationship would not have been frowned upon at all. The family of the younger party would indeed be pleased with such a match. Even as a priest, life among the tribes tends to entail fewer restrictions. Expectations are different there."

"But we're not in the jungle, we're in Miami, and here in Miami that's a crime."

"Yes, it is, but that is my point. In a very short time Cisco would no longer be in Miami, he would be back in the jungle. No more crime would be committed here, just the same as if he were cast from the priesthood and imprisoned... or dead, as he now is." He paused a moment. "I do not condone what he did, but I saw no benefit in further defaming the church when the solution was bringing itself about on its own — by God's own hand perhaps. I still do not. This should be known as a place of healing, not of shame. How can people come to us for help if they fear for the safety of their children?"

"And yet you covered it up, this action against someone's child."

"I expedited a situation that would relieve my suspicions. *Suspicions* mind you, and nothing more. I had no real proof that anything untoward was going on."

"And yet Kevin did."

"Yes, it would seem so. Direct allegations, at any rate. But he did not come to me."

"Would it have helped had he done so?"

"Perhaps. I would have thrown Cisco out sooner. That is a certainty. Perhaps there would have been no deaths."

"So you're saying it was his own fault? Kevin's own fault that he died?"

"No no, not that… No." He paused as he drew in a long, thought-heavy breath. "I am saying that it was Father Cisco's fault. I am saying that it could, perhaps, have been avoided by chance or the hand of God, but that rather it happened — by chance or the hand of God. And last of all, I am saying that I am sorry. Sorry that, for my part, I was not more decisive in dealing with my suspicion, and not more helpful to you… or at least to your office in the church."

"It was wrong, helping him to hide his crimes."

"Perhaps," Gonzales nodded, "But that is too big a question for me to know now. We must do what we think is best for the church as a whole."

Wolfe said nothing.

"Might I ask you something?" The old priest's eyes looked aside to the altar as he asked the question.

"Of course. If I can answer it."

"Was the boy killed here, in the church?"

"Yes, I think so. The weapon was probably your letter opener. It is missing, is it not?"

"Yes, it is. Cisco often fingered it when we spoke, especially if the topic was of particular stress to him. A nervous habit is all it was, something to do with his hands, to keep them busy. But if a murderous compulsion overcame him, if…"

"If the boy were nearby, and threatening him?"

"Yes," Gonzales sighed, "It's the scenario that makes the most sense. Perhaps… self defence. I suppose we'll never know for sure."

Yes we do, Wolfe thought, *Even you do, Gonzales.*

"And Father Pascal? Was he killed here too?"

"I don't know where he was wounded, or even how… but he died in the old community centre."

"But why?"

"I think he knew, or suspected that something was going on between Cisco and the boy. If he had walked in on Cisco in the old centre, or heard something from one of the kids — Father Cisco had already killed Kevin, maybe Douglas too."

"But you say that Father Pascal did not die right away?"

"No, he didn't. There was evidence in the cell that Father Cisco had tried to help him, that he had tried to keep him alive but the wounds were too severe. He told me as much himself."

"Well, that is something." The old man nodded to himself.

Wolfe didn't reply. It might be something, but it was a very, very little something.

"And Ms. Cruz is okay?"

"Yes, she's recovering. She was frightened, and in danger from her asthma, but not permanently hurt. Not yet."

"Well, perhaps Father Cisco would have had a change of heart in the end, would have spared her."

"Maybe," Wolfe lied.

"Well," the old man, seeming much more frail than he had the first time Wolfe had seen him, patted the younger priest on the shoulder and bowed his head, "I'll leave you to your good-byes. Take as long as you like, I'll see that you aren't disturbed."

"Thank you, but let the people come and go. I like the idea that Kevin has company, if that makes sense."

"It does. God bless you, Father Wolfe. I mean it. I hope you find what it is you seek."

Wolfe nodded, knowing that any such spiritual sentiment from him to Gonzales would be taken for what it was: a mere formality. He wouldn't patronise the old man with that, despite his personal feelings.

Gonzales turned and walked out through the door toward his office. Wolfe remained in the quiet, hearing the buzz of the electric lights above and smelling the slow-drifting scent of must and stale books, just as he had on the first night he had entered the little church to find his brother there, still and lifeless on the cold stone.

He bent once more to touch the floor where Kevin had lain, and then he turned and went his way.

There were legal battles revving up, regarding his diplomatic immunity, and the bishop had hinted that it might be best to make himself scarce for a while — a comment which usually led to a stay in the Vatican itself — so he knew that it might be a while before he saw the little church again. Maybe he never would.

He might even be alright with that; he hadn't decided yet. The evidence for the other case was gone and those involved would have scattered their own incriminating evidence to the wind. A new start there, too, and not an easy one, now that he had stepped on the toes of the local authorities. Might mean a new investigator. They wouldn't stop until something came of it. Things like that never stayed covered up forever; the truth will out, after all. The truth will out.

He looked once down the length of the street in either direction before stepping into the car and turning on the ignition. He tested the brake pedal once or twice before pulling out into traffic, then smiled at himself and made his way back to the bishop's mansion.

A bottle of 25-year-old scotch to share, and a decent cigar each. Wolfe took a long pull of the whiskey and let it sit on his tongue. Linger. The flavour was sweet at first then acrid, biting, that leather-sucked taste of old saddle. He smiled.

"It was good work, my friend, despite what the police might say."

"You think so?"

"Yes," the bishop smiled, "Even they think so."

"Who, the police?"

"Of course."

"You wouldn't know it from the way they're going after these charges."

"Oh, it could be much worse you know. The big guns haven't weighed in and I don't think they will. Not against you, anyway."

"Why not?"

"I don't think the regular guns will ask them to. They have to object on the surface, that's a given. We can't have vigilantes running around taking care of their own business, now can we? They're not all as good a shot as you are, for one thing."

"Well, sorry about that."

"The shooting?"

"Yeah."

"Not to worry. You've been to the Vatican, you know that even spiritual leaders live in the physical world and are not averse to using physical force when security demands it. Defence of the weak, and so on. The government was given a sword for a reason, the Scriptures say, and the Vatican is a government, don't forget that."

"Yes, I suppose you're right."

"I am." He paused. "What else is on your mind?"

He thought for a few moments, taking in another pull of smoke and a taste of the whiskey. "Why me, David?"

"What do you mean?"

"I mean that there are scores of men out there, devout men of faith, with skills like mine and a deep desire to serve God. Why would the church, why would *you*, choose me to do this work?"

"Rather than a more zealous man?"

"Yes... to say the least."

The bishop smiled. "Do you recall the story of the wheat and the tares?"

"Of course."

"Do you remember why the farmer is forbidden to pull out the tares in order that the wheat might grow better?"

"Yes. Ripping out the tares would wreck the roots of the good plants too."

"But why couldn't they do it when the plants were still very young? Before the roots get all entangled?"

"I don't know. I don't think the Scriptures say."

"But every farmer knows why."

"Why?"

"Because no one can tell which plant is which until it starts to show its colours, grows a bit, and by then everything is mixed in, conjoined, good and bad together."

"So you don't want to pull me out because I might damage the good roots?"

"No, that's not it at all. I was always better at plain speech than parables... that's painfully clear." He smiled and took in some scotch, rolling it around in his mouth before swallowing and offering an answer, a finger kinked upward as if the answer hovered in front of him. "Father Cisco thought that he was a true priest, a man who served and loved God, right?"

"Yes, that's what I've heard."

"Did you believe it? That he was a good servant of God?"

"Perhaps he was at first. Not now."

"Well, there you go."

"There I go?"

"Don't be thick, Daniel, or slow down on the scotch, one of the two." He took another pull on his own drink.

"Just speak plainly to me, it's been a long week and I don't have the patience to riddle it out with an old theologian."

The bishop chortled, despite his mouth full of whiskey. Once he swallowed, he turned a little in his chair to face Wolfe, and he set his tumbler down. He grasped the younger priest's forearm with his pale hand and spoke.

"If Cisco could think he served and loved God, so fervently, and yet be so very wrong in his view of things, then I must believe that you might believe just the opposite concerning yourself, just as fervently, and yet still be a willing tool in the hands of the Almighty."

"That's a bit of a stretch."

"I'm an old theologian," he said, settling back in his chair and bringing his tumbler up toward his lips again, "That's what we do."

Both men smiled and the bishop replenished the whisky in their glasses. The room had begun to fill with smoke and the good will of old friends and remained so until late in the night when at last, in a fog of alcohol and thick smoke, Wolfe retired to his room and to a long, dreamless night.

The following is a bonus peek at the next part in the adventures of Daniel Wolfe.

A TIME FOR WEEPING

ONE

She could see his form come from the shadows behind her. He didn't belong. Not in that place. Not in her room.

She tried to lift herself up, to flee or to fight, but her muscles would not respond. Her limbs did not move. Like she was drunk to the point of stupor, she sagged sideways in her chair, staring into the mirror at the shadowy figure. But she wasn't in a stupor. She was fully, acutely, aware. He stepped forward, a scalpel in his vinyl-gloved hand. Her scalpel.

She knew him, and as she realized who he was, what he had done and what he was about to do, everything within her strained to scream, to voice the sudden frost in the veins of her arms and legs.

But no sound came.

He stopped behind her, immediately behind her, and slid his hand down over the caramel skin of her shoulder, over the silk of her robe and into the gap. His hand cupped her breast, caressed it as he leaned down and drew in a deep, slow breath from her hair. He held it there for a long moment, eyes closed, then let it out over the skin of her neck and back.

The vinyl of the glove made his skin feel reptilian. Almost dead.

"I'd like to make love to you," he said, "I know we both want that."

She couldn't even make tears fall from her eyes.

"But I can't." He wrapped his arms around her, hugged her close and pressed his cheek against hers. "I mean I *can*, but…" he chuckled, "I've perfected this. It would be nice to share something else with you first. That first night. The magic night." He stroked her cheek, lost in thought for a moment, then met her eyes in the mirror. "Can't though. DNA. Too many questions. Too many lines drawn between me and you then. Not enough space. No static to hide in. But don't worry, what we will get to share is the most intimate of moments. You won't be disappointed."

He tightened the hug and lifted, sliding her and her chair closer to the vanity table, closer to the mirror. To her it was as if his face grew larger, and his eyes larger yet as she stared at the scalpel in his hand, her scalpel, and she remembered the feel of it in her own thin fingers… the weight of it… the keenness of the blade. She prayed, both to Mary the

2

Virgin mother and to Jesus, the son who had died for her, sweat blood in the garden with the weight of it all. She strained to ask the man what he would do to her, strained until she felt as if she, herself, might sweat blood.

But she couldn't.

"I used to be like you," he continued, "I used to be just the same. Walking around, jumping at shadows and sounds like attackers were hiding in every corner, demons waiting to grab my soul, or worse. If there is worse."

He pulled the robe to the sides, laying bare her breasts, shiny with sweat. He smiled.

"You're beautiful, you know. It's a shame the inside is such a torment, because your form is… *art*. I once killed a woman who had no idea how beautiful she was. I mean, she was no supermodel, but she was a really good-looking woman. But you know, don't you? Yeah, you do."

He stroked her cheek as he spoke, and in his words she could hear a light-hearted joy, like he was remembering an amusing story at a dinner party.

"She looked in the mirror and saw only her flaws. Too much here, too little there, this a little crooked. Shame though. No one else saw that. They saw her beauty. Outward beauty, anyway. Inside she was like you are. Like I used to be. That's no life, is it? Not life at all, really."

He leaned her forward onto the table, resting her cheek gently against the glass surface. She could hear him stand, stretch, and pace across the room,

3

toward the bathroom, but she couldn't see him. Still couldn't turn her head. Couldn't scream. Or cry. The squeak of the faucet was followed by a surge of water, and if she could have jumped in fear she would have, but all in her body was calm. All but her heart. She could feel the racing of her heart.

So she was still alive.

She tried to work her mind against the fear, against the paralysis. She struggled to move her lips. Fingertips. Toes. Nothing. She blinked, but not at will; it was some uncontrolled reflex, moistening her eyes as if in any other moment. Dry eyes in the midst of all of it.

His footsteps returned.

"When I was a boy, I was as normal as anyone else. Not like you are now, but maybe like you were before. Something happened to me too. In my case, it was a stepmother." His voice rose into a mock witch's cackle, "My wicked stepmother..." A chuckle, then he seemed to grow still. Thoughtful.

"Compared to my life with her, to the unnatural fucked-upedness of it, your experience, a rape and a beating at a party, is nothing. She was nice enough at first, but it didn't last. My dad and her were the same way. She was all giggles and sparkles for a while, then she seemed to get... bitter. Sullen, maybe is the word. I don't know. She turned into a bitch, anyway."

His hand found her thigh, ran down he length of it as he spoke, then altered its direction. Back up,

4

each inch a deeper violation, until it reached the fold where her thigh met her hip. Then he paused.

"He was the same way back to her. She gave as good as she got, I suppose, or better. After a while, my dad just seemed to work later and later. He'd leave early in the morning sometimes, even before I was out of bed, but still it was late before he'd come home. Always said they were busy down at work. Must have been a banner year, for that place, the time the two of them were together."

He blew out a breath of air, rose to his feet and shook his head. He placed his arms around her again and gently lifted her up to his shoulder. Her head sagged, her chin to his back, and she saw them then. The plastic covers, like inverted shower caps, placed around his shoes.

"It was after that year that I got shaky. I started to stammer. Started to get picked on at school, and then it got even worse – what she did, what they did... Dad being away. I hated them. I hated all of them. I hated her for what she did to me, I hated him for leaving me there with her. I hated the kids at school and the indifference of my teachers. I hated them all."

He lowered her onto the closed toilet lid and removed her robe. He crouched down, pulled her panties down over her legs and paused a moment, staring at her uncovered nudity, a pensive smile toying at the edges of his lips. He reached out and stroked her, lightly, with the tips of his fingers. The soft skin. The groove where her labia met. Probed

5

the tiny bump hidden just within its apex. Then he sighed, looking at the gloves with a kind of shame.

"The things she made me do. Sick bitch." He looked as if he were about to erupt, to explode into violence and strike her. Then he calmed again. He turned off the water faucet. And then stood.

He hung the robe on the hook behind the door and tossed the panties onto the bath mat beneath it, watching them a moment, like an artist observes his drying paint. Picked them up again. Tossed them there a second time. Then lifted her, with sickly gentleness, from the toilet to the tub, lowering her into the water.

He picked up the scalpel from the bathroom counter and set it on the rim of the tub. His eyes watched her intently for a moment and, when he seemed satisfied that the rhythmic inhalation and exhalation of air would not shift her position, he stepped out of the room.

She searched her field of view for any kind of help. Any unseen angel. Any weapon or tool, though she knew she could not use one. Her heart beat the seconds away, ticking down to… her mind would not grasp the thing.

When he returned, he held two candles and a box of matches. He placed the candles on the back of the toilet seat and lit them. A sweet fragrance began to fill the room, mixed with the temporary and sharp scent of sulphur and smoke.

He lifted the scalpel and placed it in her right hand. She was right-handed, he had noted that a long time ago. Made a note of it. He wrapped her limp fingers around it and then cupped her hand in his own, waving it back and forth in the water, like he was unwinding at the end of a long and tiresome day at work. She thought for a moment that she even heard him hum something. Wistful. Peaceful.

Then he slid the scalpel down behind her thigh and up, the blade slipping effortlessly into the skin, like the penetration of sex, but far more intimate. A cloudy red line followed the shining metal across her inner thigh, through the femoral artery and through the muscle and fat on either side of it.

Her heart kicked against her ribs. She strained again to scream, to cry, to fight. But it was an inner strain, a mental one, without effect or sign on her physical form. She felt no physical pain over the wave of shock and fear.

He moved her hand upward and over the lip of the tub... dropped the tool onto a soap dish. Then he lowered her hand to the surface of the water and let it drift from his fingers.

It fell, into the darkening red of the bath, as her heart pumped faster in answer to the call of her body for more blood. More pressure. But the pressure was spewing out from her thigh, into the lukewarm water. Dissipating with the spreading red cloud in the water.

She could feel her heart, could feel that she was still alive.

He stood and stepped back a pace. "I can't talk to many people like this," he whispered through sigh of release and relief, "But we're close, and I trust you."

From his jacket he lifted a single sheet of paper, folded neatly in thirds, and opened it up onto the bathroom counter, so it leaned neatly against the mirror. She had written it, only a few hours before, and then had watched him throw it into the fire.

But there it was.

She did not watch him long, though. Instead she watched the redness of the water, the fading away of her belly and thighs in the murk, the murk of her own vitality. The crimson smoke no longer dissipated and faded, but instead added to the growing darkness of the water. The growing darkness of her vision too.

Her heart was not racing now. Not steady. Not right. Beating. Missing. Shuddering. Jazz. Syncopation. She could feel that. The jazz...

And then it stopped.

He watched her for another ten minutes. She watched him for a much shorter time. He considered masturbating, but the blood was too much. The spell was broken. The woman was gone.

At rest.

At last.

He walked out into the living room and looked out over the city. The sun was not yet up. It wouldn't be for another hour or more. He stood and stared at the sky, waiting for the moment when he was sure that it was lighter than it had been the moment before. When it happened, he smiled.

Another day.

Another day.

And this day would be alright. No one would harm him this day. Today he was the predator… some other person the prey. But not her. She was at rest now. The fear gone. Healed.

He turned and left the apartment, letting the automatic deadbolt click into place behind him. He couldn't do up the chain, which a perfect scene might demand. No matter. Lots of people didn't do up the chain. A little imperfection only added to the realism of the piece.

He walked down the empty stairwell and, pulling on his cap, out the side door of the building, into the parking area. He kept his head low, below the line of sight of the video cameras. Didn't matter. He didn't look unusual.

And no one would be looking.

The sun was just rising over the flat horizon of the Atlantic as Father Daniel Wolfe rounded the corner and began the last leg of his morning five-mile. He'd mastered the timing, at last, bringing an end to his run and a beginning to his day as the sun rose and lowered the layer of heat down on the Miami shoreline. At least the breeze was fairly constant – a little farther inland the humidity was like a down comforter, but without the comfort.

His ribs were healing. The skin on his face had returned more or less to normal, and even his heart and attitude, dark as both tended to lean, were feeling good.

The loss of the evidence in his last case had been a secret pleasure to him; he didn't have to deal with that for now. It was no great loss to the investigation, except that they might have found evidence of who the main perpetrator was, the one who had made the videos. Probably the same man who owned them, but there was now no way to be sure. None that they currently had, anyway. Did they need to be sure? And how sure? That was up to the Vatican and, these days, that could mean almost anything.

In the past, a great deal of energy went into hiding the sins of the clergy, and into protecting men who were victimizing their flock. The forty years of accusations prior to the Maciel scandal. The failings of John Paul II – and even Benedict XVI in whom so many had such high hopes – were common knowledge among those aware of the ongoing battle against abuse by those in positions of authority and power in the church. Even with a general shift in awareness and attitude, there were pockets of the old way of thinking. Huddle. Protect. Circle the wagons, regardless of what sickness was hemmed inside of them.

Francis though, he was different. Seemed so, anyway. There were things he knew of and was active in, new programs and bold public statements, intentional actions meant to shake up the institutional church and shake out those vipers living in the shadows of the true priests and servants of holiness.

And, like all popes, there were things of which he did not know. Probably did not want to know.

There were layers of the Vatican government that, much like the American or British systems, were under the authority and even sanction of the person sitting in the highest office of the land, but were not under the leader's direct scrutiny. Plausible deniability. Shadowy operatives with questionable methods and undisclosed budgets. Handlers who answered to their superiors in only the vaguest of terms. Since the election of this 266th pope, heir to the See of Peter... this network had grown, and its activities broadened in scope even as they increased in intensity.

Wolfe's feet fell heavy as he thudded into a stop in front of one of the many luxury condo high-rises on Brickell Bay Drive, and looked out to sea. He stretched out his calves as he watched two yachts cruise past each other in the Miami South Channel. Must have been a hundred feet each, if not more. Smooth. Low rumbling of power under restraint in the no-wake zone.

He imagined the silver-haired men in sea-captain hats waving regally to one another, champagne flutes lightly held between manicured fingers... He wondered how much blood was on those fingers, had a fleeting image of it smeared over the rim of the hats.

He could take or leave the champagne. Had too much blood on his own hands to criticize theirs. But the boats? He could imagine himself on one of the boats.

Nice, he thought as he straightened up and began to walk the last two blocks back to his hotel, the Four Seasons Miami. Bishop Grippe had, as usual, spared no expense in taking care of his recovering investigator. No hundred-foot yacht, no, but a room at almost a grand a night and a masseuse that showed up every morning at half past eight to work his muscles and keep the healing process rolling along.

A guy could get used to this.

There had been meetings over the past few weeks, talks between Vatican officials and local police. State authorities. Grippe had hinted that there might have been a call in to the Oval Office. A Vatican diplomat had been bad, after all, stealing a car, obstructing police – catching a killer.

Nothing much was coming of it except that Sergeant Delaney, no fan of Wolfe's, had not been letting things drop. The few infractions that the priest had committed in the course of finding his brother's killer, and in rescuing Ana Cruz, had ruffled the cop's sense of justice – or maybe just his pride – and now he was making a nuisance of himself. Effectively.

There was even some talk of taking the reasonable degree of cooperation they'd already achieved and running with it, sending the pet priest back by private jet to Rome, to complete his recovery there and keep out of the jurisdiction of the American judiciary for a while.

Wolfe didn't like the idea much.

He liked to travel, liked visiting Rome, and even liked much of what the Vatican had to offer him. It was a beautiful place, with both a deep dark side and one of high art and beauty.

No, the issue he took was that he was an American himself. He didn't like the idea of running away from his own government, of hiding behind the walls of a foreign one. He did have an alternate identity, a Vatican citizenship, and even diplomatic status. But still, it didn't sit right with him. He would go, if they told him to.

But he wouldn't like it.

He entered the lobby, big and bright and open. Good lines and a feeling of clean efficiency. Luxurious minimalism. Calm. Best of all: cool.

He smiled to the women at the check-in counter, and nodded to the concierge before striding straight through to the elevator. Up to the pool deck and only a brief pause at the showers before he dove in, feeling the stretch and faint pain in his recovering ribs, but reveling in the ability to move once again, to flex and to pull himself through the water.

A few laps. A quiet float on his back until the sun's brightness was too much, then up to his room. The masseuse would be there any minute and he was ready for a good work-over, perhaps the pain in his ribs would be gone today. *Here's to hoping.*

When the light rap on his door finally came, almost ten minutes late, he pulled it open and stood there in his towel.

It was Bishop Grippe.

"Hello Daniel, doing well?"

"Yes," he said, recovering himself, "Very well. I was expecting the masseuse."

"Yes, I know. Apologies for that." He stepped partially into the room, but held the door slightly ajar as he continued. "I cancelled the appointment. It seems things have come to a head and something must be done."

"What kind of things?"

"For the most part, charges have been dropped and there will be no more problems... but for one."

"Shooting Cisco? Surely that can fall under self-defense. He tried to kill me, after all – and was going to kill Ana."

"No, not that. You are correct that they see the necessity of the situation. The fact that it was not your own firearm used, but one taken from your attacker, helped as well. No *mens rea* – no intention or premeditation. Besides, he'd have survived your bullet... it was Officer Cruz's that, justifiably, did him in."

"So what is it then?"

"Sergeant Delaney, he has convinced the owner of the car you... borrowed... that all should not be forgiven."

"The diplomatic immunity?"

"Fuzzy, here in the US. Had we been almost anywhere else, your status as a diplomat of the Vatican State would be unquestionable, but as you have not renounced your American status…"

"They are treating me as a citizen, rather than a foreign attaché."

"Some are, yes. Some not. As it stands this morning, we still seem to be winning the battle – slightly – but not as well as yesterday. And tomorrow? Who can say…"

"I see. So this means?"

"A flight, I fear. Soon."

"How soon?"

He shrugged. "I'll send your other bags after you. I have taken the liberty of putting some basics in this," he gestured to a roller bag behind him in the hall. "You can add to it anything you like, but be quick. The flight leaves in a couple of hours."

"I see."

"I know you're not happy about it Daniel, I can see it in your eyes, but it will have to be so for now. Once you are out of the country, and once some time passes, the woman might warm to the offer of compensation, the sergeant might find some other bone to chew on, and who is to say? We may gain a full pardon or dropped charges and nothing more shall come of it."

"And if we don't?"

"All will be well, my friend. I will see to it. All that can be done, will be done. For now though," he stepped backward into the hallway, "You'd better grab that and come with me. The plane is waiting, and you'd best spend your last hour or so on board."

Wolfe leaned back in the seat and sipped his drink. Just an orange juice for now, he'd save the harder stuff for when they were airborne, out over the Atlantic and looking down on the glittering city disappearing behind the private Vatican jet.

Now that he was on board the plane, the American government couldn't compel him to leave it. The plane was, in effect, Vatican sovereign territory, just as a diplomatic pouch was off-limits to customs officials, the entire plane was off-limits to police, homeland security, NSA, customs – all of them. To breach this protocol would be a major international incident.

Yes, he might be facing some serious charges, and some individuals would be very unhappy that the Vatican had spirited him away before official closure of the issues surrounding his latest job, but he would be out of their reach. He was already out of it, in fact, though he knew he wouldn't really feel like it until they were airborne and over international waters.

His fellow Americans were not, after all, strangers to overstepping diplomatic bounds.

He closed his eyes and leaned back in the chair. The weight of the past month – hell, the past four years – was descending on him. He had been carrying it all along, he knew it had been building up, but there was a difference between burden in the moment and burden after the fact. In the midst of the chaos and tension, a person just gets on with it, doesn't think too much about the toll it takes. It's the only way to get through. At the oncoming edge of a break though, when the stillness is just starting to seep through cracks in the tension, the burden really presses down. The tension is felt more keenly, because there's time to focus on it. He took a deep breath in, stretched out his ribs and his lungs, and blew it out. A slight shudder, but he could feel the stress ease out of him a fraction at a time. A little longer and he could breathe easy. Another hour and he could really relax.

He wasn't sure if he'd drifted into sleep or not, but he was suddenly aware of another presence, someone standing quite close to him. He started and opened his eyes, ready for almost anything they might see.

He needn't have worried.

Father Vittorio Sanchez, Bishop Grippe's secretary, stood a couple of feet away from him, in the center aisle. His face was expressionless, but Wolfe could sense the tension.

"Hello Vittorio… you coming too?"

The man shook his head.

"What's going on then… any trouble?" Wolfe didn't like it, didn't like the cold feeling creeping up in the back of his neck. He sensed danger. A trap. A trap from Sanchez though? No.

When the secretary spoke, it was with a voice raw with emotion, and worn by grief. Once he broke his stoic pose to speak, a shadow of anguish passed over his face and the façade that Wolfe had detected, was utterly broken.

"Father Wolfe. I know where you are going. I know why you are going."

"Yes? What's wrong? Is it David?"

"No, the Bishop is fine. It is… a personal matter."

"Not a church matter?" Sanchez shook his head. "Not an official matter at all?" Again, a shake of the head. The other priest seemed to be struggling to master himself. It was a strange sight to Wolfe, who had met the man some years ago and had never seen any break in his composure before – despite some pretty good reasons to get emotional.

"Tell me." He was surprised by the gentleness of his own voice.

"It is my niece," Sanchez said, his voice rising in pitch, the timbre of weeping creeping into the tone. He was barely keeping it together, and speaking made it impossible.

"Is she in danger?"

"No. They say she is… they say she killed herself." The final words trailed off into a whisper, and the man's chin sank to his chest. His shoulders shuddered a moment, then he lifted his face again, an expression of defiance coming over it, and the posture of his body changed from one of defeat to one of decision. Strength in the face of threat.

Wolfe studied him. "They say this, but you don't believe it?"

"No. I do not."

"May I ask… why?"

"Because she is afraid of heights, for one thing." Wolfe said nothing. "She did not tell people of it. It embarrassed her. She was a proud woman, successful in her way. They say she jumped from the Bay Bridge, the Rickenbacker Causeway. She never went near the water. Never liked bridges, even in cars. Terrified of heights. And yet they tell me she climbed the barrier, stood upon the edge, and dove from the top of it, leaving two little girls behind to fend for themselves. I do not believe it."

"Strange things happen, Vittorio. I am sorry for your loss, but people do strange things."

"It was not like her."

"Was she troubled?"

Vittorio hesitated. His skin flushed then, knowing what his hesitation would mean to the man who watched him; there would be no concealment there.

"Yes, she was troubled. She had been in a bad marriage. Happy, she thought, until she came to know that her husband had been… interfering, with one of their daughters. Perhaps both of them. She confronted him. He beat her. Kept her in the basement for four days." His voice cracked again but he kept on. "He beat her several times and raped her. Then he raped the girl. Then he fled. They have not yet found him, and that was almost a year ago now."

Nothing but silence passed between the men for a while, Sanchez taking a moment to recover his control, Wolfe taking in the enormity of what had happened to the man's loved ones, and so to the man himself as well. It was Wolfe who broke the silence. There was no point in trying to soften things in the face of what had been said.

"An experience like that can break even a strong mind. We can't know what something like that could have done to her. Do you think that things might have just become too much? I'm sorry to say it, but how could she have been in her right mind after an ordeal like that? How could anyone? It would make sense, after all of that, if suicide makes sense at any time."

"She was strong. Perhaps had she been alone in life, it would have overwhelmed her, but she was not. She had her mother. She had me. Most of all she had her daughters, and she was being strong for their sakes. I spoke to her regularly, Father Wolfe, and I sensed much pain. Much fear. But nothing like this. There was no despair there. Not to the point necessary for… She would not have done this thing, and if she had, she would not do it in such a manner."

Wolfe studied Sanchez's face for a few long moments. The secretary stared straight ahead, occasionally glancing down at the other priest's unwavering gaze. At last, Wolfe spoke.

"What is it you are asking of me?"

"I am asking for three days."

"For me to stay for three more days?"

20

"To look into it. To find out what I already know to be true."

"You know what's going on here, for me. You know what it is you are asking me to risk?"

He nodded.

"And what makes you think I can do this? What makes you think that it's worth the risk to even try when, presumably, others have looked at it already?"

"Because I have seen and heard much, in the past three years. My desk has been the landing place of many calls about you, many complaints – threats, even, from men of higher positions of power than Bishop Grippe or even the Cardinal. I know what you have done. I know why you have done it.

"I do not judge. I say nothing in that regard – it is not my place. I do not know whether it is right or not, good or evil, but I do know that you care about those children you help. I know that you care about those who were children long ago and needed help then, but received none. Broken people. That is your calling, Father Wolfe.

"Well I am broken. My grand-nieces are broken. My sister-in-law is broken. If you can look into this with all of your powers, for three days, and find nothing to keep you longer, then I will be silent and accept it as a mystery… perhaps my own failings to know my niece. But I do not think you will find nothing. And once you find something, I do not think I will need to ask you to stay longer. To find the truth. When that time comes, I trust you will do what needs to be done. As you always do."

Neither man spoke for a while then, and Wolfe's eyes wandered the plush interior of the plane, mentally pictured the coastline fading into the distance behind him, the soothing thrum of the engines, and the uninterrupted scotch he'd linger over as he left his troubles – and the threat of a cell – far behind him. Hell, he had even planned to watch a movie. When was the last time he'd seen a move?

True, he hadn't liked the thought of leaving in this way, with the fight still raging behind him, but he had to admit the idea had grown on him since he'd left the hotel and stepped into the safe confines of the fuselage. Sanchez stepped forward and shook Wolfe's hand in both of his own.

"I will leave you now, to think and to decide. You will do as your conscience dictates," he said, "Of this I have no doubt. Just as I have no doubt that my niece was murdered, and her children left motherless after her death. In whatever it is you choose to do, I truly wish you God-speed, and a soul at peace."

Then he turned and left the plane.

Wolfe sat there, watched the black-clad figure reach the tarmac and walk across it, disappearing into the small, private terminal.

His mind was running around in a tight circle, from point to point and back around again. What Sanchez had said was in there, in the mental machine, but it was too little information, too few data points to chew on, to draw connection, conclusions. For that to happen, for the mental circle

22

to widen and grow, he needed more. He wouldn't get more if he were out over the ocean.

Fifteen minutes later, just as the engines powered up for pre-flight checks, Father Daniel Wolfe, priest-hunter and agent of Vatican Internal Investigations, stepped over to the open door of the jet. He stood, with the air conditioning blowing down upon his shoulders, halfway between the sealed protection of the Vatican State and the heavy heat of the late Miami morning. He paused, just for a breath or two, just to remember the feeling of safety and escape, for one moment more.

And then he moved down the stairs and back into the city.

Find *A Time for Weeping*,
and other books by Jeff Spence,
today on Amazon.

Also check out

www.SpenceWriting.com

Printed in Great Britain
by Amazon